ENCHANTED NET

MYSTERIOUS FIELDS

CELIA LAKE

Cover design by Augusta Scarlett.

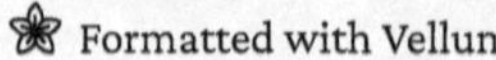
Formatted with Vellum

About Enchanted Net

Enchanted Net is the first book in the Mysterious Fields trilogy, a Victorian historical fantasy romance. Thessaly and Vitus will get their happily ever after in book 3, *Elemental Truth*. They have to solve some problems along the way.

~

Thessaly's life is laid out before her, a sparkling path toward the goals any young woman of Albion should aspire to. Her own magic is strong, she's a gifted duellist mastering the enchantments of illusion work. Now she's betrothed to the shining son of one of the greatest families in the country. All she has to do is tread the steps of the proper dance.

Vitus has just returned from a grand tour, learning all he can about stones and mines to cap off his apprenticeship as a talisman maker. Now it's time to establish himself, build his business, and craft his own future.

When Thessaly and Vitus meet at a costume ball, there's an immediate spark between them. Thessaly's marriage agreements specifically permit that, so long as she's discreet. Certainly, there's no barrier to a friendship or magical collaboration. Vitus, for his part, is charmed by her intelligence, creativity, and eye for crafting magic.

They've barely begun to get to know each other - or figure out how to handle their growing mutual interest properly - when Thessaly's world collapses. The sudden change in her life throws everything she'd expected into chaos. Vitus has no idea how to help, not without risking his future as well.

Join them for a toast in honour of recognising each other as kindred spirits, navigating the politics of Albion's Great Families, and figuring out how to live their own lives. Set in 1889, this book about the magical community of Victorian Britain is a wonderful entry point to Celia Lake's Albion books.

While many of the events of this trilogy are visible to Thessaly and Vitus, some of what happens is not. Grown Wise, a historical fantasy romance featuring Ursula Fortier in 1947, takes on those remaining questions. It will be out in May 2025.

CHAPTER 1

WEDNESDAY, MARCH 20TH, 1889
AT ARUNDEL, THE FORTIER ESTATE

"Thessaly. Five minutes." Thessaly heard her mother's comment through the door. The rap on the solid wood had come exactly on time, of course. Sioned Lytton-Powell ran her household as precisely as any general might want. Thessaly knew when she could press her luck and when she couldn't. Today - this entire week - was decidedly a time when she would do as Mama said, when Mama said.

"Of course, Mama." Thessaly called out, pitching her voice to carry without moving. Her maid was finishing the last details of her hair, using delicate charms to make sure each strand stayed where it ought. Once Alma finished, Thessaly stood, feeling the dress flow into place evenly, with the bustle settled behind her and the silk of her skirts falling to just above the floor. The weight of the gown was more than she preferred in a day dress, slowing her movement slightly, but today would not call for duelling of the physical sort. She would manage.

They had arrived at Arundel that morning, notable guests in a week of celebration. Thessaly and her parents had been shown to a gem of a guest house. It was not far from the main manor, tucked into gardens that were a tad bare now in March, but stunning in summer.

Her frock - every frock and gown she'd wear this visit - had been precisely chosen to suit not only the occasion, but the setting. She'd had dress fittings every week for months, each bit of silk and velvet and satin and embroidery debated to the finest degree. The result flattered. Of course it flattered, it was not permitted to do anything else.

The green redingote fit perfectly, the colour bringing out her blue eyes and the dark of her hair. It would contrast pleasantly with whatever Childeric wore. The pale golden cashmere dress under it was a princess cut, which felt much lighter, combined with a smaller bustle. It would be easy to sit in the Great Hall, to walk in the garden, to pose and wait politely, all of which would likely be involved this afternoon.

This dress was plain, deceptively so, other than the quality of the material and the fact that getting that kind of glow to the gold of the wool was far easier with magic. The spectacular frock was for Friday, and her betrothal. It was a confection of cream silk, embroidery, and enchantment that made her look stunning, as if she were lit by the perfect light no matter which way she turned.

Part of the debate of her clothing had been about how to dance with that fashion. In two days, well two days and a few hours, the Fortiers would announce the engagement of their eldest son Childeric. There would be toasts and joyous comments about the joining of two great families. Mama would point out that it was three, that it was the Powells - her family - that mattered just as much here as Father's. But only in absolute private, with all the wards and protections that Aunt Metaia could and would offer.

Certainly not here, where Thessaly could feel the Fortier magics sunk into every stone. It was an ancient estate, of course. This was a family that had its roots in the even more ancient dynasties of France, before the Conquest. They kept their family magics private, much as they were private about many other things.

Thessaly understood that. Mama and Aunt Metaia did, the Powells did. And Father's people, too, the Lyttons, though Thessaly knew somewhat less of those. Aunt Metaia had taken an interest in her early. Thessaly leaned to the Powell side, and her younger sister, Hermia, was likely to follow Father's line of things more.

The marriage was a coup, though. Thessaly had known that she'd marry for advantage. This was the expectation of her family, of both families. There were a great many Powells, and even with two of them currently on the Council, their overall influence was not what it had been a century ago. And Father's family was known for angling for strong magic, generation upon generation.

The Fortiers, on the other hand, had been in ascendency. Revolutions in France and the colonies had brought people needing refuge under their wing. They had turned that to their benefit, building up a vast set of client families and interconnections. And all those families owed them favours to be called in at some later time, bound by oath and magic and not a little blood.

The magic mattered here. In a slightly different world, where Thessaly had made her debut at Queen Victoria's court, she would certainly have been married already. She'd have had a season for making matches, then been paired off to someone. By now, at twenty-two and a half, she'd likely have a child, perhaps even two.

But Thessaly was a daughter of Albion, and the magical

community of Britain ran by slightly different standards. When they'd formalised the marriage agreements over the past few months, each point had been laid out, delineated and specified, just as much as the financial arrangements had been.

Her magic mattered. It was at the heart of what she brought to the marriage. She was a duellist. Her skill and strength at the art had been seen and noted. She would complete an apprenticeship in Illusion magic within the year, before she was properly married. It would demonstrate to the world she was capable magically, and that there was every expectation that her children would have equally potent magic. There were no concerns about recent intermarriage with the Fortiers, just the promise of bounty and plenty.

And if Childeric wasn't the man she'd have chosen if she had all the choice in the world, she had come to reasonable private agreements with him. He was the golden child of his family and his generation. Thessaly would make sure he shone, by pairing him socially and flattering him magically. Her own apprenticeship in illusion work was a help there.

Not that Childeric actually needed much physical enhancement. He was well-built, with golden hair like his mother's, and he wore clothing well. But her own skills would indeed be a help with the parties she would throw, the events they would be at, and all the other glittering moments of the Great Families.

Childeric would treat her with all courtesy - in public and in private - and if he did, she would back him up in public and leave him alone in private. Bar, of course, the expected and negotiated children, ideally a boy first.

Childeric would inherit the title from his father in due course, and the family must continue and flourish.

What she did with her time, outside of producing suitable heirs, was hers to decide. She could consult as she wished, she could keep up her duelling. She could even take a lover if she wished. The betrothal and marriage agreements held the usual sort of terms for that with the relevant charm precautions to avoid children outside of the marriage. A number of women of their class did, and many of the men. She was fairly sure Childeric would not seek out more time with her than required. Thessaly did not intend to be a solitary queen of ice and snow, all alone on some remote pinnacle.

That was a question she could not solve immediately, certainly not today. She knew that the signs of her betrothal had changed some of her relationships with her schoolmates. The actual announcement would change far more. Thessaly couldn't really make plans until she saw the way things fell out. Insisting on a duelling strategy that didn't suit the field of play did no one any good.

Instead, she came back to the feel of the land under her feet. This was a landed estate. Since the making of the Pact in 1484, the great work of magic that had split Albion from non-magical Britain, a Fortier had held the land magic at Arundel. Childeric's father, Lord Clovis, wielded that power visibly. Thessaly had been to a number of the other landed estates since she'd left Schola four years ago. In some places, the land magic was a delicate layer, a tracework of light and life. Here, at Arundel, it was more like a fortress of stone, if one that had a number of decorative elements.

It was certainly different from the house Thessaly had grown up in. That had a reasonable range of protections and enchantments - that was one of Father's specialties, after all. But it had very little weight of history, this sort of history. It was not a deep well of stored familiar power. Their house in Northumbria had been granted by the Lyttons, Father's family, on Mama and Father's marriage. Before that, it had been the home of a few of Father's spinster great-aunts and a widower uncle, all people who hadn't wanted to live in the bustle of Trellech, take a townhouse in London, or to live in rooms on one of the established Lytton estates.

There was one more knock, this one wordless, and Thessaly gave herself a last glance in the mirror, then opened the door. Mama stepped back, getting a good look, brushed one spot on the join at the shoulder, making sure it lay perfectly, then nodded. They walked in silence down the stairs of the guest house, where one of the estate's maids was waiting to show them across to the manor.

She knew little about how this sort of thing went among the non-magical community. Here, the betrothal was an excuse for an excess of magic on display, in every form and shape. Most of that would be far more on display tomorrow and in the days after, but all the signs of it were here now.

The Great Hall was decorated for the week already, delicate draped garlands combining a mix of seasonal flowers enchanted to hold their perfection for days and charm illusions. Thessaly could feel the warding and protective magics even more strongly here, a net that enclosed the space and made the boundaries almost tangible. And she could feel, even if she couldn't identify, the number of charmed and talismanic jewellery pieces in the room.

Her own clothing offered none of that. While Mama and Father had been thorough in their spending on her dresses, that largesse had not extended to jewellery.

Granted, it was not expected for a young unmarried woman to have much of her own. She wore only a string of simple pearls today. Mama had her wedding parure on, naturally.

Thessaly did not have time to stare, and certainly not to gawk. The family - and certain of their key allies - were all present, with the reigning matriarch seated in state at the far end. She was welcomed first by the younger son of the current generation, Childeric's uncle Dagobert and his wife Laudine. Their son Garin was only nine. He wasn't in evidence. Of course, he must be up in the nursery or some such, just as Hermia was at home. Hermia was only barely sixteen. She would not be properly out in society for nearly two years more.

Mama and Father moved on, making polite and respectful greetings to the Landrys. Mama gave Magistra Landry every courtesy. There were rumours about what she could do with her magic, and no one with sense wanted to find out the truth themselves. Magistra Landry was dressed well, her gown of silk, but she was not brightly adorned, as the other women were. Instead, she wore a glowing deep blue, not a shade of mourning, but hard to interpret.

Thessaly's classmates at school had sometimes giggled over the story, how Henut Landry had met a handsome Frenchman in Egypt, where she'd been born. She had gone with him to France, where they had lived a decade or so until he had been killed fighting valiantly at Versailles in the siege in 1870. Magistra Landry had fled Paris through a portal to Albion and come to the Fortiers, calling on an old connection of her husband's. She had been enceinte then.

Alexander, that child, was enough younger than Thessaly they'd only overlapped at Schola for one year. He'd finish this June, soon to be launched into his own career. Now, he was standing just behind his mother. He was here because he was on holiday for the fortnight, and because he and his brother and mother still lived on the estate part of the time.

Now, Thessaly just inclined her head to him, letting him bow over her hand, and then his older brother, Philip. The other girls might have pined over the romance of his father, but Thessaly had often thought Philip more interesting. He hadn't gone to Schola at all, and remained more French than of Albion and Britain's magical community. Though, of course, he'd made all the proper oaths on the Silence and to the Pact.

Philip had a sense of certainty and mystery that were twined, somehow, not at all like the average boy or man of Albion. Some people talked in hushed whispers about how he couldn't be trusted, he didn't understand what was suitable for Albion. And others flocked to that sense of difference, like a moth to flame. Philip, for his part, mostly kept at a distance from anyone outside his family. Thessaly had found him interesting to talk to, well-mannered and considerate, and Alexander even more so. Both of them treated her as a person, interesting in her own right, which was not as common as she wished it were.

That, of course, brought her to Childeric's parents. Lord Clovis and Lady Maylis were both looking splendid, the sort of confidence that came with knowing that everything was as they wished it. They greeted her parents, offering the proper formal welcome to their lands. It was the same as it had been all the times before. This was the welcome made to honoured guests who were not actually family, delineating in a few particular phrases what was and was not permitted.

It meant Thessaly could use her own magics, so long as they were not against one of the family. Likewise, she had free access to the public spaces of the manor. For her comfort, she could draw on the food, drink, and staff in all the ways expected of her class and station. Of course, they'd know if she made use of those, likely nearly as soon as she did.

Thessaly made her little bob and compliment, then Childeric bowed over her hand, playing up the formality before tucking it into his, a rare public touch. She nodded once at Sigbert, Childeric's younger brother, before needing to keep her feet and her skirts in order as he escorted her to his grandmother's chair. "Grand-mère, you remember Thessaly Lytton-Powell, of course." It had been some months, actually, not since the ball the Fortiers had hosted over Solstice week. The other times she'd seen Childeric had been in Trellech, the show of being seen at suppers and the winter's festivities.

"Lady Chrodechildis. Madam Fortier." At least Thessaly did not need to navigate the difference in titles here. She could feel the coiling magic, just as she could feel the weight of her dress and where the fabric fell, or Childeric's hand under hers. The woman before her had been Lady Fortier for forty-five years until the death of her husband some four years ago. She was a rigid pillar of propriety, determined that her husband's legacy should not be squandered. And so she kept the courtesy title, but with her forename to distinguish her from Lady Maylis, the current Lady Fortier.

Now, Thessaly bobbed a little deeper, making all the little shows of respect she'd been trained in from the time she could walk. The arch of her hands, showing she was not working magic, her lips together but not tense. She could not help her stance. Even in a formal gown and delicate slippers, she persisted in standing like a duellist, ready to move. Fortunately, the skirts hid many things, and that was one of them.

When she raised her eyes just slightly, Thessaly saw the minute nod. Madam Fortier tapped her fan on her wrist. "You may walk in the gardens. We wish to speak with your parents." Both sets, presumably, the way Madam Fortier said it.

Childeric might have baulked at the order if it had been his parents or his aunt and uncle. He had more sense than to do so here. He simply smiled and gestured. "This way, then. We'll have a look at the daffodils, shall we?"

As soon as they were away from the others, he lowered his arm. Admittedly keeping hold of it while navigating doorways was awkward. He utterly ignored the rest of the waiting guests.

Admittedly, most of the people present were a generation older, but Thessaly caught sight of Jacinthe Howard and her husband. Jacinthe, Childeric's cousin, had married Amalric Howard last year. They'd married as soon as she'd finished at Schola and before starting her apprenticeship. Thessaly enjoyed talking to them both, though she'd wondered about the speed of the wedding.

Neither she nor Childeric spoke further until they were outside. It was mild enough she did not need an additional wrap, at least. And, as she suspected, they were heading not simply for the daffodils, but for one of the estate's cottages. Some people - parents, for example - might have worried they'd go off and do indecent things in private. But no, Childeric wanted to relax with his friends. Never mind that she couldn't relax, not wearing what she was right now. She waited until they were well away from the house. "Really, Childeric, today?"

Childeric and Sigbert had taken over the vacant cottage

without actually asking permission. Over the last year, it had turned into a spot where they could play cards, gamble, and generally not be bothered. It had a significant lack of regular sweeping, comfortable seating in any sort of structured gown, or other amenities. Also, a distinct lack of books.

"If it weren't for you and your parents arriving, I could have been riding all afternoon," Childeric said. "Tomorrow, though..."

It wasn't as if Thessaly was going to win any arguments. "I can't sit down there, in this frock. There'll be dust." Or other things, even less kind to the fabric than dust. If she stayed with him, she'd be cordially ignored by whatever nearby friend had got free for as long as they played.

"Go for a walk, then, if you like. An hour and a half, shall we say? Enough time for a game or two." By now they were at the cottage, and he swept off without waiting for an answer from her. Thessaly wondered if anyone back in the Great Hall would realise they'd separated. Albion, at least, did not chaperone her daughters as much as Victorian England did. Especially not when, like Thessaly, they were quite capable of defending their own honour. But they did notice who was where, when, and with whom.

What she wanted to do was find the salle and at least work through some drills on her own. That wasn't an option. It would require an entire change of wardrobe, the sort of cleansing charms that would disarrange her hair, and everyone in the vicinity knowing Childeric had left her alone. She sighed and resigned herself to a slow and stately walk around the orchards. She'd have chosen different shoes, if Childeric had given her any warning of his plans.

CHAPTER 2

MARCH 22ND AT ARUNDEL

By Friday evening, the estate was teeming with guests. A massive pavilion had been erected on the great green lawn to the west of the house over the past day. Now, through the windows of the Great Hall, she could see it lit with glowing charmlights, each and every decoration sparkling with magic. The grass had been covered by a dancing floor, smooth and perfect, with paths to protect the dresses of the ladies present. The whole thing had also been warmed to be comfortable without a wrap. Not that too much skin was bare, of course. Not among the guests.

Here, tonight, there would be three sets of bare shoulders, a flagrant demonstration of raw magical potency. One set belonged to Lady Maylis and one to Laudine Fortier. The third were Thessaly's. They were an overt sign, bright and sharp as some of the electric lighting now more common among the non-magical. It shouted that the Fortiers were powerful enough to ensure their complete protection. Other women, lesser families, might worry about some potion that would harm or at least embarrass, applied to the skin. The Fortiers did not.

The reality, of course, was that Thessaly had been layered with complex - and expensive - charmwork before dressing. It had been done by Magistra Landry, who at least had not expected Thessaly to make small talk. It had been a particular gift, after several days of being surrounded by chatter and commentary, unless she was entirely alone and asleep.

People gossiped about Magistra Landry, how she had ancient and exotic - and terrifying - magical skills at her disposal. She had been born and educated in Egypt, and of course they had approaches to magic largely unknown in Albion. If someone from Albion had done this work, it would have meant several steps - a bath, the careful application of alchemical lotions, retouching as they dried, then charms beyond that. This was far more efficient, potent magic anchored in a brush of an ointment mixing oil with finely ground herbs.

Some people Thessaly knew refused to be in the room with Magistra Landry, as if some of that might rub off. Thessaly did not know her well - certainly not enough to consider a first name. But today, the older woman had been thoughtful and careful, explaining what she intended and making sure Thessaly understood how it worked. Not all the details, of course. There wasn't nearly time for that and certainly Magistra Landry would not be inclined to share her secrets.

And Magistra Landry had been efficient, thorough, covering the slight crescent of skin that showed if Thessaly lifted her arm, the nape of her neck, and up to her hairline. She took the care to make Thessaly turn and move in any way that might happen during the dancing. It was not the sort of thing one would do routinely, but it was a show of power, and she would do it again for her wedding. It had given Thessaly a chance to get more of a sense of the level of Magistra Landry's skill and the controlled strength of her magic. People might well fear the harnessed power she felt. Certainly this was not a woman you wanted to make an enemy of.

But here Magistra Landry was, lending her skills to a minor detail of a betrothal of the Fortiers. Thessaly wondered how the older woman thought of it, whether she resented being at their beck and call for something admittedly trivial in the grand scheme of things. On the other hand, the Fortiers had helped her build her resources. And their help had let her raise her sons into competent magicians themselves, starting here and then in Trellech once she took up residence there.

Once she was fully dressed and arranged, Thessaly had been quietly escorted to the Great Hall, via the back of the house, to wait for the right moment. Her mother and father were already out among the guests. She had glimpsed them in a waltz. The older women among the Fortiers had already been out among their guests for an hour or two, but Thessaly had been asked to wait until the formal announcement. Now, Childeric appeared, bowing to his grandmother, then his mother, before offering his arm. "Father says it is the hour." He then paused and took a step back to admire Thessaly's gown, circling her. "My, Thess, you do look lovely. Quite the thing."

It was excellent that he appreciated it, though Thessaly had been hoping, perhaps, for a little more in the way of specific compliments. Of course, he was in full evening dress. There was a nod to the Fortier heraldry of black, gold, and purple in the flowers in his buttonhole and the jewelled amethyst and jet clip that held them.

Her gown did the same thing, a golden shimmering cascade of silk the shade of the champagne that would be served at the announcement. The bodice and train had touches of purple, and there were over two hundred delicate pearls gleaming along the bodice and skirt. It was all woven enchantment too, and not illusion work. Hours upon hours of work and swaths of magic in the design and weaving had gone into making it glow as if with its own light. Thessaly looked stunning in it, and she wanted to make the most of the evening.

They made a lovely procession. Magister Dagobert went first, escorting his mother, as his wife had remained outside to see to the guests. Lord Clovis escorted Lady Maylis, of course, and Childeric had offered his arm at the perfect angle. They made their way out, picking up the metre of the music as soon as they could hear it, step by steady step. People parted in front of them, leaving space on either side. Magister Dagobert saw his mother to her chair on the small dais at one end of the dancing pavilion. Then she nodded, as the other two couples took their places and Magistra Laudine appeared from the crowd to stand beside her husband. Sigbert appeared from the other side, attentively positioned by his mother's elbow, while Childeric and Thessaly posed.

Her parents stood on the other side, waiting to come forth for their part in the announcement. She could see the Landrys, a little further back. The men were elegant in their evening wear. Magistra Landry was resplendent in a gown of deep faience blue that made her brown skin seem like copper in the charmlight. The sheer numbers in the gathering were a potent sign of power in themselves, hundreds of people here just because the Fortiers had bid them be.

Thessaly could see a few of the others she knew from her Schola years, dotted here and there. Not every landed family was here, but the ones with children and heirs around her age all were. Genevieve Donovan was over there, though her husband Marcellus was sitting down beside her. He must be having an off day. Temenos Sibley was with his parents, and there was Ignatius Knapton, with his wife - they'd married young - and his sisters. She didn't see Lionel Baddock. Perhaps he'd had a relapse of whatever had been ailing him the past year or three. Before she could look for others, Lord Clovis began speaking.

"Good evening, good evening! You are most welcome to Arundel this evening. All who come with good will are welcome here for our festivities." It was a sensible welcome, ritually speaking, bounding it not only by time but by intention. "We welcome you for the celebration of Childeric's birth, the completion of his apprenticeship, and, we are delighted to say, to announce a betrothal."

Now Thessaly's parents came forward, Mama's hand resting on Father's arm. Further back, near the opposite end of the tent, the light shifted a little. Thessaly could see Aunt Metaia standing with Cousin Owain, among a little knot of the members of the Council. Even Council Head Rowan and her husband were here, and that was a social coup. They did not always attend events like this. Thessaly wondered if that was because of the Fortiers, or far more likely due to Aunt Metaia's friendship.

Besides their cousin, Aunt Metaia was closest to the head of the Council, Hereswith Rowan, and Thessaly could see them leaning together, watching. Thessaly could see several alchemists, too. There was Romulus Heath, who

Thessaly would love to talk illusion work with, if she got such a chance during the gatherings over the next few days. And there, further away, were Hesperidon Warren and his wife Griselda. She knew they were closer connections of the Fortiers.

"The Fortier and Lytton-Powell families are delighted to announce the betrothal of our son, Childeric Fortier, first-born of the land's line, to Thessaly Lytton-Powell, eldest daughter of Sioned and Harold Lytton-Powell. We ask you to raise your glasses and toast." The toast was given first in archaic, rhyming French. It was not quite an oath, but Thessaly could feel the way it tugged on the magic. Suddenly, those well-wishes and blessings were honed into something with her at the centre, the light through a faceted gem. Then someone was holding a cup, and she took it, drinking at the same time as Childeric. She did not swoon, but it was a terribly near thing. The light and the magic and the sheer presence of so many people, all intent on her every move, suddenly rushed in. The glass was plucked from her fingers while the guests applauded, then the music began.

Childeric immediately swung her into the dance with no pause for breath. Here, at least, they were well-matched. Thessaly was, if anything, more nimble on her feet. Her duelling skills gave her an advantage there. The music was chosen to let them show off the chassez and hop of the mazurka. Each time she leapt, she felt the skirts follow her down a second later. Each time she spun, there was some other glittering enchantment that caught her eye.

Every eye was on them. They had the entire floor and covered it over and over again. She spun, and she heard Childeric call out an incantation, three high-pitched beats in perfect archaic French, and then there were golden rose petals cascading down. Each one glowed with magic, each one matched the golden yellow of the heraldry. This was not romance, this was about the display of magic and power and delicate control, hinting at less delicate uses.

When the dance came to the final bow, Thessaly was on the edge of breathlessness. She was more fit than Childeric in the ordinary way of things, but the work of making all her skirts go just where she intended added a layer of complexity. The dance had been a touch more draining than she'd expected, even with the flurry and nerves of it all and the need to make a perfect showing. No matter, she was in excellent health, she could and would see the evening through with the necessary vivacity.

Fortunately, the next dance was a slower and more stately waltz, and it was with Father. From there, she was handed off to dance with Lord Clovis, with Magister Dagobert, their sister Bradamante's husband Yves. From there, she danced with other notable men of the extended family and their close allies. There were quite a few dances with Father's brothers and the other Lyttons, too.

All of that was interspersed with quadrilles and other set dances. She had, of course, perfected the ones the Fortiers favoured. She'd practised them throughout the winter, tracing the measures repeatedly, dragging in whoever was handy to be her partner. Most often Hermia, honestly. Hermia had been good-natured about it, and willing enough to learn dances she couldn't enjoy in public for another year or two. Nonetheless, Thessaly had wondered if she were taking advantage of Hermia, or of her sister's sometimes visible admiration and imitation.

Late in the evening, though - nearer one in the morning than midnight - she found herself on the edge of the gathering. The more senior adults were finding quieter pursuits, disappearing to the manor's public rooms for conversation and chairs, or more stately dances. The sea of people - the client families and such - had thinned out as well. Those not of the same status as the Fortiers knew their role was to come and swell the numbers, but not stay too late.

Oddly, Thessaly felt entirely on her own. Childeric was in one corner, chatting with a knot of yearmates from his time at Schola. He was enough older that their social sets from school didn't overlap much, but there were fewer people there than she'd expected, given the size of the guest list. A number of people between Childeric's year and Thessaly's had already said their farewells around midnight.

Adamus Mortimer had bowed out, so had Odile. Odile and Cosi and Thessaly had been the three of similar background in Fox House in their year, but of course Cosi was expecting again. Neither travel by portal nor a late evening was considered appropriate for her right now. Odile had pled exhaustion before eleven, leaving with her husband before Thessaly had any chance to talk to her.

That was the thing she was discovering at the moment. Plenty of people wanted to talk at her, to make a point of congratulating her. Very few wanted to actually have a conversation, much less hear how she was or anything remotely personal. She was here as a gem set in the line of the Fortiers. That was apparently all that mattered. She'd expected much of that, but perhaps not from everyone who'd offered it.

On any other night, she might have migrated toward Aunt Metaia. But Aunt Metaia had talked with Mama and Father briefly, and since then she'd had the sort of deliberate expression on her face that meant she was repressing a dozen things it was better not to say. There, at least, Thessaly had the promise of a better time to talk soon, next time she visited Bryn Glas, Aunt Metaia's home.

Thessaly was considering her options when there was a courteous voice at her elbow. She felt the presence of his magic, before anything else, the way she sometimes woke at something shifting in the night. "Might I fetch you something cool to drink, Thessaly? And perhaps escort you with a charmlight for a breath of fresh air during this dance?"

That was Philip Landry, still impeccably put together. She nodded, once. It at least offered a chance for a pause and possibly some actual conversation that stretched beyond congratulations and a compliment on her gown. He returned within a minute, glass in hand, calling a charmlight in the other. The light caught on his hand, a flash of turquoise and some green stone on his ring. He offered her his arm as soon as she took the glass, escorting her out through one of the openings in the pavilion, onto the paved walkway.

They did not go far. She was not remotely dressed for it. But to stand outside, under the stars, that was refreshing. She - and Childeric - were expected to see the night through. There was at least an hour or two more for her. The sky above was remarkably clear. Even the weather and the stars had obeyed the Fortiers' expectations, and the moon was only barely rising, a glimmer on the horizon yet.

"My congratulations, of course. I had not yet had a chance to make them properly." Philip offered a little bow, then gestured up at the sky as he went on. "In our traditions, the stars are gemstones strewn across the sky, and tonight, you are among them. May it bring you all the blessings you wish." It was courtly, more than that, it was kind.

Thessaly inclined her head. "Thank you. How lovely a

sentiment." She would acknowledge that he hadn't needed to say it, or that way, here, in the quiet. "Are there particular stars of note, then, do they match gems? Or is it more the metaphor?" The stars seemed a far more pleasant conversation than anything she might say about the betrothal or the wedding to come.

Thessaly knew what was expected. She knew what the benefits would be, for herself and for her extended family, and she was going into it with her eyes open. She and Childeric had come to their own terms about things. Certainly once the focus of the wedding was over and done with, she would have more freedom in private. He would not burden her unduly. Philip wasn't of that sort of family, but he knew by now how that was played. They didn't need to discuss it.

"Ah, mmm." Philip looked up toward the rest. "Sirius is of particular note, but not tonight. There, though, is Spica. If Sirius marks the beginning of the year, the flood of the Nile upon which everything depends, Spica is the mark of the harvest. And you know the other lore, perhaps?"

Thessaly had done exceedingly well in her education at Schola, including in her Astronomy class and the later specialist lectures in chronological and locational magics. "The sheaf of wheat the parthenos holds. A maiden who is unattached, whole in herself." Her mouth twitched. No one but Philip could see. "Not exactly what one thinks of at a betrothal."

"She is also Astraea, justice unfolding, Persephone, queen among the dead, Isis with her magics bringing grain and civilisation. The shade of your gown calls it to mind with the gold of the harvest and the land. Though Spica, of course, gowns herself in blue. It is a favoured colour with us. We do love our faience and our lapis lazuli and our turquoise." His mother's dress, tonight, that made sense, and then he lifted his hand and she saw a flash of the brighter turquoise stone on his ring. "In some customs, Spica's star is the emerald, but that would not do for you tonight, or in this mode."

It made her smile again. "No. It signals the wrong sort of things." Just then, there was a cough behind her, and Philip turned to look over his shoulder.

"Alexander." There was a brief phrase, in fluent Arabic - if it had been French, Thessaly would have understood, of course - then Alexander bowed to her. "I am bid to see if you will return to the dancing. May I take your glass?" Thessaly handed it over without complaint, offering her hand to Philip to escort her back.

"Your brother was kind enough to keep me company for a breath of fresh air, but I am quite renewed." It was true, a few minutes on the grass and in the open air had been most restorative. As soon as they were back in the pavilion, Childeric swept her up again, this time into another of the couple's dances.

When they came to a stop again, some time later, only the resilient few were left, and Childeric walked her back in silence to the guest house. It took her last dregs of energy to stand long enough for Alma to release her from the dress and bundle her into a nightgown. Tomorrow, there were more festivities, an afternoon of sport and a pavo match, followed by a banquet. Those would come entirely too soon.

CHAPTER 3

APRIL 8TH AT THE DESCHAMPS FAMILY HOME

"Vitus, dear boy. You do look well. Come, let me get a good look at you." Vitus had just stepped into the parlour, finally able to see his parents and brother for the first time in a year and a half. Well, his parents, at least. Lucas was nowhere to be found.

"Mama." He stepped forward, taking the hands she held out to him, and bending to kiss her cheek. She also looked very well. When he left, she'd been slowly recovering from a lingering cough, the kind everyone had worried about. Now, her eyes were bright, there were roses in her cheeks, her hair had a good shine to it, and he hadn't heard her cough yet. "You look wonderful, and also it's excellent to see you." He then took a step back, pivoting and holding out his hand to his father. "Papa, the same. I am very glad to be home."

"Grand, boy, grand." They were informal tonight, just the family. Vitus was wearing much the same sort of thing as his father, dinner jackets, though Vitus's needed a bit of tending. "I thought we'd go in for supper before asking you about your travel, but I hope the journey went well, even with the delay?"

Vitus had begun in Calais before six that morning. He'd shepherded two trunks of his own and two smaller ones full of quite heavy materia onto the ferry, then the train. That had been better than dealing with an exhausting wait for customs at the portals in Paris. The ferry and train had taken a full eight hours. Then he'd had to guard them through an unexpectedly long wait for the portal in London.

"There was some unusual delay at Bedford Square. I ended up going across to Southwark, and the deliveries had priority." He'd had two hours there, though at least at a table with tea and a place for the trunks. His parents had been out for a call when he'd finally got home. Odd to call it that, after so long away.

Before he could get lost in his thoughts, the door opened. It didn't quite bang against the wall. Vitus was wrapped in an enthusiastic hug, the breath almost knocked out of him. He didn't quite lose his balance; he had, in fact, expected this. Lucas was not at all moderate in his emotions, and the entire family had no idea where that came from. Also, he'd picked up at least a bit more height and a noticeable amount more muscle while Vitus had been away.

"Pax, pax." He thumped his brother on the shoulder. "I'm not going anywhere now. I didn't know if you'd be home."

"We've a lot to catch up on. My last letter might have missed you? I'm on leave for a fortnight yet, not sure about my next orders after that yet. There's a chance I might make Cavalry Master in due course." Lucas took a step back, eyes gleaming. "Did you bring me anything?"

"Lucas!" Their mother pitched it to carry. "Is that really the first thing you say?"

"Pardon, Mama. It's so very good to see you, Vitus. You have no idea how much I've missed you. Did you find anything I might like?" Vitus looked utterly unrepentant.

Vitus reached up to ruffle his hair. Elder brothers could take certain liberties. "I missed you too. And yes, I have some books for you." He'd spent hours haunting used book stores, stretching the funds he had as far as they could go, looking for things Lucas might like. He'd struck on a trove of cavalry books in a mix of languages, but of course, the illustrations carried a fair bit, and Lucas had a knack for reading languages. Or at least he did if they had anything to do with horses.

Their father cleared his throat. "My dear, may I have the honour?" He offered Mama his arm and there was the little procession from the parlour to the dining room. Once everyone was seated, Papa raised his glass. "Welcome home, Vitus. Do, please, tell us about your travels. We've read your letters over and over, but they rather hint at stories instead of telling all the details."

Vitus beamed. He waited just a moment, nodding at the housemaid who brought the food around. "Thank you, Jane." He then settled in. Vitus had given this some thought, and not just today. He'd known his parents had made a number of sacrifices. They'd not only saved to fund his travel, but for his apprenticeship in the first place. And again for keeping Lucas in sufficient horseflesh for a cavalry officer, as well as his other necessary accoutrements. He would gladly tell them as much as they wanted to hear about his travel.

Now, Vitus laid out what he'd learned, months each with four different talisman makers. He'd gone from Paris to Vienna to Florence to Geneva. He spun out two or three tales from each place, the joy of learning about a new city and what made it itself. That kept them going through each new course to the sweets when Vitus wrapped up the last of his stories.

"Oddly, it kept making me wish for home. Here, and Trellech, and London. Not that the Seine isn't glorious, or the Duomo in Florence, the different squares and features. But I am glad to be back." He added to Mama, "And I have gifts for everyone. Some lace and ribbons for you, Mama, and books for Papa and Lucas, of course." Also, some handsomely carved pipes, but he'd set those in the smoking room for later. They all kept such things just to the one room, because of the influence on the materia, and particularly on Vitus's work and Mama's jewellery.

It felt good to be at home, in a household that had changed remarkably little while he'd been gone. There was his bedroom upstairs for private space, along with Lucas's and his parents', of course. Papa had his office and the smoking room and Mama had the parlour. They came together in the library and the dining room, one for quiet and the other for congenial conversation. Each piece did its part, it was like setting a gem in a way he'd not consciously realised before this trip.

"Aren't you thoughtful, dear boy. Now that you're back, when does Magistra Niobe expect you?" Mama inclined her head and shifted slightly so that Jane could tidily clear away the other plates and set out the cheese.

"Tomorrow morning, Mama. She thought it best - and I agree - to figure out our strategy and then set to on Monday." Vitus was nearly done, formally, with his apprenticeship. It was, as always, the 'nearly' that mattered here.

He still had to produce at least one notable piece, solid journeyman work.

It didn't need to be a master's piece, not yet. That could come in a few years. Though if he managed it now, that would be a useful coup indeed. However, creating something both innovative and visibly effective, the sort of effective that could be discussed at a guild meeting, was not easy to arrange. It was far more likely he'd make something competent but not yet adding to the larger art of talisman making.

He and Niobe had talked about options in their letters back and forth. But the actual pieces he made would depend on the intersection of the gemstones and minerals he'd brought back for her and on what requests her workshop received. And, unspoken, whether any of the patrons involved would be willing to have him do the work rather than her.

Magistra Niobe Hall was not that much older than Vitus was - thirteen years. But she was in fact a prodigy who'd earned her mastery by the age of twenty-six, the age Vitus was now. He wouldn't equal that, but he had hopes of it before he turned thirty. She had been willing to take him on for a lower fee than she could have commanded, and she'd treated him more than generously. And then she'd arranged the visits of his last year, calling on several old favours and trading at least one for the future. He owed her more than he could say, and he wanted to do her proud.

"Well, then." Mama folded her hands. "And you'll be staying here, then? I told Jane and Cook to expect so."

"If it's not a bother for the moment." Rooms in Trellech would be vastly more convenient. But it was also more expensive. He'd be watching every coin or hint of one, at least until he could start getting commissions in his own right. Past that, in fact, because he'd have to pay for his materia in advance, and minerals and gems of talisman quality didn't come cheap. What he'd brought back should be a big help, of course, but at least two-thirds of those were intended for Niobe. "I don't expect I'll be out late, at least for a little while to come."

"That is considerate of you. Perhaps tomorrow evening we might talk through the social calendar, and see which events we should attend?" And which they should subtly note that Vitus was now home for. "You missed quite the affair at Arundel. Did our letter about that at the equinox reach you?"

"No, I can't say it did. But I was moving about a fair bit the last week or two." Vitus inclined his head. "The pleasant sort of affair or the scandalous sort?"

"Oh, entirely proper. You know I wouldn't gossip if it were the other." Not about the Fortiers, certainly. His family, the Deschamps, were more or less a client family to the Fortiers. Not by location, not anymore. Papa's father had moved the family from Sussex to Somerset in the previous generation, when Grandmama had inherited this house. It stood in a pleasant but undistinguished magical village. It was well-positioned for access to both Trellech, via the portal, and to non-magical England, via the railway. Vitus smiled and inclined his head to acknowledge the reality of the situation.

His mother went on, with barely a pause. "It was a betrothal, absolutely no detail spared. Childeric will marry Thessaly Lytton-Powell. She looked terribly well. There were pieces in the Trellech Moon about her ensembles afterwards. A fine eye for colour and for tradition, both, though more than one commentary I have seen noted that she is rather on the sharper edge of the season's fashions. It was quite the event, a ball in an outside pavilion for the betrothal itself. There were many events before and after, through to the Monday. Your father and I were honoured to be invited for quite a few of those. Such a performance on the Saturday, with illusionists and singers and aerialists."

"I'm glad to hear it, Mama. And I hope you found it enjoyable." His father's chin moved just a fraction, which meant Papa had found it professionally profitable, then. Good. That was a relief. Papa had not found himself with a particularly viable sort of magical talent, but with an excellent head for records and numbers. But he was enough of Albion he had not found it comfortable to make his place among the non-magical, as Lucas had in the Army. Instead, he was a man of business who handled matters for a number of families, providing confidential advice and assistance. It was, however, a line of work that depended far too much on reputation and current fashion for comfort and security.

And that was true even more with the Fortiers than with some. Not that Vitus was up on the latest gossip there. It wasn't the sort of thing Mama or Papa would write about, nor anything Lucas would track as directly. But the Fortiers were known for sharp dealings - enough that people recognised the name well into the Continent. Vitus would need to find someone who could fill in the news sooner rather than later. Possibly Mama in private, in a few days.

"Perhaps we might withdraw?" Papa suggested it offhandedly. "Will you wait for us, my dear?"

"I am a trifle tired. I think I will retire." She stood and all three men rose politely. Mama came around, kissing Vitus on his cheek, then Lucas, then going around to Papa. "I shall read, though. Tomorrow, dear boys."

That left the three of them to retreat to the smoking room. Vitus presented the pipes, with a brief explanation of the artists who'd carved them, as well as the pipe tobacco he'd brought back. His father raised an eyebrow, and Vitus said, half-laughing, "I worked it off over several Saturdays helping him do inventory. It was quite informative, actually."

From there, they settled into a comfortable conversation about matters in the neighbourhood and among the closer family acquaintances. Vitus had not missed as much as he'd feared. Mama's letters, in particular, had been informatively thorough. When Papa also retired - nominally because he had an early meeting, and really because he wanted to talk to Mama - Vitus stood. "Come up to my room, would you?"

Lucas followed him, dropping into the chair by the bed immediately after Vitus closed the door. Vitus brought the warding up, instinctively and automatically. "How is Mama, really?"

"Much better, honestly. She tires easily, still, but the rest is vastly improved. Magistra Niobe sent around a stone. Mama sleeps with it."

Vitus blinked. He had not known, and it was one more kindness he owed Niobe for. Of course she'd think of that sort of thing, and of course Mama must have stopped in to the workshop in Trellech more than once. Vitus had certainly given her plenty of reason, little tidbits of news and stories that weren't about what he was learning that Mama would have enjoyed sharing. "I hadn't known."

"It shows." Lucas shrugged. "I'm glad you're back. I'm hoping to stay posted here. Cavalry Master's an excellent post, decent pay, and I'd be able to come see you. Supper weekly, probably. But I worry. Papa does too, even if he won't say anything about it."

"I'll talk to Niobe about it. And maybe see if there's a Healer who might have other ideas." Whatever plagued Mama, at least it didn't seem to be progressing. It wasn't consumption. The Healers had checked for that, more than once. Colds and catarrh just lingered, on and on, and had in some form since Vitus could remember, though they ebbed and flowed, better and worse. Then he sat on the bed, toeing his shoes off. "All right. Books first or gossip?"

"Books. Then gossip. I won't be reading them right away. Those?" Lucas had caught sight of the stack on the table. "Are those all for me?"

"Don't even ask me how many used bookstores I went through. Or how many times I made ridiculous equine noises when my language skills failed me." He was better now, but he'd started his book searches early, long before he'd gained much functional fluency in any of the relevant languages. "Thumb through, and then we'll chat." It was indeed good to be home, and to have things be as he expected.

CHAPTER 4

APRIL 9TH IN TRELLECH, WALES

Vitus paid the carter, dropping a couple of extra coins in his hand once the man had helped him unload the two trunks. The carter brushed his thumb across the coins, then nodded, pleased. "Thank you, sir. Let me know if there's somewhat else."

"I will. Not today, though." Vitus waited until the man had turned the pony cart around and back through the alley onto the street. Then he knocked three times on the door, good steady thumps. It opened before he could knock a fourth time.

"Don't be silly. Of course you're still on the wards. Here, pick that up, I'll take the other end. I can't possibly greet you properly with them in the way." Niobe was right there, shawl pinned around her shoulders, her hair up. She looked extremely well, and as if she'd barely aged at all. They didn't speak again until they got both trunks back to the workshop at the other end of the ground floor. It hadn't changed, with the long workbenches and grinding stones, with the windows that let in as much daylight as possible. Once they'd set the two down, she turned her hands on his arms. "Let's have a proper look at you."

Vitus waited, knowing she'd take in what he was wearing, as well as the rest of it. He had made all the talismanic accoutrements he was wearing, cufflinks, tie pin, and, of course, the watch fob. He'd been lucky enough to do a favour for someone who had some pieces of citrine from one of the Bavarian mines.

Amethyst would have been a lot easier to get, especially in Austria, but he'd not wanted to suggest he was of Fox House. The golden yellow matched his own Salmon House, even though the citrine had been nearly as costly as a good topaz, due to rarity. And, he was vain enough to think the flash of bright gold drew the eye to his hands, where a fair bit of his skill lay. She considered him, head cocked, then grinned. "Buttons, too? That's clever. Come, tell me all about it."

Vitus smiled, giving her a proper bow. "It's good to see you, too. Talking before you look at the treasures I brought back, then?"

"Oh, yes. Stones are patient. I am not always. Tea's ready. Sit, sit. You look well. The trip back wasn't too bad, then?" She bustled about to fetch the teapot from the small room off the stairs. It didn't sit out in the workroom, of course. Too much stone dust and such could get into it. "I'm not expecting any clients today. We can take our time, properly."

Given that cue, he began with the trip, and the various minor delays and the current state of getting stones through customs. Then Vitus looped back to the beginning of his travels, pulling out his notebook to keep track of the dates. As he went, he undid the cuff links, then pulled out the tie pin, then finally the watch fob, in the order he'd made them. They were, of course, designed to work together.

The cufflinks were a fairly standard protective design, averting the ordinary sort of ill fortune or minor harm that could sometimes come anyone's way. The tie pin was a much more delicate piece. He'd had to learn three new design techniques to make it properly. It helped him present himself as someone worth listening to. It wouldn't make up for gaffes, but it would incline someone to hear him out if he didn't put his foot in his mouth. He'd explained both, with Niobe pulling out her jeweller's loupe to look at them, asking questions about the design along the way.

"And the watch?" That had been three solid months of work, the last three, before the stop in Geneva to get the watch to complete the piece. "Designed to help me understand what's truly needed, so I can best judge whether I am the person to provide that." It came out stilted. Vitus tried not to flinch at that.

Niobe reached out a hand, a finger tapping on the back of his before she picked up the watch and fob to look at it closely. "You're nervous about it."

The usual sort of thing was a piece that let you shine in the best light, that was thought the optimal way to bring in business and build your reputation. Niobe had laid it out before he left. She'd had him do all the research reading in the library and from her own collection. And then she had left it up to him what to do. The more he'd thought about it, though, the less comfortable he'd been with it.

Now Vitus looked at his hands, not at her. "Not what I'd originally researched, no." He cleared his throat. "I came to the conclusion that I found the usual sort of thing uncomfortably manipulative. Not in all cases, of course, but in some. Enough that I wanted to invest in making a signature piece that did something different. Went about it in a way I wanted to use day in and day out."

"Also," Niobe said, "A much more difficult problem, as you're working on multiple layers. Presenting yourself well is simple enough, in terms of construction. This?" She kept looking at the watch, which at least meant she wasn't peering at him. "This is four layers, isn't it? Not three."

Vitus nodded once. "A net around the edge, to bring in the information that's needed." He let out a little hitch, a half-breath. "Then clarity, to understand what's there. Followed by refinement, to understand what is needed. Finishing with self-awareness, to decide if I am a suitable person to provide that."

Niobe put down the loupe, then slid the watch back into his hand. "Look at me, will you?"

He looked up, meeting her eyes, and then was startled to realise she was smiling. The watch was in his hand, so was the fob. He knew how that felt now. He'd had enough time with them both, even if there were still nuances to learn. "I am exceedingly proud of you. Not many would make that sort of decision, not when you know how custom usually runs, what you were sure I'd expect."

The last few words made him blink, suddenly uncertain, but at least reassured he had not disappointed her. Then she was pulling something out of her bodice, a long chain with an oval locket on the end. He'd seen it once or twice before, but never for long or up close, and he'd thought she always wore it. Now she pulled the chain over her head, holding out the locket to him. "Get your loupe out. Have a look at that. Take your time."

They were, in fact, orders, and she was his apprentice mistress. Even if he weren't utterly curious, he'd have obeyed. He twisted a bit, to get better light, then worked his way through what he could see. Three tiny gemstones, suspended from the locket proper, set one above the other, shading from pale green through emerald, then the engraving on the locket itself. "Drawing from the Etruscan revival?" Vitus glanced up. "But not your work, the goldsmithing."

She laughed at that. "No. I traded with Mercurius Hazel, it's his journeyman piece." She didn't have the delicacy of touch for that, and there were plenty of reasons goldsmithing was its own mastery. "But the design was all mine, and all the gem work. You can open it, too."

Vitus went back to looking at it, then started making notes with one hand, while looking at it. It took him at least five minutes. That was long enough that Niobe had refilled both their cups of tea. Finally, Vitus offered it back, closing it gently and making sure it latched. "The bottom stone, the chalcedony, is the warding, here, the anchor for it. One of them." He corrected himself quickly.

"One of them. No sense in having a single point of failure, even if this one is quite secure." Niobe was definitely amused. He'd started with the easiest.

"And then, the middle one, the chrysoprase, that is something about drawing people whose custom you want and averting ill fortune. The smallest stone, the diamond, is a layer of that discernment. Who would make your reputation, to put it bluntly."

She beamed at him. "I want to work with interesting people, who I can actually help. I also want to make a good living at it, thank you. When you came in, I was sure I wanted to keep you around. It was just a question of how." Niobe gestured. "And the locket?"

"The interior looks like enamel, but it's stone, isn't it?

Lapis on the left, citrine on the right. True citrine, yes?" The feel of it was echoing what he wore. "From Brazil?" She nodded once, and he went on. "Amplifying appropriately." He then gestured with the end of his pencil. There had been no pictures in the locket, which was curious, actually, but he would not ask about that.

"Just so. And the outside?" Niobe slipped it back around her neck, though she left it visible.

"Near enough what I chose. About the discernment, and giving you information to discern with. Trusting that people will see your skill. The ones you want to, anyway."

The last part of it made her laugh. "Exactly. And it works well for me. Yours is a distinct style - we can discuss in detail at some point. Was the back of yours based on Petrus Minor or Elezar Three?"

"The second, more. But Petrus Minor has that really interesting comment in one of his letters about the applications with intent work. How to get what the actual intent was, not the projected intent." Vitus raised a hand. "Later, yes. More to the point, when I have all my notes - they're in the trunks - and can give you the citations and quotes."

"See, there are reasons I chose you. More than a few of them. Before we get to the trunks, though, now you know I approve. What are your plans?" Niobe had settled to look at him square on. Not that Vitus wanted to duck this. This was what mattered.

"I need to build my reputation. Related to yours, and independent from you. And figure out, erm."

"How to build a clientele without taking from me." Niobe raised a finger, gesturing at the fob. "That won't be a problem. You and I are different people. We can now delineate who suits best. And it's not as if I'm unwilling to consult after you leave the nest. I certainly hope you'll be willing." Before he could say anything, her chin lifted, warning him she had more. "Not as an obligation. Your obligation to me is done when we finish your apprenticeship. But I hope, very much, we will be collaborating for many years to come, and be friends, as well as colleagues."

"That's your end game." Then he blinked. "Oh, the pattern on the back, with the drops of gold."

"Exactly. Easy to add more, as appropriate. Well, for Mercurius or someone of his skill." She turned her hands palm up. "Acceptable to you?"

Vitus was nodding before she finished speaking. It was far more generous than he'd expected, and she no doubt already had ideas about how to ease the way. "Where do we start?"

"Ideally, we'd find someone with a visible need. An engagement that requires a new ring or a wedding gift. A Council challenge, from someone with the resources to commission a work and time enough to make one, but of course we can't count on that. The weddings and betrothals are rather more frequent."

"One of the heads of school or perhaps one of the notable professors retiring, someone else beginning," Vitus agreed. "I gather I missed quite the betrothal party for the Fortiers, but of course they'd use their own family pieces." He hadn't yet hunted down the coverage of the engagement ring, but it would be in one of the papers, and he was curious. "I don't suppose you have the latest gossip about that?"

"And if they do commission a wedding piece, it'd probably go to Gallagher." Ambrose Gallagher was highly skilled. But Vitus was now absolutely sure he ran to the conventional piece to draw in custom. He did solid work, but not imaginative designs. However, he had far more of the custom of the best of the Great Families, if they didn't keep someone on retainer privately. "I do not position myself to get more than the most public gossip about the Fortiers, but I can think of a few people who might know more. Or you have your own society connections. But no, I can't imagine you'll get the offer of any pieces for Miss Lytton-Powell. Maybe for a gift or two, but nothing that would make your name."

"Even with Father's connections. I'm not established yet, and the wedding's set for, what, next March, I heard?"

"Once Miss Lytton-Powell finishes her own apprenticeship, yes. And winter's such a rush, you know that. You might pick up some commissions for that, though, especially if we could get some pieces made up to show the range of your skill by, oh, June."

Vitus considered. "The thing I haven't figured out how to show is the distinction between my artistic ability and my magical. It'd be possible to make plenty of pieces that aren't expensive but are quite effective, but of course convincing people of that is the trick."

"Just so. Perhaps we should look through the stones and see what you might work with?" Niobe pushed back from the table. "I intend for you to start out with a reasonable stock. That's why the amethysts and a number of other less expensive stones. Not that I didn't want to rebuild my own stock, and honestly, it's so much better when someone has a look at them."

"The emeralds from the Alps were surprisingly good quality for the price." Vitus offered. They wouldn't make stunning jewellery necessarily, but they'd be effective in talismanic work. "And there's quite a lot of excellent amber, and that's always good for magical pieces of varying kinds."

"What did you find in the way of agate?" Niobe waited for Vitus to join her, and then they lifted the first of the trunks up onto a bench so they could better unpack it.

"Some interesting colouration, absolutely. And I found some unusually well-proportioned peridot, too, on the way back. Here, let's start with that." He lifted out the tray, rummaging for the compartment that had those. It was good to be back, and it was even better to know he'd made the right choice in Niobe's eyes.

CHAPTER 5

APRIL 26TH IN TRELLECH

Thessaly considered her options. They were rather more limited than she'd prefer, given the setting, her clothing, and her social obligations. The evening had begun well. It was her third year attending the St. George's Day gala, one of Albion's most notable costume balls. There were hundreds of people throughout the Opera House's public rooms. From where Thessaly stood on the balcony, she could see people forming up for the next dance.

Of course, the date had been chosen for convenience, not precision. With St. George's Day falling on a Tuesday, and just after Easter Week, of course it was on the next Friday. It had meant a week of people making final choices about costumes and getting final illusion work done, so Magistra North had been busy with consultations. And Thessaly had been kept busy helping.

And then there were many gatherings before and after the gala itself. There wasn't one at Arundel. The Fortiers were less enthused about English saints, even as an excuse for a party, but Thessaly had three or four invitations to parties after the gala. She'd have to see where Childeric was planning on going. He had refused to decide the last time she'd talked to him.

And now Childeric was nowhere to be seen, and he should have been easy to spot. He was costumed as the Sun, glowing slightly with illusion and charmlight, enough to brighten any corner he stood in. When she'd seen him earlier, he'd been in fine fettle, gesturing and laughing and gathering people around him, like moths to a flame. Of course, she had no part in the illusion work of his costume. The Fortiers had someone for that, a specialist kept on retainer. And besides, most of the work had already been arranged before the betrothal.

Once she was married, she would not need to have a professional reputation. She might turn her skills to small things. She could do illusions fit for amusing children or for some family gathering that involved charades or small plays put on for the guests at a house party. But whatever she wore, in the years to come, would likely be someone else's magic. Just as it would be someone else's sewing and weaving and every other skill that went into a frock. Thessaly appreciated other people's skills, but she wanted, wistfully, to be able to display her own, without being judged for it. Any of her skills, whether that was illusion work or duelling.

That wasn't true tonight. She had been tempted, at first, to pick a swordswoman or a Musketeer or something of the kind, a nod at her own duelling prowess. But she had promised Childeric explicitly and his parents implicitly that she would not show him up in public. Making her own skill that visible meant people would remember and perhaps comment.

She might be one of the top rank of duellists in her age range, up to a decade or so older, at least on a good day. And she was clear that part of the reason she was marrying Childeric was because the strength of her magic and her ability to use it were visible, any time she duelled. Despite all that, apparently it was now time to keep that light under a bushel, unless she was actually in the duelling salle. No one had come out and said it, but in the month since the betrothal, Lady Maylis and Lady Chrodechildis had both made specific comments about it. Thessaly wasn't fool enough to miss them.

So her costume was nothing that would remind people of that set of skills. Thessaly had made several consultations with Magistra North, her apprentice mistress. Finally, she'd gone for a subtle bit of illusion work, or at least as subtle as a twining dragon that coiled around her could be. It had certainly been an interesting project to design, and she'd learned a great deal from it for the next time she did something like this.

The head came up over one shoulder, curling down to rest across the bodice. Its wings were tucked against its back, scales of peacock blue and turquoise shading down to deeper greens and purples against a blue gown the shade of a summer sky. No one had yet noticed the details, and that was interesting information. Mind, the half-mask she wore didn't exactly obscure her identity. But it made people have to work for it, especially if they didn't see her next to Childeric or his parents.

Looking down to the dance floor, Thessaly could see the senior Fortiers clearly enough. They had chosen quite conventional costumes. Lord Clovis was dressed as his namesake, in proper Merovingian robes of a deep blue-purple. His long hair was gleaming and loose rather than pulled back, and he looked every bit a king. Lady Maylis looked serene and elegant in long brocade robes and Queen Clotilde's translucent silk veil over her hair, both a striking scarlet red.

They had a small horde of people ebbing and flowing around them. The crowd would make a smile and nod and bob to them, as people outside of Albion might have done to a King and Queen. She'd only seen Sigbert briefly. It hadn't been long enough to identify which of the many possible heroic knights was his inspiration. He had forged off into the crowd as soon as they arrived.

Her own parents were not here. They didn't care for costume parties, and Father thought it was a great deal of fuss and bother to come up with a suitable outfit. An unnecessary expense, he'd declared. That was why Thessaly's costume used a gown she'd already owned with the illusion doing much of the work and needing only a relatively reasonable set of materia to work.

However, Thessaly expected to see Aunt Metaia at any turn. Her aunt had a long list of people to talk to, since these events were at least two-thirds business for anyone on the Council. Aunt Metaia, however, had let Thessaly help with her costume, and Thessaly wanted to know how people were taking it. There she was, in the opposite corner from the Fortiers. The illusion work was holding up well, too, and Thessaly let herself feel smug. Consistency and stability were some of the trickiest and least appreciated parts of a competent illusion.

The costume was a rather lovely take on an undine, all watery blues, curves, and swirls. Aunt Metaia's skirts appeared to pool around her ankles like she was always standing in a few inches of water that made them shift and bloom. The illusion work that made strands of her hair appear to do the same was a deft touch, if Thessaly said so herself.

Thessaly had had enough of the dancing for the moment. The masks made it possible for her to dance as many dances as she wished. And to dance without anyone becoming nervous about whether Childeric or his family might take offence at a hand that lingered a hair too long. Thessaly had amused herself, through several sets, in contemplating which of the men she danced with might be worthwhile for further conversation. Of course, she couldn't tell much from just a dance, it limited what one could talk about. If - more like when - she eventually took up with someone for her personal pleasure and his, she wanted conversation to be a part of it. Conversation mattered near as much as well as the more physical and as yet unknown pleasures of the bed.

Mind, duelling gave her an advantage on spotting people. The way people moved in a duel carried over into dancing. Temenos Sibley, there, was in a deep scarlet red, a knight on a mission. He had a habit of standing with his heels together and his feet at a right angle. Awkward, if he had to move quickly in any direction. That had to be Gerold Teague. He had been a few years ahead of Thessaly in school, but she'd know the way he took a stride anywhere. It was just slightly shorter on the right, from a slight knee injury.

Thessaly was fairly sure that the pair over there were Gaius and Felicia Roberts, brother and sister, rather than a married couple. Their costumes didn't complement that way, and besides, she could usually pick out Felicia by the way she held herself. She was a much better duellist than her brother, overall, though Gaius was clever about it. If someone could combine his eye for strategy with her skill in making use of it, that person would be near impossible to defeat.

However, there was no one she much wanted to talk to. Several of the women where she'd have had reason to speak to weren't there, due to having small children. If she talked to any of the male duellists, Childeric would likely be put out, or at least there was a chance he might be. She did not need that bother in her evening, not remotely. Best if Thessaly kept those conversations somewhere less public, like the next time she was in one of the salles in Trellech. And while she enjoyed duelling Felicia, the woman's conversational skills tended toward a sharp eye for gossip that Thessaly couldn't indulge in at this sort of event. Far too much chance that someone might overhear.

She was just about to go navigate the stairs - people always picked costumes that took up more space than they realised - when she realised someone was just behind her. "Oh, I beg your pardon." She turned, her skirt sweeping the floor behind her.

The man bowed, quite low, and with no hesitation. "Mistress." Then he straightened up. His own costume took her a moment.

He wore a long frock coat better suited to historical dress, all in a muted grey, over a matching shirt. The grey was like stone with slashes in the fabric, where shades of amethyst purple were bunched up to make shapes. It could be better with a little illusion work, but the sewing was well done. "A mine, master? Amethysts?" Once she had the idea, it was obvious.

He grinned - his mask matched his outfit, a muted grey.

It didn't hide his smile at all, or his eyes, which also lit up. "Just so, Mistress. You have a keener eye than most."

She slipped one foot behind her to curtsy properly. She made the sinking and rising gesture she'd practised for hours of her life so it looked smooth and not like a particularly precise sort of torture. Thessaly considered for just a moment, then shifted her fingers, focusing on her intention. Along the curve of her shoulder, she knew the dragon would open his eyes, blinking slowly, appearing to shift and rearrange himself. If this man had seen the tail as it undulated down her train, it would twitch.

The man took a step back, and then clapped his hands once, delighted. "Oh, you are far beyond me, Mistress. Are you hiding here from the valiant noble knights, then? Or am I keeping you from some treasure or quest or whatever it is dragons do with themselves when not dealing with such bothers?"

It made her laugh, picking up on his honest enjoyment. This was exactly what she had been hoping for, someone to have a bit of a verbal duel with her. She shifted again, and the dragon blinked once more, and then did that thing cats do when they wriggled into sleep. She'd based him on a cat, as it was far easier to study a cat than one of the custos dragons, who had a different shape, anyway. "I was considering the dancing, but I think I'd prefer a breath of fresh air. I do not see my escort handy, either."

The man considered, his head cocked. "Perhaps I might fetch you a glass of punch? I gather the terrace is warmed, if you would prefer that. And well-lit still, this time of night." Later, it would be a spot for people who wanted an assignation or at least to arrange one. But it was not yet midnight and plenty of the people who would be in and out were at least nominally innocent young women and spinster aunts.

"That would be most kind. Or wine, if that is easier to find." She had paid little attention to the refreshment table up on this level when she went by. There'd been a knot of people around it.

The man nodded and gestured at a courtly bow. "I will be back shortly, Mistress." He took two steps back and then turned smartly. Thessaly considered, and migrated down the balcony toward where it opened up overlooking the broad terrace and courtyard at the back of the building. Whoever he was, he was efficient, because he returned in only a couple of minutes, handing her a glass of wine before offering his arm.

The terrace was not even particularly crowded, and they found a space down at one corner, still well-lit and visible, but away from the din. Thessaly hadn't realised how wearing that had been until she could hear herself think again. She took a breath, settling herself and letting her train fall into place, before turning to the gentleman. She inclined her head. "Thank you for the glass and the thoughtfulness. Do you wish to remain a mystery, or may I ask who I am thanking?"

It made the corners of his mouth turn up. "Vitus Deschamps, Mistress. An apprentice talisman maker. Though I hope not an apprentice for too much longer."

Thessaly considered the lists of people she had memorised, not least for the betrothal, when she'd been expected to be able to say something suitable to any person who might speak to her. "Your parents are Master Claud and Mistress Joceline, yes? And you have a younger brother." She couldn't quite keep from looking up, searching her memory.

"Lucas." He supplied the name promptly. "He is not much seen in Albion society. I am impressed. Nor is he here tonight, actually. He's a cavalry officer, based in Somerset, but with limited leave."

That was intriguing, actually, to have a family who diverged quite like that. She knew the Deschamps were a client family to the Fortiers. There was some distant family connection, a few generations back, cousins or a cousin marrying in, something like that. Relevant enough, as it was, that she knew the name, not so powerful that she needed to worry about offending out of season. It begged the question of whether she shared her own name or not.

Etiquette - the sort of precise etiquette wielded like a weapon - said that anonymity gave her an edge of power, a chance for a conversation without her current social state interfering. Reality - in that same circle - said that whatever she said or did would make it back to Lady Maylis, eventually. Or to one of her relatives, which was as good as the same thing.

Instead of deciding immediately, she asked him another question. "I have not seen you at other events, at least recently, have I? Though I suppose at most of them you are not impersonating a gemstone mine." The lack of clarity on the crystals kept making her fingers twitch and want to do something to improve it. Not that it was a poor costume, it just could be stunning with a little touch or three.

"I have been travelling the past year and a half. A series of visits with talisman makers in Europe. I am an apprentice to Magistra Niobe Hall, she was kind enough to make the arrangements." Ah, the sort of thing where she'd traded favours. Not everyone got that kind of opportunity. Magistra Hall didn't do work for the Fortiers - nor for the Powells or Lyttons - but she had an excellent reputation.

In particular, she was known for turning down requests she did not care to take, for whatever reason. Which was almost certainly why the Fortiers, Lyttons, and Powells preferred others, who could be relied on to fulfil requests as required. Thessaly nodded once. "I know her reputation, of course."

"You are learned, Mistress." Deschamps made another slight bow, lifting his glass in acknowledgement. "And I can see you appreciate magic in its many forms."

CHAPTER 6

APRIL 26TH IN TRELLECH

Vitus was not at all sure of his footing in this conversation. It was as if he had found himself in some new European city, still only beginning to grasp the language and the way the streets went together, or where the river was. There was usually a river, that much he'd learned. The non-magical world ran on them, and the magical folk preferred them.

This woman, whoever she was, didn't seem far from his own age. But he wasn't sure if he knew her. None of the mannerisms quite fit with the women he'd gone to Schola with, not in his house or his year, anyway. That still left quite a few options. But the illusion work was skilled, and it wasn't a design he'd seen before. Not that he was up on the most recent work in Albion, of course, and he also didn't know every illusionist currently crafting in the art form.

She considered, then inclined her head. "Thessaly Lytton-Powell." The name rolled like the dragon she wore roaring to the sky. He'd heard her name recently, of course, twice over, but more than that, she came from two of the most powerful families in Albion and was marrying into a third.

Before he could do something ill-considered, he made another bow, careful to keep it elegant. “An honour, Mistress. May I also compliment your dressmaker and your illusionist?”

That made her smile, something that didn’t seem terrifying. She shifted her fingers slightly around the glass, and he saw the dragon move, another sinuous twist of the magnificent head, before he realised suddenly he had made a gaffe. Vitus swallowed. “Pardon. Your dressmaker, alone. Your illusion work is - I don’t think I’ve seen anything like it. Might I ask about it?”

She blinked at him several times, then she held out her wineglass to him. He took it, unsure what she was doing. She reached behind her head, tapping the ties that held her mask in place twice, so that the fastenings loosened, then lowered the mask. He wasn’t sure if she’d used charms to enhance her looks - smooth her skin, bring roses to her cheeks, that sort of thing - but she looked stunning. Flowering with the abundance of her magic, that was a way to put it, something no charm could ever quite duplicate.

She was also young, younger than he’d guessed with the mask on. They had overlapped at Schola, if briefly. He had a faint memory of someone who looked enough like her, though that someone had been a firstie when he’d been a fifth year. And in Fox or maybe Owl House, not his own Salmon. No, it must be Fox. Someone from a family like hers must have been.

Now, she lowered the mask, indicating several small embroidered strands in different colours along the edge of the mask. “These anchor each point, and by focusing on them, I can adjust the illusion so it moves. The other part is, well, more or less a dance, certainly a performance. It comes out a little differently each time. It is not a rigid precision." She considered, then added, "Your brother would not approve of it as a military drill."

Vitus laughed. "Ah, but my brother is a cavalryman, and horses do not precisely behave the same way each time, either. It is a delightfully organic piece, and with much more nuance in the colour than I've seen in many illusions. It's the range." He glanced back toward the rest of the gala. "I am wondering how many other people appreciated it properly?"

"My aunt. But she had the advance knowledge to do so." Mistress Lytton-Powell let the mask drape from her wrist by one loop of ribbon. She wore it charmingly like a dance card, then reached out for her glass. Vitus made absolutely certain not to fumble with it.

"If this is what you create when you are encouraged in your work, it is a pity more people do not notice." There, that was a gallant statement. "Are you apprenticing then, or do I insult, and you have completed it?"

"Oh, not for nine or ten months more." Her tone shifted, the kind of thing those of Fox House read in their infinite subtlety, and Vitus had to work to understand in all the implied layers. "Illusion work - if not this form of it - is a suitable skill for a society wife of the Great Families."

"My congratulations, of course. My parents were at your betrothal. Mama was telling me how grand the festivities were. I am sorry I was away, and missed the chance myself." He glanced over his shoulder. "Will your betrothed object to find you talking with another man? Or will his parents or yours?" It suddenly seemed an excellent idea to gain more information on that point.

"Childeric is off with his friends." There was a clear

neutrality there. She was not placing any judgement anywhere near that sentence. That was most curious. "And he and I have discussed matters. A conversation somewhere public and well-lit for a few minutes is well within our agreements. A hint of scandal is not. You understand, I am sure."

"I understand that those are deep waters, not ones I normally navigate, Mistress." Vitus let himself smile. "I must trust, then, that you will let me know should I overstep. And of course, I do not wish to keep you from the dancing."

"I did want a breath of air. I will go in soon enough." Mistress Lytton-Powell turned to him, looking him up and down. "Actually, may I adjust your costume? Would you mind terribly?"

Vitus blinked. It was certainly not a sentence he'd expected, or an offer. "What sort of change, please?" He thought quickly through what he was wearing in the way of his own work, just cufflinks, tie pin, and a protective talisman under his shirt.

"It's rather a lovely design, your amethyst. But I've been itching to improve it. And you seem like a gentleman who wishes the proper translucence and shading in his accoutrements. Something as much like stone as it is possible to wear?"

She turned her hand up, palm flat, the mask bumping against her skirts as she moved. "May I? The amethyst first, but I also hope for an improvement in the surrounding matrix." Before he could ask anything further, she added, "It will wear off overnight. I don't have any of the fixatives handy. Obviously." She gestured at her skirts. "I might carry them beneath my skirts, but I'd worry about breakage. Some people are so clumsy on the dance floor."

She obviously did not permit that sort of clumsiness, the way she moved so deftly and gracefully. Vitus was clear it was a skill she'd spent endless hours perfecting, but he appreciated it all the more for that. Now, he nodded. "If you wish, I will not deny you." He said the words in all gallantry - and honestly, he did not wish to offend. But something in them had more of an echo than he'd expected, and he did not know why. "Should I stand in a certain way?"

"Just your arms at your sides, away from where I'm working. Here, let me have your glass as well. They should be safe enough here for a moment." Mistress Lytton-Powell considered the railing. "Or if not, I suppose there's no one right below just now." She balanced the two glasses on the flat of the railing and then turned back. "It won't take very long." Then she tsked once. "Your suit, is it wool or a wool-silk blend?" Those were the two most likely for Albion, and in spring.

"Wool." He knew the silk could affect enchantments. Plenty of the men inside were wearing something of the kind. Anyone who routinely wore protective enchantments like armour in their clothing, rather than their accoutrements. "I've talismans in my cufflinks, tie pin, watch fob, and a pendant, if that might affect anything."

It made her raise an eyebrow, but then she nodded, and before he could ask anything further, he could feel the effect. It was rather like a paintbrush gliding over skin, a tactile sensuality that reminded him of running his hand along the stone of the mines themselves when he'd visited. His other experiences of illusion work had been less sensual. As her hand moved, he could see the way everything shifted. She was using the embroidery and purple cloth as the base to form crystals that stuck out at different, realistic angles. They formed a broad line from one shoulder down to the opposite hip, rather like a sash or even a sword belt, made of gemstone.

Then she considered, bringing her gloved hand to her lips for just a second. There was something more like a pulse of magic. Now he could see the suit take on a shimmer more like stone, and with little cracks and shading. It faded out a bit as he craned his neck to look at his shoulders, but the effect was more visible across his chest.

"There." She sounded pleased. "Thank you for that. It was bothering me. You were very close with the fabric. Do move. I want to see how the effect adjusts."

Given the instruction, Vitus took a step back, then forward, reaching for both glasses again and offering hers back to her. She took it, lifting her glass in a silent toast, and he touched his glass to hers. It rang, suddenly a little louder in the surrounding quiet. He could feel and see how the crystals looked like solid stone, but they shifted as he moved, like living rock. Or the scales of her dragon, now he thought of that. "I am simply sorry, Mistress, that they will not last. Like a Fatae tale, I suppose, fading away with the dawn."

"Should you wish to discuss a more permanent piece, I'd be glad to do so. At the moment - you know how this goes, I'm sure - you would speak to Magistra North North. Her shop is north on Trivium Way." She nodded in the general direction.

"I know the place." He did. It was just down from the stationery store his father preferred. "I would like that, though I should probably consider if I wish amethyst or something else."

"The purple suits you. And the range of it." Then she cocked her head. "Though you weren't in Fox House, I think."

"Salmon," he agreed. "But much as I like citrine, it doesn't suit me well to wear. Not in this sort of quantity, anyway." He had somewhat mousy hair and the paler yellow did no favours. "I love lapis, but that's even trickier to manage in a costume."

Mistress Lytton-Powell got a speculative look in her eyes at that. Vitus knew that look much better. In anyone of Salmon - or anyone in the Four Metals, for that matter - he'd have immediately pegged it as a sudden contemplation of an interesting magical problem to solve. "I might have some ideas for that, but it needs a layered effect, and getting the veining right is a trick. I will do some research. Do call."

Before he could say much more, there was a voice behind him. "There you are, Thessaly. I've someone I wanted you to talk to." Vitus turned to see a woman, perhaps in her forties, coming toward them, or rather floating, as if she were in a small lake or pond. It was an impressive costume, if far more showy than Mistress Lytton-Powell's at first glance. Her mask made him unsure who the older woman was.

"Aunt Metaia." It gave him the beginning of a clue, but then Mistress Lytton-Powell turned. "This is my aunt, Council Member Metaia Powell. Auntie, I have been discussing some illusion work with Master Vitus Deschamps. Oh, and I meant to ask about your work, we haven't had time. I will think about the lapis lazuli." That seemed heartfelt, actually, not just politeness.

Vitus offered a bow. "Of course I won't keep you. I'm glad to see your glass to safety, though, if I may serve in so small a way. Your costume flatters, Council Member. May I guess your niece had a hand in it?"

It won him a flash of a smile, something full of an

approval Vitus didn't entirely understand. "Oh, a man who uses his eyes properly. Yes, thank you, Thessaly did the work, and splendidly. Do come along, dear, or we'll never find him again."

They both smiled at him - their smiles made it obvious they were related - and Vitus just bowed once more as they went off, saying nothing further. He was left alone with two mostly empty wineglasses and a surprising number of questions. He couldn't do anything about those, but he could go show off her work and perhaps have a few conversations that might lead to eventual clients in due course.

CHAPTER 7
MAY 3RD IN TRELLECH

Thessaly was normally a fairly patient person. Today, though, was testing every grip on her calm she could muster. Magistra North was unhappy with her, and with good reason. Thessaly had missed not only May Day because of the rites at Arundel, but also April 30th and yesterday, May 2nd. Now it was Friday, and half of what Thessaly wanted to do would take several days of work in a row to set up. She could scarcely start now.

Magistra North had left her strictly alone all day, as if ignoring her would make the problems go away. On one hand, that was an apprentice mistress's prerogative. Magistra North had long since earned every bit of respect for her time and skill that she demanded and expected. And it wasn't as if Thessaly would make an argument about fairness. Even when that was true and valid, people rightfully assumed - given Thessaly's background - that she was doing it for some other reason than correctness.

Besides, it was hard to argue with someone who was on the opposite side of the building. And it wasn't as if Magistra North didn't have cause. Thessaly had heard the commentary and concerns about the failures of apprentices in her year, and a few years on either side. People who had an awful run of ill health, or who just weren't up to standard. She'd talked to Aunt Metaia about some of it, but Aunt Metaia hadn't had an answer either.

It meant there was pressure on the people who were apprenticing to finish, and to meet - exceed - the expectations of their field. That was true in Alchemy, in Healing, in the things that kept people alive. But for all people assumed Illusion was an optional art, Thessaly knew perfectly well how important it was. Illusion work, lasting illusions, was essential in keeping non-magical folk away from Silence-kept spaces or magical homes or places where they could get hurt by magic they didn't understand. Aunt Metaia did quite a lot of that work for the Council and for private clients.

Even if Thessaly never did much direct consulting, she could take on that role at Arundel or other properties in the family. It would free up illusionists to work on other spaces. Or it would be a way to offer a contribution to the well-being of those in Trellech. The sort of thing where other women, like Mama, might organise a philanthropic luncheon or raise funds with their gifts and talents.

All of it meant Thessaly couldn't argue with Magistra North's irritation, even if she had had little control over it. Instead, Thessaly had spent the day getting her workroom in order. She could not start the new projects yet, but she could lay out everything she'd need for them come Monday. She had the materia in the protective storage over on the worktable. Thessaly had also set out and comprehensively annotated her notes, then written up the steps in sequence.

The project at hand was a lasting illusion, projected and formed onto a carved piece of wood. The technique was most commonly deployed for children from families rich enough to have a substantial piece of magical work in the nursery. It was also sought by the occasional theatre who could afford it on a larger scale. It was, however, an excellent technical challenge, both in the crafting and the artistry.

It had also involved sanding a board smooth and preparing it for the fixative and applying that, which had given Thessaly far too much time to think. And mostly, Thessaly had been thinking about the past few days. That might in fact be dangerous to indulge, and yet simultaneously necessary.

The rites at Arundel had been both fascinating and frustrating, in about equal parts. She certainly knew the basic theory of it. She'd earned near enough top marks in Ritual class in her year at Schola, but there was always a distance between the theory of the thing and the application. Professor Hayes had hammered that into them, especially once they got into the practical exercises. Every ritual depended on many factors in the moment, much like the difference between a play on the page and in the theatre.

The Powells had their own customs, of course. Usually she spent the seasonal turning days with Aunt Metaia and that side of the family, rather than Papa's. The Lyttons had rituals, of course, but they ran on a different cycle and schedule. The Powell rites weren't about the land magic, though, not formally. They had to do with the continuation and flourishing of the family and those they supported. There were the customs to bless the fields, give thanks for the harvest, for health and happiness, and to offer propitiation when that was called for.

The Arundel rites hadn't been like that. And worse, she hadn't even been able to talk about them with anyone. Her parents hadn't been invited, and when Thessaly had tried to talk a little about them, no one had wanted to listen. Maybe she'd get a chance in private with Aunt Metaia on Sunday. There was a garden party, but after everyone left, they might get half an hour, maybe longer. She could write a letter, but somehow putting magic on the page always flattened it, like someone just learning the rudiments of illusion. It came out like drawings where the dog's legs had bends in the wrong places or some of the mediaeval illustrations of dragons that looked more like a misplaced crocodile.

That just brought her back to how trying to put her thoughts into words kept stalling. For one thing, a fair bit of the Arundel rites had been in French, and not modern French, either. There'd been something that had been - Thessaly had followed about one word in four - a particular sort of duel in words and poetry. It had classic forms. She thought it was possibly a mesh of ritualised couplets strung together in different combinations. It had built enchantments, though, a web of magic that built up piece by piece, into something like a net.

It had not been a surprise to the others there, though she'd caught Alexander Landry nodding at some particular detail here or there. But of course, he'd grown up with those as the rites he knew. And he had a particular interest in Ritual as a magical form, though Thessaly knew that he'd also had several out-and-out arguments with Professor Lollard. The gossip about the volume and range of those arguments had spread outside Schola quickly. She hadn't had Lollard. He'd begun helping Professor Hayes with some of her classes as she approached retirement or when a ritual needed a second.

The good part about it, such as there was one, was that

the Heir's role wasn't terribly complex. She wasn't likely to need to have a vast stock of magical poetry memorised by next year, anyway, but she might be called on to scatter flowers. Or do something with flowers. There had been an awful lot of precisely chosen flowers, and not just for the usual materia reasons.

It had, however, also been a tremendously long couple of days. Lady Chrodechildis had mentioned - but not fully explained - that their traditions came from older and even more powerful times. They were anchored first in the great Merovingian courts, then transformed and woven with arts from Aquitaine, brought across the Channel in the Conquest.

The night before had involved a feast, more French poetry, a sort of pageantry, which had not, she thought, been essential to the land magic, but rather a custom of the family, a chance to show off their wealth and power. There had been illusionists, all competent but not terribly imaginative. Or, she thought now, not permitted to be imaginative, and that was an interesting and also worrisome concern.

They'd all been men, all skilled, but also curiously restrained in their arts. The feasting and pleasantries had continued after the dawn rites. There had been processions to the four corners of the manor's immediate grounds. Someone had to make the traditional blessings on the water and the earth, and every garden in those bounds, down to the kitchen courtyard herbs.

She'd ended up entirely fatigued, far beyond what she'd done in the day. It had been complex, yes. It had been long. The day had involved four complete changes of clothing, starting with ritual dress in the morning, then a day dress. Then she'd changed in the afternoon for a more formal gathering with a larger guest list. It had ended with a last change into evening dress, with a pause for an hour's rest in a wrapper between afternoon and evening. That should not have tired her so much, though, that she needed to sleep half of the second away.

Thessaly felt the approaching presence before she heard the footsteps. That was just good sense, both as an apprentice and as a trained duellist. Magistra North's magic had a definite signature. It meant Thessaly was standing facing the door, head properly inclined, when Mistress North knocked once and opened the door without waiting for a reply. "Thessaly?"

"Ma'am." Thessaly raised her eyes the proper amount.

"You must not let your betrothal interfere with your studies. I should not need to say this." Magistra North looked at Thessaly straight on. "Do not make me call attention to it again. If you need to take additional time besides the Solstice break, let me know in good time."

"Yes, magistra." Thessaly weighed her options. "I am all set up for Monday. Is there any reading you suggest I do as well?"

That brought a slight pause, then Magistra North walked to the worktable, pulling out a piece of notepaper, and writing a few things, the pen scratching at the paper. "Several articles. You have all of those?"

Thessaly peered at the list as it was handed over, all neat copperplate writing. "Yes, magistra. Monday, then?"

"Your betrothed is waiting for you. None too patiently. Kindly arrange for him to meet you elsewhere in the future, if you don't mind. We've not space, for one thing."

Thessaly blinked. "I had not expected him, magistra, but of course, I'll let him know. I'm sorry he disturbed your work." She waited a moment for the nod of acknowledgement, then Magistra North swept out of the room. Thessaly gathered up her things, tucking the notes into a small leather portfolio that was delicate enough to carry in public. She added her shawl and made her way downstairs as swiftly as possible.

Childeric was in the front parlour, looking impatient. "There you are, Thess."

"I didn't expect you." She came over as he stood up and pressed a kiss on each of her cheeks. "I - were you waiting long?"

"Long enough." He shrugged, but in a way that made it clear it had been too long and also her fault. "I needed to check some things on my own, and also with you. Walk you to the portal, then?"

She nodded, and once they were outside and there was more space, she slipped her hand through his arm, a proper escort. He did the thing right, of course, walking at her pace and minding the sway of her skirts, putting himself between her and the traffic on the street. Childeric didn't speak again until they were about halfway to Portal Square.

"I need you to get free two afternoons next week. Tuesday and Friday. Maman has some people she'd like us to have tea with."

Thessaly didn't quite stop, but it was a near thing. She swallowed, gathering all the words she'd been taught for when she had to disagree with something, but do it with absolute politeness. "I'm afraid that's not possible, not on such short notice. I've already promised Magistra North I'll be available."

"Maman said it wouldn't matter. And after all, your illusion work is lovely, of course it is. But you're scarcely going to need to keep good relations with others in the field."

Now she stopped, and she tried to get her face to look baffled rather than furious. She was fairly sure she was failing, and the two expressions didn't exactly have much common ground. She turned away for a moment. When she looked back, Childeric was standing there. Finally, what Thessaly mustered was, "It's a part of our agreements - the formal ones and the informal ones, you did promise. I'm given freedom to complete my apprenticeship to Magistra North's standards. Besides, I'm just getting into the really challenging part." Also, the most interesting parts.

He dismissed that last. She'd wondered if he might. "It won't matter when we're married. Of course, you can still do that sort of thing. It's certainly more suitable to the family than flower arranging or purely ornamental embroidery or some such. But you needn't strain yourself now."

Thessaly took a breath. "Still. Magistra North has just been quite firm with me. She's upset I missed three days this week. I'm afraid I can't ask for more, not until at least after Solstice."

"You can explain it to Maman, then. Before Sunday." He held out his arm, elbow crooked, pointedly. "Tea today, or will you find time tomorrow? Maman is at home to callers in the morning."

Tomorrow, it would have to be tomorrow. "I need to get home. Mama and Papa are having a few family guests for supper, and I need to be ready. Please convey my greetings to your mother, and I'll call in the morning." At least doing it in that order, she could consult with Mama and maybe one or two other people on how to navigate an additional complication.

Childeric nodded sharply, and then walked off again, with no warning to Thessaly. She didn't trip over her feet, thankfully. Once they were in motion again, he picked up an easier conversation about something he'd seen in the shop windows earlier. He could be entirely charming - and decidedly amusing - when he chose. And yet, once he left her at the portal, she found herself feeling at sea again. She wanted nothing more than to go home, sit, and rest for a little.

CHAPTER 8

MAY 9TH AT THE FOUR METALS SOCIETY HOUSE, TRELLECH

"How is it, being back?" Vitus looked up. The gathering of the Four Metals was more or less wrapping up, a lunchtime discussion. He'd only made it to two other of the society gatherings since he'd returned to Albion, between the family demands, sorting through plans with Niobe, and a few minor commissions. Today's talk, however, had been about symbology and simplification or decoration of the same, all relevant to his professional interests.

"Amayas." Vitus nodded. Amayas Robson had been a few years ahead of him at Schola, also in Salmon House, but he'd gone into an entirely different line of magical inventiveness. He had a knack for making devices, mostly those designed for secure storage, with a range of locks, magical protections, and decorations. Sometimes the decorations were also protections, of course. "Busy, of course. And you've gone through the same thing, beginning to establish yourself."

"Ah, yes. Chasing the perfect commission that will simultaneously show your particular skills without stepping too much on the toes of anyone else in the field." Amayas offered a quick grin. "I'm glad you're not in mine, actually, the way you were asking questions."

Vitus had thought about that aspect of it. "Fortunately, Niobe thinks training someone up to a high standard reflects well on her. And she's always getting more requests than she can handle. It's just a matter of convincing a couple to consider me."

"Which is part timing and luck, and part the whim of the client. None of which are certain." Amayas considered, then crooked a finger for one woman to come over. "Merryn, you remember Vitus Deschamps, yes? He just returned from the Continent last month. You two want to talk carving techniques sometime, I expect."

Amayas melted away at that, leaving Vitus to stand and make a little bow, then figure out what to do with himself. "Mistress Penforth." He'd start with politeness, even if the Four Metals generally only gave a brief nod to formality within their society house walls. Merryn was a bit older - perhaps late thirties - and sedately dressed. She was Cornish, Vitus remembered. Professionally, she did something with stone carving, making warding and boundary stones. Within the Four Metals, though, she had a reputation for cunning little automatons, and she sold them as a sideline.

"You needn't." It might have been sharp, but she had a lovely smile, even and relaxed. "You're apprenticing with Niobe, if I remember correctly? Almost done, I'm assuming. You had that question about connective engraving."

"That, and the difference between a fully detailed symbol and one that is simplified. I know the answer is to do a duplicate and test it, but that's not so easy when the stones are expensive." Vitus spread his hands out.

"Deschamps, Deschamps." She cocked her head, considering something. "You might have a word with Philip Landry, if he has a moment. Not one of us, of course, but he's consulted on a few projects I've worked on. Tell him I suggested it. That might actually help. He's got rather an interesting line of discussion about the shifts from fully detailed hieroglyphs to hieratic and Demotic. Something about the way the shapes carry meaning and it's the meaning that matters. Even if the original pure form, as some people have it, would have all the minute details."

"I don't know much about any of that. And I'd not have thought to ask him." Vitus considered. "You think well of his work?"

"Don't believe all the gossip you hear, mmm?" She snorted. "Oh, he absolutely has secrets and all sorts of magics I've no idea about. But he's also got new ways of thinking about a problem. A very Four Metals sort of thinking, in his own way."

Vitus nodded. He'd never have considered the approach without active encouragement. "I can send a note, at least, and see what comes of it. Thank you, that might help me figure out a way forward. You use some techniques related to layering, don't you? Not bind-runes exactly, but related approaches?"

That got her off into a good five minutes digression on historical and modern applications. Also, she laid out the benefits for boundary markers, and how to make the things look appealing as well as being useful. None of it was entirely relevant to the current problem Vitus was trying to sort out. Niobe had given him a piece of jasper with an awkwardly placed conchoidal fracture, already too small to be worth shaping further if they were to do any carving. His assignment had been to figure out something that would work with the shape as it was.

When she paused, she then laughed. "You are very polite. That will take you far."

Vitus let himself smile. "It's no difficulty to listen to someone both knowledgeable and passionate. Besides, isn't that what we're here for, all of us with our own pet projects and wanting someone to appreciate them?"

Merryn tilted her head again. It reminded him of some watchful animal. "Not everyone does as you do." She then gestured. "Next week, Wednesday, perhaps supper beforehand with a few other people? We might have some ideas for making further connections. I suspect you're going to say Daedalus Briggs' devices aren't your sort of thing, but you really should come. It's how he talks about them that will intrigue."

That, of course, was the reason he was here today. He wasn't fool enough to turn down that kind of invitation for a more intimate gathering that would lend itself to back-and-forth conversation and perhaps further introductions. Vitus nodded. "I'd be delighted. Send me a note with when and where?" He'd make it work, though he hoped the restaurant wouldn't be too dear. He reached into the inside pocket, pulling out his calling card and writing a note with the message address. A few minutes later, after two other brief nods at people he'd like to talk to more soon, he was out the door, walking back toward Niobe's workshop. She wasn't expecting him at any particular point, thankfully, since he'd already been longer than expected.

He was turning right from Trivium Way onto Caelum Road when he spotted an unexpected figure. That was Philip Landry, properly turned out, but pausing by one of the newspaper stands. Luck was with Vitus. The carters were out in force at the moment, making deliveries. Despite that, he crossed the street without risk of life or limb. Landry hadn't moved from his spot.

Vitus nodded once. "Pardon, Magister Landry?" He would begin politely for several reasons, starting with the fact he was asking a favour.

The other man blinked at him once or twice, then said promptly, with the sort of speed that suggested he kept a large roster of names and faces in his head. "Vitus Deschamps, isn't it? I heard you were back from the Continent."

"Three weeks ago, yes. It was a most educational trip, though I am glad to be home. Might I ask for a moment of your time? Magistra Merryn Penforth suggested I ask if you'd be willing to consult about something I'm working on. Suitable arrangements, of course, for an hour or so." Vitus was of the class - as were the Landrys - where business was done and consulting fees were paid, but where naming a number in the open was decidedly considered déclassé.

Philip Landry inclined his head. "Perhaps we might walk and you can tell me the scope?" He gestured with one hand. His voice was a pleasant baritone, though with a hint of an accent to it.

"I was going back towards Magistra Niobe Hall's workshop," Vitus offered. "But if you were going another direction, sir, I'm glad to walk with you."

"That will do well. I was heading a little further myself." They picked up a steady walk. Before Vitus could say anything further, Landry added. "My younger brother is to make a Grand Tour. He leaves in July. Paris, first, of course, for the Exposition Universelle." His voice was pleasant, entirely conversational, but giving the French name for the World's Fair rather than the English. "Perhaps I might ask you to suggest places to visit or avoid, as part of our conversation?"

"I would be glad to." It was an easy enough thing to agree to, especially if it eased the way. "A focus on what area of study, may I ask?"

"Ritual, primarily, but of course, that encompasses many other fields. Your own focus would have been mineralogical as well as the crafting of talismans, I assume?" Landry glanced over at him.

Vitus nodded. "I'd be glad to write a letter of introduction or two. I can certainly pull together my notes, depending on where he expects the trip to take him." Then he took a breath. "I've a particular piece I'm working on, where space, shape, and size are considerations." As they covered the next block or two, he laid out the basics, what Merryn Penforth had suggested, and then waited.

Landry listened attentively, then nodded. "I could go over enough you could make sense of some of the literature in an hour." He considered. "You are a young man, setting up in the world." He named a number, and added, "And whatever you feel you can pass along from your travels."

It was decidedly on the low side. Vitus considered. "I wouldn't wish to undervalue your expertise, sir."

"My choice." The words came out bluntly. Then Landry offered a smile. This one put Vitus a bit on edge, for all the danger in it didn't seem aimed at him. "It does not require much effort on my part, just my time, and I will look forward to an hour talking about a topic too few appreciate. Perhaps you might call on me in my rooms, oh, next week?"

They made the arrangements after considering their various obligations, settling on Thursday week. Vitus considered, then said, "Pardon, may I ask another question? Related to the Fortiers."

There was another of those shifts, of Landry rearranging himself, as if he might need to act in some new way. "Yes?" The reply was entirely neutral in tone.

"I had the pleasure of meeting Mistress Lytton-Powell at the St George's Day gala. She invited me to call on her for a professional consultation, but I—" His voice trailed off. "I did not wish to give offence, either to her, or to her fiancé's family."

"And I would indeed know something about that." Landry nodded once, though he was silent for long enough that Vitus was sure he'd overstepped somehow. "If she made the invitation, she considers it within her bounds. I would not, however, seek a meeting in some private place. The seeming of the thing, you understand, rather than the risk of it?"

It took Vitus a moment to think that through. "I thought her illusion work skilful. And more than that, artistically innovative. As someone who looks to make works of magic that combine function and form, it caught my eye."

Landry inclined his head. "Her family has brought her up well, in all the ways one means by that sentence. Call on her in her apprenticeship, when her apprentice mistress is available. But yes, I think you might have mutual interests, in the way your magic is expressed." He shrugged once. "I would put in a word for you, but I do not expect to see her to speak to for at least a fortnight. I have a number of other obligations."

"Of course, I wouldn't expect you to extend yourself on that point. You barely know me." Vitus nodded. "I appreciate that. I'll send a message and ask her to let me know if there is a convenient time." It would let her decide, or let her dissuade, if her comments at the gala had been pure politeness.

"I hope your family is also well? I suppose the next event of note will be the Midsummer Faire." Landry offered it agreeably. "Or perhaps the Council rites?"

"The latter, I expect. We were honoured with an invitation this year." It would be a fantastic opportunity to remind people that Vitus and his skills existed. Papa had exerted himself on that count, dropping a word in a couple of relevant ears. "Mama is quite looking forward to it. And then the Faire, yes, that's always an enjoyable outing." And a necessary place for him to begin to establish himself.

"I will hope to see you at one or the other, then. Please remember me to your mother. She has always been delightful to speak with." Landry then touched his hat. "I should be off. Thursday next, you needn't bring anything other than whatever you use for notes."

Vitus nodded. "Thank you for your time, and the time to come." He watched Landry walk off, further into the crafting quarter, before turning down into the courtyard that led to Niobe's workshop. He had the sense, strong but hard to pin down, that Landry had been pleased to have a conversation about skill and knowledge that was comfortable for him. And that, simultaneously, that it was a change from other conversations in his life. The information about Mistress Lytton-Powell was, however, welcome, and he would figure out how to send a note round in the next day or so.

CHAPTER 9

MAY 11TH AT BRYN GLAS, WALES

Thessaly had just finished the fourth round of drills when she heard her aunt. "Tea, dear?" It was a lovely day out, warm and dry enough that Thessaly had come to work through her duelling exercises outside in the meadow beyond Aunt Metaia's more structured gardens.

She had not actually been able to set up a duel this month, either in the past or soon. And June would be worse, between the Council rites and the Midsummer Faire. Thessaly had hopes of one in a week or ten days, depending on whether a couple of people could get free. It had to be a couple, for propriety's sake, and ideally at least one other woman. Palantina Monkton and her brother Decimus, maybe, or Eveline and Cuthbert North, but both pairs of siblings often had other obligations. She'd have to hold her thumbs for good luck and hope.

"Coming, Aunt Metaia." She wiped her face off with her handkerchief, then looked around to make sure that everything was fit to be left. She undid one lingering cantrip in the southwest corner and mended a bit of torn up ground ten feet from her. Then she considered the knees of the pantaloons she was wearing under her calf-length frock. Aunt Metaia approved thoroughly of rational dress, especially for active pursuits, but she did not approve of grass stains at the tea table. Nor did she approve of letting stains set and making more trouble for the maids later.

Fortunately, another charm took care of that one. One final bit of magic pulled all the wisps of hair that had come loose into a tidier form. Thessaly felt quite suitable to be good company again. She had come up here in a burst of frustration, after a somewhat aggravating morning being quiet and attentive while Lady Maylis was at home to callers. Even though she'd just been sitting there - with Childeric beside her for about half of it - she'd turned up at Bryn Glas feeling exhausted and out of sorts.

By the time she made it back to the table on the garden terrace, Aunt Metaia had settled in. Three kinds of scones and several small decorative pastries stood on the tiered stand, along with neatly sliced sandwiches. "Oh, tea." Thessaly let out a relieved sigh. "Please do thank Cook for me?"

"Are they not feeding you at home? I swear, Thessaly, every time you come here, you seem to be starving. Though you worked up an appetite, too." Aunt Metaia settled into her own chair. She was wearing one of her favourite forms of aesthetic dress, a loose peacock tea gown over a darker blue underdress, uncorseted. The fabric, though, was radiantly gorgeous. The shade shimmered from blues to greens to a hint of purple like the bird, a far richer weave than Mama normally wore at home. "Has the tree stump been thoroughly defeated, then?"

Thessaly ducked her chin, because that was an edged question. "Thank you for the chance. I wanted to scream most of the morning." She felt far more alive here, she realised, than she had at Arundel, or even at home. As if she could flourish here and not there. That was an uncomfortable thought, and unhelpful to boot, and she set it aside.

"A particular frustration?" Aunt Metaia poured the tea, without looking directly at Thessaly. That was pointed, too. Aunt Metaia might be Thessaly's favourite aunt by far, and Thessaly was fairly sure she stood high in Aunt Metaia's list of favourite relatives. But that didn't mean Aunt Metaia wasn't terrifyingly competent in her own right, and by the standards of Albion's Council. She was an acclaimed Mistress of Illusion, far beyond Thessaly's own skills at the moment. She also held an equal mastery of Sympathetic magic, and she was entirely adept in any social or academic duel.

"Lady Maylis asked for me to receive callers with her. It was," Thessaly broke off, because there was no good way to say this. "It was very rigid."

"And how do you feel about that?" Aunt Metaia's voice was calm, comfortable.

Thessaly considered. "I know making a good marriage is expected. For my sake, for the family's sake, for the sake of the next generation. Childeric can be charming, and I know I'm very lucky that his family thought me suitable." Aunt Metaia knew all of that. The Powells had been a powerful family for many years. But neither they nor the Lytton's - Papa's family - had held the land magic, at least not any of the lines that led to Thessaly.

Aunt Metaia nodded. "The Fortier lands are flourishing, both magically and otherwise. They've had a charmed generation or two, as well. Two handsome sons in the current line. A nephew, and then of course there are Bradamante's children." That was the sister between Lord

Clovis and Magister Dagobert. She'd married out of the family, but of course remained close with her brothers and mother.

"And Arundel is a stunning estate." They'd talked about where Thessaly and Childeric would live, as part of the betrothal agreements. The time between the betrothal and marriage was partly to fit up the entire first floor of the manor at Arundel for their particular use. By the wedding, they'd have their own drawing room, workroom, study, and library, as well as adjoining bedrooms. Sigbert had rooms above, where Childeric was now, and the other end of that floor was the nursery. Lord Clovis and Lady Maylis had the ground floor on that wing, with the kitchens and staff spaces in a courtyard off that side of the house. "And Lady Maylis hinted they might also see about a town house in Trellech in due course. Besides the family one."

Aunt Metaia nodded, tilting her head. She was considering saying something, Thessaly knew that look. "And you know, I'm sure, that there aren't too many people your father considers suitable among people around your age."

Thessaly grimaced. "No. Mama and I went over that. I know the lists as well as anyone, of the Heirs and notable families. Ignatius Knapton was promised young, and Temenos Sibley's still in his Guard apprenticeship, it's not suitable for him to marry. Lionel Baddock shows no signs of marrying yet, he refused any discussion of it."

"Also, Lionel Baddock's looking for someone with a larger dowry than your father would settle on you. As are a couple of my colleagues on the Council. The Grimly boys, or Gaius Roberts or Oswald Martin." Aunt Metaia pursed her lips. "Has Harold ever discussed that with you?"

Thessaly blinked. She'd known Aunt Metaia was not entirely pleased with Father for some reason, but no one had said why. "Not in detail, other than that I've read the marriage agreements." That had, in fact, been curious, but no one had included her in the financial discussions. "There's a settlement for me, but no dowry." The settlement would come from the Fortiers, with an increasing amount as she fulfilled the terms of the agreement when it came to children.

Aunt Metaia nodded. "Just so. Now, I believe it's your life and your marriage, and you have as much right to know the financial details as anyone. More than me, for example. Your father has disagreed, but I was hoping he'd do the right thing once the arrangements were settled. Apparently not." That was decidedly disapproving.

Thessaly looked down, uncertain what to say. Aunt Metaia reached out to touch her wrist and went on. "It explains why Harold was so pleased the Fortiers thought you the best choice, that they wouldn't require a dowry. And you bring a great deal to the marriage. Strong magic, good health, excellent breeding, sparkling intelligence, but there are no direct intermarriages in your line and the Fortiers for generations." Thessaly glanced up to catch her aunt smiling. "As to a settlement of your own, I have some thoughts, dearest. I'll let you know more soon. Still in progress, right now, don't ask."

Thessaly said, mock-primly, "I would never. Besides, it's rude." Besides, she knew Aunt Metaia lived comfortably, but she had no expectation of any of that coming to her.

"And we can't have that." Aunt Metaia was teasing. "And they are treating you well? Besides the social tedium?"

That was a harder question to answer. "I told you last week about Childeric pressing me about the apprenticeship. Magistra North has been so kind, and so helpful. I know you arranged that. I want to learn as much as I can, even if I won't use most of it where anyone can see. And I keep thinking about how you talk about needing more people to help with the illusions that keep people safe."

"For one thing, who knows what the future holds." It was one of her particular motifs. Aunt Metaia was known for shifting one way and the other. She made the most of the tools that came to her hand at the moment, for what she wanted to do. Now, a good half the time, that involved some sort of twist, because Illusion magic was excellent for both pranks and getting people to see something in a new way.

Thessaly nodded. "I am not yet old enough to be permitted the interesting things, though. I have to establish my reputation first." She said it solemnly enough, but then she met Aunt Metaia's eyes. "At least, that is how things go, yes?"

It made her aunt chuckle. "You must show you know the way things work before you can toy with it, yes. And I have heard the gossip about you being someone to watch to set fashion, rather than follow it." Then she paused, sobering. "If you are sure you want to walk that path. It will, of necessity, be a narrow one, with everyone watching you to falter for some time to come."

Thessaly shrugged.

Aunt Metaia said nothing for a long moment. Finally, carefully, she went on, "A betrothal is not the same thing as a wedding. If you changed your mind now, any time before you marry, I would support you. I want you to know that."

Thessaly blinked, then she swallowed, unsure how to respond for a moment. Then, slowly, she put words together. "That means a great deal, Aunt. You've always been so kind, and so clear. It's been such a gift. But I know how the property entailments lie, and of course there's

Hermia to think of. And I..." She let out a huff of breath. "Making a living as a consultant, a specialist, that is also a hard road. I know that much."

"I suppose you saw enough of my younger years." Aunt Metaia nodded. "Now that I am on the Council, everyone will leap for my touch on their magical projects." She had specialised in long-standing illusion work, at least when it came to what she did for others. That kind of magic went into renovations and remaking rooms or buildings entirely, anchoring it in appropriate materials. Thessaly had much more of a visible gift for the more flexible, like clothing and costume. Like the costumes for St. George's Day. "I suppose I cannot blame you for wanting comfort. Even when it comes with tedium."

That made Thessaly smile a little. "And the agreements give me a fair bit of freedom, at least in private. My own workroom, time for duelling, all that. As long as I keep up the necessary obligations. I won't be bored."

"No. Though it is not, I hope I have demonstrated, necessary to marry to avoid boredom. I, for one, am rarely bored." They'd more or less finished the tea sandwiches and baked goods. "Come in, will you? I wanted to show you a few things in the library." Aunt Metaia rose, and they went in.

Thessaly had always loved this house. It was far less formal than home, certainly less than any space she'd seen at Arundel. Aunt Metaia had gone full heartedly for an eclectic collection, full of mediaeval ornaments and vibrant colours. Vines taken from an illuminated manuscript climbed along the entry wall, carvings with little individual faces peeped out of the woodwork, stained glass framed the tops of the window. The sofas and chairs had soft cushions, not itchy horsehair.

The library was Thessaly's favourite, even beyond the cosy little bedroom that was hers whenever she visited overnight. The walls were lined with bookshelves, there were three kinds of chairs in front of the fireplace as well as a plush rug, and every book seemed to hold wonders. Behind the shelves and on the walls that weren't covered by books, there were scenes to match out of myth and legend. Those were full of magic with touches of illusion that meant they shifted slowly over the course of a day.

Aunt Metaia went over to her desk. One side was stacked high with books, which meant Aunt Metaia was deep in some project or another. The spins were turned away from the room, toward the corner. Aunt Metaia pulled a couple of titles from the other side of the desk, where three books had been waiting. "On loan. I tracked down copies last week. You'd been asking about that challenge with lapis lazuli."

Thessaly nodded. "He hasn't called, but I'm still interested in the problem. Lapis lazuli is nuanced, not straightforward. Not the shape, not the veining, not the shades of it."

"I heard a little more about Deschamps." Aunt Metaia waved a hand. "You know I've all sorts of connections. He seems to have been accurately forthcoming with you. Likely to finish his apprenticeship within the next few months, especially if he can establish his own clientele. Magistra Niobe has been vocally pleased with him, and putting him forward. And he has an excellent reputation for thoughtfulness. Not brashness." Aunt Metaia considered. "In trade, as is his father, but you might reasonably dance with him once in an evening without a scandal."

The way Aunt Metaia put that made Thessaly snort. "Mama was pointing out that now is about the proper time for me to consider where to be giving my patronage. I am delighted with my dressmaker, of course, and my shoemaker. I would consider a new milliner. Mine keeps needing to be dissuaded from entire birds. It might be the fashion, but the balance on one's head is a problem. Besides, well." Thessaly found the tiny bird eyes to be distracting, honestly, when faced with them. And while that wasn't a problem when the hat was on her head, it was when she was waiting to put it on. "But you're right. I could cultivate some connections. Would you recommend considering him in that vein?"

"See how he sets about his work, but you might consider a small commission over the summer. Even though the Fortiers have their own preferred talisman makers, you might want something as a token for your husband-to-be or someone else in his family. Having your own sources preserves the secret better."

Thessaly nodded, then considered. "Aunt Metaia? You understand the dynamics of it, but you never married." Now she'd got herself into this sentence, it was suddenly tangling around her.

"Oh, that." There was a laugh. "There was some pressure to, of course, but I'd made a case for my own work. And there was no, hmm. Politically obvious match for me. No particular benefit to the family."

"Didn't you want, I don't know?" Thessaly stalled again. She did, in fact, want children, in due course, and marriage was the way toward that. "Your own family?"

"I have you. And there's Hermia." Thessaly's younger sister was reaching the age where Aunt Metaia could talk more in depth with her about magic and enchantment. "I like a baby or a toddler, but much better when they can go back to Nanny and their mother. Even you, dearest." Aunt

Metaia shrugged. "I enjoy being able to talk to people in depth. And children grow into that, but they don't start there. I am quite content. Also, I rather suspect I'd not have ended up on the Council, or at least not when I did, if I'd had children. Given the timing."

Council challenges were risky on every level, magical and physical. And emotional and mental, as well, from what Thessaly knew. Aunt Metaia had been not yet twenty-five when she made her challenge, decidedly on the young side. If she'd married as Thessaly would, she'd have been a year married, maybe the perfect age to be expecting or have had a baby within the last few months. The two things did not go together at all well, no.

Thessaly just nodded. "Thank you, aunt. Would you show me the books, perhaps? Or would you be able to show me Warrington's Third? I still don't quite have the knack for it. It comes out blotchy for me. Or did you have something you wanted to talk through?" Thessaly gestured slightly at the desk. "You have a lot of books out, I see."

"That's still in the early stage, not fit for talking about. As to the knack, there's a trick there, the shape of your hands. We can certainly do that. Talk here, and then the workroom, and I'll see you off in time for supper at home. How's that?"

Thessaly went through the mental maths, well worn, about how much time she'd need to change into a suitable gown for supper at home. They ate on the late side, usually half eight. It would give her and her aunt an hour, plenty of time for a little experimentation.

CHAPTER 10
MAY 16TH IN TRELLECH

Vitus had found Landry's rooms without difficulty. The directions had been quite clear. They were along one of the streets off Trivium Way with smaller shops, quieter places like a tailor's or someone who did ordinary domestic enchantments like keep-cold boxes and stoves. The first-floor rooms were popular with young professionals, living on their own or with a friend. The flats that included the second and third-floor rooms were often taken by young families. Vitus had gathered in his travels that most folks didn't like small people who charged across the floors in the wee hours living above them, but magic at least helped with muffling the noise here in Trellech.

Vitus checked to make sure he was not early. It wouldn't do to presume on the other man's time. He knocked at the undistinguished door, just a plain brass nameplate that read only "Landry". A moment later, the door opened, revealing a simple parquet floor, well tended, the walls painted a pale brown like parchment. Landry was wearing a sleeveless ritual robe in dark blue over a charcoal suit, his hair pulled back. "Deschamps. Do come through."

With one gesture he closed the door, then gestured to one across the hallway, putting himself between Vitus and another door on that wall.

Vitus went through. Naturally, he would not be rude. And even if he'd been inclined to rudeness in the first place, he would not have done it to any of the Landrys, for about five good reasons. This room was both what he'd expected and nothing like it. The first thing he saw were bookshelves lining one wall on either side of an unlit fireplace. The mantel was lined with a mixture of photographs and sculptures.

Vitus might have expected elaborate Egyptian sculptures, but nothing like that was visible. Not other than four small stone figures and a painting above the mantel that seemed likely to be some particular landscape in Egypt. It certainly had sand and dramatic colours in the sunset. The photographs were quite ordinary, curiously humanising. There was one of Landry with his mother and brother, quite recent. On the other side, there was one likely of Landry at about the age of ten, with what must be his father as well as his mother. A matched piece suggested grandparents on his father's side, given both their complexions, even in the daguerreotype image, and the shape of the cheekbones and nose.

The statues, however, were a series of four men, all crafting unspecified objects. Vitus could identify one as a gem cutter immediately. Of course, he could spot the tools of his own trade. The others, though, were harder to make out at a distance.

A large desk stood at the far end of the room, under the window, to make the most of the natural light, but there was a table with three chairs near the door, and a sofa and two easy chairs facing the fireplace. More bookshelves lined the entire right side of the room. Vitus glanced at his host for a sign of where to sit, and Landry waved him toward the fireplace. "Your question does not seem to call for significant note-taking or design work, but if the table would be more comfortable, let me know. I copied out some examples of texts to discuss."

It was a curious set up. The room was obviously set as a room where many things were done by the man who lived here, but it was not set up as any kind of workroom. Vitus knew a little about Landry's skills. He'd thought materia played at least some role in them, and there was no sign of materia storage at all. There wasn't even the sort of ordinary household apothecary chest that many people kept on hand. Vitus tried not to stare, instead sitting down and tucking his feet out of the way. Landry took the chair nearest him.

Vitus took a breath. He wanted to ask a dozen things about the layout of the rooms, why Landry had chosen this presentation of himself. Landry obviously periodically did consultations here. The space was set up for that, and Vitus knew he didn't have offices elsewhere. He'd checked. But this was a more personable sort of space than he'd expected. Magistra Landry had a fearsome reputation as a consultant, the sort to approach cautiously and only at sufficient need. She did not explain herself; she never had, but her work was impeccable.

Her son, however, seemed to work in a different mode. Philip Landry had also built up a reputation as a skilled specialist, but he was decidedly seen as more approachable if also still foreign. Merryn's comments had suggested that and Vitus was indeed finding it so. No one knew Landry well - he had not gone to Schola, nor was he in any of the societies. And he was not a member at either Bourne's or

Wishton's. That last was curious, because if the Fortiers had extended themselves, they could have sponsored him, even given how much of his background was not of Albion. Before Virtus could wander too far down that train of thought, Landry spoke. "Now, let's see."

"Before the explanation you're so kind to offer, I brought along notes about my travels. I included several letters of introduction that might be of interest and not, perhaps, as readily available through your own sources. Gems and minerals, as you noted. And two hotels I would recommend avoiding." Vitus reached into the portfolio he'd brought, pulling out a file folder with twenty sheets of paper clipped together, along with three letters in unsealed envelopes.

That last one made Landry's mouth shift just for a moment. "What brings you to recommend against them, then?"

"I presume your brother would prefer to spend his magic on other things than avoiding pests, for one. The other, mmm." Vitus tried to figure out how to put this. "The proprietor's daughter would very much like to be married, or failing that, cause herself a scandal. I did not find it remotely restful or supportive of my studies."

It came out more primly than Vitus had meant; not that he was opposed to a mutually agreeable tumble in the right circumstances. He'd had several on his travels, even. Having Maria Antonia turning up in his bed on no notice had not been comfortable. Vitus had been quite worried about what her older brothers might do to anyone who found themselves in that situation.

Vitus coughed and added, "I have a younger brother as well. He's two years out of Schola, Boar House. He is perfectly capable of taking care of himself, as I am sure yours is. But that is no reason not to spare them unnecessary and unproductive difficulty."

Landry nodded, taking a moment to glance through the notes. Then, Vitus was rewarded with a slow smile, perhaps an agreement at the desire to spare younger brothers avoidable problems. "These will be of great help in the planning. That is much appreciated, and generously done. I assume you bring the same attention to detail to your talisman work?"

That got them off into an agreeable conversation. Vitus was careful to keep it brief. He began with an overview of how he went about things, as he drew out his sketches and plans for the piece that had brought him here. Within ten minutes, Landry was nodding along. "I don't know the theory here as well as I ought. Most of my work is not in the directly material, but you're looking for something, like, hmm." The older man glanced up, clearly thinking through how to put it.

"Do you know Montfort's treatise on inscription?" Vitus offered.

"Hah!" Landry nodded emphatically. "Let me grab that. In fact, you can show me what you're thinking." Landry stood, rolling upwards with a physical ease that surprised Vitus a bit. He moved like a duellist, like Lucas did, rather than an academic swot, always bent over his books. He went across the room, precisely pulling out a book from the shelves with due care for the book itself. "Here we are, yes."

Landry passed it over, coming back around to sit down. Vitus thumbed through carefully, looking at the right-hand pages to find what he wanted. It was about a fifth of the way in, on the right, bottom half of the page. He did not have a perfect memory the way some people did. But he had a gift for remembering what the text had been shaped like, how it was laid out, and it was decidedly handy in this sort of situation. “Like this.” Vitus passed the book back, open to the illustration of working a complex talismanic inscription down to a simplified but potent one.

“Oh, yes. I thought you might think of that one. Right. If I were to do the same thing with a text, is that what you’re thinking? Are your inscriptions more commonly linguistic or symbolic, then?”

“More commonly symbolic, but it’s not uncommon to build a word or two into the piece, to anchor the intention. And in some pieces, there is a word that activates the enchantment, and if so, that word is often built into the inscription.” These were not professional secrets, they were visible to anyone who cared to look at enough talismanic pieces. Or, for that matter, read a representative sampling of the literature. He pulled out a couple of sketches of what he was working on, passing them over.

“Ah, yes. Let me sketch a few things, then.” Landry stood, coming back with a small wooden lap desk. He took out pencils and paper, then sketched out a column of text three or four characters wide, the pencil strokes turning into hieroglyphs. Then he wrote the line again, and again, each time the shapes shifting until they were still distinct letters, but far less of a depiction of some bird or beast. “Here, you see the progression, yes?” He held it so Vitus could see.

“And in this, the, pardon, I don’t know how to ask this entirely. Do the shapes themselves also hold magic?”

Landry blinked at him, as if that were not an expected question at all. “It is not something we talk of much. But among my mother’s people, it is thought that the very act of writing is magical, that words do indeed hold magic. To a degree beyond how Incantation is taught in Albion, as I understand it, though I do not hold a mastery in that magic as it is counted here." His finger tapped the page. "You name a thing and it becomes so. And yes, each shape has, pardon." He cleared his throat. "I am not used to discussing this in English. Each shape has a symbology to it, associations, of what it is, which of the many gods it is associated with. Gods." His brow furrowed. "Does that answer your question?"

"Enough, thank you. And these other two forms of writing, the hieratic and the Demotic, do they hold magic the same way?"

It earned Vitus a laugh. "Ah, if I were writing an inscription," Landry said. "It would be the hieroglyphs by preference. But if I were, mm, designing a border for something, to frame an act of magic? Perhaps I would draw on the pattern of the Demotic, a rhythm in the design, do you see?" He sketched out a couple of shapes, repeating the same three repeatedly to make a line.

Vitus peered at it, considering. "May I ask what it says? If it is private, of course, you need not say."

It got another of those blinks, before Landry ran his finger under the text, word by word, reading it out in the original, and then again to translate it. "Ptah, the Disc of heaven, who illumineth the world by the fire of his eyes." He glanced up at the mantel, then said, "Ptah is a god of crafting, of enlivening what is made. A god for talisman makers, certainly, as well as for others." He nodded once at the wall away from the window. "I have a workroom, of course, though I tend to more complex ritual forms at my mother's townhome. As I said, most of what I make is not done in stone as you do, but ink on papyrus if it has physical form. And yet, I turn to the crafter, more than to others." He hesitated.

Vitus cleared his throat. “If I make offerings, they are most commonly to Vulcan for the crafting. Though I do not work in hot metal or the forge, he is also a god of crafters.” Also, a favourite among those of the Four Metals, which is why Vitus had picked up that inclination in the first place, but he wouldn’t say that here.

“Ah.” Landry nodded once. “Here, let me look at your inscription, and see if I might suggest applications of the idea.” That took up a fair bit of time, passing the commentary back and forth. Vitus found himself talking more freely, as they went, about the challenges of establishing himself. Landry was not forward with his advice, but he was not shy about offering it when relevant to a particular topic, including how he selected the rooms they were in.

Vitus had been right that the presentation was deliberate. Landry had wanted an ordinary street, a room that suggested a serious scholar and magician, without being intimidating. His mother, on the other hand, had an imposing townhome in a well-off neighbourhood of Trellech, a bit to the north. Most people never saw beyond the most formal parlour. Certainly not the library, which Vitus took to be one heart of the home.

“And your brother, when he returns?” Vitus started gathering his papers together. He knew they were almost out of time.

“Ah, should he wish to set up in consulting, then we might take a house together. We will have to see. He is more inclined to formal ritual, and the spaces that requires are more difficult to arrange.” Just then, the clock chimed from the tower outside. “I would be glad to speak again, when time allows. I might have a commission for you in a month or two. It depends on how something plays out.”

“I would be glad to discuss at your convenience. You

have been generous with your knowledge and your time. I won't keep you further." Vitus made his goodbyes warm - he really was grateful - but brief. A minute or so later, he found himself walking down the steps, out to the street. Thoughts - and new ideas for how to go about his work - were swirling around in his head. He rushed off to Niobe's to write them down fully before they tumbled out.

CHAPTER 11

MAY 17TH IN THE MAIN TRELLECH LIBRARY

Thessaly was utterly immersed in what she was doing. That was turning out to be a problem. She was up on the top of one of the small rolling sets of steps in Trellech's main library, in one bay far to the back of the main reading room. She had a couple of books already waiting on the table in the middle of the bay, along with her gloves. She was trying to hunt down at least two more.

Magistra North had recommended additional reading before Monday, but she hadn't had a complete reference for the chapter she remembered. It was in one of the books by Hezekiah Applebloom. There was an entire row of them, and many of the chapter titles were not as illuminating as to the contents as they ought to be.

That was the problem with illusionists all over. They - Thessaly included - enjoyed playing with appearances.

Now she reached for the next volume, then over-reached. If she'd been in duelling gear, it wouldn't have been a problem. Today, she was in entirely proper skirts and bustle and shoes without nearly as much grip as might be sensible. She wobbled. Then there was a hand under her elbow, another at her back, steadying her. It felt comfortable and secure from the first touch.

"Pardon, Mistress." The voice below her and to her left was oddly familiar, but not one she knew immediately. Someone she'd gone to school with, maybe. Thessaly used that bit of stability to reach for the book she'd actually wanted, then cleared her throat.

"Thank you. May I come down now?" The hand at her back moved away, until she couldn't feel the pressure, though the one under her elbow didn't do the same. She retreated backwards down the steps, making sure her feet were solidly under her before she looked to see who had helped her. Then she blinked several times. "Oh! Master Deschamps. A pleasure to see you again." She did her best to make it sound warm. Thessaly hadn't expected him, not here, but she was in fact pleased to see him, if also a trifle confused.

He flushed, just slightly, then tipped his hat to her. "Mistress Lytton-Powell. I am glad to lend my assistance. Or to do so again, if there is another book you would like fetched. I hope you are well?"

"I am. Though I was waiting for you to call. It has been four weeks, after all. I had several thoughts about your question about the lapis lazuli, and I have done some preliminary experiments. Though of course, it depends a bit on the foundational materials you had in mind - cloth versus stone, and so on. And naturally, the duration you were hoping for."

Master Deschamps ducked his chin. "Mistress." He then closed his mouth, as if unsure how to go on. "I am perhaps wary of your position. Considering a number of factors."

Thessaly took a step back to better consider him. And to

better arrange her skirts, so everything fell into place. Her gloves were off. It was difficult to thumb through pages with them on, and she couldn't fix that now. Besides, they were in a library, and libraries had their own rules of etiquette within Albion. He also took a step back, bowing slightly, as if that would ease whatever uncertainty he felt.

"My betrothal." Thessaly tilted her head, naming what she was sure was the problem. "I can assure you, Childeric is nowhere near. A library is not particularly his natural habitat. He is off having a pleasant ride with some of his friends, I believe. And his parents are at Arundel. I have no chaperone and do not need one - we are in a library, of course, a respectable location. I am betrothed, not immured in a tall tower with no access to the outer world."

"But you are, Mistress, betrothed to the son of a powerful family, who are known to..." His voice trailed off. But really, there wasn't an entirely polite way to finish that sentence.

"Who are known to hold grudges. This is not worth a grudge. And I am the daughter of two other powerful families. But again, not immured in a tower. Father wouldn't dare. Besides, Aunt Metaia would have argued him out of it long since." That was true, too. Father was firm about how things were done, a proper Victorian father, but he deferred to Aunt Metaia - and to Mama, honestly - on matters of magic and manners. Especially when they overlapped, as in this case.

"You and I know that we have had conversation - twice now, and the first was most pleasant. But there is the reality and the seeming, and we both know that some people confuse the one for the other." He gestured for a moment at the books. "That is, in fact, your art."

Thessaly slowly inclined her head. "That is accurate

enough. Are you worried? I would not keep you if you are truly concerned, though I am grateful for your helpful hand. Also, I am enjoying the conversation." The last month had brought home to her how much she'd enjoyed their first conversation. She'd felt free to express herself there, not contained and limited. He'd listened in a way she found enticing. It certainly wasn't how she felt around Childeric or Sigbert or their family.

He seemed to think she was assuming it'd be an indiscretion. Or, more reasonably, that the Fortiers might see it as one. It made sense, and yet it didn't, and that was puzzling and confusing her.

She had wondered - especially after that conversation with Aunt Metaia a fortnight ago - about the different ways her life might have gone. Or might go. It wasn't as if she didn't have options and choices and possibilities. Thessaly knew she would do her duty by Childeric, by the agreements. But while he could be exceedingly charming and flattering, nothing about how he did that made her heart beat a little faster. None of it provoked even as much reaction in her body as a good duel, the combination of challenge and physicality and how one matched with the other person.

It made this conversation more complicated, feeling something she hadn't felt before. This wasn't an assignation, of course it wasn't. But even if it were - which it wasn't - she had options. She knew her agreements with Childeric thoroughly and precisely. And now, they came rushing back.

Father and Aunt Metaia and three specialists in ritual language and oaths had gone over it on her side of things. She could spend her time where she chose, even bed who she chose, so long as there were due precautions against pregnancy outside her marriage. It would be better to avoid the more delicately risky forms of bedding until she'd had at least one child. But there were options there. Aunt Metaia had talked through some of them and made it clear she'd share more details or suggest specialists if Thessaly had any interest.

The other way round, well, that was a different question. Thessaly was fairly sure Childeric was bedding someone, though she had not exerted herself to find out who or how long it had been going on. Not yet. All the signs she had seen suggested nothing that put her at risk. More to the point, both Mama and Aunt Metaia had agreed with that analysis. They both had much more experience spotting that sort of thing in the wild, a Mistress who thought to displace the legitimate wife, or wife-to-be. Not that she'd say that here and now.

Thessaly expected Childeric would be much the same in bed as he was in the other areas of his life. Skilled and deft enough, because he'd consider a lack of skill to be a failure. But he'd be far more about what he got out of the experience than what she did. And if she wanted in-depth conversation or magical debate, she would have to find it for herself, and elsewhere. Possibly with his mother or aunt, but that was more delicate than finding it among people her own age.

She could - and planned to - use her social influence to cultivate that sort of discussion. It would not only keep her from utter boredom - a key consideration - but it would also let her support and encourage people who could use it. Aunt Metaia did that. Mama did it, though in a more limited way, seeing as there was less money on Father's side of things, and thus less independence.

But she couldn't deny, now she'd thought a bit more,

that she liked it when this man, Vitus, the one in front of her, touched her. She liked how his magic felt, though she didn't have the language to describe it. There was an openness, a sureness, a comfort with himself that was appealing, even before she considered anything else. And she couldn't deny that maybe she was responding to that.

Still, they were back at the fact this was a library. She certainly would not suggest anything improper here and now. Thessaly had certainly read her share of romantic tales, but she wasn't actually sure how one proceeded from a bit of fantasy to something real, anyway. If she were inclined, it would require more study.

The silence grew. He was the one making this odd and awkward. It was all entirely him. Finally, she raised an eyebrow at Master Deschamps, as pointedly as she could manage. He cleared his throat. "I do not wish to make enemies. Not when I am still establishing myself." There was a tiny pause, then he added, "Or after."

"Well, no. You are sensible. And forward-thinking, not inclined to let today's choices destroy tomorrow's. But will you trust me, that a conversation will not damage anything? And that I am interested in what you are working on, besides the question of the lapis lazuli illusion." She glanced around. "Do you have a few minutes? Perhaps we might sit and talk for a little while. Enough that you will be reassured that no member of the Fortier family is going to emerge from the shelves like an avenging ghost."

His mouth opened and then closed again. She could see him swallow. "If you insist, Mistress. May I get your chair?" The thing of it was, he had fine manners. They weren't the sort that was entirely about the show of it, or even the show of his magic. They were practical, like Aunt Metaia when she was at home. She set the two books in her hand down on the desk in the library bay while he came around to pull out a chair. Thessaly arranged herself with a little shift of her weight and magic so the bustle would not bulge in awkward ways. She let herself sink down to sit on the front half of the chair precisely as she'd been taught. Not that either bustle or corset really permitted much else.

After a moment's hesitation, he sat down at the short end of the table, at an angle to her, but without the table between them. She kept her feet tucked under her chair, her skirts falling around them. She was sure that brushing his ankle or foot would startle him into fleeing.

"There. And thank you, you know just how to be a help. Far too many people are about form over function." She set her hands on the table, considered their lack of gloves again, and decided to ignore it. Besides, at least two-thirds of the reason for gloves had to do with magical interference. She was confident both in her own ability to spot that in this setting and the fact Master Deschamps seemed exceedingly unlikely to try something of the kind. "What brought you here this afternoon?"

"Oh. Erm." He cleared his throat. "Mistress Lytton-Powell, I was thinking about a question that Niobe - Magistra Hall - posed to me. About which stones take which types of enchantments most elegantly. A number of stones can be made to suit, but the question of which ones make it..." He looked up, searching for words, "Smooth. To purpose. Comfortably." He looked back at her, meeting her eyes deliberately.

There now, he was actually engaging. That was excellent. "Do call me Thessaly, please. Otherwise, we shall be forever making the simplest comments." Her double-barrelled surname just made that worse. "I don't know the materia nearly as well as you must, but, oh, something like amber or perhaps citrine for light? Or I saw a piece done with pearls that tended toward a glow, that shimmer of something beautiful and perfect."

"As you wish. Thessaly. And I am Vitus, then, please." Then he was nodding enthusiastically. "Just so, yes. Though pearls are rather tricky to work with. Any sort of inscription into the nacre is likely to damage the pearl and cause it to flake and destroy itself over time. In that case, the enchantments lie in the entire structure. They might be anchored by talismanic pieces for a central focal bead, or perhaps in metal spacer beads or something of the kind."

"I'm sure that complicates the design as well, magically." Thessaly offered. "Competing influences, something of the kind? I was looking for an article about something related, about how many layers of illusion or enchantment work are practical before you begin to have contradictions. Or that is the idea, anyway. I've not read the chapter yet."

Within minutes, she'd pulled the books over, thumbing through to find what she was looking for. A minute or two after that, his hand brushed hers, as they were peering at the page together, until he jerked his hand back. "Pardon."

"I did not mind." That had come out entirely too prim. "I hope we might become friends, even if you are nervous about it right now. In due course. More meetings in the library or perhaps a tea shop or some other suitable place."

The thing of it was, she enjoyed his touch, the simplicity of it, the way he didn't presume to reach for more. This still wasn't an assignation, and she did not want to make things difficult again, but now she was wondering about what it would be like to have one. With him, in specific. She couldn't remotely tell him. He'd bolt into the street. And if there were signals you gave to hint at willingness, well, that had not been included in any of Thessaly's education.

Vitus withdrew his hand carefully, folding it into his lap. "I enjoy your conversation a great deal." He wasn't quite looking at her now, as if he couldn't speak and talk at the same time. "And your ideas fit well with mine. The expansion of what I'd like to do, I mean. I - erm." The sentence tumbled down into a pile of innuendo that she was fairly sure he hadn't actually intended. He did not seem a man of that sort. But she did like his company, in ways she wasn't sure how to describe. Maybe it was just that he listened as much as he talked, and that was decidedly novel at the moment.

"Then we will have to see when we might find time again. Do come round to Magistra North's when you get a chance. Or write me there, and we can make a proper appointment, if that would reassure you. She's quite interested in the question herself, actually, and she might have some useful references for you. Or connections." There, she could lay that lure out. Magistra North had in fact mentioned that she was always on the look out for suitable talisman makers who could work to her standards. His apprenticeship with Magistra Hall was promising that way. Then, before she could say much more, they heard the bells.

"Oh, I beg pardon. I need to get home. I promised to escort my mother to something." Vitus pushed back, then offered a bow. "Again, yes. I will write and find a time. Until then, Mistress - Thessaly." Before she could do more than smile and nod, he was gone, and she was left looking after him. Once she was sure he was not returning, she stood again, and went back to hunting up the books she wanted.

She could not get the thought of him out of her mind. Vitus Deschamps did not have Childeric's classic handsomeness, but he was more than pleasant to look at. He leaned forward, letting his interest show, not an aristocrat's disdain, and that was appealing. And he'd listened to her. He hadn't interrupted; he hadn't seemed bored at all. By the time she set the books she didn't need on the cart to be reshelved, she'd begun to wonder what it would be like to have him hold her hand. Or perhaps dance.

Certainly, she didn't know any detail that would make him unsuitable for a private assignation. Vitus had been trained to discretion, that was part of his work. He came from a family known for probity and good sense, given his father's work. He was from the crafting class, but that didn't matter since they wouldn't be discussing a marriage. It came down to whether she was interested, whether he was interested, and whether they could sort out something mutually agreeable.

Perhaps - no, for certain - she'd also figure out how to study up on how one might delicately suggest an interest. If she could bring herself to ask Aunt Metaia, maybe that would help. She certainly couldn't ask Mama. Even if she decided she wasn't interested in Vitus, just the idea of the option, it would be good to know for the future.

CHAPTER 12

MAY 18TH AT THE DESCHAMPS HOME

May 18th

Saturday evening, Vitus joined his mother in the drawing room while they waited for Papa and Lucas to return. Papa had had some business in Trellech, and had promised to meet Lucas at the train station in good time for supper. Vitus was making himself useful as a tool for the winding of yarn.

Or, more precisely, Mama was winding yarn. Vitus was holding his hands a steady length apart, deep red yarn looped around them, while Mama wrapped it up into a ball. She had begun by wrapping it around her fingers, and now she was twisting the ball this way and that. They had been talking about nothing much in particular, before his mother asked, "What was it like living outside the Pact?"

It was a question Vitus had thought about a great deal, but one he'd barely discussed. Niobe had her own experience travelling on the Continent, but it had been a decade before, and with all the constraints of being a woman of the age and class that required a constant chaperone. Hers had been magical, of course. But it meant that she had never ended up alone, needing to deal with whether she might reveal her magic by accident. Vitus, on the other hand, had walked miles across various cities, exploring all sorts of places.

And in truth, it had taken some getting used to on his return. The Pact was the great triumph of Albion. In 1484, King Richard - the Third, but in Albion, he was so often just Richard, the only one who mattered like that - had made a great treaty. Those humans with magic would leave the Fatae alone, other than some specifically negotiated places like the Belin in the mines, or those who tended particular groves and ancient portals. And in turn, the Fatae would not lead mortals astray, and they had taught Albion a number of magical skills, including the crafting of portals, half a dozen healing techniques that saved lives every week, and various protections. They were bound by the Pact, what Vitus's teachers at Schola had described as a country-wide geas, made real and whole by each and every person sworn to it.

Within Albion, if someone attempted to use magic near the non-magical, anything they might understand as true magic, the Pact would stop them. That person's greatest fear would rise up inside them as a warning. If they did not, if they pressed on, fear was a powerful distraction and motivation all by itself. Sometimes, rarely, people died of it, pushing through the fear to some foolish action. But in the main, it worked well. And if a few people of Albion lived through chaos by what looked like pure luck, that wasn't revealing magic, not in and of itself.

"It was different. It's odd being back. Walking around Trellech, where all the magic is visible, all the time." He used his right thumb to nudge a strand of the yarn into a better position to unfurl. His mother tugged gently at it as she kept winding her ball. He found that satisfying in a way he didn't know how to describe, a particular physical contact between them. "It took getting used to, on the Continent. But it was easy enough for me. You know I've never been prone to a lot of show about it unless I'm working. And that part was all in magical workshops. No worries there."

"And people who have magic just - do what?" Mama glanced up at him.

"They live their lives. Mostly in their own little facets of the world. They see these families socially and not those, and if you don't have magic yourself, you'd never know they did. Sometimes it causes a difficulty when a girl falls in love with a boy, or a boy with a girl, and they're from different sorts of families." Vitus looked up at that, and that was a mistake, Mama definitely noticed.

"There's a story there, then? I hope with a happy ending?" Mama blinked once, then she looked back down at her hands. The shift of the red yarn was rather hypnotic. Soothing, in a particular way, as well as practical.

"Oh, when I was in Florence. Not the Rossi, I was working with Marco Rossi. But a cousin of theirs, Marco's parents are the head of the family. Gianni, he fell for a young woman, Renata Casini. He had magic, of course, like you'd expect, and she didn't. The families didn't trust each other much. They didn't have all the other connections that made a match sensible to anyone who wasn't twenty and madly in love. Also lust." Vitus had to smile. He'd heard this story from both Marco and Renata while he was there, complete with the replicated tirades of several sets of aunts and multiple grandmothers.

"And what happened, dearest?" Mama glanced up again.

Vitus shifted a little in his chair. There was noticeably less yarn between his hands now, and more give as a result. "In the end, Marco's family had her - just her - over for supper, suitably chaperoned by a woman both families knew. They explained it to her. They had a potion ready, one that blurs the memory for a few hours. She was reasonable and delighted there was a simple enough solution. Her parents know now, she said, but they treat it as a folk custom that works, as much as anything."

That part confused Vitus, though of course he hadn't said so to them. Coming from Albion, it felt like a dangerous risk, and one that could come back and bite like a viper without warning. "And now, she doesn't have magic herself, but her children seem likely to - they're still a bit young to be sure. And they're thrilled. She could get Marco's brother apprenticed. His magic isn't very strong, but he's turned into a grand smith, making door hinges and latches of all things. But Florence needs a lot of them. They do wear out."

"Oh, well. The dears." Mama, Vitus was clear, would be quite happy to have grandchildren of her own, sooner rather than later. A moment later, she confirmed that. "You could think about marrying now. Or if not marrying, at least see who you might make a match with."

"You are putting the cart before the horse, Mama, in your fondness." Vitus kept his voice even. It wasn't her fault she'd touched a sore spot. "I need to establish myself before I'd feel able to commit to supporting a wife. Even if she were also a crafter, with her own work, as seems likely." At least, that was the way the sensible logic ran. "And besides, a lot of the women I'd be interested in are already betrothed or married, or they're still finishing their own apprenticeships."

Mama peered over her glasses at him. "Have you been counting them up, then? When you go to your club or about your day?"

He had, actually. "I am human, Mama, and I do hope to marry." Now he looked down. "Some of them are not for me, though." Vitus cleared his throat. Then there was absolutely no good way to finish that sentence.

Lucas saved him in the end. Behind him, there was a clatter of sound, the door opening, Lucas swooping in. "Mama, you look well. Vitus, you look well occupied. How are you both? Papa's just putting his things away. He'll be five minutes."

"Mama was encouraging me to marry, or at least look at likely prospects." Vitus said, while Mama picked up the ball of wool she'd dropped in her skirts and wound the last bits up more quickly. "If you meet any likely women, do introduce us?"

"It seems unlikely, but I will indeed. Anything for my brother." Lucas clapped him heartily on the shoulder. "I need to make the last train, but that gives us a few hours. What sort of things are you looking for in a wife, then, beyond a tolerance for your being late to supper?"

"I am entirely on time today," Vitus said, with some attempt at dignity. He couldn't help thinking of Mistress Lytton-Powell - Thessaly - yesterday, though, her face popping into his head as entirely unavailable and yet also a fair bit of what he thought he might want. She was beautiful, and that was relevant - he was a man who loved beautiful things, his work was making useful things also beautiful or beautiful things also useful. But that wasn't what mattered. She was clever and opinionated and undeniably skilled at her own magical arts. She had taste, which absolutely did not reliably run with the magical skill, as he knew all too well from his own work. And she, for whatever reasons she had, seemed to enjoy his company.

He certainly couldn't forget the moments he'd touched her. She hadn't shifted away from his touch either time. There had been something steady there, in her magic, in her person, even when she'd just nearly toppled off the steps. It had simply been comfortable for him, and he shouldn't allow himself to want more of that, no matter what she said about being inside her agreements. Wanting wouldn't get him anywhere good.

He said, after a moment. "Cleverness, kindness, competence of her own, whatever her form of magic might be. A good eye for beauty and the world, noticing things." Vitus glanced up at his brother. "I did mention to Mama that most ladies who might suit are already betrothed or married, or enough younger they are not yet done with their own apprenticeships."

"I will think about it. Who knows, perhaps something will come to me late at night." At that point, Papa came down, and they went into supper. Late that night, once Mama and Papa had both retired, Vitus offered to walk his brother back down to the station. He could use the time to think.

They walked in silence until they were on the road. Lucas cleared his throat. "Is there anyone, then? Suitable or unsuitable?"

"Already promised elsewhere. She made it clear a conversation was no problem." He cleared his throat. "And she offered to consult with me on a project." Vitus thought for a moment about not saying more, but he'd already come this far. "Thessaly Lytton-Powell. Betrothed to Childeric Fortier, but she was rather fierce about not being immured in a tower because of it."

"Huh." Lucas considered that. "She duelled at Schola. Not in public much. She had private tutoring. I wouldn't have known about it, but Harald Totham was in her sessions. He'd talk about it sometimes. He was a couple of years ahead of me, in Boar, you remember? She was good, even by his standards, and he's been around some of the best, given his family. What's she doing besides the betrothal, then?"

"Illusion work. Didn't I tell you about the gala?" Vitus glanced at his brother. The moon hadn't quite risen yet, so he had a lantern with a charmlight, set to look like a candle from any distance at all.

Lucas paused for a step, turning toward him. "You didn't mention a name. Someone like her, then. Clever. Competent. A different sort of magic than yours, but illusion. She'd appreciate the art of the thing, wouldn't she? We don't give you enough of that at home. Papa and I do tend to the functional." Lucas considered, and Vitus braced himself for his brother to ask more about her. Instead, Lucas changed the topic. "Is Mama intending another scarf for me, do you know? The chaps will mock me if it's that red."

"For the orphans, or whoever needs one, I'm fairly sure. But she didn't say. I'll find out." Vitus considered his brother. "Something more sombre would be appropriate?"

"Black would do, or a grey. I can't wear it in uniform, anyway. Or if you wanted to encourage her to a blanket, I could use one of those come winter. There are draughts, and I can only magic away so many before someone notices. That could have some bright in it, make the place a little more cheerful. I've a room of my own now."

"That's got to be a delicate balancing act. I could probably do you some talismans that would keep them from your bed. Or something of the kind. Let me think about that. I might need to experiment."

"Best of brothers." They were most of the way to the station. Lucas patted his shoulder again, and they shifted over to talking about nothing terribly obviously magical. It gave them a little to catch up on the latest personal news of various cousins.

CHAPTER 13
MAY 21ST IN TRELLECH

Thessaly had only been at the salle for twenty minutes, just long enough to warm up and have one bout. She'd been looking forward to this for weeks, it felt like a yearning like the night before a birthday and anticipated presents. The session promised enough of a challenge to keep her busy, though two people were running late. It wasn't her preferred salle or her preferred set of partners, but it was what she'd been able to schedule given her apprenticeship and the increasing social demands the Fortiers were making. Thessaly had been prompt. She'd changed into rational dress, suited for duelling, before everyone else was ready.

She'd started paired up with Herman Phipps. Herman was not one of her favourite people - he had absolutely no conversational skills - and he was not one of her favourite duelling partners, either. He thought that strength made up for skill or delicacy of touch. Thessaly was certain she'd have a bruise from a concussion charm on her décolletage in the morning. That was, however, what alchemical creams were for. And a fichu with a good illusion charm to back it up.

Thessaly had won the match tidily, after drawing it out to about six minutes. Master Forester had asked her to when they were getting ready. He'd wanted to get a better measure of Herman's stamina - and what skills collapsed when he tired. He knew Thessaly was more than skilled enough to play a match out as requested, at least against someone of Herman's quality. And he'd naturally sweetened the request by promising her a bout at the end of the session, which would keep her on her toes. Especially going into it tired.

They were a few minutes into the second bout when there was a knock on the door. It didn't disturb the duellists - Lambert Kellan and Decimus Monkton were well matched and better trained. The knock came again, louder, but before whoever it was could demand again, Decimus pulled out an interesting trick, bringing Lambert's feet out from under him. He fell to his face in the dirt of the floor, gesturing immediately to signal he yielded. Decimus immediately offered him a hand up. It was only once they were standing and Master Forester was clear there were no lasting injuries that needed tending that he called out, "You may enter."

To her surprise, the person at the door was Father. "Just here for my daughter. There you are, Thessaly. We've somewhere to be." Father's voice was all bonhomie. "Do change, promptly, please."

"Father?" There were so many things Thessaly wanted to ask, and so few she actually could. Anything she said here and now would turn into gossip. She was absolutely certain of that. And well, Father had been more pointed about certain matters, the last fortnight or two.

"I thought I'd mentioned last night, but your mother suggested perhaps you hadn't heard me." He absolutely hadn't mentioned it, but of course she couldn't argue.

Thessaly swallowed down a lump of feelings. "Master Forester, I beg your pardon. I must have forgotten this morning. May I write to see about rescheduling, when convenient to you?" It would put the numbers off for this session, and Thessaly had arranged enough such sessions to know how much of a bother that was. "Father, it will take me a few minutes to change. Perhaps you'll wait outside? I can come out of the changing room to the foyer, so everyone else can get on without further delay." Otherwise, she'd be waiting for the end of a bout to cross the salle safely.

Father nodded once, briskly, and strolled off to the entryway. Thessaly ducked off to the changing room. She had no idea where they were going, but it wasn't as if she had a change of clothing with her. She had the dress she'd worn for her apprentice work. It was a serviceable and reasonably flattering gown of deep brown with copper and green touches, but it was three years old and beginning to show it a little around the cuffs and hem. And she certainly wasn't wearing her best corset. She'd put on the one most suited for duelling today, like a sensible person.

Fortunately, the corset didn't need help, and one of the salle's staff was still in the changing room, so Thessaly could get a hand with the buttons up her back. Within ten minutes she was tidy again, though her hair only managed it thanks to a couple of hastily applied charms to keep the wisps from coming down. There certainly wasn't time to braid and pin it again. At least Herman hadn't been too challenging, and the current frock was cut high enough that whatever bruise was darkening wouldn't show.

Father was pacing back and forth in the entry, but of course there wasn't anyone to see him. Just the usual protections. Those wouldn't care about pacing, only about someone trying to enter the salle without warning. Thessaly ducked out of the side door, stopped, clearing her throat. "Father?" Then she hesitated, but going into this with no information would be worse than whatever came of asking. "I really didn't hear you say anything last night. May I know where we're going?"

"Sortis Hall. Your uncles are expecting us." His chin twitched. "We've a portal reservation in eight minutes. You took longer than I expected."

He took off, striding along, utterly ignoring the fact that she had to scamper to keep up. Well, at least the more visible parts of the scampering were hidden by Thessaly's skirts. She'd worn the boots with the best soles, but she was still out of breath when they reached Portal Square, just barely on time. Three minutes later, they were through the portal, coming out on the cobblestones outside Father's family estate, the main one. Like the Powells, they had properties across Albion, but this was by far the oldest and largest, the heart of the family's interconnections, nestled into Wiltshire.

Father took off again, but slightly more slowly. Without speaking, they went straight along into the house, then into Uncle William's formal study. It was all dark wood and oxblood leather, every detail chosen to be explicitly masculine - and explicitly exclusionary. Thessaly trailed her father, half a step behind. It was only once she was in the room and Father was closing the door behind her, that she got to see who was there. Uncle William, Uncle Edgar, and only Aunt Amia, Uncle William's wife. Thessaly liked Aunt Lysanne, but everyone on Father's side of the family felt she hadn't really held up to the family standards.

"There you are. Have a seat, Harold." That was to Father, of course. "And you, Thessaly, here." It was not a chair either by Father or by Aunt Amia, but between her uncles. Thessaly sat, because again, arguing would not do any good. "Now, Thessaly, we wanted to have a word or two about how to make the best use of your marriage."

Thessaly folded her hands in her lap, matching Aunt Amia's pose as perfectly as she could. If she did what Aunt Amia did, it would be harder for her uncles to find something to complain about. Aunt Amia had long since mastered every piece of that art, and she was teaching it to her daughter and son. "Yes, Uncle?"

"Now, we're quite pleased that Harold could come to an agreement with the Fortiers. But it is time, Thessaly, for you to do your part for the family. And to set an example for your younger cousins, of course." There was a small hoard of them between her uncles, though Aunt Amia's children, as Uncle William's second wife, were still something of an unknown quantity. Charles was at tutoring school, preparing to go to Schola a year from September. And Margot was still in the nursery, though she'd had some early indications of magical promise.

"Of course, Uncle. I understand that." She glanced from Uncle William to Uncle Edgar, then back.

"Now, it was quite difficult sorting out a proper match for you. Far more difficult than it was for Ferdinand and Henry." His sons by Aunt Esme, his first wife, were solidly married, with little cousins in the nursery now. "Or for Lily and Mark." Those were Uncle Edgar and Aunt Lysanne's two. "We wanted to match you to someone who would extend the family connections, of course, but also the family magics and tendencies. Now, despite some other concerns, no one here will bother to argue with the strength of your magic, and your skill and speed at wielding it."

It was something, she supposed. She also offered - besides the combination of two lines of magic and a whole host of Powell family enchantments in her head - excellent marks at Schola. Both in theory and in practice. Not that Uncle William mentioned that. "Thank you, Uncle."

"However, it was unexpectedly difficult to find a match for you. Not just due to Harold's choices in certain areas, or your mother's preferences, though both of those were relevant." Thessaly had spent five years living and breathing Fox House and its subtleties, and Uncle William was being more obvious than usual. He was not pleased with Father about something and he was rubbing Father's nose in it. He was also displeased with Mama, but that was as usual. "There is rather a dearth of suitable partners. Several we'd considered, during your schooling, turned out not to be up to snuff."

Aunt Amia chimed in, "There's a fair bit of gossip about it right now, actually. More than the usual number not completing their apprenticeships. Of course, it's always a trifle hard to tell. People don't talk about it, naturally."

Thessaly considered her years at Schola, but she'd have to go back and look at lists to figure out if the numbers were significantly different. Her year didn't seem so much different from those a year or three older, up to Childeric's year. And it was a bit early yet for those more than a year or two younger than she was. They were still in the earlier stages of apprenticeship or whatever they were doing next. And of course, some, like Cosi and Odile, had gone on to marry promptly, and weren't doing an apprenticeship at all. "Thank you, Aunt. And Childeric is who the family - everyone - felt best."

"In all respects. An excellent family, thriving estates, sons with strong magic." Uncle William leaned forward. "Now, we need to discuss your social calendar, on your own and preferably with Childeric, for the rest of the season. And give a start to considering the winter festivities." Even though it was May, of course everyone was planning ahead.

Father cleared his throat. "Your uncles have generously agreed to assist with some of your frocks. But for that reason, knowing which events you will be at is a consideration." How many new gowns, whether they were for events with a particular colour theme or costume, and most importantly, who would make them.

Thessaly inclined her head. "That's very generous, Uncle William, Uncle Edgar. Aunt Amia, I am sure you have some ideas already? You always have such an eye for dress." There, that was deftly navigating a thread between who was providing the money and who wasn't, while acknowledging that Aunt Amia would have a fair bit of say. Her Uncles - and Father - cared that the dresses and gowns and whatever accoutrements sent the right message. They did not deal with any of the bother of making it happen.

"We'll schedule a time with my modiste in the next fortnight to get a start. She's already considering fabrics." Aunt Amia's modiste was, well, a trifle stuffy and fond of more ruffles than Thessaly cared for, but she did fit things well. "It's not the sort of thing we'd leave in your Aunt Metaia's hands. This isn't her realm of understanding at all."

Uncle William snorted. "And besides, she's cautious with her money. As she ought to be, I suppose, but unwilling to extend herself for you as we are." Oh, that was definitely her uncle digging in a thorn about Mama. And also about Father's finances, now. Thessaly was sure of that, even if she had no idea of the details. Father did not discuss such things with her, even though - as Aunt Metaia herself had pointed out - some of it definitely concerned Thessaly directly.

Now, Thessaly chose the proper reply, deflecting from the unpleasant jibe. "I expect to have tea with Lady Fortier - and Childeric, of course, and some of the other family - later this week. I assume I may directly inquire with her? There are, well, there are all sorts of nuances to the landed estates I don't understand yet. Never mind the Fortier customs in specific." None of which the Fortiers had actually explained to her, though they might have mentioned it to Mama. This, at least, would give Thessaly a direct reason to inquire.

"Oh, yes. And of course, if she prefers her modiste, defer to her judgement, at least so far as any family engagements go." Aunt Amia bobbed her head, entirely ignoring the larger question of the demesne estates.

Uncle Edgar picked up. "Now, the other thing we wanted a word about is to get a better sense of the range of the Fortier assets. How they deal with who they know, as well as the more physical sorts of things. You've been out at Arundel now enough to have a sense of who is seen and not seen at smaller events."

This was the sort of sharp observation Thessaly had expected someone to pick up. "I do not have all my notes, uncle. I apologise. But I can certainly talk about the gatherings I've been at." She could remember well enough who had been at some event, even if she would have to check her records on which one. Like Mama had taught her, she kept lists of that sort of thing, to avoid repeating the same frock or conversation topics too often. It was habit by now to come home and scribble down what she remembered while Alma took her hair down and brushed it.

From there, the conversation wound along, working through the events that Uncle Edgar knew about, with Thessaly filling in the smaller teas and less formal gatherings. They didn't finish until nearly suppertime, but Father chivied Thessaly off toward the portal when her Uncles didn't ask them to stay for supper. Once they got home, she'd discovered they'd missed supper there as well, and Mama was annoyed. Father had gone immediately off to Trellech and one of his clubs. Thessaly had given up on the evening and had a tray in her room. Then she settled down to go through her notes for a summary for the next time Father's side of the family needed an accounting.

CHAPTER 14
MAY 24TH IN TRELLECH

Niobe had had appointments that morning in London. Vitus had spent the first part of the day in the library going through newspapers and magazines from while he'd been gone. There was an entire list of items that weren't urgent, but where it would be a help to have notes on them. Vitus had been as methodical about it as he was about any other line of research. He'd put in the request slips with the library two days before, just in case what he wanted was in the off-site storage.

When he'd turned up Friday morning, the librarian on duty had shown him back to a small and bare cubicle, with a stack of bound volumes on a cart, a book stand and snake set up to hold the pages open where he could read it. She wasn't someone he'd been introduced to by name, a woman of middle age with a steady way of going about things that he didn't want to interfere with.

It was a degree of effort they hadn't gone to before for him, and some hint of his confusion must have been visible. "We understand you're nearly done with your apprenticeship, Mister Deschamps." The librarian's voice was mild.

"And we are glad to assist with whatever resources we can share."

"And perhaps like it when I do my best to make it easier?" Vitus asked, risking a little.

"The advance list is not, shall we say, what everyone manages, sir. Let us know if you need anything else? You mentioned you might want another set next week?"

"Yes, Mistress. I don't know how far I'll get in these, yet," Vitus gestured. "And I think I might get to the volumes still stored here. I'll let you know as soon as I figure that out. And I'll be done with the room by half-past twelve."

She nodded and went out without another comment, closing the door behind her. Charms kept the room from being stuffy. The lighting was well positioned. And as it turned out, Vitus was in a good mindset to make serious headway. He'd been away for eighteen months, and he got through a full year of the relevant papers and journals.

It left him confused, though. He'd been focusing on a few specific things in each issue, updated each week. Every week, the Trellech Moon ran a list of updates to apprenticeships. That sort of information was almost always public knowledge, because the results were public. Because, as Papa had explained to him early, it let people know who to watch for, or who to ask when they were early in their career. Mama had added the clipping about Vitus's apprenticeship to her scrapbook, as she would the longer piece when he completed his apprenticeship later this year.

Along with the beginnings and endings, there were always a handful of other announcements, and those ran once a week, on Wednesdays. Vitus had never been entirely clear if it was because Wednesday reliably had a bit more spare space. It might instead be a nod to Mercury's association with communication and trade. There was no reason it couldn't be both.

It was about noon, and that meant he had time to think about it. The numbers of people starting apprenticeships were about what he'd expected, most of them in late August through September. There was always some variation for particular people's schedules. Occasionally people started at other times of year, or they changed apprenticeships for some reason. Death and illness didn't skip over someone just because they were a master of a particular magical art or craft, unfortunately. Or sometimes one was postponed or on hiatus for some reason.

For women, that could be because they were expecting, of course. Mama had not gone into the details with him - she wouldn't until he got serious about marrying - but Niobe had been a lot more pragmatic. Some kinds of magic were known to be inimical to an unborn child - experimental alchemy or a fair number of duelling's standard approaches. Some, it was a lot less certain. Taking the portal fell into that category, and so did many kinds of talisman or ritual work. Some kinds of magic were generally safe, such as a lot of materia or sympathetic magic work, or those forms of incantation that didn't rely solely on the body's own vitality.

And sometimes men had something come up or change. They didn't suit with their apprentice master or mistress. Some decided to go into a different line of magic. In sadder cases, there was a death or illness in the family that changed the obligations. If someone inherited the land magic, obviously, they might pause their apprenticeship until that was more settled, or might never resume. It depended on why they'd done the apprenticeship.

Now, though, he was fairly sure there was a pattern that

confused him. He made a note of the last set of volumes he'd like next week, and brought the card out to the librarian at the desk. "I'm all set for this week. Same time next, if that's convenient, and this is what I'd like." He hesitated. "Actually, could I add a handful of the guild annuals?"

"As you like." The librarian considered, then pulled out a slim bound volume. "Here's the list, just write down the proper title and that signifier, here. That's what we need to get it from storage."

Vitus took the volume and his request card over to the counter nearby and skimmed the list. In the end, he asked for the annuals from the last ten years for alchemy, protective magics, and incantation. Niobe had all the volumes both for the talisman makers and for the gem cutters, of course. When he brought it back, he cleared his throat. "Is this too many?"

The librarian glanced over it. "Ten years. A specific project, then? No, the annuals are fairly short, the public ones. Or they're bound together. We bind every three years for the protective magic and incantation guilds, I believe. We'll have them ready for you."

"Thank you." He made a slight bow, and then escaped into the late spring, pausing to buy a pasty on the way to Niobe's to tide him over for lunch. By the time he got back to the shop, Niobe was putting her things away, and he dropped the box of pastries he'd added to his order on the table. "Good outing?"

"Very satisfactory, yes. You might just get to come along next time." Whatever she'd been doing, it had made her cheerful. "How was your morning?"

"Statistically confusing. I don't know if what I'm seeing is a fluke or what. Do you have a minute?" Vitus swallowed. "Relevant to, I don't know, the larger state of the field."

"All right. I'll make tea. It seems like a tea sort of conversation. And you brought pastries to sweeten the request." She gave him a smile, bustling off to sort out the tea, while Vitus sketched out his actual thoughts into something like an organised list. When Niobe came back five minutes later, she settled down, pushing a mug over. "What's the question?"

"Are more people than expected not finishing their apprenticeships?" Vitus watched her, and he saw her eyes widen, like he'd hit on something he shouldn't have spotted.

"Why do you say that?" Niobe's voice was calm, the sort of calm that she put on for consultations with new potential clients. It was utterly pleasant, just the right notes of warmth. If he hadn't heard her don it like a cloak a score of times by now, he might have missed the shift.

"Because I was looking at the announcements. There's fewer people completing. Fewer announcements of it. More notices about someone on hiatus or who's getting married or something, without finishing." Vitus tapped his notes from that morning, which had the names. "I left Schola in 1881. Guard apprentices who were in school with me finished up last year. Alchemists, within a year on either side, usually." Talisman crafting was one of the longer apprenticeships, about as long as Healers or the Guard, because it required the gem cutting skills first, and those weren't fast to learn.

Niobe nodded, but she said nothing further.

"I noticed it with the Guard. There's what, forty people a year who go into Guard apprenticeship overall, perhaps five to eight of those from Schola. Not all of them intended for the Guard proper, some want to be analysts or focus on warding, or whatever. And not all of them finish, for whatever reason." But he tapped the notes again. "Last year, while I was gone, there are announcements of three not finishing. Four the year before. And that's not normal. And two alchemists, and usually it's only one. Both of the ones this year, and both last year, were men, so it's not because of marriage or the fact they're expecting a child, either. Besides, the notices imply most of them aren't intending to come back."

"No." Niobe took a deep breath. "Do you remember Montgomery Allen? Two years behind you in Salmon, he was apprenticing with Theseus Whitsun."

Not someone either of them was close to - Master Whitsun favoured the posh crowd, though often the ones with more money than sense. But he was a deft gem cutter. Vitus nodded. "I don't know Montgomery well, other than through the House. Different interests when we were in school." More to the point, Allen hadn't been in Four Metals, and that had taken a lot of Vitus's time and been the heart of his social circle.

"Theseus gave him every chance. Allen's a deft gem cutter. He'll make a good living at that. But the enchantment work for the talismans itself? Something went wrong every time. Anything beyond, oh, Porthos second rank." Which was, in fact, a degree of enchantment most people could manage their fifth year at Schola if they'd been focusing on the skills. Vitus had succeeded at all but the last two exercises in his fourth year. And he'd comfortably learned the fourth and fifth rank enchantments in the first two years of his apprenticeship, though some people took three years at it.

"Anyone else like that?" Vitus asked.

"I've heard a couple of other stories, but other fields, mostly. But Allen was supposed to be very gifted. He'd been working with Theseus on and off from the time he started Schola. Poor man's been rather upset about it. Allen's his sister's son. Allen, too, of course, but at least he can focus on the gem cutting."

Vitus nodded slowly. "And the Guard and such?"

"There's more of them. I think the numbers show more. Was that also your impression?"

"Going through the lists, yes. I asked the library to pull the annuals going back ten years for alchemy, protective magics, and incantation. I know you've got the talisman makers and gem cutters both." Vitus spread his hands. "Is that why you were worried about me?"

"Yes, and no? I didn't see any signs of anything being wrong with you. Feel any signs, more so, really, given our work. Very tactile, our profession." Niobe let out a puff of breath. "But I didn't want to say anything. People get suggestible. And I wondered if it were something in Albion, if something would change while you were away. But you seem to have done well with the travel, but also done well now you're home and settled in."

Vitus nodded. "There's a difference out there, of course. The Pact's not in play. But in my work? I can feel some of the variations of location. Austria has that lovely ley to work with, Magister Lenz's workshop, outside Leipzig. And then Vienna felt entirely different, of course."

Niobe chuckled. "It does." She leaned back. "There's been a little conversation among masters of the guilds, but nothing conclusive. It seems to be less of a concern more recently, the last couple of years, but it's terribly hard to tell. In some cases we're sure of, it only seems to become relevant once people get into more advanced work, more that draws directly on their skill and vitality, both."

"And that leaves gaps in apprenticeships, doesn't it? Not only, um. Individual ones."

"Some people rely on the apprentice fees. And some people, honestly, do their best work when they're teaching. And we need a certain number of new folks - especially Healers and the Guard and so on - but apothecaries and whatnot, too."

Vitus frowned. "I didn't check the numbers for that. Or the people who might reasonably have gone to Alethorpe or straight into apprenticeship."

"I won't ask you to do that. For one thing, I can do that myself, or we can get someone to do it, more likely. I don't think anyone actually looked at that, in terms of the specifics. At least not that I've heard about. But I'd not mind your notes on the annuals when you read them, to pass along."

"Of course." Vitus let out a puff of breath. "You were worried it might be me, too? Whatever it is?"

"I was. I'm a little less worried now. Sunlight dispels ghosts. Isn't that what they say?" She leaned over, patted the top of his hand. "Right. Why don't you set up the signet you wanted to work on? I think I have an idea for how to do what you want with the different depths without a risk of fouling it."

Vitus offered a little smile. "I'd like that." It was a lovely bit of topaz, and he didn't want to spoil it or have to cut it down further.

CHAPTER 15

MAY 25TH AT BRYN GLAS

"It's still not right." Thessaly didn't turn around. They were in Aunt Metaia's workroom. She knew right where her aunt was. Thessaly could feel her, ten feet back, across the room, and about three feet to the left. Thessaly was trying - and failing - to get a proper complex illusion to take. She'd somehow made the time to make and apply the gesso, the bulk of it earlier last Saturday, so it had time to dry.

Now, it was refusing to behave. Oh, not the gesso, precisely. Thessaly was fully willing to accept that certain materia had opinions about how, when, whether, and in what circumstances it was best used. The recipe Aunt Metaia preferred - and thus the one Thessaly also preferred - involved rabbit skin glue, marble dust, titanium white. And at least seven drops of honey from Aunt Metaia's beehives. That was not the problem, not exactly.

Getting the illusion to hold was the problem. She'd tried twice, and she couldn't make it work. The images fluttered there for a moment and then faded, like a rose wilting out of season and before the eyes.

"No. Talk me through it, then." Aunt Metaia sounded amused rather than annoyed, and that was enough to get Thessaly to turn around and look. Aunt Metaia was wearing another of her favourite aesthetic gowns - there was no one in the house besides the staff and the two of them. This was a rich green with gold-embroidered ribbon adding subtle touches over a paler green undergown. Thessaly was wearing one of the ones Aunt Metaia had gifted her for times like these. She had five in the wardrobe upstairs.

Mama wouldn't let her out of her bedroom in one at home, even just to the portal. Mama had extremely precise ideas about how one dressed and moved and acted in public, and no degree of informality was permitted within those standards. Her clothing was armour and protection. Thessaly knew that, even if she yearned for something different, and a fight on a different field. This gown was a muted lavender over a darker purple, and it made Thessaly think of fields of the flower, something soothing.

Now she took a breath, turning to face her aunt. "It's not flowing properly. It is not the materia. I am confident it was mixed and applied properly. Not only by my skill, but you checked it. One of us might miss something, but both is unlikely."

Her aunt snorted, but nodded her agreement. Thessaly went on. "It is not the current weather, it is an ordinary enough sort of day. Neither too dry nor too utterly damp." Both could affect the humidity of the room, and thus the finest nuances of the casting, but they were of Albion. They were used to dealing with humidity in a range from damp to soggy to utterly waterlogged on a regular basis. She'd have far more trouble in a desert. Thessaly considered. "Me, I suppose." It was the factor she couldn't bring into line.

"Talk to me about that, then. How do you feel today?" Aunt Metaia took a couple of steps forward.

"Unsettled." It was the first thing that came to mind, and Thessaly could and would say it here, rather than guarding her tongue. If she couldn't trust Aunt Metaia, here, at home, there wasn't anyone she could trust.

"Your apprenticeship? Your engagement? Things at home?" Aunt Metaia considered. "Come sit. We'll have tea before we try again. Tea often helps." One hand on Thessaly's waist guided her out toward the library, and Aunt Metaia summoned a tea cart. Five minutes later, there was tea steeping and a plate of Welsh cakes to nibble on.

It had given Thessaly time to figure out some words that might describe what she felt. "It's nothing specific. But I was out for supper at Arundel last night, and I am still getting used to how they do things. Not the manners. My manners are fine." At the moment, she was leaning an elbow on the table, which was decidedly not permitted anywhere else.

"I'm sure they have their particular ways. Do they explain much to you?" Aunt Metaia reached for her own teacup. "Or are you expected to work it out from first principles and etiquette guides on your own?"

It made Thessaly almost choke on her tea, and she set her cup down pointedly. "The latter. With occasional raised eyebrows when I misstep. I am getting fairly good at the eyebrows. They are all expressive with them. I wonder if it's hereditary."

"Maylis and Laudine did not start as Fortiers. Though I grant that Chrodechildis was a distant cousin." Aunt Metaia considered. "Though Maylis and Laudine both come from Third Families, they're related more generations back."

Unlike the Powells, who were Fourth Families, even if they were one of the most notable ones. They were part of the families who had come up through Wales and Scotland, ancient magic pushed to the borders of the island by invasion after invasion. "Eyebrows." Thessaly said firmly. "And Childeric won't explain. Not that I expected that much, but even less than I'd expected. He's busy with something."

"And he's not bragging about it to you? The boy doesn't understand how to carry through with a project, does he?" Aunt Metaia scoffed, then her expression softened. "I'm sorry, that must be terribly frustrating."

"It is. For one thing, I might have ideas. He's, I don't know, frustrated about something. Like he was last year, when he couldn't get Fulgett's Triad to come out right." It was a particular new duelling technique, and Thessaly had picked it up in under three goes. Childeric had taken five months, though admittedly he was not very steady about doing his drills. And he'd only managed it once, when she had been doing bouts with both Childeric and Sigbert, before Childeric had declared he didn't want to duel her again. "Yes. It's like that. Frustration and pent-up energy, and an edge of something, but he won't explain it at all."

"Is he also frustrated, expressing it the same sort of way, at his parents or his grandmother, or his brother?" Aunt Metaia poured herself a little more from the teapot, fiddling slightly with the lid.

That one, Thessaly had to think about. "A bit more deferential to his father than usual, actually? But I thought that was mostly the betrothal being settled and him finishing his apprenticeship, and I don't know. Growing up a bit. Maturing. Realising that petulance doesn't go with his looks, charm is much better." She sighed. "He's certainly much more fun when he's inclined to be charming."

Aunt Metaia considered. "The offer still stands, if you change your mind. I'm going to keep saying that, I suspect, until you're actually wed. Just in case."

That brought Thessaly's eyes up from the table, tilting her head to peer at her aunt. She was also doing things with her eyebrows, she was fairly sure. It was contagious. "Nothing's changed. I knew what I was agreeing to. And it's not as if I'd get a better offer." She cleared her throat. "And Father and the uncles made it clear where they stand, the needs of the family."

"Ah." Aunt Metaia considered. "They have been very set on you making a match with Childeric, indeed." It was a decidedly neutral statement, deliberately, and Thessaly focused on her aunt's face.

"You don't approve?" Then Thessaly caught herself. She knew better, she'd been trained to better, even though the slip wouldn't matter here. "Pardon. You have opinions, you've expressed them to Mama, but this isn't your decision to make. Or advise on, other than making it clear to me, in private, that there are alternatives."

Aunt Metaia nodded once, confirming Thessaly had laid it out properly. "Your parents - and your father, in particular - have reasons. They're even understandable reasons. But they are not much about what's best for you, as much as what's best for the family. Those are two different things. I worry about what it will mean for you."

Thessaly nodded. "I— well, I am expected to marry someone. Talking with the uncles made it clear there aren't many other options, not for our sort of family. Of the other people who are heirs or likely to be, the others are all promised or in need of a dowry, or both."

"Quite." Now that was a bit of sharpness. "And your uncles have opinions about the dowry and marriage settlement. And your father is guided by that." It was a precise and nuanced commentary, and Thessaly could not figure out how to ask about the money side of it. It wasn't anything Father discussed with her, and not the sort of thing she'd ever talked about with Aunt Metaia in this sort of context. "There's Jupiter Delwyn, but he's both younger and in line to be heir but not heir yet."

"No, and I don't think I'd like Noctua Delwyn as a mother-in-law. Lady Maylis has strong opinions, but with the Delwyns, I think there's no chance of being myself, ever. I'd lose any time there was a disagreement with anyone in the family." She shrugged. "It's a series of choices, and Childeric can be quite decent when he wants to be."

"There are a number of ways something might be better or worse. You know enough about the political maths, how it's not a straight line, or even more complex maths. And your mother made choices the same way, with her eyes open to what they were." Then Aunt Metaia got distracted by a take on it. "Curves and volumes and such." Aunt Metaia waved a hand at Thessaly's torso. "Even if you bring pleasant curves - or at least curves Childeric ought to be appreciating properly - to the equation."

That broke the tension a little, and it was Thessaly's turn to snort. "He used to at least look." She had to count back. "Not that he ever presumed too far."

"Not least because you can trounce him, formal duel or no, and you both know it," Aunt Metaia agreed. "I suspect you could even do it without disarranging your hair an iota."

"That is something to aspire to as a standard." Thessaly would have to contemplate that, how to be optimally effective with the least physical movement, especially any that might be noticed. It allowed - well, the bustled skirts allowed - for a number of foot placements, in reasonable shoes. She could do a number of things with finger positions, as well, never mind incantations and charms. All in all, that would be a pleasant challenge to sort out, though she hoped not to need any of the resulting skills.

It brought her back to the essential issue, however. "No. He's distracted. It's not that he's trying to be dismissive, exactly. Whatever he is, it's not about me. It's about something else."

"Huh." Aunt Metaia sniffed. "All right. Tell me if you discover what it is, then. Perhaps we can sort out better what to do about it. And I suppose you'll have the usual sort of things coming up, where his attention will not be divided. The Council rites, and then the Midsummer Faire."

"Exactly. And I have excellent new frocks for both, and really, when Childeric is being social, he really can honestly be lovely." That was the thing. She didn't love him, but until the betrothal, she'd generally enjoyed her time with him. He wasn't terribly interested in the exact things she was - or when he was, she was better, and she tried not to rub it in. But they had plenty of overlap in other ways, and of course, a whole host of young men and women of their age and social status to gossip about. Which could, in fact, carry quite a few conversations. Perhaps she ought to try that again.

"Yes, dearest?" Aunt Metaia was leaning back.

"I was thinking I ought to collect some gossip, and see if that gave us something to talk about. Is there any that you'd find interesting to share? Or useful to the family, or whatever else it is you have in mind?"

"Oh, now, that's an interesting question. And we all know plenty of couples where what keeps them happy together is a bit of mutual social plotting. Is there anything you've heard that seems likely?"

Thessaly wavered. Her mind got stuck on Vitus, because part of the gossip recently had been about his costume at the St. George's Day gala. Not about him directly. He'd kept his mask on, but about the effect of it. Her aunt raised an eyebrow, in her own mode of it, and Thessaly blushed. "You remember Vitus Deschamps? I was talking to him when you came to find me at the gala."

"Ah, yes. Respectable family, not our league, but I gather Niobe Hall's quite pleased with him. And he is a handsome young man. I saw him in passing - the other side of the street, not to speak to - last week in Trellech."

"I bumped into him - well, he saved me from a tumble on the movable steps - in the library Friday week." Thessaly ducked her chin, then looked up at her aunt. "We talked. He's..."

"Ah." Aunt Metaia considered. "You know your agreements, of course. And I am not someone to discourage you from pleasure. In those places it might reasonably be found."

"Aunt Metaia!" That came out pitched and startled. Aunt Metaia had in fact made it plain she was no untouched maiden, but this was a bit more than she'd said. Thessaly wondered if her aunt could in fact read minds, given Thessaly had been thinking about asking her about how she might open a conversation with Vitus about something beyond decorous conversation. Now she had an opening, but she wasn't sure how to position herself to move into it smoothly. Duelling gave her the mode she wanted, but not the words, here.

"You know your mythology perfectly well. It is possible to be an independent woman - a sovereign lady, a parthenos, whatever we call ourselves, in whichever language." Aunt Metaia was leaning back. "Not that I have recently, mind. I've been far too busy."

Thessaly blinked several times, then ventured, "And also, whoever you might take up with might have political aspirations, and that's exhausting?"

Her aunt laughed, though it was a bit hollow. "That too. That's the trouble with ageing. You know far too many people's quirks and, even worse, the things that entirely put you off them, in any form of congress. Perhaps the seasons will change and I will be inclined. Perhaps I will not. Either way, I have had my grand times." She waved a hand. "You should have some too, that is all I am saying. And if Childeric is not forthcoming, he knows what the agreements are."

Thessaly ducked her chin again. "I prevailed on Vitus to call me Thessaly. And he's coming around this week to talk about the lapis lazuli illusion. Finally." Then she sat bolt upright. "I think I have an idea. Can you give me five minutes to set something up?" One of the articles she'd been reading at the library touched on what she wanted, a way to better lay groundwork for an illusion, but she'd need to work through how it felt in practice. Reading about it was not remotely the same as doing it.

"Of course. I'll be along then."

Thessaly brought the last fragment of Welsh cake to her mouth, chewed, and abandoned her tea as she went back to the workroom.

CHAPTER 16

MAY 30TH IN TRELLECH

Vitus was, honestly, only half paying attention to the conversation at the start. He'd spent the afternoon at Magistra North's workshop, talking through the problem of lapis lazuli and illusions with Thessaly. The actual conversation had been extremely informative.

Vitus brought several samples of different grades of lapis with him. Niobe's lectures on the topic had been exceedingly thorough, and he'd also made excellent notes at the geological specimen collections he'd visited over the past few years. Vitus had taken pages of notes, but also come away with several samples of Thessaly's work, all carefully layered into a folder with sheets of protective paper between them.

He was supposed to decide which he'd like embedded into fabric and provide a suitable outfit for it. The one he'd worn for the gala would do once Mama picked out the amethyst work and pieced in something suitable for the base for the illusion work. Thessaly had made it clear she wasn't intending to charge him for anything other than the materials. That would involve some lapis that would become powder, but he'd expected that. The best way to make something seem real was to anchor it in reality, after all. Once the illusion was set, he'd be able to call it up again with a little more powdered stone.

It would give him an excellent excuse to call again, though perhaps not until after Solstice. It had become clear during the conversation that Magistra North was tolerating his visit as a useful educational moment, but that Thessaly had limited time for such endeavours. The time wasn't a problem, there wasn't another masked ball until autumn. Costumes could so often get too warm and unwieldy in the summer months.

They hadn't had time for any private conversation, and Vitus kept telling himself that was entirely to be expected. And for all Thessaly had made it clear she was not letting herself be limited by gossip, he was still entirely wary of someone objecting on her behalf. That was a problem he absolutely didn't need. He already had more than enough challenges to be going on with.

So, apparently, did other people, because Vitus caught a snippet of a complaint. "I still don't understand why it didn't work. It was splendid on Thursday. Then, when I was demonstrating it last night, nothing worked properly. It was as if all the magic were drained out, and when I tried to replenish it, that too drained out like nothing I've seen."

That sort of comment was quite common in the Stream's conversation rooms. Salmon House was known for people not only with many skills, wide-ranging skills, but also a desire to tinker constantly. Normally, though, the experimentation wasn't so ardently mechanical. Vitus cleared his throat, turning around to the people just behind him who'd been talking. "Pardon, I couldn't help overhearing. Perhaps explaining it to someone else might help? I find that in my own work."

Two women and two men stood there. He didn't know any of them entirely by sight. Vitus thought that one pair - a dark-haired man and woman maybe six or seven years older than he was, going into their middle thirties - must be Olivia and Oscar Hemmings. They were twins who'd been the scourge of several teachers at Schola. They were also the reason for about thirty specific rules about what not to do in Salmon House proper or with the provided materials. They were apparently responsible for at least half Professor Marrington's hair being pure white.

He made a slight bow. "Vitus Deschamps. Recently returned from the Continent and finishing my apprenticeship with Magistra Niobe Hall."

The four of them nodded, and the other man stuck out his hand. "A few years behind me, then. Marius Collins. You know of the Hemmings. I suspect everyone does, even if you've not been properly introduced. They were travelling before you were. This is Aline Holder, enchantments."

Olivia grinned, the sort of sharp grin that put people on notice. "Oscar and I find our hands in all sorts of particular novel problems. Marius is working on some devices to better detect poisons in the water from industrial processes. He's hoping to bring it to the Council and the Ministry for broader deployment."

"If I can get it to work reliably." Marius looked entirely beleaguered. "The most recent trials have been going swimmingly. We've been able to verify the results through other methods. The device is meant to be much faster, and allows us to pinpoint the source of problems so that the proper people can go in and take steps."

Vitus considered for a moment. "That is the sort of

thing that Council Head Rowan is interested in, I know that. And Council Member Warren, too." There'd been a number of pieces in the Trellech Moon about that. It was a particular focus of his. "Where were you testing it successfully, and where did it have problems?"

"It's been quite solid approaching cities. We did some trials around Sheffield, at different distances." Something in the way Vitus had gone about the question had apparently been reassuring to Collins. "And then some in London, though of course, London has its own complications. And some here in Trellech, to confirm that it would work when there was a great deal of magic in the vicinity."

That answered a question Vitus had been about to ask. Substantial magic, whatever form it took, could warp magical devices if you weren't quite careful. "Schola island?"

"A few quirks to the results, but within norms." Marius folded his hands behind his back, the sort of gesture people made when they were inclined to gesticulate and knock things over. Lucas did it, when he was trying to be proper or when there were delicate objects about. "That's what made today so frustrating. It was if all the ordinary rules of magic stopped working, at least for a little."

"May I ask where you were testing?" Vitus said.

"Out in Sussex, the southern Weald." Marius shrugged. "And I can't think why it would have changed there."

Vitus tilted his head. "The Weald's an odd place, magically. It remembers being a forest, for one thing, and, blast, what's the word?" He searched back through his memory. This was not made easier by the fact he was fairly sure the last time he'd discussed it was in French, and rather in passing. "Anticline." At the last moment, he managed to give it the English pronunciation.

"Pardon?" That was Oscar.

"Anticline. That's the name for the formation. It runs through the Weald across the Channel to Dover. Unusual landscape, and a number of magical implications." Vitus blinked several times. "Pardon. I've just been terribly esoteric, haven't I?"

"Yes." Three of the four of them said it in unison, with Aline trailing by half a beat.

Vitus tried to gather himself. "Um." That was not gathered at all, that was far too close to imitating a gaping fish, and The Stream had plenty of other fish already, in a variety of forms. "I'm a talisman maker." The twins twigged to it fairly quickly, and he added for the others. "Knowing the geology of where the stones come from sometimes matters a great deal. And I am just back from seeing an awful lot of mines and mineral specimens, as well as the insides of dozens of workshops and such."

Marius made a small understanding noise. "All right. So what's different about the Weald? Or wherever we actually were. We'd taken the train to Littlehampton, then horses north, I don't know, eight or ten miles up the Arun?"

"I know the land there a bit," Vitus considered. "My family is a client family of the Fortiers. The bigger parties, you know, or the times we can be useful." He got an uncertain nod from Marius and Aline, but the twins were more familiar with how that worked. It made him guess that the other two came from backgrounds not so tied into the Great Families. "Tell me more about what happened?"

"The readings looked like they were what we expected nearer the coast, but then something, I don't know, changed. And the whole thing went haywire, and then it stopped working. Do you really think it was the ground underneath, or the rock, or whatever?"

"I think it's worth doing the work to check it out. Compare where your device has worked, look at the geology there. Or, I don't know. Where the portals are. Maybe someone opened a portal at just the wrong time. The Arundel portal would be, what, a mile or two, depending where you were."

Marius got a very thoughtful expression. "That's a lot of work, but it's at least somewhere to start, which is more than I had when I got here. Look, let me buy you a drink? Do you have time to chat a bit more? What are you up to, then?"

A handful of minutes later, they'd claimed a table and chairs. Marius had bought a round of drinks for everyone, and they were comfortably tucked into sharing tidbits back and forth. None of them had answers to Vitus's particular needs. They were all older, but in that ground where they were established in their fields, but not able to be notably generous with someone setting up. Except, that was, with their information. Olivia and Oscar shared a couple of names of people who might be interested in encouraging innovative talisman work - or at least starting with competent. Vitus felt he could offer competence within his scope.

From there, Vitus asked a bit about how they'd gone about establishing themselves. Now they were into a second round of drinks, all four were more relaxed. He got several excellent pieces of advice, about how to set up, how to talk about what he did and where. And also a pointer or two for thinking about rooms to let. Better yet, they shared a few stories of things that had gone wrong for them, or at least sideways, and recovering from them.

The conversation easily shifted from that into more general gossip, catching up on various stories while Vitus had been away. Olivia told a couple, then pursed her lips.

"You're enough younger, actually. Do you know anything beyond the public about Cyrus Smythe-Clive? Such a horrible thing." Vitus tilted his head, because he wasn't placing the name immediately. Olivia said, "No, then. Awfully tragic - actually, maybe you didn't hear. Cyrus married Tanith Cooper."

"Fox House, four years behind me." Then he swallowed. "Oh. Mama wrote." That came rushing back. It had been the sort of unthinkable news that got shared for kind reasons and because people liked to share misery. Though in Mama's case, it had been so Vitus didn't offend at some later point.

"They seemed thrilled, wonderfully happy. And she died, leaving him and their just-born daughter. Horrible time. Our families know each other fairly well, though of course Cyrus and Andie are enough younger, we're not friends, exactly." Olivia shivered visibly. "That it could come on so quickly, and his sister apprenticing as a Healer, even." She took a sip of her drink before going on. "He's just thrown himself into who knows what. Immersing himself in something. No one sees him, even allowing for mourning, which, of course, he's got every right to do."

Vitus considered, thinking about who he knew. Thessaly would have overlapped with him, actually, and in Fox House, though he'd have to check the years. "I might know someone to ask. Does anyone have any sense of how the daughter's doing?" They'd married very young - both of them still in their apprenticeships. But Tanith had been a brilliant alchemist, the sort who got listed in any number of the top alchemists of their generation. Besides the human loss, that she'd been loved, that was something Albion couldn't afford. Creative alchemists were rare.

Three of the four shook their heads, but Aline offered a

quiet comment. Vitus had noticed she didn't speak unless she had something purposeful to say. "At home with a nursemaid. But the Coopers are apparently, well, they think he's not fit to raise her, and they should have the chance. It hasn't come to anything before the Courts yet. But my Mama knows a cousin of the Coopers, Nimby Wallace, and I gather it's partly because they're making sure everything's utterly in order. Not the sort of play you get a second chance at legally."

Vitus nodded. He'd ask Papa more about that. He might know something about it. While Papa's work focused on the business side of things, and for excellent reason, knowing about the interpersonal feuds was absolutely essential. "I'll ask the person who might know when I get a chance. It might be a fortnight or more. She's got obligations for Solstice."

"Well, so do many of us." That got the conversation aimed in a much more genial direction. Marius had a booth at the Midsummer Faire to demonstrate some of his other devices. Olivia and Oscar were giving a lecture there on mending charms for unusual circumstances. In the end, the five of them planned to meet up at the Faire, at the least, and perhaps regularly after that. Vitus took himself off home feeling rather pleased with the day all in all. If he did not have solutions for his problems, he had at least made more connections who might help in time. And good company in several forms was a definite joy.

CHAPTER 17

JUNE 1ST AT THE TEMPLE OF HEALING, TRELLECH

"Now, is there anyone you'd like to make sure you get a few minutes to speak with?" Aunt Metaia paused, just before they entered the gardens proper. Thessaly could hear the buzz of the people beyond, like bees but at more pitches. This was one of the great benevolent gatherings of the summer, bringing people to gossip and chatter and raise funds for the Temple of Healing and their patients in need.

Mama and Father might appear at one of them, but today, Aunt Metaia had been the one to make the donation for their entrance. Thessaly was certain it was a generous one, though subtly conveyed in an envelope. She'd seen the way the woman at the gate had reacted to the slip with the sum to be claimed from the bank in due course. Aunt Metaia made a point of being at this sort of thing. She considered it one obligation of the Council. And, of course, it was also useful for whatever her current projects were.

The gardens would be glorious, of course. They were some of the most diligently tended in all of Albion. The people in them would be just as brightly dressed, showing off their summer frocks and parasols and whatever other accessories.

The entire feel of the place was different from Arundel. That was nagging at her now. This, for all it was a space of no small amount of pain and suffering in the course of eventual healing, felt hopeful. Arundel felt like it was waiting for something. It wasn't something out of a gothic novel, not exactly, but it did feel like there was an uncomfortable emptiness somewhere, just out of sight.

Though perhaps it was also the company. Being with Aunt Metaia felt glorious, as it always did. Even when they were behaving as women of their station ought to in public. Of course, Thessaly preferred their time in private, when neither of them fussed about upright posture and their best manners or the approved topics of conversation. But even with those restraints of society in place, she loved watching how Aunt Metaia wove through the world.

Thessaly considered the question. At school, she'd spent most of her time with the other duellists. At least when she wasn't working on an assignment or essay or practising Incantation or Enchantment or some such for an exam. Now, it was complicated for her to talk to them socially, particularly in any relaxed form. That was hemmed in, limited to scheduled sessions at one of the private salles, and she wouldn't be able to do that until after solstice. Her time was so full of dress fittings and social obligations with the Fortiers. Anyway, duelling wasn't sociable, not the same way.

Of the girls she'd been closer to at Schola, a few would be here. More would be home with small children or expecting one, and few of the women of her class lived in Trellech all the time. Some of that was worries about the portals, but of course a new baby was apparently entirely exhausting, even with nursemaids. Thessaly would presumably find out herself in due course, but not for a bit yet. Wedding first, then the rest of it.

The other half were still busy with their own apprenticeships, and they'd drifted in different directions. Oh, it was a pleasure to chat when they ran into each other. They did from time to time, somewhere like these garden parties, or in the Fox's Den, the Fox House club a little south from here along Trellech's Club Row.

Thessaly also had her own membership at Bourne's now. Father had insisted on sponsoring her. But navigating that socially was even more complex than the duellists, and she hadn't bothered for months if she wasn't with Childeric. There was a particular form of social warfare played there, about the precise choices of clothes, charms, and hair among the women. She could play that game and win it, but she also knew it to be absolutely exhausting. And whether or not they were there together, Bourne's meant dealing with Childeric and his expectations. He spent a fair bit of his free time there, and so did most of his closer circle. Anything she did would get back to him immediately. That was entirely too much bother.

Now she shook her head. "I will let you know if I do." Aunt Metaia, on the other hand, had a plan for today. She had various bits of Council business to do, not that she'd specified it to Thessaly. A word in a number of ears, arrangements to get together before the Solstice rites. But she mostly wanted to introduce Thessaly to people she didn't know yet who would be interesting.

Aunt Metaia thought about the world and the people in it in a way Mama didn't. Mama and Father treated their connections as levers to move the world, but Aunt Metaia went about it differently. She wanted to see what was individual about someone, what made them smile or lean forward. What caught their eye, Aunt Metaia had put it that way once, and what they ignored. It was curious, because by any reasonable measure, Aunt Metaia had more actual influence and power. Far more than Mama and Father did, more than Thessaly could herself hold now or likely in the future. Yet, Aunt Metaia thought Thessaly could do the same. Insistently.

Aunt Metaia was younger than Mama by eight years, but that eight years made a lot of difference in terms of energy and willingness to finish the argument. Thessaly knew they'd been arguing about introducing Thessaly to a wider circle of acquaintances - among other things - for the past few weeks. Maybe longer. Mama had finally thrown her hands up and said she certainly couldn't stop Aunt Metaia doing what she was going to do. She'd then turned around and told Thessaly to be properly appreciative.

Now, her aunt steered them both through the guests, nodding and smiling at several people along the way. They made a pleasant pair to look at, at least. Thessaly was wearing one of her newer gowns. It was a muted green with decorations from white to golden yellow, with a few ribbon roses echoing the real flowers in the decorative garden beds. Aunt Metaia had not, for once, chosen the peacock green she favoured. Today she was wearing something to match Thessaly's green, but darker, like mature leaves or grass in a meadow.

The introductions went well enough. They'd gone through four, all women a little older than Thessaly, with a range of different specialities. One - Gwendolyn Harrow - had an interest in Enchantment that might be a good mesh with Thessaly's interests. Another, Christel Williams, was someone Thessaly remembered slightly from school. She was three years older, she'd been in Owl House, but now she was wrapping up an extensive apprenticeship in Ritual magic.

Thessaly turned around, after that, considering whether to see about getting a glass of punch or some such, when she found herself two steps from Vitus Deschamps. They were over on the edge of the party standing on one of the paved pathways that ran from the Temple itself down to the wards at the far end of the space. Aunt Metaia had found someone to talk to, and the woman Vitus was with - his mother, perhaps - patted his arm and turned to speak to someone else.

"Master Deschamps." Thessaly offered her gloved hand, and he bowed over it, habit standing in for decision. "Delighted to see you. Not your natural habitat, I expect?"

It made him blush for an instant, then chuckle. "My mother asked if I would escort her, and of course I was glad to." He looked over his shoulder, as if he wasn't certain where she'd got to. Then he turned back when he was reassured it was not far and that she had already found a conversation to enjoy. "You look lovely, of course, very suitable for the setting. No illusion work today?"

Thessaly found herself smiling, the sort of smile that made her mouth and eyes crinkle. "Not today, no. I didn't want to compete with the garden. And it's a bit of a trick, if you don't know what's blooming. If this were, oh, at Aunt Metaia's, I could plan the frock and illusions to suit." She gestured with one hand, then glimpsed Aunt Metaia clearly giving her a little time and space.

"If I do not get a chance to speak with your aunt, please convey my greetings and well wishes." That was entirely stilted, but there was a little quiver at the end that made her sure it was some sort of nerves.

"Oh, of course. I haven't made progress on the lapis lazuli illusions yet. Yesterday rather got away from me. I was hoping to do some more reading tonight and tomorrow, though, it's such an interesting problem." It was, too, and she'd very much enjoyed working through it with him. Magistra North had also thought it an excellent problem, suitable for her attention.

"No, of course." Vitus spread his hands. "I had an interesting discussion that evening. Actually, you might have a thought about it?"

Thessaly inclined her head. "Of course, on what topic?"

"I was at The Stream. I found myself in conversation with someone who had been working on a device to better measure the effects of industry upon the rivers and streams. He's done a number of tests already, but they were up along the Arun, not terribly far from Arundel, as he described it, and they had some odd readings."

"My." Thessaly inserted one of the appropriate noises here, while she thought. "May I ask what sort of odd, or is that a trade secret?"

"He didn't get terribly specific, and he's terribly busy between now and solstice, though I expect to go round and see more of it after the Faire. And I'm afraid we of the Stream can get terribly arcane about what we're trying to do."

Thessaly snorted, then covered her mouth to muffle the sound. "Honestly, there's an entire line of jokes about how each house is terribly arcane. It can't all be the Owls."

"I'm sure no one dares say such things about Fox. At least not where anyone of Fox House could hear." That made her laugh even more audibly, which was out of mode for this sort of gathering.

"Ah, you'd be surprised. Not everyone has tact. Or tactical sense. What did your friend say?"

"Friend might be stretching it, at least yet. Agreeable acquaintance, at the moment. I suggested he look to the geology, that can sometimes cause changes in magical response. I'm sure you know that, as well?" Vitus took a half step closer, still at a polite and proper space.

"Indeed." Thessaly considered the problem. She'd been at Arundel for a range of magical events now, including May Day's land magic rites. She'd duelled there, which was a decided help. There were undercurrents there, but there were on every landed estate and every estate of a powerful family, and the Fortiers had been both for centuries. "It's hard for me to distinguish the family magics from the rest of it. I do not find that my magic runs differently there, on the whole. But I have, I admit, not attempted the more delicate sorts beyond personal habits of dress and hair." She inclined her head, teasing just a little. "I have not yet tried the more elaborate illusions there."

"Good afternoon. Thessaly?" Aunt Metaia's voice behind her was a pleasant alto.

"You remember Vitus Deschamps, Aunt. He bid me to convey his good wishes to you, of course." Thessaly turned to look at her aunt, who came up beside her, offering her hand.

Vitus bowed over it properly, then straightened. "I hope you are well, Council Member. It's a pleasure to see you both. Thessaly was very generous with her time on the topic of lapis lazuli on Thursday, and then I had a conversation with an acquaintance. You must have a wide experience of the way magic responds differently in various locations. There was an odd occurrence near Arundel, but not on the estate properly, and I was wondering about the geological features of the Weald being in play."

No one else would have noticed it, but Thessaly knew her aunt well, and she knew Aunt Metaia was now paying close attention. "My usual line of work lies in Illusion and Materia work, but yes, I have found that. Certain places seem to restore and prolong magical effects, others seem to drain them unusually quickly. There is a whole line of theoretical work on it, but I admit I've found the practical analysis lacking. Not remotely rigorous enough. All of the published reports tend to be the author's pet locations or an excuse to travel to where there is excellent fishing or shooting or other sport."

That made Vitus chuckle. "Ah, that is a problem. If you have titles to recommend, I would be glad to consider them, though. Any bit of information might be a help. I suppose you don't know of any other cause of issues, a known one, such as, I don't know, one of the Fatae portals?"

It was a bold question, actually, and Thessaly was rather impressed with Vitus for asking it. The Council's primary role, by one count, was to mediate the agreements of the Pact. They were charged with making sure that both those humans with magic and the Fatae, the various magical beings of Albion, did not cause trouble. "Step on each other's toes like the worst sort of dance," was how Aunt Metaia had put it once.

Her aunt paused for a moment, letting them see she was weighing what to say. "By the Arun, within a few miles of Arundel. No, there's no particular Fatae site there. And this was recent, the problem? Not near to May Day itself?"

"Earlier on Thursday, from what they said," Vitus offered. "Ah, not anything that might be more obvious, then. I suggested he look at the geology, see if there are any patterns there. I'm quite curious what turns up, or if the device behaves itself in other locations." Then he caught a movement. "Pardon, my mother." He did not dash away. He waited for a proper dismissal.

Aunt Metaia smiled at him, beneficent. "We certainly will not keep you from filial devotion." She left a moment for Thessaly to say something, and that was entirely deliberate.

Thessaly smiled as thoroughly as she could manage. "Truly, a pleasure to see you twice in a week. My good wishes to your mother and family, and perhaps we'll get time next week or the one after to confer again?"

"I hope so. Mistress, Magistra, a good day." He waited just long enough for Aunt Metaia's nod, and then immediately went to his mother, offering his arm.

"That is a pleasant man, and one with good manners, attentive to his mother," Aunt Metaia said, considering. "Also, a man with pleasant features and better brains. I hope you get more chances to talk soon, then." It was a very approving sort of statement, also bold.

Thessaly could feel the blush rising in her cheeks. "As you say, Aunt. Now, I was just thinking I might bring you some refreshment. Before there are more people you wish to introduce me to?"

"Grand. Ah, I see Lady Teague. I'll have a word with her. Come find me there."

Thessaly nodded and went off in search of the refreshments. A glass of lemonade would be just the thing.

CHAPTER 18

JUNE 5TH IN TRELLECH

Vitus found himself far too busy to do more than think of that meeting with Thessaly at the garden party in brief little snippets. Mama had several young women to introduce him to. Of course she had. They had been pleasant, and certainly the sort of woman he might aspire to as a wife. All three were daughters of men of the professional classes, a suitable match for Vitus. Two were the eldest daughters of different senior clerks in the Ministry, well used to helping a household and a family run smoothly. The other had been the only and much treasured daughter of a solicitor and his second wife.

None of them had any interest in talking about his work. Oh, they'd made the proper sort of pleasant comments, but they had asked no questions. They had offered no thoughts of their own about relevant aspects, or even their own interests and magical skills. It was hard to tell from five or ten minutes' conversation constrained by the setting and the company, but Vitus had got the impression that none of them had aspirations beyond family life, some proper number of children, raised well, to continue on like their parents.

Vitus was not a radical, nor was he revolutionary in his ideas. But he had dreams beyond steady competence. He wanted to create talismans that made a difference in someone's life, or ideally in multiple people's lives. Keep the head of the household well and hale, and his entire family would prosper. Or hers, for that matter.

That had sent him on a long and promising chase through the literature in the next few days, both in the main library in Trellech and in Niobe's own collection. He didn't have answers for any of it, not yet. And if he came up with set pieces, talismans that could be reliably replicated, or only with minor changes for circumstance, they would need a tremendous amount of testing.

On the other hand, pieces that removed some of the exhaustive personalised work could be sold at a lower cost, especially if he could also source materials to match. Jet was not inexpensive, especially in larger pieces, but it was certainly less costly than many other gems. If he could get something that would suit in quartz or agate or something of the kind, even better. Those were abundant, and a talisman didn't actually have to be a stunning piece visually.

Vitus had come up for air from that research on Thursday afternoon. It was just in time for Herrick Blades, who'd been a year ahead of him at Schola, to wander into Niobe's shop and mention a lecture that evening. It was part of a series that had apparently been running for months, comparing non-magical innovations to magical ones, and seeing where they might connect or oppose each other. Herrick had off-handedly mentioned plans for supper after, saying Vitus was welcome to come along. They had a room at Bourne's, the more the merrier.

If nothing else, it would be an excellent chance to see, be seen, and hopefully be interesting to potential future clients. Or perhaps, even to a potential patron. Vitus hadn't needed Niobe's nudge to agree. He was glad he kept a reasonably good suit for such evenings in her spare wardrobe, rather than needing to dash home via the portal and back.

When he turned up the steps into the Rosamunda Hall, the most esteemed of Trellech's lecture halls, the place was only about half full. Not the best turnout, but it was getting on for solstice. Vitus also supposed that the audience for a discussion of sound recording was, in fact, perhaps a tad limited.

The lecture itself was interesting, talking about the limitations of non-magical sound recordings and the variety of methods they were made. Magic allowed for a much wider range of pitch and timbre. On the other hand, magical methods not only required a specialist to do the recording, but also to make any copies. The non-magical gramophone recordings were much simpler and less costly to reproduce. The discussion of the benefits and challenges once they reached the discussion and debate portion of the evening got quite lively, though everyone was, in fact, in favour of a wider range of recording options.

The organisers had left fifteen minutes at the end to share other related news. Some of the chatter was about attempts in the United States to do long-distance power transmission. Only the bare bones had come through the telegraph, but one man shared the news there had been a successful transmission in the United States, just two days previously. There had been a successful project in Germany, running between Miesbach and Munich a few years earlier. Vitus had heard something about it when he was there. He put his hand up once or twice, only to lower it when the conversation went elsewhere. After time was called, Herrick nudged him. "Coming?"

A small troupe of them - perhaps a dozen men and four women - went along down to Bourne's. They were shown promptly into one of the gathering rooms, with trays of sandwiches and bottles of wine already out for refreshments. The group spread out, and once everyone had food and a seat or at least a bit of furniture to lean against, Herrick cleared his throat. "What were you wanting to say back there? Oh, yes. You chaps - and ladies - may not remember. Vitus Deschamps, talisman maker, year behind me at school, recently back from the Continent."

Vitus managed a slightly awkward bow, given he was holding both a plate and a wineglass. He set first the glass down, then the plate on a side table. "Put me on the spot, Herrick." He got the tone on the nose, teasing the right amount, because Herrick started grinning. Two men who'd been talking turned their attention to Vitus, and Vitus realised they were a couple of the extended Fortier associations. No one he knew well. They were just enough younger, in that odd gap between people who might have gone to school together but hadn't known each other well. But they'd been in Fox, at least two of the three, so there wasn't even that overlap.

"Oh, I was curious about this work in America. I had someone go on at me, at some length, about the Miesbach-Munich transmission, back in, erm. 1883, I believe. Maybe 1884. Long enough ago the details were a little fuzzy once he'd had a few drinks." That got a laugh. Everyone here knew that sort of conversation. "A somewhat longer distance, maybe, didn't whoever it was say, what, fourteen miles?"

"How long was the other?" One woman leaned forward, looking interested. "And why did it stop?"

"Thirty-something, I think." Vitus spread his hands out. "And it was a steam engine, if I remember right. Hard to keep it up all the time, I guess." He wrinkled his nose. "Things will go wrong with them, especially in constant use."

That got a murmur of sighs, because yes, they all knew enough about the sometimes explosive foibles of steam engines. "Do you know anything more about the details, the voltage, or anything?" That was one of the men Vitus didn't know, leaning forward with his elbows perched on his knees.

"Not really my field, obviously. Other than that I have an interest in electron." Half the faces cracked into broader grins, the others looked baffled. "Amber. One of the original names for it, and where the word for electricity comes from."

"That gives us somewhere to start. Or will all the discussion be in German, do you think?" One of the Fortier connections piped up at that, and his friend elbowed him.

"The library gets some of the German papers. I don't know how long they keep them. Though I'm sure it was reported in London, if not here." Vitus wriggled his hand. "I mean, that's another illustration of non-magical and magical. We don't all hear the same information, and we don't all know what to do with it, do we? If it doesn't fit into our world, how we do things, it doesn't stick."

That got the group off on a cheerful round of increasingly loud debate about how to handle that. Of course, people had magical specialities, and of course those could take a tremendous amount of time. It left little space for other things, especially for those apprenticing. Vitus managed to sit down, as other people got up to pace, and eat his sandwich while listening.

Two of the women were ardently arguing for the need for broader education. Or, at the very least, that someone should start an evening school that covered things relevant to the magical community, a more formalised and structured version of the current lectures. Both of them lit up at the idea, and others began encouraging it. Someone pulled out a notebook to scribble down ideas and names.

Herrick bumped Vitus's shoulder with his hip as the conversation shifted around. "Not going to volunteer for it?"

"I'm glad to come to the lectures if I can, but adding one more thing right now? I've got plenty I'm trying to manage. Once I've got my own business established, maybe I'll have space for anything else in my head."

That got a laugh from Herrick, and he pulled over a chair to chat more about what he was up to. Most of it wasn't entirely relevant to Vitus and his immediate future either, but Herrick was doing some interesting research around some of the synthetic dyes and whether they had any use for magical applications or not. They were wrapping that up when the gathering started breaking up.

Vitus looked up to find the two Fortier connections standing, apparently waiting to get a word in edgewise. "Pardon, Deschamps." The one on the left, who was brown-haired, waved a hand. "Louis Montague, if you've misplaced the name. Look, are you perhaps free and going to be at the Council rites or the Faire, after? Some of your ideas are interesting. There's someone who might want a word."

His companion - blonde, more wiry, also perhaps a little more cautious - elbowed him suddenly.

Vitus did his best to ignore that. Their business was their business, after all. And it wasn't like his answer was private. "Both, most likely, though I'm not sure which days at the Faire yet, other than that the Fortiers offered me an afternoon at their display booth on the Wednesday." It ran for over a week, and not only could he not tolerate the crowds every day, he naturally had other work. But Mama had wanted to see the flower show. And Lucas had wanted to get free for some of the pavo matches and the horse sales. Vitus would happily go with either of them.

"We'll be in touch, perhaps, then. Or someone will be." Louis was about to say something else, and that was when Vitus saw something he didn't understand. He knew what it was, but he had no idea why. Louis's face - and his body - had stiffened, the kind of thing that signalled he'd brushed up against an oath sworn on the Silence. He could see the fear there, the way Louis immediately went pale and stopped speaking. Most people took the hint immediately, thankfully. And of course, Vitus wouldn't press further.

Now, he just nodded, giving the social courtesy that nothing had happened. "Of course. Perhaps I'll see you at the Faire." Then he glanced to check his pocket watch. "My, is that the time? I ought to get going. I've an early appointment in the morning." He stood, adding, "Herrick, grand to catch up, and I'll think about if I've come across anything about the dyes that might be relevant. Talk to you soon, I hope." A few more farewells, and he was out the door, out of the club, and well on his way to Portal Square to get a portal home. It had given him a lot more to think about, most of which he was having no luck untangling.

CHAPTER 19
JUNE 8TH AT ARUNDEL

Thessaly stumbled, trying to keep up with Childeric. They were supposed to be taking a sedate turn around the gardens before tea. Childeric was not making that easy. Especially since Thessaly was wearing the sort of frock one wore to have tea with the soon to be family by marriage. It had rather more frills and fripperies than she'd choose for outside exertion. "Childeric, please."

She was feeling a bit out of sorts, overall. They'd been sent outside to take the air. Arundel itself seemed pleasant, the gardens coming into vivid and impeccably tended blooms. But being with Childeric was not remotely soothing, even in such surroundings. She kept having to guess what he was going to do next, and feeling one step behind. He stopped, wheeling around, at first looking annoyed, before it smoothed out - like ice melting - into something kinder. "You should have said something, Thess."

She had. Or at least she thought she had by using words like 'just a moment, please' and 'my shoes aren't fit for this'. He'd brushed by that, five minutes ago or more like ten now, until they were at the far end of the gardens, about to loop around toward the duelling salle. "I'd appreciate slowing down a little. My slippers aren't designed for these paths." She was feeling every pebble under her feet, and that was not her favourite.

"Doesn't that mean you'll be on the path longer?" He had a point, and just to be annoying, he added one of his more charming grins. Thessaly couldn't get Aunt Metaia's comments, the quiet ones, out of her head, though. About how Thessaly theoretically had other choices. They were very theoretical, though, since the betrothal agreements had oaths behind them. If he could be charming all the time, it would be much easier, honestly.

"But I am less likely to slip. You're wearing good solid shoes." Then she took a breath. "More slowly, at least until we're on the bigger paving stones. And look, you seem out of sorts. Is there anything I can help with?"

Childeric immediately shook his head, but he did offer his arm and set off walking more slowly, in keeping with the actual surroundings. "It's a family matter."

Thessaly bit her lip, trying to figure out how to say 'but aren't we going to be family' in a way that wouldn't immediately annoy him more. After trying out and discarding several options, she settled on a mild, "Oh, and there's nothing there you can talk about?"

He glanced at her, then shrugged. "You know how it is, of course you know. All the family expectations, and people wanting to get the most out of something. And of course I want to do my best. Father was on at me about something earlier, that's all."

"You shine, when you're at your peak." Thessaly offered it as a compliment, and it was accurate enough. "I won't pry, then. It's just, well." She let out a little huff of breath. "I worry that I'm missing something, you know? That will be a problem for later, because I didn't notice it now."

That made him laugh, suddenly entirely cheerful. "Oh, don't worry about that at all. If there's something to know, someone will tell you. Probably me." Childeric granted her another of his entirely sunny smiles, the kind that every woman she knew wanted to have directed at her. "I promise."

There really wasn't a good argument to be made about that. Or rather, if she argued, she'd be saying straight out that she didn't trust him, and that wouldn't go anywhere useful or pleasant. "Thank you, then. Now, what have you been up to that you can talk about?"

He hadn't asked her about her apprenticeship, not since he'd turned up at Magistra North's a few weeks ago. No, it was more than a month ago, now. Time had slipped by. Childeric considered for a moment as they walked, the kind of pause that Thessaly expected was him sorting through what he could share. Not whether she'd be interested, he didn't weight that highly in his decisions. Besides, she was interested in many things. "Oh, the usual. A spot of duelling, a spot of gaming. There was this excellent horse race last week, I'll come back to that. But I had a chat with a chap, oh, last week sometime, about an interesting Incantation application."

"I'd love to hear about it." Thessaly made her reply immediate and warm, squeezing his arm slightly with his hand. "Please. Go on?"

It got him started on a long spiel about a particular approach. He did the thing he often did, of simultaneously explaining things she knew very well in unnecessary detail and then brushing over the parts she didn't. Here, he covered things she'd had in class at Schola - which he must have known, he'd taken the same class. And then he entirely breezed through the newer implications, a couple of articles she hadn't read.

"What was the title of that one again? I'd love to look it up?" She got that in during a brief break in his words.

"Oh, hmm. Something like 'The Words and Values'. I can look it up, I suppose, if you remind me after tea. I have notes somewhere." That phrase would not help at all. It was a common enough term to turn up in the literature. And he'd just referred to the person he'd been talking to as Maz, and she was pretty sure that was a nickname. She made a mental note to ask him after tea, yes.

By this point, they'd come down along the long edge of the gardens, and the salle rose into view as they crested the slight hill. She could see Garin, Childeric's young cousin - Dagobert and Laudine's son - out playing with a hoop and stick. It was one of the more popular of the magical children's games. It helped a child learn to apply charms to guide the hoop and improve their precision and grasp of magic.

She leaned a little into Childeric. "It must be hard, Garin being on his own. You and Sigbert had each other to play with, and Garin doesn't have anyone."

"No, it's nearly as many years to the Mortimer cousins. They're still babies." Childeric paused, half-turning to her. "Do you think about children very much, in the specific, then?"

It was rather an odd question. She and Childeric were certainly committed by their agreements to doing their best to have some. Thessaly decidedly understood that was part of the general expectation of being a married woman, though, of course, not every married woman did. And there were people like Aunt Metaia, who'd ignored that whole line of things. Here and now, she nodded. "Of course I've thought about it some. And Hermia's enough younger I've, I don't know, seen her grow up, when I was old enough to pay attention. And she's six years younger. That's enough of a gap we didn't play together much, not like if we were closer."

Not that Thessaly hadn't - didn't - enjoy time with her sister, but with that sort of difference in the ages, one or the other of them generally had to adapt to the other. Hermia had not gone to Schola. The Ministry had offered her a place at Alethorpe, and their parents had turned it down flat. Alethorpe was for girls and boys who needed to work for their living, who needed to become experts in magical crafts. Not for a Lytton and not for a Powell, they'd been unified on that point.

Instead, Hermia was studying at a small day school run by an intimidating older spinster in Trellech, learning a variety of skills suitable for a woman of good breeding. It included a bit of magic, of course. There were many and varied charms for enhancement and hostessing. But she was also learning also how to make conversation in a range of circumstances, play the pianoforte and the harp, and do suitable delicate painting of appropriate subjects. Mostly, that apparently involved still lives of rosebuds. No suggestive drooping petals were allowed.

It had, on one hand, created a bit more of a gap than Thessaly had wanted. She'd so much looked forward to sharing Hermia's stories of Schola. On the other hand, Hermia seemed happy enough, and she certainly read enough books on her own to float in knowledge for decades to come.

Childeric nodded once. "I'm glad you're. How does one put this, considering the situation we will find ourselves in?" He waved a hand. "I've not had much to do with Garin. And of course, there will be a nursemaid and nanny and tutors. You won't need to raise a finger about any of the tedious parts."

"As you say." Something in her tone hit him wrong, and she could see that. She leaned to kiss his cheek. "If you'd rather go off and do whatever you've been thinking about, I could meet you back up at the house in, I don't know, half an hour?"

"If I come back without you, someone will be annoyed. Probably Grand-mère." Childeric considered. "Where are you going to be?"

"I thought I might go lend a hand with Garin, if you wanted time. You could meet me back here?" Thessaly hadn't really formed the thought until she spoke, but it was a fine and reasonable one.

"Forty-five minutes, then. And mind you don't muss your dress." She was about to object that she knew far more about managing her frocks than he did, when he offered that charming grin again. "Grand-mère will notice."

"Of course. See you in a little, then." Childeric nodded once, dropping her arm, and wheeled about, heading off on a beeline for - well - somewhere. One of the outbuildings, maybe. There was a whole cluster of them off that way.

Thessaly waited until he was a good thirty feet away. Then she picked up her skirts a little to make her way down the hill and into the hollow where the salle was. "Garin, do you want some help with that? I've a few minutes."

Garin looked up at her, blinking as if he weren't sure what to do with the offer. He was nine, and Thessaly couldn't help thinking he was not suited to be a nine-year-old. He had a certain amount of inherent dignity that didn't suit the age. Solitude - being alone among his cousins in age - had given him a self-possession or an interior focus that contrasted sharply with most of the other children she'd known. "Thank you, Mistress Thessaly." He also had a formality to his manners, though admittedly she was both not yet a cousin by marriage, and she was an adult. He had to call her something other than her bare forename.

"The hoop? Or something else? I'm not dressed for duelling, but I could get you started on a few drills, if you liked?" A lot of the idea of future children was rather opaque in her mind, still. But she kept getting flashes of what it would be like to teach someone - Garin's age or a little younger - the basics. She couldn't tell if it was a boy or girl, and besides, children's clothes for active play overlapped a bit. But she could see, she could even more clearly feel, the movements and the early charms for aiming and protecting.

"Oh, I'd like that. Sigbert said you're very good." He looked around, as if sure one of his cousins was going to drop out of the open air. "Even better than Childeric, he said."

It made her laugh. "I have promised not to duel Childeric in public. You can work out the answer from there, I hope? Don't tease Childeric about it, though. You know he wouldn't like it." Honesty made her add, "And I don't think either of us would like being around when he feels like that."

It made Garin tilt his head. "In that case, I definitely would appreciate you showing me a few things. In the salle?"

"That's probably more sensible, isn't it? It's not a problem, I have permission to use it. And I'm not going to show you anything complicated today. I'm not dressed for it, and I need to be presentable for tea. Come along, then." She took the steps over to the salle, pressing her hand to the door to open the warding. She did the same again inside on the panel to bring up the charm lights, feeding a little of her own magic. "Now, you've had a few lessons already, haven't you? Can you show me what you know? I'm going to go find a target you can aim at."

That would be both tidier on her end - she was perfectly capable of levitating it rather than wrestling it in place physically - and better practice. More to the point, it was something he could continue on his own with someone else supervising. She went off to the storage to find one of the simple targets, while he positioned himself. "Right handed, we're going to want to talk about your feet in a second. Don't you let me forget."

As she turned away to rummage in the storage, she caught a glimpse of Garin smiling, then waiting patiently for her to come back. She considered, setting an alarm chime on her watch, clipped to a fold of her bodice, to remind her when it had been half an hour. That way, they'd have time to clean up and she could tidy her hair.

CHAPTER 20

JUNE 18TH IN TRELLECH

Vitus had taken the afternoon to go look at plausible shops to let. There was nothing suitable near Niobe's workshop in the crafting quarter, certainly nothing he could afford soon. The spaces he could afford had awful lighting, the ones that had the light he wanted were far out of his budget and would be for years yet. And there weren't exactly many of either, just two with terrible light and worse floors, and three entirely out of his reach.

The problem with talisman work was needing space for the equipment on one hand, keeping in mind that grinding wheels did need appropriate flooring, for both weight and vibration reasons. But also, it needed a space that could be sufficiently secured. Especially given that the working tools were probably worth something to a burglar and the collection of stones in progress or waiting to be worked certainly was.

Niobe handled the latter with extensive warding, though she also took other precautions. At least half her stock waiting to be worked was in the bank vaults of the

Scali, and they'd ensure secure delivery as requested. That also cost, though, and getting them to come across town outside of the Crafting quarter cost even more. It looked like he might have to, though.

He could, however, make do with an ordinary flat, if the floors would take the grinding wheels, unlike the alchemists. Sensible people didn't want to live in a building with a commercial alchemy lab in it. Between the smells and the chance for entirely unwanted magical explosions and more subtle, but possibly more upsetting, effects. A home stillroom was one thing, but anything beyond that was tightly licensed and restricted to specific areas of town and buildings with additional protections. Talisman work, however, could be done in a second bedroom, if the other conditions suited.

He didn't particularly want to move out of home - he enjoyed meals with his parents, and with Lucas when Lucas could get free. But he wasn't entirely opposed to it, if it made sense. It simplified some of the security measures if he lived on the property. In that case, his presence could be anchored into reinforcing the warding and alerting him immediately if something was wrong.

The flat he'd just seen was fine, he supposed. But the light was only decent in one room. Ideally, he needed two with good light, one for a consulting room and office and one for a workroom. Plus, he supposed, a bedroom. The bathroom had been small and cramped. The kitchen was tiny, though there had been a landlady and housekeeper who saw to the building, including meals if he wanted that.

Maybe something better would turn up tomorrow, or next week. Well, likely not next week. Everyone more or less went on holiday for the Midsummer Faire, whether people had booths or exhibitions or not. He made his way along the street, past the various smaller shops, heading back to Trivium Way. He'd just turned down the street for Niobe's workshop when he heard someone calling out his name. Down the street, just to the south, he saw Philip Landry, his mother, and his brother.

Landry waved once, and Vitus walked down that way, nodding, but first tipping his hat to Philip's mother. "Magistra Landry, Magister Landry, Mister Landry." The last one made Alexander Landry look amused, more than offended. It was the proper term, given he hadn't yet even begun his formal apprenticeship. It was interesting seeing them together, and not in formal dress. Alexander was still growing into his adult height, Vitus thought, and possibly his shoulders would also fill out more.

Philip Landry offered a smile. "We were about to see to the last of the luggage for Alexander's travels. You are just the person who might have proper advice." He considered, and without glancing at his mother, added, "Please, do call me Philip, if you prefer."

Magistra Landry inclined a head. "A pleasure to speak. Philip spoke highly of your intellect after your consultation." From anyone else, Vitus would have been crowing with delight, but from her, he was sure he was missing about five layers of meaning, at least three of them dangerous.

Alexander stuck out his hand, glanced at his brother, got a brief nod in reply, and added. "And Alexander, if it's easier."

"I'm glad you thought so well of me. And please, do call me Vitus." It was only polite to offer the same, especially to his elders. "The consultation was a tremendous help, actually. I'm just finishing the piece now, but it's come together better than I'd hoped." Vitus hesitated a moment. "Philip, perhaps we might find a time after Midsummer Faire for some further conversation? And I happened across a piece of turquoise. If you were minded for any talisman work in the future, I thought I would see if you had an interest first." He stumbled a little over the offer. The three of them were looking at him intently, and with matched confident gazes.

Philip looked at his mother this time, just for an instant, but then he nodded. "Once Alexander is off on July first, shall we say? I expect we'll be tending to various odds and ends until then." There was a quick glance at his mother, before he added, "And the Fortiers have a call on my time for a project, as well." It was a neutral enough comment, but Vitus got the sense it was not the way Philip would have chosen to spend his time at the moment. It made visible that both mother and son - sons, perhaps - had obligations there.

Magistra Landry nodded once, as if there were some undercurrent that made sense to her sons. "Just so. I hope you have some pleasant plans for the solstice and the Faire, Master Deschamps? Are we likely to see you in the Fortier tent at all?" From her, the formality and the courtesy title he hadn't quite formally earned was a nod at treating him like an adult. He was fairly sure of that, anyway.

As to the tents, that was still something of a nebulous delight. Many of the landed families took tents at the Faire to show their particular local wares or highlight crafters and artisans. Others took tents to watch the pavo and bohort in comfort, rather than crowding into the stands. The Fortiers did both, though Vitus didn't think either Childeric or Sigbert would play any matches this year.

"The Fortiers offered me an afternoon at their tent, along the Winding Way. On the Wednesday." It was not likely to be a particularly busy day. But Wednesday at least suited the work he did, and perhaps having fewer in the crowd would mean more chance to talk to people interested in his work. If they'd been favouring him, he'd have had time on the Saturday or on Sunday afternoon, or perhaps the last day of the Faire. "And I hope to attend, of course, several other days. There are quite a few lectures on the Monday and Thursday I'm interested in, particularly." He hesitated, then added, "And my family is invited to the Council rites this year, and my mother is looking forward to that."

"Ah." Again, Magistra Landry was near impossible to read. "We will see you then, I hope." Her mouth curled up slightly. "And I have no daughters, so you need not fear being prevailed upon to dance."

It was a common problem, for all Albion's upper society mostly ran to as many daughters as sons. But women who were expecting rarely travelled, and it made the dancing uneven in the younger generation. Vitus considered, then took a slight risk. "And I have no sisters, so Philip and Alexander are safe from the same."

It made the two men smile, and from Alexander, at least, it was a fairly honest smile. He added, "Ummi has made sure I am sufficiently skilled as a dancer to partner her. Philip doesn't care for it."

Vitus blinked. That was a piece of information he hadn't expected. Philip snorted, clearly at ease with his brother teasing him. "The truth is, Alexander has had more cause to learn it. I can manage, but I am not, mmm." He searched for the word, visibly enough Vitus was sure of it. Alexander murmured something in a language Vitus didn't know at all, and Philip nodded. "I am competent, but not decorative. Duelling training both is and is not a help."

"Do you duel then, Alexander?" Vitus would not ask Philip, not directly, though that answer implied something. As had the way Philip moved during the consultation, that suddenly popped into his mind. But Alexander had just finished Schola, and not only was it potentially part of his study, but there was the Duelling Club, and various other activities of the kind. It was certainly a less threatening inquiry, a less personal one.

"Oh, yes. Protective and Martial magics, as well as Duelling club." Alexander shifted his weight slightly, and Vitus noted he did not brag about his skills, not like others did. "Do you? I've been trying to figure out who to arrange a bout with, to keep up my skills, before I leave. Besides my brother."

Vitus held up his hands. "I am not fit for that. I had the basics at school, and I do not quite have two left feet - I am a competent dancer - but duelling? Not my skill. I do work in stone, so I suppose it makes some sort of sense. Stone is rarely quick to respond."

It made Magistra Landry chuckle, as if actually amused. "I appreciate a man who knows his own limits. I told you, Alexander, you ought to see if Thessaly has a little time. Of course, I don't know her current standard." She glanced up to consider Vitus again, and Vitus did his best not to shrink from her evaluation. He felt all of a sudden like all his conversations with Thessaly were on display, as innocent and simple as they had been. As public as they had been.

"But Master Deschamps - Vitus - is here, and Thessaly is not." Alexander pointed out, with admittedly entirely correct logic. "I should say, sir, I appreciate the notes you gave Philip. He did a trip of the same kind, but it was years ago, and not all the same places I'm going."

Philip cut in, his voice a smoother baritone than his

brother's tenor. "Time in Egypt, though, with some of Ummi's extended family. And you will like that."

"And that is not somewhere I have experience. But for what I could share, I am glad to. I don't feel it's necessary to make all my own mistakes, when I can learn from other people's adventures and perhaps make different choices in a few places."

"Just so." Philip was definitely amused now as well. "You did share admirably detailed notes. I was expecting, I don't know, a page or two and perhaps a letter of introduction." He considered. There was a glance at his mother and her minute nod. "Not everyone chooses to extend themselves on our behalf."

Vitus considered the possible answers to that, then he said, feeling his way through and trusting to trained instinct, "One theme of my apprenticeship has been figuring out not only what I wish to do, or which skills I might wish to build, but how to go through the world. Perhaps more than all the lore about the stones and materials and inscriptions." He nodded once at Alexander. "And as I said, I agree with the idea of sparing a younger brother the discomforts that serve no purpose."

A little to his surprise, Magistra Landry nodded, an unusual four times, emphasising it. "Just so. You are fortunate, then." Her eyes moved from Vitus to where he had come from. "I gather you are establishing yourself?"

"A slow one, but that is my aim, yes, Magistra. I was just coming from looking at a possible flat for a workshop, but I'm afraid it wasn't all I was hoping for." Vitus gestured with one hand. "Magistra Hall, my apprentice mistress, is glad to share space with me for a while longer, but I do not want to impose on her longer than necessary. And I know she hopes to take another apprentice sooner than later. She has an eye on a few who are entering their last year at Schola, I believe."

Alexander considered, "I would be glad to call on her, if anything I might share would interest her. I admit I would like to learn a bit more about talisman work, beyond what Ummi has taught us. We have a number of family techniques, mostly for ritual purposes." He said the last a bit hurriedly, as if he were unsure if it might give offence.

"I'd be glad to speak to her and see if there's a convenient time. You're leaving at the beginning of July, then? I will see if she's free before then, and may I send a message round?"

Alexander reached into his pocket, pulling out a slender calling card case of engraved copper rather than the usual silver. "We're here to Solstice Eve, then at Arundel through the Faire." Vitus nodded, glancing at the address, presumably also Magistra Landry's home, before slipping it into his own pocket.

"Of course. I should be able to send a note around." The bells chimed, and he'd lost half an hour somewhere. "Oh, my. I should get back. She has a client calling in half an hour, and I can make myself useful fetching and carrying. I do hope we'll speak again soon."

"And I." Philip offered his hand, and Vitus shook it, then Alexander's. He bowed over Magistra Landry's, who dismissed him with a slight smile. As Vitus crossed the street, he glanced back to see the three of them continuing south toward, presumably, their further errands.

CHAPTER 21

JUNE 20TH AT BRYN GLAS

"Here, dearest, close your eyes. I want you to try something on." Thessaly was perched on one of the silk-covered benches in Aunt Metaia's bedroom, as they were getting ready for the festivities at the Council Keep. Aunt Metaia had been out with the more private Council rites all last night and this morning into the early afternoon. Everyone had retreated to their homes or other suitable places to change for the evening's formal presentations and dancing. They had an hour before they had to think about leaving, at the least.

Thessaly was already dressed. Collins, Aunt Metaia's housekeeper and lady's maid, had put her hair up beautifully, swoops of it gleaming in the light, looking exceedingly elegant. There were flowers to add, the last touch, but those were waiting until just before they left.

The gown was designed for the summer. It had swaths of golden silk, the shades of a perfect sunset, over a deep red underskirt, the bodice shading from gold up to white. She had long silk gloves, perfectly cut and charmed to fit her hands, that would stretch to the puffs of the sleeves. A nearly invisible layer of delicate lace protected her bosom from magical harm. It was the most adult gown she'd worn yet, in some ways. These were not the pastels and demure cuts of a young woman not yet betrothed, in keeping with Albion's current fashions for that sort of thing.

Aunt Metaia's gown was a brilliant peacock green over an underskirt shot with silver thread, like the cool beauty of a shimmering pond or a hint of snow on Snowdonia. Not, of course, that the great and looming mountain had snow at the summer solstice. But Aunt Metaia did favour reminding everyone that every season came and went and came again, and that the cycles mattered.

She obediently closed her eyes. "Yes, Aunt?" Behind her, she could feel Aunt Metaia's presence, the weight and power of her magic, before she felt the brush of silk against silk. Then there were hands reaching around her, and the cold weight of metal against her skin through the lace. A necklace, whatever it was, and much more substantial than she'd expected.

"There. Look at yourself, do." Aunt Metaia gestured at the mirror in front of them. The necklace was nothing she'd expected. Thessaly brought her fingers up to touch it, a parure of ovals set with garnets. She knew it, of course she knew it. Aunt Metaia wore it regularly. The colour shaded from brighter red nearer the back, to a deep red, the colour of blood, at the front. That was a single larger teardrop garnet, drawing the eye instantly. That wasn't all, though. She could feel the magic in the piece.

"Aunt Metaia?" Thessaly turned her head. "Mama will think it far too adult." Though Mama had told her earlier not to bother packing jewellery, her aunt had something for her. "Does she know?"

"She does." Aunt Metaia let her fingers rest on Thessaly's bare skin, warmth against warmth. "It's a talismanic piece. Protection, that's why it's garnet. The central piece is one I wore for my challenge. You can wear the pendant on its own, that's the one with the greatest talismanic work."

Thessaly's fingers brushed it, trying to get a sense of it. "It's stunning. But are you sure you don't want to wear it?"

"It wouldn't go with my gown, dearest. And besides..." Aunt Metaia considered. "It is time for you to have it."

There was an odd quality there, something Thessaly noted, but did not understand. Of course she noted it. This was Aunt Metaia, who loved her, who she loved back wholeheartedly, and without the complications of loving Mama. Aunt Metaia had named that herself years ago. There were obligations to parents, and from parents in return. How she was with others in the family, how they were with her, that was more of a choice on both their parts. It was a deliberate choice in how it felt and what she made of it.

She twisted to look up at her aunt, and her aunt waved a hand, summoning another one of the padded benches with the pull of her magic, then settling down onto it, facing Thessaly. "There's something I wanted to talk about, dearest."

A serious something, then, a terribly serious something. Aunt Metaia could look like that, had looked like that, but always at other people. Never at Thessaly. Thessaly had been nine when her aunt challenged for the Council, too young to be there for it. But she remembered Aunt Metaia looking like this, discussing it with Mama, insisting she was going to do it, and do it in her own way. And Thessaly had seen it since. That was most often when some piece of political manoeuvring or personal benefit had run up against Aunt Metaia's instincts and ethics and sense of what would be done. "Yes?" Her voice cracked a little, even in so short a word, and Aunt Metaia patted her hand.

"I am worried about you, dearest. Or rather, I am worried about Childeric Fortier, and you are so near him, within easy reach."

Thessaly blinked several times, unsure of what to say. "Aunt?" When in doubt, an interrogative appellation worked well. She'd learned that at Schola, in several of her classes.

"Will you promise to hear me out? To trust that I may not have experience in marriage, but I have experience in observing men - and women - and their ways?" Aunt Metaia squeezed her hand once.

"Of course, aunt." Why wouldn't she hear this out? Thessaly expected it would not be comfortable to hear, or Aunt Metaia would not be nervous about how she took it.

"I would like you to pay attention to how he treats you tonight, and in the days to come. How he treats other people." Aunt Metaia took a little breath. "The problem with some men is that the more power they have, the more likely they are to abuse it. Some women, too, but here we are concerned about a man."

Thessaly opened her mouth, wanting to protest that he had not done that with her. And then she closed it. Because she remembered what he'd been like the last few times they had been in each other's company. None of it was an obvious twisting of power like that. She swallowed. "What does that look like that you've seen?"

There was a sudden sigh from her aunt, both hands grasping Thessaly's. "Thank the gods and the ancestors. You're not fighting me. I couldn't bear that." Aunt Metaia took a breath, settling herself a bit. "He was charming with you, to begin, wasn't he? I saw some of that in public, of course, but also in private?"

Thessaly thought back. "He was charming in private, too. He does know how to be." Examples seemed called for. "Childeric would ask about what I was working on. He would give me some small token. A book of interest, tickets to a concert, not just the usual sort of flowers that are dictated by etiquette, telling sentences in their choices." The language of flowers had a lot to answer for, honestly.

"And then you were betrothed. What changed?" Her aunt hesitated for a second. "When did it change?"

"That week. Before we were formally betrothed, actually. He'll go off on his own or with Sigbert and his friends. Gaming, cards, maybe other gambling. Or he'd go riding, in ways I couldn't join him. And of course he won't duel me." Her mouth twitched. "Not going to be a marital hobby, he sulks for days when he loses, and he always loses." Other people, other women who were entirely competent duellists, might throw the bout, at least sometimes, but Childeric knew exactly how much better she was. "He's rather exhausting to be around, actually. Though that's probably as much the pressures of the family, the expectations."

"But he hasn't tried to hurt you. Push you, force you to do something, grab you tightly. He hasn't left bruises?" Thessaly glanced down at her arms, which were bare and the proper pale white of her class and station. The bruise from last month's duelling had long since faded, and she hadn't had the chance to acquire more that way. Those were honest bruises, not what Aunt Metaia meant.

She shook her head. "No. But I - now you say it, I've wondered if he might, once or twice." She looked up, meeting her aunt's eyes. "What do I do?"

"You've explained why you made this choice. And I can't say you're wrong. It would secure your family's position for the next generation. There are not any other particularly palatable choices on the horizon. And Childeric can be very charming. How is he when he is around his family, with you? Other than Sigbert?"

"Charming. Pleasant. Especially with his grandmother. Of course, she sees everything and knows even more. I don't know what kinds of charms and tools she has built into Arundel. Not the gardens, though, or the salle, or outside spaces, I think. That's where he's been abrupt." Thessaly could at least work through it now, pulling together the threads of the relevant patterns. "Do you think he'll get worse?"

"I think there's a chance." Aunt Metaia let go of her hands, turning hers over. "He had to be charming until the betrothal was secure. He needs you, too, mind. There aren't so many women from a background the Fortiers would consider who are unmarried and within a few years of your age. And you are not vain, my dear, but you know you're one of the most attractive." Thessaly snorted, bemused. But Aunt Metaia was right, of course. They'd been over this multiple times.

Some were already matched, or had not flourished as expected. Some who might be considered were far too young - one of the Alvey girls, for example, might make a match with Garin, but they wouldn't do for Childeric, not in the next decade or so. The Great Families no longer reliably pledged their daughters under the age of ten, and besides, it wasn't like Childeric was inclined to be patient about whatever marital rights applied.

A couple of women of her generation seemed well enough, but there were hereditary concerns in their families, the sort of thing the Fortiers would avoid. A couple of others would have refused to follow the Fortier customs and would have insisted on Childeric marrying into their line, with all the implications of that. And Childeric was his father's Heir, and the Fortiers did not make that sort of match, had not since the Conquest. "Does that give me any leverage, then?"

"With his parents and grandmother, yes. With Childeric, I do not know. What I am going to tell you here and now is that if he behaves in the way he seems he might, I will take issue with it." Her fingers lifted to touch the jewel she was wearing, a faceted aquamarine. "With every bit of power at my disposal, magical and social." Aunt Metaia raised an eyebrow. "We can discuss the sensible strategy later this week."

Thessaly nodded slowly, thinking it through. "And tonight?"

"Tonight, pay attention to how he treats you. And watch how the men there treat their wives or their fiancees. And vice versa, though it's more often men grasping at their power than women for all sorts of reasons." Aunt Metaia tilted her head, thinking. "Watch Lord and Lady Teague. How he treats her. How he has for years. There are others."

It made Thessaly shiver. Not someone she wanted to get close to. Mabyn Teague had come from an extremely wealthy family, and she was enough older they'd only overlapped in Fox House for a year. Now, she spoke little among others, unless her husband was elsewhere. And he was almost always around. "Yes, Aunt." She took in a breath and let it out. "I'll think about it."

"And like I said, dearest, if you do choose to break the engagement, I will back you with every resource at my disposal." She stood, bending over to kiss Thessaly's forehead. "I understand why you said yes, enough. And it would mean a battle with your father that would have consequences. But I will do my best to make sure you have choices, whatever is required. Now, will you help me choose a ring or two? Then Collins should be back to make sure our flowers are perfect."

"And once we've slept tomorrow, there's the Midsummer Faire. Far more pleasant. How do you think the pavo matches will go? I can't decide which of the tournament teams are most promising." That, at least, was a far more diverting conversation topic. Thessaly was a competent rider, but not at the level required for a pavo match. On the other hand, she appreciated skill at it no end, and it gave the players fine form.

CHAPTER 22

JUNE 20TH AT THE DESCHAMPS FAMILY HOME

"Sit, dear." Vitus's mama gestured for him to sit in one of the chairs she kept for these chats.

Vitus sat, and promptly. It was a custom before the formal social events. Once she was dressed, she liked to have a little rest and a chat while she finished the details of her preparations. Vitus knew it was partly to cover for the fact that dressing, in and of itself, could be tiring for her. He was not intimately acquainted with the layers of a lady's wardrobe, but he knew they were numerous, with various laces and buttons and needing to stand in this position or that so everything could be properly done.

Once she was dressed, while she was fixing her hair, she enjoyed having one of her sons or Papa join her, depending on who was handy. Papa was still tending to some last-minute arrangements. Lucas could not get leave, and so it was Vitus's role to provide conversation. Or to be nudged into doing what Mama wanted, as seemed to be the more accurate description. "We should coordinate, dear. Before we arrive."

"Yes, Mama?" Vitus knew what was coming, but he couldn't quite bring himself to ask the obligatory question.

"Business opportunities first, or matrimonial ones?" Mama glanced at him, clucked her tongue once. "Don't think you're getting out of the second conversation, but we can start with business."

"I need to make my name, yes." Vitus knew this was true. He and Niobe had discussed it endlessly. He and Mama and Papa had as well. Vitus had spent far too many nights awake at three in the morning staring at the ceiling. Awake and staring, despite knowing perfectly well that ideas were scarce at that hour and also rarely good ones. "And that means finding a few well-placed clients who need talismanic work done. Ideally, a betrothal. Or a Council challenge, but one can't predict that. I don't even know who would consider it, if there were one tomorrow." He held up a hand. "Theo Carrington has aspirations, I've heard, but he's young yet. And I don't have a direct connection to him besides being at Schola at the same time." Not the same year, though. That would have allowed some connection.

"Who else, then?" Mama leaned back slightly. "And if Theo Carrington was on the Council, he'd have less time for flirting or whatever it is he does that's beyond flirting."

"Mama!" Vitus did his best to sound mock-horrified, because that amused his mother, and she could stand to have more amusement. "My innocent ears."

It drew a smile from her. "You know perfectly well what I'm talking about, even if you do not indulge."

That brought them smack around to the matrimonial discussion, and Vitus ceded to it, rather than fight it. He was saving his resources for the evening's events, which would be delicate navigation all round. He didn't know who he'd end up talking to, or how it would go, but he could be certain it would be complex and demanding. "All right."

He took a breath and let it out. "It's not that I disagree with the idea. The right marriage might bring more opportunities, for me, for Papa, or for both of us. Connections and all that comes with them, not to be too crass. With any luck, it would also bring a fair bit of pleasure for me, company for you, and I don't know what else. But I find it difficult to get my head around it in the abstract. I adore stones in the abstract, what they might become, the available potencies of a garnet or sapphire or amethyst, or lapis lazuli. But that tells me very little about that particular stone, what I will love most about it."

His mother snorted. "And I cannot persuade you to work from the list of stones, as you put it, available to you?"

"Most of them do not entirely appeal, for one reason or another, though I admit that's more a matter of taste than any flaw in them." Vitus ticked off on his fingers. "Hannah Morris, perhaps. She's of a good family, but I heard some gossip that makes me suspect she's seeing someone. The Stream, Mama, which is why you didn't hear it." It strongly suggested that whoever she was seeing was not from Hannah's own Fox House, but another Salmon, too.

"Hester Wallington?" She was from a well-off family. They'd made a lot of money in wool over the generations, and now in woven cloth. Hester was pleasant enough, but Vitus had very little sense of her personality. She was the sort of woman other people described as 'efficient' or possibly 'self-effacing'. Hester had, in his experience of her at Schola - she'd been a year behind him - preferred the library over any other location. Vitus appreciated a library, but not as his only source of sustenance.

Vitus also couldn't imagine what it would be like to be married to her. He had a fear he'd walk into rooms all the time and not realise she was there. Or, and this was perhaps worse, her family would take pity on them, and be generous - Hester was known to have a substantial dowry. Another kind of man might find that compelling. Vitus just wanted to step gently away from it, and leave her to her books and the inside of her head. There was no space for him there.

And whatever else he wanted in a marriage, he was holding out hope it might be an active sort of partnership. Vitus wanted to come home from his workshop, or whatever the appropriate geography was, and talk with his wife. He wanted to hear her ideas, perhaps she'd read something during the day, or had a thought during her own work or events. He wanted the sort of marriage where he might help her wind her yarn like he helped Mama. Or they could take turns reading a serial out loud, as well as perhaps going to lectures and concerts. And he wanted someone who would at least consider travelling with him, to go look at the places the stones he worked with came from.

"Alexandra Smythe-Clive?" His mother suggested it, almost idly, into the silence.

"Still in the early years of apprenticing as a Healer. They have some quite stringent rules around nepotism when it comes to materials, so it would be a challenge as much as a benefit on the business front. And she's spending all her spare time, what there is, with her brother and her niece. Not the time, mother, not the time."

The Smythe-Clives were a social step above the Deschamps. They were not strongly aligned with any of the landed families, which was actually rather interesting. Alexandra and Cyrus's father was a specialist in arcane kinds of law, though as a researcher rather than a jobbing solicitor. They had family money. He didn't need to work for a living, just take on questions that intrigued him.

Cyrus had been training as a ritualist, though Vitus had no idea how the death of his wife the previous year had changed that. That was the thing. Cyrus had loved her. Everyone who'd seen them had known that, had known it was mutual. Their choices about marriage had been uncommon. Albion's Great Families - and also the notable ones - tended to marry only after the apprenticeships were completed. It was another reason he wouldn't consider Alexandra. Not now, not for some years. Healers were too important.

"Griselda Warren has a sister. A younger sister, as yet unmarried." His mother said it, and then immediately turned to consider her face in the mirror.

"It would mean being Hesperidon Warren's brother-in-law, and he is uncomfortably ambitious. Much too much like flying too close to the sun and all the wax of my wings melting," Vitus pointed out. "Though I will grant you a range of connections and in varying directions." Hesperidon Warren was relatively new to the Council. He'd made a successful challenge seven years ago, a year into his marriage. "And Dido Talton is apparently almost betrothed to Adamus Mortimer. Don't suggest that."

"I heard that her family is rather pleased with the arrangements. I suppose there's that. I wish her well." Mama wrinkled her nose. "Adamus always struck me as a tad too martial for comfort. Oh, I know Lucas is in the cavalry, but that's different somehow."

"It is different, dear Mama, because Lucas is somehow able to take off his military mode with his uniform pieces.

Or even when he hasn't actually changed. I think the horses help, though."

"Oh, well. Your brother does whatever it is he does there very well, I must say." She fiddled with a ring, then thought of another name. "Laodamia Hastings, though she's not yet done with school."

"Too young for me, Mama." It wasn't uncommon for the woman to be younger, but that was more than a few years. "And I gather she's quite talented in sympathetic magic, planning on an apprenticeship. Niobe knows Timothy Wallace quite well. They're finalising the arrangements this month, apparently."

His mother chuckled, agreeably. "All right. No marriageable misses on the horizon. Are there any other prospects for business? The Sisleys, perhaps? Actually, let me count up."

Vitus knew what she was counting. There were several young Heirs at the moment. Those men - well, and Jenifry Alton - still at Schola but old enough to have been formally declared as heir to the land magic, whatever customs their families used for that. It made them the right age and station for their families to consider pieces made for them, for the adult obligations they were taking on.

"Matthias Sisley, nephew to Lord Phineas Sisley, his sister's son." Sisley's father had married into the line and taken the name. The Sisleys ran to that kind of connection when the direct line wasn't an option, and Phineas had no children of his own. Vitus didn't think that a terribly likely commission, though he'd make the attempt. Lord Sisley wasn't known for generous spending on anything beyond his own research interests.

"Richard Edgarton, heir to his father, Lord Anthony Edgarton. Temple Carillon, Heir to Lord Ambrosius Carillon. They both might be interested in talismanic work, perhaps. Jenifry Alton, the only child of her father, Lord Siward Alton. He might like a piece of jewellery for her." Too young to consider for marriage, and whoever married her, she'd hold the title in her own right in due course. He counted through in his head. "And erm. Didn't you mention one more while I was gone?"

"Oh, that was a sorry tale, Justin Hareward. His father died unexpectedly, some sort of accident, I believe, and he's now Heir to his grandfather. They're still getting used to it, but at least he's a year out of Schola. They might be interested in a piece, actually. Worth having a conversation, letting Lord Hareward know you're available."

Vitus spread his hands. "As you say. I think my best choice is to wander and see who wishes to talk. There's the Faire to consider, that's a time for more conversations, less obvious."

The problem with the Council rites was it was a time to see and be seen. People made and kept notes on who spoke with whom, for how long, and whether it seemed a pleasant conversation or a tense one.

"I suppose I must let you do your own work. Would you come and put this on for me, dear? The clasp is a little too tight for my fingers." Vitus came around behind her, his thumbnail working the clasp. It wasn't the clasp that was a problem, he thought, but that she had more aches in her fingers. Like the cough, she'd seen the Healers. A few things helped, and none mended it. Perhaps he'd talk to Niobe about a talisman she could hold that would warm to ease the aches. That would be a practical sort of gift to bring home. It ought to work in a bit of agate or carnelian and set in a ring or bracelet. Bracelet, most likely, that would be more comfortable with aching fingers.

CHAPTER 23

JUNE 20TH AT DINAS EMRYS, THE COUNCIL KEEP IN WALES

The Council Keep was glowing with light and filled with people. They spilled out from the keep itself into the walled courtyard, the charmlight lanterns leaving very few shadows. Of course, Thessaly took in the shadows as well as the light. She was a duellist, after all, and while she didn't expect to call on those skills - not in this gown - she couldn't avoid thinking that way.

Childeric, on the other hand, was blithely chatting away here and there. He kept stopping every two or three steps to talk to someone new, tugging Thessaly back and forth on his arm. She couldn't drop his. That was improper, but she hated how he didn't even seem to notice he was making it difficult for her. It was the first of the Council rites since their betrothal, though, and it meant she collected quite a bit in the way of formal congratulations. Also, more than a few glances that were at least somewhat envious, but that was to be expected here and now.

Once they made it inside, Childeric deposited her with his mother and grandmother while he went off to find his father and line up for the proper presentations. He had claimed the token gift for the presentation. This summer, the gift was a box holding a series of ritual tools carved and decorated from a Sussex cow horn. It was generally considered a relatively neutral material for the purpose.

The presentations went smoothly enough, at least. Everyone knew how to keep things flowing. There were near a hundred and fifty demesnes to go through. Even if there were a number of quite young Heirs present, they had fathers - or the occasional other relative - to guide them. It was an excellent opportunity to chat quietly and an even better one to decide who to save a dance for, or to arrange to talk to later. Dagobert and Laudine Fortier were already working on that. She'd seen them chatting with three or four other couples, a few minutes each time, before moving on. It was deft, and Thessaly appreciated watching their skill in action.

Finally, the presentations were done and Childeric came over as the music struck up for the dancing. "Of course I'll claim the first dance, Thess. As soon as the Council has trod the patterns, do come." On the one hand, there was no reason to be on her feet for the extra time. On the other, Thessaly enjoyed watching the Council Members dance. It was a series of ritual dance steps, flowing from period to period, style to style.

As usual, Hereswith Rowan, the Council Head, led things off with her husband. He was gallant with her, as he always was, a shift of bows and courtesies. But Thessaly had noticed how he watched his wife, with unfeigned adoration. Council Head Rowan gave less away by her look and seeming. She was steady, hard to sway by shallow needs, but determined to follow through.

Aunt Metaia was paired for the dancing with cousin Owain Powell. They'd been a year apart at Schola, and despite being somewhat distant cousins as the Great Families counted it, had got on well ever since. As Aunt Metaia put it, he wasn't the sort of family for the more intimate gatherings, but the next step out, and she knew what to expect from him. Watching her now, she also liked him, and that was something Thessaly hadn't really noticed before.

She seemed to have some particular comment for him tonight, because at least once, Thessaly caught an odd expression on his face, like Aunt Metaia had said something unexpected. Then he'd swing her around in the curves of the dance, and when they were facing back toward Thessaly, the moment had passed. The dancing finished, and he brought her up to end in front of Thessaly and Childeric. Childeric made his bows, very proper, very charming, pulling out the charm for them he hadn't bothered with for Thessaly. Now Aunt Metaia had called her attention to it, she couldn't stop seeing the problem.

Instead, Childeric swung her into the dance, the sort of showy thing that led off the general dancing. She had to focus on keeping up with him and making sure they both looked good. That was not only her feet, but the shimmer of illusion magic that drew the eye to them. Nothing forbidden in this space, of course not. She'd checked the list with Aunt Metaia well in advance, of what was permitted, what was welcome, and what was neither.

Once that was done, he deposited her outside the dancing floor, kissing her on the cheek. "Save a dance for me later, Thess. I've people to have a word with." He disappeared off into the crowd, and while she was tempted to keep that eye-catching illusion up so she could spot him easily herself, it seemed far too much like undesirable effort.

It left her on her own to decide what to do. She could see Council Head Rowan had paused. Aunt Metaia had come up to Council Head Rowan and Rowan's companion, Bess Marley, who occupied the socially complex position that was part organisation, part company, and part assistant. A moment later, Mistress Marley broke off from the two of them in search of someone else. That was not for Thessaly.

Across the room, she could see Childeric's mother, Lady Maylis, glance his way, then turn back to her conversations with Leda Grimly and Griselda Warren. Both their husbands were on the Council, and both couples had been invited to the May Day celebrations, a sign of a closer connection. Or a desire for one, and Thessaly wasn't entirely sure which way that went, actually. She waited a moment to see if Lady Maylis wanted Thessaly to join them, but apparently not.

Thessaly could mingle in search of a dance partner. She could chat with people about either her apprenticeship or duelling. She set off on a stately circuit of the large hall, toward those not dancing yet. At that point, she caught sight of the Edgartons, and she did, in fact, have something to ask Richard. He was seventeen, just finished his fourth year at Schola.

Thessaly made a polite bob to Richard's mother first. Lady Edgarton was an imposing figure. She was Lord Edgarton's second wife, later in his life, something over thirty years younger than he was, married to produce an heir. They were civil in public, but Lord Edgarton generally found plenty of reasons to be elsewhere, given the opportunity, leaving Richard to tend to his mother's whims.

"Lady Edgarton, a pleasure." The way to handle formidable women of her generation was a certain amount of formality and lashings of giving due deference. "Richard, also a pleasure to see you here. I was talking to Alexander Landry last week about some of the Duelling Club events this year at Schola. Perhaps I might ask you to escort me to get a glass of punch while we talk about that, if it's not to your mother's interest."

It worked, in this case. Lady Edgarton nodded once and Richard promptly offered Thessaly his arm as they crossed over to the tables set out on the long wall opposite. He was obviously dutiful, attending on his mother, but just as obviously eager for a short break. "Landry is - may I ask what he said?" There was a hint of nerves there.

"He thought you were quite skilled. We were in the salle at the time. He talked through the sequences you'd tried. A bit more work on being able to use your magic to give you the ability to launch from your back foot, perhaps. Have you seen Franquemont's Second Treatise? There are a series of drills that you might find handy, and most of them don't require a partner."

"No, Mistress, but thank you. Is that anything like Hildebrand's Sixth? We tried that in one of our last class sessions." They had, by this point, reached the punch.

"Ah, not entirely. Hildebrand focuses on the terrain, Franquemont on the relationship of your body to the terrain. A nuance, but a crucial one, sometimes." Thessaly permitted him to retrieve a glass for her, and they withdrew a little to chat more. She was able to get him diverted into a discussion of the other duellists, and comparing his commentary to Alexander's was just what she'd wanted.

Thessaly was, of course, keeping an eye out for possible bouts to arrange. Richard was not quite in her league yet, but he would be within the year if he kept going as he was. And from what Alexander had said, he might well exceed her given time and thoughtful training. After he'd talked with enthusiasm, she asked, "You're still intending to go for the Guard, yes?"

If he hadn't been so much younger, she'd consider holding out for him as a potential husband. But the age difference was not a help in that direction, and it was difficult for a Guard apprentice to be married.

"Yes. My mother's, well, she has pointed out I needn't. But I would like to serve beyond the land magic in due course." At that point, he offered his arm again. Thessaly discarded her glass onto the tray of one of the passing servants, and they made their way back to his mother.

"I wish you luck with it." By the time he had bowed to his mother again, Thessaly was ready for the more complex dance of the party again. She made her farewells and then turned around, considering her options for the next dance. She could see Lord Ambrosius and Lady Hespasia Carillon, almost certainly talking books. They were known for it.

Their heir, Temple, was standing behind his mother's shoulder, not quite hiding the fact some of the conversation was over his head. He was a clever enough young man, she'd heard, but within his own interests. Not wide-ranging. That was how Hermia had put it.

Temple was a couple of years younger than her sister, but he was one of the people Mama was eyeing as a potential match, especially if they actually took to each other. Mama would not have considered it without Thessaly's betrothal, but the Fortier connection absolutely opened doors and would continue to do so. She'd have to remind Mama to see about arranging some social outing that included Temple in the next few weeks.

She saw Alethea Witham, and got a word in. Alethea was delighted to consider a duelling session once the Faire was over, and they planned to set that up in the coming week, by note. The other woman was just a year out of Schola, apprenticing in Sympathetic magic, but her apprenticeship schedule was less gruelling than many. Alethea suggested adding Septima Palgrave, daughter of one of Aunt Metaia's colleagues on the Council. Thessaly was willing enough, and proposed Palantina Monkton, if they wanted four women. She promised to sound them out by note if she couldn't catch them tonight. That was something lovely to look forward to, excellent.

From there, Thessaly turned, and she saw Lady Teague. More to the point, she saw Lord Teague. It brought back, immediately, what Aunt Metaia had said about it. It wasn't anything that Lord Teague was doing right now, in this very moment, but she was watching Lady Teague's body language. If it had been a duel, she'd just have taken a hit, something that hurt. She was trying not to let it show because that would make the next one worse. Lady Teague's body was all about the stiffness, the barely repressed certainty she'd done something wrong.

Worse, Thessaly had felt that herself, tonight. Not as badly, not yet, but certainly when Childeric had disengaged from her after the first dance. It wasn't that he couldn't have other plans; it was how he treated her in the process. How he didn't have any care for her. There was distance from a lack of care to harm, but watching the Teagues, Thessaly began to realise it was a much shorter one than she'd thought before tonight.

Maybe there would be some chance to talk in the coming days, or at least offer her a distraction. Mabyn Teague had been a fifth year at Schola when Thessaly had been a first year. It at least permitted a social connection with no need to be entirely too formal about it. She'd look for a chance, perhaps during the Faire.

From there, she turned to find Jacinthe Howard and her husband Amalric. She made a little bob of her head. Jacinthe was cousin to Childeric, the daughter of his aunt Bradamante. And the Howards had married last year, right after Jacinthe finished at Schola. "Jacinthe, Amalric, a pleasure to see you. I hope you're both well? And the cat, Amalric?" Amalric was well known for a small black cat, near enough entirely a familiar, who normally considered his shoulder her natural habitat.

"All well, thank you. You look lovely this evening. I do hope Childeric has admired the effect properly." Jacinthe was easy to talk to, at least for Thessaly. She had her own magical interests in Incantation, like Amalric, but they honestly seemed to enjoy each other's company. "And Onyx is also well, other than complaining at length when we went out." She laughed, a sound that Thessaly knew had been trained into being pleasant, but which was also solidly real.

They talked for a little, mostly about plans for the Faire, as Thessaly was interested in which lectures and performances they recommended. Asking an Incantation specialist about performances was often informative. She made note of several she'd not have considered on her own. Then she caught Jacinthe peering over her shoulder. "Pardon, I see Uncle Clovis. I wanted to catch him to ask something. Do excuse me for a moment."

Amalric didn't go with her. Thessaly shifted a little so she could see Jacinthe and her uncle. It was the kind of thing she did automatically in these social gatherings, so she would not be surprised by someone coming up behind her. And besides, it provided all sorts of knowledge about what was going on. Jacinthe was saying something earnest, leaning in, when Clovis shook his head sharply, sending her away with only a word or two. Thessaly completely missed what Amalric had just said to her, but then excused herself to find some other conversation, with fewer treacherous spots.

CHAPTER 24

JUNE 20TH

Vitus had been making his way through the Great Hall, a slow pass where he'd paused to talk to people here and there. He and Niobe had talked through who to speak with, as well as his conversations with his mother. There'd been no hope with Hesperidon Warren. He was swarmed with people wanting his time and attention.

There'd also been no chance with Lord Phineas Sisley. He'd made it clear three sentences in that he wasn't interested in talismanic work, without ever actually using the words. He'd just strongly implied the family already had sufficient pieces. He preferred ancient pieces re-endowed with magic. That was that.

Conversations with Lord Siward Alton had been more promising, thankfully. That was especially true since Vitus had noted that he knew of an excellent supply of topaz to match a piece that Jenifry was wearing. What he had in mind would take inscription and enchanting well. Vitus was glad he'd correctly pegged Lord Siward as someone who liked to indulge his daughter. He'd equally spotted

Jenifry as someone who very much wanted all the shiny delights to be hers. It would not be the sort of piece that made his name, but it might lead to other connections, and it was a straightforward sort of commission.

He'd also had a brief but promising conversation with Lenore Wallace, and with Psyche Milton, both of whom were looking for pieces for daughters who were coming of age. Both had asked when he'd be at the Faire, and he'd promised to have a few initial thoughts sketched out when they talked. They both wanted the usual enchantments to go with jewellery for social events, something that put the wearer in the best light physically and encouraged sparkling conversation. That sort of work was the bread and butter of a talisman maker. While it wouldn't make his name, doing it well would be a boon to a steady income. Do a piece that someone liked, that meshed well with their magic, and they'd want similar ones to go with other outfits.

He was just considering another turn around the Great Hall when he saw Thessaly again. She had just finished a conversation, the sort that meant she wasn't looking back, a far more successful Orpheus. It made his heart beat faster. That was not an emotion he ought to be having about her at all. And yet, there she was, determined and graceful. Also rather stunningly dressed, and he was sure he'd heard something about that garnet in the past. He angled himself, so she might see him, and to his surprise and delight, she turned, before gesturing. "Perhaps you might escort me for a breath of air?"

Of course, Vitus offered his arm, as well as pleasantries. "At your service, Thessaly. This way? You look lovely today. I hope you've been having a joyful solstice?"

It was still pleasantly warm out, though the sun had set

at half eight, a good two hours ago now. The courtyard was lit with charm lanterns, more than enough light to see. And more than enough to avoid the corners where people who'd gone in search of privacy for more intimate reasons. Not that anyone was crude enough to consider outright indecency here, everyone with sense knew they didn't know enough about the protections and charms in this keep. But they could arrange an assignation for later, simply enough.

Vitus and Thessaly ended up strolling north of the main tower, though Vitus didn't suggest the steps up. They wouldn't be kind to an evening gown. "Are you warm enough, or may I offer a charm?"

Thessaly tilted her head. "I'm tempted to say yes, just to see what you offer. But I am quite warm, thank you. I hope you've been having a good evening?"

"Oh, yes. A number of conversations in hope of later work on offer, mostly, but it is always good to see who's here to be seen. Your gown suits you very well, as I said, and also your aunt's. But I admit, I'm exceedingly curious about the garnets. The pendant, especially."

Her hand came up to touch it, silk-covered fingers obscuring it for a second, then she lowered her hand. "Aunt Metaia gave it to me outright earlier today. She's worn it on and off for ages, including in her challenge for the Council." Vitus saw her shoulders shift. "Perhaps I might employ you for a consultation about it, when we're past the Faire? So I best understand what it can do, and how to help it settle to my needs?"

"I would be delighted." Vitus made a slight bow. He thought back to what he knew about key pieces. "It was made by Mariel Alderscroft, wasn't it?" She was one of the talisman makers Niobe had looked up to, two generations older, and she'd died a decade ago.

"It was. Aunt Metaia told me the basics, of course, but I know that's not the same as having someone with expertise look at it. I'd much rather you than someone else." She leaned in a little, and he was sure it was deliberate. She couldn't be flirting. Surely she wasn't.

"Glad to. In good light and with all my tools handy, of course, but we can arrange whatever space you'd feel comfortable in." He gestured back toward the hall. "I'm a little surprised not to see you in the midst of the dancing?"

"I promised Childeric another dance tonight, but..." There was a brief twitch of her shoulder, and something in it caught his attention like a poorly angled facet on a jewel. Not that it was obviously wrong, but it was not shining the way it ought to. He made note of it, but he didn't know what to say.

Of course, he had to say something. The silence was drawing out, more and more obvious, and she also wasn't saying anything. He cleared his throat. "I would also be glad to offer you a dance, if you wish."

Her face lit up, and he knew it wasn't the talisman. It wasn't designed for that. It was all her, without artifice or magic. "I would enjoy that very much. When we're ready to go in, please." The shape of her shoulders changed again, something that underlined the shift in mood, and he smiled back at her, knowing he must look at least a little ridiculous.

"Do you have plans for the Faire?" It was the obvious question here, and it would at least get them back onto what felt like safer ground. She smiled at him again, and yes, she did. If you had asked Vitus what she'd be interested in, he'd have guessed about half of what she said. She was hoping to see several of the pavo matches. She knew people playing on the relevant teams.

There was a duelling demonstration of particular interest, though she was not taking part as one of the duellists and seemed a little put out by that. Thessaly apparently had a fondness for some of the agricultural shows, including the oxen. She added after a moment. “And some of the kitchen item demonstrations. Not that I cook, but I find the banter fascinating. It’s actually useful in illusion work, the way people talk about what they think people will like.”

That wasn’t an angle Vitus had thought about directly. “Huh. You mean the language about why you should pick this device over that one?”

“Like that. What vocabulary they choose, it, what’s the word?” Thessaly looked up, visibly thinking hard. “If you listen to the hawkers, they describe common fantasies, common desires. A lot of illusion work is based on that, how to satisfy the eye one way or another. I suspect it’s the same for talismans, yes?”

“Yes.” Vitus could hear the calls of the men and women in the vast barn full of booths. Certain words enticed, particularly, and those booths would be ringed by people listening and buying. Selling a talisman didn’t work the same way, but learning to describe what was on offer more that way might well be worth doing. “That’s going to give me a lot to think about. If you know when you’ll be wandering through the halls, perhaps we might meet up, if it’s convenient?”

“I’ll have to check the diary and the schedule for the Faire, of course.” Thessaly said. “But I’d like that. Mama finds it tedious and lower class, but she admits it’s not actually a problem that I enjoy the booths. Naturally, if we see anyone of our sort there, the standard line is being aware of what new items might be helpful for the housekeeper and staff, though I don't really have an excuse there, it's not like I'd be running my own household once I'm married. Never mind, I can claim I'm scouting things for Aunt Metaia's staff. Company would be delightful." Then she lifted her hand again. "Perhaps we might go in and dance again? I should probably be visible."

"Dressed as you are, more people should have the opportunity to admire you, yes." Vitus offered it with as much gallantry as he could manage, then held out his arm to escort her. As they were coming in, the music picked up a waltz, which was well within his dancing skills and not too energetically demanding. They swung into the patterns of the music, passing other couples. Thessaly was beaming. Once they'd made a turn around the dance floor, there was an honest joy at the physical pleasure of it she wasn't hiding at all. Vitus felt triumphant that he could be so close to it, that he hadn't marred it for her, with some awkward comment or misstep, with either foot or tongue.

It was a long waltz, longer than he'd expected, and when they finished, he offered his arm again to escort her from the dancing space. She glanced around, then frowned. "Do you see any of the Fortiers?"

Vitus looked, first faster, before he made himself settle to the steady view that didn't skim over knots of people in the crowd. The hall had thinned out a bit, some people gone to side rooms for quieter conversations, some gone home. But no, he didn't see any of them. "Your aunt, yes. Your mother and father, there." They were tucked in a corner behind several other people. "My mama will have noticed. Shall I go ask her?" He hesitated. "Bring you some punch back, as an excuse?"

"I'd appreciate both, thank you." She took several steps further out of the way, and she was fidgeting slightly. It was noticeable because normally she didn't do that sort of thing. He'd noticed all her gestures were normally deliberate. It went with the illusion work or maybe with the duelling training. As Virtus went, he made a note of who was still there. Magistra Landry and Alexander, but not Philip. None of the Fortiers he could see, though he saw Jacinthe and Amalric Howard talking with several people from Amalric's year at Schola. He could see Hannah Morris, no gentleman hanging on her attention, and Ilanit Rosen. He couldn't see the two men in the group. They had their backs to him.

"Mama." He bent to whisper in her ear. "Have you seen where the Fortiers went? Thessaly Lytton-Powell wanted to know." His mother was seated in one of the chairs at the side.

"Left, I am guessing for the portal, I don't know. Ten minutes ago? Rather early for them, and none of them stopped to say their farewells. Lord Clovis, Lady Maylis, their sons, and Dagobert and Laudine Fortier too. I think Bradamante's still around somewhere, and I've seen both the daughters I expected to recently." The eldest of Bradamante's daughters had moved to France with her husband a few years ago, and thus no one factored her into the social calculations the same way. His mother sniffed slightly. "Abrupt, but I don't know if anyone commented about it."

"Thank you, Mama. I'll bring you some punch in a minute, shall I?" He kissed her cheek, then went to gather up a glass for Thessaly, bringing it back to her. "Mama says they left, all together, perhaps ten minutes ago. A bit abruptly, she thought, but no idea why."

He was about to hand the glass to her, when she was in fact wringing her hands, little twists that moved the gloves against her fingers. "Oh. Oh dear. I, no, I promised Childeric a dance, of course. Do you think they were angry? Does your mother mean angry, when she says abrupt?" Then her hand came up to her mouth. "Pardon. I'm..."

"You don't want Childeric to be angry at you." It came out of Vitus's mouth before he could stop himself from overstepping. He managed to stop before asking why she was afraid of that, why she thought he'd be angry at her in particular. "Here, may I escort you back to your mother? Or your aunt seems to be on her own at the moment." He rather thought her aunt was far more soothing than her mother, from what he'd gathered so far.

"Aunt Metaia, please. You are kind." She didn't speak again as they circled around to where her aunt was.

Vitus made a slight bow, then said, "Thessaly was a trifle concerned that the Fortiers had left with little notice. May I fetch you punch as well, Council Member?"

Her aunt tsked, gently. "Thank you, no, but you are most considerate for offering. Please, don't let us keep you, I will reassure my niece." It was a kind dismissal, but a clear one, and it was obvious to Vitus that Thessaly was in sensible hands now. He made his bow, and turned back toward the punch table, so he could keep his promise to his mother.

CHAPTER 25

JUNE 21ST AT THESSALY'S HOME

"Thessaly, wake up." A moment later there was a hand - Mama's hand - shaking her awake. They hadn't returned from the Council Keep until well past one. It had taken more time for the evening gown to come off and her hair to be brushed out and braided for sleep. It had taken far longer for her to actually fall asleep, not until perhaps three.

Thessaly rolled onto her back, tangled in the sheet and light blanket. "Mama?" Then her mother's face came into focus, not just the face but the rest of her. "What happened?"

"Your Aunt Metaia is missing, and they want someone to come do the tests to find her, a blood relative. Will you get dressed quickly, and come? You know more about where her things might be, if the Guard have questions." Her mother looked incredibly pale, as if she knew already that the answer to whatever had happened was not likely to be good.

"And I'm also on the warding. She was meeting someone. Wasn't it Thirza Remmerton? Or was it Alice Bovey-

Potts? No. Thirza." Thessaly pushed up on her elbow. "I'll get dressed as quickly as I can. Ten minutes, maybe fifteen."

Her mother nodded once, sharply, and went off. Presumably she was going to put on something other than the wrapper she'd pulled on over her nightgown. The wrapper sufficed to speak to one of the Guard who had called, but not for outside the house. One of the maids appeared as she was leaving, bustling about to find a suitable frock. "The blue, please, I think. It's clean, and..." And it would do for whatever this was, if they ended up waiting at the Temple of Healing or something. Thessaly refused to let herself think about other things.

"Yes'm." Twelve minutes later, she was in the frock. Her hair was coiled in a simple braid and bun and firmly fixed with both hairpins and charms. Thessaly took a moment to gather up a book and a reticule in case they were stuck waiting somewhere. Her reticule sensibly held the sort of minor portable apothecary set that might be useful to have on hand.

She met her mother in the foyer. They shared a portal with four or five other magical households nearby, and fortunately, it was much closer to them than the others. Mama nodded once, approving, and then they went out, set the portal for Aunt Metaia's, and walked through.

The portal on the other end was near the ancient castle, now mostly ruins and a bit of tower, near the grove and the duelling meadow. The space around the portal was rather crowded, and there was a certain amount of purposeful chaos involved. Thessaly wondered at first why they weren't at the house proper. The portal stood perhaps three hundred feet away, and down the hill. But of course the warding would have kept them out.

"Magistra Lytton-Powell, Mistress Lytton-Powell. We

appreciate your time. I am Captain Euphemius Farrow. We would like to begin with access to the property, through the warding, if you can provide that, and then a few drops of blood for a location charm. I also have some questions to help the process overall." He said the last few words a little awkwardly, as if he'd usually put some other phrase there, like 'assist our investigation'.

"Of course, Captain." Mama said. "In what order would be best?"

"If we might have the blood for the charm first, that takes a few minutes to prepare, and the ambient magics in the house might interfere. But then we would like to see the house, if you are willing."

"And you are - worried my sister is missing?" Mama asked, her voice catching, most unlike her.

The Captain nodded once. "Magistra Remmerton reported her absence to us and mentioned that the staff had the day off, and that you both would be the best for any of the locational charms. A close friend of the Council Member, I gather?"

Mama nodded once, then one of the junior Guards came over holding a clay disc the size of her palm. Mama removed her glove with precise little movements, then turned her palm up for the prick of magic. Thessaly held still, not sure what to do here. Once that was done, Captain Farrow led the way up the hill to the front of the house. "The layout, Magistra?"

"The house here, with a garden on two sides. A road runs around to the back, but it's used rarely, just for access to a hut up the hill a few times a year. The grove is there, tucked in the curve of the hill."

Captain Farrow nodded. "And you are both able to open the warding, Magistra, Mistress?"

Mama nodded. "Thessaly spends a fair bit of time here, and I am Metaia's next of kin. She didn't marry." It was a fairly ordinary sort of arrangement.

"May I ask when you each last saw Council Member Powell, and when each of you were last in this house?" Captain Farrow had pulled out a small notebook as he walked, but he waited at the door. Thessaly took a breath and placed her hand on the warding stone, the panel at shoulder height, and then opened the door once she felt the magic recognise her. As she turned back, she saw one of the Guards murmur something in his ear, and he nodded once without explaining.

Mama nodded. "We were at the Council rites last night, of course. My sister left before we did, not long after midnight, when there were a number of people still there. We left after one, perhaps one-thirty." She hesitated, a little at a loss.

Thessaly picked up immediately. "I was the last one here. I joined my aunt as we dressed. I was here from three in the afternoon until we went to the Council Keep at six." She considered what she knew of the magical implications. "We were in the library, a brief stop in her workroom, and mostly in her rooms on the first floor."

"So you would know if anything looked out of order? Or where the staff might be?" The Captain nodded. "Please. It will take us a minute or two for the charmwork, given the ambient magic here. Perhaps we might speak further in the library or the parlour, whichever room you think best." He was glancing around the space. Thessaly was sure he was not only taking in the house, but if anything might be a clue of some sort. "And please speak up if something is out of order or not as you'd expect. That might be important information."

Neither Mama nor Thessaly deigned to reply to that. They certainly knew their fundamental magical principles of sympathy and contagion. Instead, Thessaly led the way to the library, where it looked out on the garden. “The staff have the day off. She always gives them Solstice night and the next day for the Faire. It is not a large staff. Evangeline Collins is the housekeeper and acts as lady’s maid. There’s a cook, one maid and one footman and a stableman. Along with gardeners who come in for the day and so on.” She gestured. “The cook and housemaid have rooms in the attached cottage. The housekeeper has rooms over the carriage house. Aunt Metaia likes her privacy. The footman sleeps in rooms over the stable with the stable hand.”

Captain Farrow made several notes. “And the other rooms here?”

Thessaly glanced at her mother, but Mama just nodded once. “A dining room, workroom, and study on this floor, as well as a kitchen and the servants’ hall. Aunt Metaia has rooms upstairs, a sitting room and bedroom and a bathing room. There are three guest bedrooms, one for me, one for Mama and Papa if they stay, and one for my sister Hermia or another guest. She didn’t invite people to stay often, outside of family, but I am here overnight at least once a month, often more frequently.”

That got her a long, steady look, as if Captain Farrow were weighing several pieces of information. His questions turned to the night before, if Aunt Metaia had been in any particular mood or had any concerns. “Just so. Might I ask you, Mistress Lytton-Powell, if you would walk through the house with one of my Guards? I would like you to see if there is anything out of place or that seems odd? Or, of course, if you find any sign of your aunt. Though,” he paused, “we do not think her to be in the house proper.

Guard Ellingsworth, if you would, take notes, as we discussed." The Guardswoman was a bit older than Thessaly. She'd have to be. The Guard had a long apprenticeship. She had dark brown hair in a pinned up braid and looked very official and efficient in her uniform.

"Of course." As the Guardswoman escorted her out to go through the rooms, she heard Mama summarise the previous evening. Not all the specifics, of course, but a general sense of the night. Thessaly was thorough in her exploration of the house, opening doors, going in, looking around, but there were no unusual signs of anything. Upstairs in the bedroom, Thessaly considered. "That's the gown that she wore last night." It was hung on the wall by the dressing screen, so it wouldn't crease. She considered the other clothing. "I would have expected her nightgown to be here, but her wrapper is missing, too. That's a teal silk with silver embroidery."

Before she could say anything else, there was a sound. "Please come down." It was Captain Farrow, calling up the stairs. Thessaly turned, coming straight down, the Guardswoman behind her. Captain Farrow set off through the garden, toward the back gate, then he stopped a little short. "Please wait here."

There was a sudden and painful pit in Thessaly's stomach, because being asked to wait seemed a bad thing. To call them out and have them wait, especially. She couldn't hear anything from beyond the gate - the warding was very good here, for privacy - but then Captain Farrow came back.

He took his hat off, and Thessaly knew, even before Mama grabbed at her arm, fingers digging in. "Magistra, Mistress, I am very sorry to inform you that Metaia Powell is dead. May we escort you back to the house until we have begun to learn more? And may I send someone for your husband, Magistra?"

"May I see her first?" Mama's voice was as sharp as Thessaly had ever heard it. "May we see her? We will not approach or interfere. Just." She swallowed hard. "She is my sister. My younger sister."

Captain Farrow looked uncertain for a moment. "If you stay well back, and if you are certain you wish to." He coughed. "She is not, pardon." He tried again. "She is not visibly injured, if that eases you any."

"Please." Mama made to go forward, and Captain Farrow moved ahead of her, carefully opening the gate with a handkerchief, and from the lower bar, so as not to disturb any evidence, presumably. Mama and Thessaly moved behind him, then he guided them in a broad circle around on the road.

Aunt Metaia lay there, on her back, hands folded on her stomach and her eyes closed, though she looked like she'd been startled by something. She was wearing her wrapper and Thessaly could see the nightgown under it, no corset. It was what she'd have changed into, once she was home and here for the night, and it meant she'd been lying here for hours, hours and hours. Before she could say anything, Mama's grip tightened. "Thank you, Captain. We will be in the library."

Thessaly could not argue with that. She wasn't entirely sure she wanted to. Part of her wanted to stay, wanted to keep whatever vigil she could, because that vigil was at least something she could be doing. But Mama's fingers were relentless, and there was nothing for it. The only thing she managed to say was, "Council Head Rowan will want to know immediately." Every Guard's head shifted to look at her, and Thessaly had to swallow hard against her body rebelling. "They are. They were friends. Close friends. And she can offer whatever resources you might need."

Then Mama was tugging her away, and Thessaly went. There were no staff in the house. No one had said if they might put on the kettle. Aunt Metaia kept one in her study. So she and Mama just sat, in the library, silent. It left Thessaly entirely too much time to think about the conversation before they left yesterday. And worse, to think about the glance or two Cousin Owain had given Aunt Metaia, and what it might have meant.

CHAPTER 26

JUNE 21ST AT THE MIDSUMMER FAIRE

Vitus had drifted through his morning, honestly. He'd come to bed around two, and he'd dreamt of the dancing, of the patterns made by dancers on the floor under the charmlights. There had been loops and patterns in his dreams of how the shadows and light played against each other. And he'd dreamt of the way Thessaly had felt in the dance, the silk of her gloves against his skin, the strength of her hand against his.

He'd woken around dawn, to stare at the ceiling and wonder about the scope of her worry. It was not something he could do much about, not something he could help with, other than seeing her back to her aunt. He knew that. She was far beyond his help, for all sorts of reasons, starting with Father's reliance on the goodwill of the Fortiers.

It would probably be better business practice if he could bring himself to figure out how to ask if she might consider commissioning a talismanic piece. Or if her aunt might. Instead, his thoughts kept coming back to her, as a person who laughed and smiled and chose to spend a little time with him, when she had a world full of other choices.

He wasn't infatuated. Or, no, he was. But it wasn't - automatically - a bad thing. Probably not. As long as he kept his head, as long as he didn't let his heart get away from him for too long. He needed to marry in due course. He could not marry her. It would be unkind to whoever he married, whenever he did, to have Vitus pining after someone else. Courtly love was all well and good in a story or a tale of ancient romance, but he had always thought it terribly unfair to a living wife.

Vitus had managed to get his antecedents tangled, even given the fact that one of them was entirely hypothetical yet. But she had said herself that her agreements with Childeric Fortier and his family had space for a conversation. She'd demonstrated that, twice, and that they also permitted a dance. He could, like a sensible adult, actually ask her what was specifically permitted in her agreements, and then bide by that. Or rather, bide by whatever she chose, given that, because there was no reason to assume that she wanted more than conversation and perhaps a dance with him.

There, that was a plan. It was even a suitably considered plan. Lucas would approve of him thinking through the various potential outcomes. Vitus did not think Thessaly would dismiss him out of hand. For one thing, she was a duellist; she was presumably comfortable working within the confines of a set of agreements within the moment. For another, she was born to the sort of family that made their agreements carefully and precisely. But also a family who also knew what they did and did not include the way they knew where their foot or hand was.

Vitus was not so confident there, but he had his own skills, of articulating desire into something that could be scribed in stone and brought to life with enchantment. He had to remember those gifts and the knowledge he had didn't go fleeing into the night, useless and far away, just because this was a different sort of magic. He had time, too. Her situation was known, his situation was known, both more liminal than they would be in a few months. Well, he hoped a few months for him, with the establishment of his own business, and after her wedding festivities were well over for her.

He could therefore enjoy what she felt fit to offer, conversation and magical theory, and perhaps a few more dances. It was for her to set the pace, and he would follow. In that context, Vitus could soothe himself, perhaps, with some tales of the troubadours and courtly love. Mama had insisted he learn enough of the language involved to please Father's Grand-mère, who liked the old customs. There, now he had a decision and a path forward, and he could sleep.

When he woke again, it was past ten. Their maid had left a tray for him, under stasis, with eggs and toast and jam, and Vitus ate, scanning the paper for the day's news. He thumbed through, checking the schedule for the Faire's events, and writing out those parts he was most interested in. That done, he dressed and packed a satchel for the day. He had no obligations at the Faire, not today, but it was a good time to get his bearings. He'd missed last year's, of course, and things were always moved around.

And he was a sensible man who wanted to scout out this year's culinary treats so he could decide where best to spend his coins. There was always fierce competition when it came to baked goods, but people often came up with particular designs or works of spun sugar, or some such, that were worth considering. Besides, they often gave some hints about trends in colour or fashion that mattered to Vitus and his work.

"Mama, I'm off. Shall I bring you anything home?" His mother was settled in the parlour, her knitting in her hands.

"Information about what is on offer. Did you sleep well?" She peered up at him. "Well enough, then. You were back late."

"Did I wake you? I'm terribly sorry. Yes, I did. I don't think I'll be late tonight. I should be back for supper." He bent to kiss her on the forehead. "Information it is, and as much of the gossip as I can gather." Then he was out the door, into the sunlight, and down the road to the portal again.

When he came out on the other end, the Faire was already in full swing. It had started the night before with a feast and dancing, while the Council rites went on far more formally elsewhere. He'd never seen that. It was intended more for the working class of Albion, in their many forms. Farmers and fisherman, of course, crafters and crofters and those servants who could get leave, anyone who could get a night off. From here, it'd be ten days of festivities, allowing anyone with a half-day off or more to get some time at the Faire.

Vitus wove through the crowds, agreeably nodding here and there to people he knew. It was too loud and too chaotic for much actual conversation, at least along the main paths. And besides, Vitus always thought the people who blocked the path - terribly easy to do, for women in bustles - were being a trifle rude. It made things difficult not only for the people behind them but also for the stalls around where they stopped.

He paid for a map from one newsboy stationed to sell the things, as well as the evening paper when that had been printed. That let him plan his day. Vitus intended to circle through all the booths, to see who was where, and then check the schedules for the landed estates, to see who he particularly wanted to see. He, fortunately, could come out as many days as he needed. Though for the sake of his feet and his shoes, he was hoping it would be more on the order of three or four than all ten.

It did decidedly require some planning. Two hours later, he'd done his initial circuit and got his bearings. He retreated to the seats near one of the outdoor show rings to sit and transcribe half a dozen scraps of paper into a proper schedule. Also, of course, to eat some of the first round of his selection of pastries. Vitus had made good choices, one with a marmalade glaze, a lardy cake, and a Bakewell tart. He kept the marmalade to bring back to his mother, and the Bakewell tart for Papa, and the lardy cake was scrumptious. They'd started winning prizes, that stand, five years ago, and their cakes seemed to get better every year.

The ring was, when he looked up, full of what looked like the initial rounds of sheep. They were being led out into the ring, around, then into place, over and over again. An announcer was explaining some of what was going on, though, of course, it was full of specialist terms that Vitus did not know. Horses he could do, and some things about cows, but sheep. Well, he just enjoyed looking at sheep.

Checking his watch, it was nearly three, and he stood, intending to make another pass. Now he had a better idea of his specific schedule for conversations, he could check what lectures might be on offer. They set up a large barn as a lecture hall. It was an excellent chance to learn about other specialities, or perhaps find a shared topic for a later conversation.

It wasn't until he was circling back to the main paths through the Faire, that he heard the newsboys. "Council member dead! More in the evening paper." He glanced around, focusing on the boy nearest him, who was waving a slip of paper, certainly printed in a hurry. He went over, pulling out a coin for it.

"What's the news, boy?"

The boy thrust the somewhat roughly printed page at him, pocketed the coin. "Council M'mber Metaia Powell."

Vitus felt the ground drop away from him. The boy immediately turned away, waving his arm, shouting, and Vitus retreated, automatically back toward the portal, before stepping out of the line of the crowds. He'd just seen her last night, alive and well. Shining, in fact, other than whatever her worries might have been about her niece.

And Thessaly, Thessaly must be heartbroken. Vitus assumed she must know if it was going to be in the paper. Someone must have told her. Surely, before it was shouted all over the Faire. The slip of paper had no real details - those would come in the evening paper, whatever they'd been able to get to press in time. Just that she'd been found dead at her home in Wales, that the Guard was on site, and that enquiries were ongoing.

Of course, she was a Council Member. Anything that happened to the twenty-one of them was automatically news and major news at that. The thought crossed his mind - to be shoved away immediately out of human decency - that it would mean a Council challenge inside a few months, and that would bring him opportunities. That was for later. Now, he dithered about whether to go home and talk to his parents, or to do something else. The news would be raging along Club Row in Trellech. But he wasn't at all sure he could cope with people picking it apart and forgetting there were people grieving and hurting, and someone dead.

He was saved from dithering forever by the arrival of the papers from Trellech, smack at six in the evening. He followed the carter to the newsboy, bought the edition. They didn't get the evening paper at home. It didn't arrive until after eight, far too late to be useful. Then Vitus retreated out of the line of people again, to read it. The front page had more to say, but not a great deal more information. It said that Council Head Rowan would have a longer statement in tomorrow morning's paper, but that she grieved with the Council Member's family.

There was a brief bio, the sort of thing the Trellech Moon kept handy for any newsworthy event, all the sketched lines of someone's life. Vitus found his mind filling in the commentary after each sentence. Council Member Powell had been born into the well-known Powell family. Yes, those Powells. She had gone to Schola, as you'd expect. She'd been in Seal House, which wasn't nearly as expected. Then it laid out her specialty in illusion work, especially illusions meant for long-term use, like around Silence-warded villages and estates. And naturally it gave a précis of her time on the Council.

There was no funeral notice yet, but there was a note that arrangements would be announced in tomorrow's paper, and that donations to the Temple of Healing were welcome. That was also entirely usual, if one didn't want to be entirely inundated with flowers. Or more importantly, at that political level, if one didn't want to reveal one's home address to everyone and their sister.

It was all what Vitus expected, and he knew that was

wrong. He didn't know what was wrong, or what it meant. Or even if he'd ever find out. For now, though, he'd go home and tell his parents. Then he'd figure out what, if anything, he could reasonably write to Thessaly in this situation that would be simultaneously kind and also appropriate if - when - someone else read it.

CHAPTER 27

JUNE 21ST IN THE LATE AFTERNOON

Thessaly sat there, her hands folded, not at all sure where to look or what to do, certainly not what to say. After they'd waited in the library at Bryn Glas for half an hour, one of the Guards escorted them home. Some part of her knew that meant they'd be searching the house, but as they were leaving, she'd seen the local Lord - Caderyn Prichard - out by the portal. That meant they could test people under the truth magic. Then she'd seen Mrs Collins, the housekeeper, come through.

The combination meant that they could search more gently. Aunt Metaia had explained that, years ago, that the truth magics needed someone able to cast them in the first place, and then to ask the right questions. Lord Prichard was skilled, magically, he could do the basic truth charms on the fly if he needed to. Enough that they could be sure Mrs Collins had no part of whatever had happened, and then she could walk them through the house. At least things would be put back properly, after. Where they ought to be.

Once they'd got back to their own home, the Guard had

stayed with them. Mama had told Thessaly to go change, and Thessaly hadn't needed to be told that it should be her mourning dress. Mama made the habit of always having one in her wardrobe, just in case, updated every year for fit and a little for style. Thessaly had only worn hers twice. Both times had been actual funerals in the extended family. They had been the sort of deaths that people had seen coming for months, if not years, in people who had had long and good lives.

Her maid laced her into the dress, made of a fine-woven wool, that would feel stifling soon. It had almost nothing in the way of trim, but that at least meant she was not dealing with the stubborn, unyielding nature of crepe. She added a single jet pendant, one that had come down to her from Grandmama. Then she descended the stairs to find Mama and Father in the parlour.

"We will have a few necessary callers, I suspect," Mama said, her voice rough. Father was not a demonstrative man, but he came to stand behind her as Mama sat in her preferred chair, a hand on her shoulder. Thessaly felt even more alone, suddenly, and she couldn't let it show. "Hermia?"

"I've told her. She is staying up in the nursery with Fitchley." Fitchley was a distant cousin on the Lytton side. She'd been governess to both girls when they were younger, and kept on to help run the house now they were older. That made sense. Thessaly would have to go talk with Hermia later. Whenever later actually was.

"Callers, Mama?" Thessaly felt she could at least ask about that.

"Cousin Owain, I expect. Perhaps someone else from the Council, perhaps he might do that part. And not today, I expect, but tomorrow, we should assume the Fortiers will call, or some of them. Childeric and his parents, at the least. You will want to be available for that." It wasn't an offer of comfort, it was an expectation, not that Thessaly needed it spelled out.

Thessaly nodded. She was running the calendar in her head now. Some part of her mind was frantically scurrying through all the tiny fragments of things she knew anything about or had any control over. Formal mourning for an aunt or uncle was three months, generally. To the autumn equinox or the day after, that would make it. Thessaly had obligations outside the home, her apprenticeship. She could at least leave the house once the most immediate rites were tended to, and callers received. A fortnight, perhaps, if she remembered correctly from Grandmama's funeral.

There were ways in which the formalities could have been a relief. Everyone of their class, everyone of Albion, knew the mourning customs. Or if they didn't know the specifics - there being a range of faiths and practices in Albion - they knew the rough outline. They knew what to ask about, who to ask where it would not be awkward. Right now, people would ask along Club Row what the Powell customs were, whether there were things to be brought or sent.

Being on the Council, Aunt Metaia having been on the Council, didn't change that. Though it probably changed where the funeral would be. Bryn Glas, her home, certainly wasn't set up for it, and it didn't have its own cemetery. The principal family estate, up on the coast, had its own, with vaults and tombs going back centuries. That hadn't been Aunt Metaia's home, but it would be where she stayed, almost certainly. Difficult to visit, without a lot of visible fuss, for one thing, unlike the cemetery that ran around the edge of Trellech, to the south.

None of this was helping. Nothing could help, and Thessaly knew she was spinning in circles, mentally, because she didn't want to think about the enormity of what this meant.

She'd never get to sit with Aunt Metaia again. Nothing like just last night, talking and being comfortable. Knowing that Aunt Metaia loved her, always loved her, chose to love her, and what that meant. Thessaly hadn't figured out the breadth of it, and now she never would. There'd be no looking through books in Aunt Metaia's library, and then trying out something new in the workroom. There'd be no more of the glorious chaos of colours on the walls, in the furnishings, that shouldn't possibly be pleasing together and absolutely were.

The house would go to someone else, someone in the Powell family. That was how it had come down to Aunt Metaia, and Thessaly didn't know the details. But she knew there were details, that some solicitor or senior member of the family would deal with them. The house would be changed, painted to something neutral and plain. Like the parlour here, which had colour, but, well, largely slate blue. The red parlour was across the hall and kept for more formal guests.

Before Thessaly could think of much else, there was a knock and a murmur. "Council Head Rowan to see you, with Council Member Powell, Mistress." That was to Mama, and it was a question. Mama nodded just once, and the maid showed them in.

Thessaly didn't even know which name to use in her head now. Aunt Metaia had been clear Hereswith Rowan was not only a colleague, but a friend, for all she was thirty something years older than Aunt Metaia was. Had been. Now, she looked like she'd been crying, there were smudges under her eyes, and she was leaning on cousin Owain's arm a little. It was odd, too, to see her without either her husband or her companion, both of whom helped her keep the Council running in various practical ways.

Magistra Hereswith - her mind had apparently settled on something, the more informal - went immediately to Mama, and bent to kiss her cheek. "I am so terribly sorry, Sioned. And to you, Thessaly, it must be such a shock." She stood, coming to press the same kiss on Thessaly's cheek. "We have, I fear, a few urgent necessities to discuss. May we join you? Is there anything you need for your comfort first? I have a selection of potions on the way, as well."

That was considerate. Mama kept the apothecary cabinet well-stocked, but Thessaly was sure she'd be utterly unable to sleep tonight, and they did not keep many sleep potions in the house.

Mama nodded once. "Please, sit. And Harold, please do sit. You are a comfort, but this may take a little while."

Magistra Hereswith nodded, and took one chair, leaving Father and cousin Owain to take the other sofa. "First, we would be glad to host the funeral at the Council Keep. It will be a day or two at least, the Guard said, before we might do so, that will give us time to plan."

"That is generous." Mama's voice didn't sound like she really thought it was. Her control was not as it usually was. "You would prefer that?"

"Metaia's will indicated that. We keep a copy of those preferences on file, in case of need. But it would also be our honour. I did not know her as well as you did, nor the ways you did." She included Thessaly in that, a specific look. "We have space for the many people who might wish to attend, and spaces to be more private if those people are overwhelming. We have the staff to make sure all is done properly. She preferred her burial on the family estate."

Mama nodded. "I expected that." She lifted her fingers to her face, then put them down. "I hadn't known her preferences, not for that. She only mentioned she had settled them. And..." There was a slightly pained frown. "Updated them recently. She said it was an ordinary matter, nothing unusual."

"Three weeks ago, yes. It's fairly routine to update them. Everything has been properly notarised by the Courts, they have a matching copy in their vaults. Of course, we'll make sure all the ordinary steps for confirmation are taken." Magistra Hereswith inclined her head. "There are provisions for you, Sioned, and also for Thessaly and Hermia, though of course we must wait for the proper time for that."

"Of course," Mama murmured in response. "Metaia was always generous with what she had."

Magistra Hereswith's face shifted, too fast for Thessaly to make sense of it, but she ended with a pleasant smile. "Now, I have a little more news from the Guard. They are investigating thoroughly, of course, and they will make reports to me at least daily. I am glad to have you join me for those, or to inform you at whatever level of detail you wish."

Mama shook her head. "The outcome, please, or if there is any information we might assist with. I assume they will have more questions to come."

"Tomorrow, they believed. There was another case that came to their attention as I was finishing up there, and they wanted to finish their investigation at Bryn Glas before speaking further with you. Please don't speak about the last couple of days with anyone outside the family who wasn't present until they do." It wasn't phrased as an order, but it was one. Politely put, delicately phrased, but absolute.

Thessaly, though, was barely restraining herself. She wanted to flee, to at least wash her face or her hands, to scrub and feel something other than numbness, whether it was cold water or the scrape of a nail brush. But she also knew Mama wouldn't tell her details about anything she missed. So she stayed, her hands folded into her lap, the knuckles increasingly pale with pressure.

Magistra Hereswith kept everything moving gently. She walked Mama - and Father and Thessaly - through the steps, and what their parts in it were. Cousin Owain offered to coordinate pallbearers. He checked if there were colleagues of Aunt Metaia's who would want to be asked. Thessaly could suggest a name they did not already have. Her voice did not crack. She did not burst out in tears. And if her voice was smaller and weaker than it should be, she would take what she had there.

Magistra Hereswith also offered one of the Council's staff to help coordinate callers and the condolence letters and such, and Mama accepted with relief. Father had a secretary for business matters, but he was better with ledgers and charts than with people. And Fitchley did well with household matters, but she got flustered by people with influence. Finally, the two stood, having other things to tend to. Once they were gone, Mama nodded at Thessaly. "You may have a tray in your room if you wish. I'd prefer you keep whatever you say to Hermia appropriate, but you might see her, as well. Your father and I have a number of matters to tend to."

It was a dismissal. Thessaly stood, automatically smoothing her skirts out, and nodded. "Of course, Mama.

Please send someone for me if I can be of any help. I'll be with Hermia for a little." Once she left the parlour, she paused to ask the maid if she could have a tray up in the nursery with Hermia, and she went up there.

Hermia immediately fell into her arms, sobbing the way that Thessaly hadn't allowed herself to do. Holding her younger sister wasn't the same, but she was glad at least someone was weeping, that someone had the chance to.

CHAPTER 28

JUNE 22ND IN TRELLECH

"I'm about ready for a break." Vitus looked up. Niobe had planted him at the table by the window, with the best light, as soon as she'd seen him that morning. He hadn't slept well, and it showed. She stretched, something in her shoulder popping. "Go make the tea, please? It is a reason for having an apprentice."

It was also an old joke, and Vitus grinned at it. He'd spent all morning and into the early afternoon documenting some of the more common stones about to be added to her stores. Each one got measured and weighed, evaluated for the quality of the stone for magical use, and noted in three different ledgers. It was both tedious and satisfying at the same time, and he could do it when his thoughts were fuzzy and distracted. He wouldn't have trusted himself with gemstones today, but agate? He could handle agate, and chalcedony, and quartz.

He stood, and went off to the little kitchen nook by the stairs to fill the kettle and put it on. Then he sorted out leaves for the pot and got the cream out of the keep-cold box. He added a couple of biscuits from the tin. They were there to be eaten, but he'd have to see about picking some more up soon. When the kettle sang, he filled the pot and brought the tray back.

Niobe had settled in her chair, across the table from him. "You're here, and not at the Faire. And you said you'd be here for the morning."

Vitus nodded. "You heard the news yesterday? Council Member Powell? Metaia Powell."

"Terribly sad. And the newspaper near enough said this morning it was murder, not mishap, though I suppose it will be another day to confirm that."

"I'd met her, two, no three times, all briefly. Solstice night, in fact." He picked up the pot and then set it down. His hand was shaking.

Niobe considered him and then picked up the pot and poured the tea herself. "What is it that's got you unsettled, then? Besides the obvious."

"I'd like to send a note to her niece. You remember, she was working on how to do lapis lazuli in illusion work properly," Vitus hesitated, but he had to say something. With Niobe, best if it were the truth. Saying it out loud, though, even here, felt raw, as if he were saying far more than the words.

Niobe snorted. "I do not keep track of everyone you meet, Vitus, but I do indeed remember Mistress Lytton-Powell. You have mentioned her more than once, and it's clear you..." She stopped suddenly, then cocked her head. "Oh."

Vitus could feel himself blushing, and he certainly couldn't meet Niobe's eyes.

"Does she know?" Then Niobe's voice changed. "A condolence note, right."

Vitus shook his head no once, then he managed to look

at Niobe's shoulder. "I was worried, when we talked in the library, that I was overstepping, she made it clear she knows what her agreements with the Fortiers cover and don't. I realised last night I could ask her what that means. Obviously not right now, not for a while, not while she's..." Now he looked up. "She and her aunt were easy with each other. Happy. The way we rarely see in that sort of family. Not in public."

"Precious little in private, some families," Niobe said with a sniff. "But she's right. Whatever her marriage agreements are, they are almost certainly specific about what is permitted. Talking in the library, not a problem, certainly. Other things? Ask her. Or there may be some things that might be an issue during the betrothal, but not once she's married. Or with precautions."

Now Vitus was blushing again. "It's not like that." He had been refusing to think about that, in fact, especially in the last half day or so. "She has a good mind. An interesting mind."

"And she's also an excellent duellist and dancer," Niobe said, pushing a mug over toward him. "All right. Condolence note. What do you want to say?"

"I'll have to go round to the Stream for the proper address for the mail." Whichever portal it was. "You've never done anything for her parents, have you?"

"No. Other branches of the Powells, and a few of the Lyttons, though not the main line of them. They have a reputation for sharpness that's well earned, and not a kind I much want to be around." Niobe reached out to take a biscuit, nibbling on it while she thought. Vitus let her think. "Do you know much about her parents?"

This seemed rather a tangent from what Vitus was thinking about, but he knew Niobe had reason to ask, even if he did not know what that was yet. "A little, but they weren't at the Fortier events until they started planning for the betrothal."

"And you were away for most of that." Niobe tapped her fingers on the table and then pulled out four stones from the pile Vitus hadn't sorted yet. Amethyst, citrine, plain quartz, and an ametrine. She lined them up on the table. "This, here, that's the Lyttons. This is the Powells. This is Thessaly Lytton-Powell." She tapped the amethyst, the citrine, then the ametrine. "And this is Metaia Powell." That was the plain quartz.

Vitus snorted, softly. "And ametrine, trystine, whatever name we're using for it, is the combination of the two." So the sympathetic magic indicated, besides the way that crystals of the stuff mixed back and forth, shade to shade, from purple through lavender into golden yellow and distilled sunshine. "The Powells have been powerful, on and off, for centuries. And there are many of them."

"And they notice if one of their own has been threatened. Whatever their internal disagreements, they come together outside the family. Sioned Powell is the elder sister here, by seven, eight years. She did everything expected of her, went to Schola, found herself in Fox House, and married well. She married Harold Lytton, and the Lyttons were sufficiently wanting the marriage that he took her name. Well, she took his, as well."

"I assumed." That part was basic maths, in terms of families. Rare for the man, unless there was a land magic inheritance at play, but not unknown.

"Now, while they're comfortably off, by almost any reasonable person's standards, they are not what the Great Families consider wealthy. They have, as a couple, nothing in the way of land holdings. Some investments, some consulting. Harold Lytton-Powell upholds his family's reputation for being sharply skilled at magic, the kind that commands high prices and only taking those contracts he's interested in. Enchantments, a range of them, but including the sort of thing suspicious husbands install in rooms when they think their wives are breaking the marriage agreements. Not always kind or pleasant, but competent." She tilted her head. "I've heard gossip that he's not fiscally sound. From the sound of it, I'd suspect gambling debts, but I'd not hear the details of that."

Vitus frowned, opened his mouth, then shook his head before trying again. "And Sioned Lytton-Powell?"

"Philanthropy. She's quite good at it, getting other people to give money or horrendous items for auctions that sell for ridiculous sums, all that. No one wants her annoyed at them, or she won't help with their next pet cause, and she has a few closer friends. But not many. Metaia is - was - always far more freely minded, in just about every dimension, and in a wide circle. No one expected she'd challenge for Council, but once she did, no one was surprised she succeeded, if you get the idea from that."

"Lucky, skilled, skilled enough to use her luck, or something else?" Vitus knew the possible threads there as well as anyone.

"Ha!" Niobe chuckled. "Skilled enough to make the best use of her luck. Until, I suppose, it ran out." She tapped the quartz. "She was Seal House in Schola, that gives you an idea too. Though we don't have their aquamarine down here, and besides, it would spoil the quartz-based metaphor. Twisting and darting under the waves, where the eye couldn't follow. She had a reputation as a prankster. Metaia was the year ahead of me at Schola. And oh, she managed to set it up so that everything in Seal House - all the outer walls, and all the inner, too - turned turquoise, all at once. Mistress of illusion work, especially buildings. A definite shock, but no lasting damage to anything. She did much of the work on illusions around Silence-warded spaces the last two decades. Not just her, fortunately, but she pioneered a couple of techniques that are far more stable, and she did her work thoroughly. She'll be missed there."

"And the Council?" Vitus considered, though now he was looking at that ametrine.

"Well-respected in her role, doing a fair bit of illusion work for them, of course, especially around the guarded portals and other locations where there's more of a Fatae touch. She was close to Hereswith Rowan, and friendly with many more." Niobe lifted her eyes. "I've heard rumours she was in Four Metals, though rarely at any general gatherings, actually. You would know that better than I."

He'd told her about his own membership - Four Metals was a secret society, but they were not as ridiculously restrictive about it as some. Besides, a lot of the work of making things involved knowing crafters who had specific skills and inclinations. But he'd never seen Metaia Powell there. "Huh. And Thessaly?" Now he reached out to touch the ametrine.

"Magically gifted - well, you spotted that already, didn't you? Sharp-eyed young man that you are. Marrying a Fortier would set her family up, including her younger sister, and that would matter to her. Born to consider family before anyone else, from both sides." Niobe weighed her next words, Vitus could see it. "More like her aunt than her mother, and from what I've seen, she doesn't have as many trustworthy friends as she should. Several married, young children at home, or they're expecting. No portals.

From what has come through in the newspapers..." Niobe paused. "If she came to me asking for a talisman, I think I'd be suggesting one that would ease her way to true friends. Not just a circle of pleasant acquaintances."

Vitus nodded slowly at that, leaving the implications of the last part for later. "So I should, um...."

"You should go write a condolence note that makes it clear you are thinking of her. That you are sorry for her, as a person who has lost someone she loved, and that you see the shape of that stone accurately enough. You could offer her a talisman, if you wanted to make one, for sleep or ease." Niobe considered with her head cocked in the position that meant she was working through what we had in stock.

"I can't imagine there's anything she'd feel guilty for, so no need for the jasper, even if we do have some lovely pieces right now. Amethyst, maybe. That's a house stone for her, in Fox, and it would go with mourning dress. Not rose quartz, unless and until you have a talk about her agreements in more direct forms. Entirely too suggestive at the moment. Howlite, maybe, for all it's a modern discovery, I still argue that it's calming in suitable ways. How about I pull a few pieces for you this afternoon, and you can look tomorrow? It wouldn't be bad to make one up, even if she'd rather not have the piece. I'll cover the cost of the stone."

Vitus let out a breath. "That's very generous, of course. And it would be something I could offer, she'd understand. It might help just a little. Better than flowers or something like that."

"I am sure they have abundant floral arrangements and wreaths by now. And you could let her know you hope to attend the funeral, that you have a memory of her aunt, one of the times you met her. There. Off you go, find the address. The Stream will have some suitable notepaper for you too." The Stream, like all the Schola House clubs, kept supplies on hand for this sort of thing. He could find properly black-bordered notecards, as well as get it put in the post properly. "And if you go now, it should make the three o'clock. Get to her before supper."

Vitus stood. "You don't mind my not putting everything away?"

"Of course not. I'll pack this up. You can come back to it when there's time. Off you go." Niobe shooed him off with a wave of her hand.

Fifteen minutes later, he was in one of the small writing rooms in the Stream. It took him seven versions of the note before he hit on a combination of phrases that were both sincere and gentle, undemanding of the reader. He expressed his condolences. He wrote that he had been taken at the St. George's gala not only by Council Member Powell's costume, but by their obvious affection for each other. Vitus said, as simply and plainly as he could, that he hoped that memory would bring some pleasure again in due course. And he offered the stone, suggesting amethyst and howlite. Or that if she had some other preference, he'd be glad to see what he could do, for a talisman for sleep and ease. He sealed it up and went off to consult the directory for the address.

As he got closer, he heard a cluster of voices. "Won't be in the paper until tonight, apparently, but he died yesterday, or at least there was a fuss at his flat. Guard in and out. Penelopes too." That meant an investigation, certainly, but that 'he' meant it wasn't related to Metaia Powell.

"Pardon, I couldn't help overhearing..." Vitus cleared his throat. "May I ask who?"

"Landry. Philip Landry." One of the men cocked his head. "You'd know him a bit, wouldn't you, Deschamps?"

"He was kind enough to do a consultation for me a few weeks ago." Vitus said it automatically, while he was trying to keep his feet under him, metaphorically and physically. "He's dead?"

"Found in his flat last night. That's what I heard. More in the paper, but it won't be out for a bit. You sure you're all right, old man?"

Vitus waved off the offer of help. "A shock. Pardon, I've got something I need to get in the mail." Before he could get dragged into conversation, he found the address he wanted. He dropped a few coins for the club's messenger boy to run it to the mail sorting immediately, rather than wait. Then he went out again, feeling like he needed a long walk somewhere with no one around to see if he could get any grip on his thoughts.

CHAPTER 29

JUNE 22ND, LATE AFTERNOON, AT THESSALY'S HOME

Thessaly had a headache. Worse, she felt trapped, and that she absolutely couldn't let any of that show. She had spent the early afternoon in the parlour with Mama, sorting condolence notes and messages into various piles. There were those that needed a reply promptly, some detail relevant to the funeral or the immediate future. Some had to be read and tended, for a reply later, after the funeral. Some were brief notes and wouldn't get a personal reply, just a printed card thanking them for their kindness.

What she wanted to do was go and duel, but she was not to be out in public. There would be the funeral, and that would be public. Then she would be expected to be at home for a fortnight, at least, for callers, supporting Mama. She wasn't to go to her apprenticeship. Though she might reasonably retreat to her own room or some other quiet place on the grounds with a book or something of the kind. If the weather held, she might go outside into the garden or orchard. She didn't know how she felt about the fact it was sunny and mild. And it was Aunt Metaia who had loved a garden beyond all reason.

She and Aunt Metaia had been supposed to be at the Faire today and tomorrow, taking in all the joys of it. There should have been cakes and fizzy drinks, flowers to consider for next year's garden, lectures to attend, and dancing to be had. The Faire ran to the delightful abundance of country dancing, as well as the partnered sort, people in vast rings or lines.

"You should rest before supper, Thessaly." Mama didn't bother looking up from her desk. "You needn't hover."

Thessaly was doing anything but hovering. She'd been sitting in the corner of the sofa, her hands folded, for the last twenty minutes. Probably twenty minutes, she'd lost track of time again. The only possible thing to do was go upstairs. "Of course, Mama. I'll be down for supper."

As she came out into the foyer, Master Harris, the man Magistra Rowan had sent over, was just coming in. "Oh, Mistress Thessaly. Third post just came in, there were a few for you, let me just sort them out. Is your mother in the parlour still?"

"She is, yes." Now Thessaly had to stand awkwardly, waiting for him to sort through the envelopes. There had been ten in the first post before she'd come downstairs, and six from the noon post. All had been school connections, nothing demanding, and she'd sent back replies to the first two batches already.

Master Harris made a slight bow. "If you have any replies to go out this evening, I'll be taking the last mail down with me when I leave. Half-seven."

"Thank you." She inclined her head. He really had been a help. He'd done all the things someone else could do. Master

Harris had seen to the post, laying out notepaper and envelopes for Mama. He'd even run out and fetched some additional black sealing wax when it was clear they'd run out sometime today. And he'd been helping with all the other logistics, making sure everyone's clothes for the funeral were in good form. He'd even arranged for Mama's dressmaker to come out for a fitting for her and for Thessaly tomorrow morning.

He finished the sorting, flicking through the envelopes one last time to check. "Five for you, Mistress." Master Harris handed over the envelopes, the top one with the Fortier seal showing. None of the Fortiers had come around, and none of them had - unless there was a note in this batch - written Mama and Father, either.

Thessaly just nodded once more and retreated upstairs. Once she had the door to her room closed and warded - for privacy and sound, both - she settled at her desk and reached for the letter opener. It was cunningly made like a fencing foil, not that she fenced like that, but it was a reasonable physical representation of duelling. Aunt Metaia had found it in a little shop on one of her trips elsewhere in Albion, and brought it back delighted. There was something absurd about opening a letter with a sword, miniature or otherwise, but it certainly worked well.

The one with the Fortier seal was from Childeric. He only wrote a few sentences, his condolences, that his parents were writing separately. They all sent their deepest sympathies. There'd been a family matter to tend to, nothing for her to worry about. The Fortiers would be at the funeral but he wouldn't be available until then.

Thessaly put it down flat on the desk, setting down the letter opener along the long edge to hold it open. "What am I supposed to do with that?" It actively discouraged any sort of response, and she had no idea what to make of it. She only had more of a headache.

The next three letters were all from people she'd been at school with. She set those aside. It would be an excuse to come up promptly after supper, and none of them would be demanding to answer. None of them were people she was terribly close with, though Eveline North had sent something that was less stilted than most. And there was a note here from Cosi. The note wasn't much, but it was hard to write a meaningful condolence note, Thessaly was finding. Certainly most people weren't good at it, whatever good meant in this circumstance.

The last one made her stop again. The seal in the wax on the back wasn't familiar, but it was Salmon House's golden yellow. Thessaly opened it, laid it out - the sword opener on the other side of the page this time - and then stared at it. Something in it burst all the things she'd been holding so tightly free, and she braced her elbows on the desk, sobbing into her hands.

One tiny part of her mind was glad she'd already set the privacy charms, no one would hear her. She had her own en suite bathing room, she could wash up and pull herself together before supper. Then all of it was just about crying in a way she hadn't let herself do yet, hadn't dared allow. She cried until everything was salt and aches and her head hurting more and differently, and her neck complaining of the strain.

And yet, it also helped.

All for a letter that had just been human and kind and thoughtful. Childeric had kept to a few formal words, no sign of actual care. Vitus, here, had thought about what might be a help. He'd barely met Aunt Metaia, but she'd made an impression on him. Of course she had. And he'd offered something that might actually ease a tiny bit of her aching despair.

Suddenly, she desperately wanted to see someone like that. Someone who thought about Thessaly as a person who was hurting. Not the silhouetted cameo shape of a young woman in mourning, treading the expected steps of a dirge for the appointed length of time. She'd write back to him. In a moment.

First, Thessaly went into the bathing room to wash her face and try to do something with her hair. Everything felt messy and sticky. She washed her face first with soap, then with the little washing grains, followed by the preferred apothecary potion for clear and glowing skin. Taking her hair down was easy enough, and the brush strokes were almost soothing. She brushed for the full one hundred, one of those ridiculous traditions that people kept anyway, and then she went to work coiling it and pinning it up.

Only once she had it partially pinned, she remembered viscerally and painfully, the conversation with Aunt Metaia as they were getting ready, just two nights ago around this time. All of a sudden, her legs wouldn't hold her, and she went down in a heap of skirts on the floor, hitting the tile harder than was good for her. She immediately pushed to brace her back against the wall, and then she was lost in crying again.

Only it wasn't just crying, it was something deeper than that, like a whirlpool made of edged memories. Aunt Metaia had been worried about her. Aunt Metaia had changed her will three weeks ago, after the betrothal, after she'd first been concerned about Childeric. Thessaly had seen those odd expressions, Aunt Metaia, cousin Owain, that conversation with Hereswith Rowan.

What if this was all Thessaly's fault, or her doing? What

if loving her had meant Aunt Metaia's death? It didn't matter that the logic wasn't smooth and obvious. She could feel the tug of it, the way it had weight and gravity and reality that she couldn't ignore. Thessaly wrapped her arms tighter around herself, and it didn't help.

She spun there, barely linking one thought to another, for what felt like hours, but maybe wasn't. The gong hadn't gone for supper yet. At least, there was - when she got her eyes cracked open - light from the window that hadn't changed much. Slowly, painfully, she unclenched each finger from her skirts, then managed to kneel, then stand. She knew better than to lean on the basin, and to use the windowsill instead, less likely to give way under her weight.

Finally, she was standing, and she looked a mess all over again. This time she started with a tidying charm for her dress. She'd ask the maids to tend to it more tonight. Thessaly washed her face again, trying to concentrate on the sensation of being aware of her body rather than fleeing from it. Cosmetic charms touched up the worst of the misery of her eyes, at least to look at. She didn't trust herself to fix the rawness and soreness. It was far too easy to do herself an injury that way. Finally, she put her hair back up.

When she emerged again, it wasn't yet four. Thessaly sat down at the desk, pulling out a pen and a piece of black-bordered paper. Painstakingly, sentence by sentence, she asked if Vitus could come meet her tomorrow afternoon, around one. She could get away for a walk for an hour or so. She wrote out and then sketched directions to the orchard down by the river. He could get there without going near the house. She wouldn't be seen once she'd gone over the top on the hill, but she'd still be on their property, inside the warding. Finally, she said that yes, she would be grateful for a talisman, especially one of his making, and she would be glad to hear his thoughts on that. If tomorrow wasn't convenient, perhaps the day after. And then, that the funeral was the twenty-fifth, at the Council Keep, at one in the afternoon.

It was not an elegant note, or a clear one. But it was readable. It was somehow unsmudged by tears, and it said what she meant to say. It would have to do.

Just before half-seven, she pulled herself together. Thessaly checked the mirror one more time. She looked pale and worn and not good at all, but in ways in keeping with this degree of mourning. She took the letter, slipping it into Master Harris's hands as she came down the stairs. "Just the one to go out tonight, thank you. I'll have some more in the morning."

Mama came out of the parlour a moment later, and Thessaly turned to her. "I have a dreadful headache, Mama. I'll retire and take a potion as soon as we're done with supper."

Mama fussed about timing for the dressmaker, and whether what they had planned for Hermia was suitable. Thessaly didn't have to do anything but nod and ask a question or two until Father came out of his office, and they went in to supper. The meal itself was quiet. Mama and Father largely talked about various correspondence they'd received.

The only comment about Thessaly's was Mama's. "Did you have a letter from Childeric, dear?"

"Yes, Mama. A brief one, he said he wouldn't be able to call. There was something needing his attention. That he'd be at the funeral."

In any ordinary time, Mama would have scrutinised the

text of Childeric's note and whatever his parents had sent, word for word, pen stroke for pen stroke. Today, she just nodded, visibly tired herself. "Indeed."

As soon as she could, Thessaly made her excuses, handed her dress over to her maid, and collapsed into bed. She took her potion - her temples were pounding, now impossible to ignore. She lay there in the dark for what felt like ages, before finally drifting off, her head in an awkward position, mostly under a pillow.

CHAPTER 30

JUNE 23RD NEAR THESSALY'S HOME

Vitus spent the morning at Niobe's, doing the rest of the stone sorting. Niobe had kept watching him, not in annoyance but as if she were puzzling out the inscriptions best for an unusual stone. She also kept him in tea, while her own morning went to finishing up the accounting for the quarter, due tomorrow. He knew she was a touch worried about him without her saying a word.

And to be honest, he was a touch worried about himself. It wasn't like him to be this unfocused, to have all his thoughts cascading one way or another. Thessaly had sent back a note by return post. It must have been, asking him to meet her at one that afternoon. She'd included directions from a portal he didn't know along a walking path to an orchard, and instructions to wait until she let him in through the gate. He could do that.

More to the point, he would. Vitus had packed this morning with that in mind, a blanket that folded up small and tidy. He'd picked up a couple of bottles of lemonade coming through Trellech on his way to the workshop, and he intended to stop by one of the cafes for something to nibble on. Of course, Thessaly might not have much appetite. But perhaps she might, if it wasn't in the middle of whatever her family was doing. And the cakes would keep, if she didn't.

At noon, he ducked out, leaving Niobe with her lunch, and headed for Portal Square by way of his favourite of the Trellech bakeries. Half an hour later, he was through the portal in good time, coming out along a country road with several branching, smaller roads radiating out. There was a path, just as described, circling down around what looked like a small shop and portal post drop. Vitus made every appearance of being someone out for a walk in a new spot.

It was perhaps a mile and a half to where the path curved against a gate to an orchard. It was June, of course, so the apple blossoms were well and truly gone for the season, but there were small apples forming on the trees. He didn't have to wait long, maybe five minutes, before there was someone coming down the path from higher on the hill, inside the fencing. Vitus stepped nearer the gate, where he'd be more visible, while doing his best to look like he wasn't lurking if someone came along the path. Not that he'd seen anyone since he got onto it.

When she came closer, he could see she looked awful. Oh, she'd done the usual sort of charms so it didn't show as much as it might, but she was pale, her eyes were sunken, and she wasn't moving freely. The black dress she wore made her look like something out of an engraving, except for the brown hair, pulled up and away from her face, with a simple black bonnet pinned on top and a veil pulled back over it. She touched the two posts of the gate, frowning in concentration, then did a little quick pattern of taps with her fingers. He could feel the sudden shift of the warding, a space big enough for him to enter, and she opened the gate to let him in.

"Thessaly." He bowed his head slightly as she closed the gate behind him and redid the warding. Then she turned back to him, and he had to think of something else to say. "I'm so sorry. I'm sure you have many people saying that, offering to help."

Her mouth twitched. "I am glad you came." It was five words, each one dropping into the world like pebbles into a still pond, with weight and gravity, sending out ripples that would go in all directions. "I— there's a bench?"

"Wherever you'd be most comfortable. I brought a blanket to sit on, I wasn't sure what would be available." Vitus hesitated, but better to put all his resources out at first. "I've some lemonade and some little cakes. I didn't know if you might want something to eat. And a few stone samples, if you wanted to see if one felt better than the others."

"Oh." That took her by surprise. Instead of saying more, she led the way back up into the orchard, to where a remarkably ordinary bench sat, under a grove of apple trees. "No one will come down here, not today. I've an hour or two, I said I wanted fresh air, and Mama's dealing with calls that would be easier if I weren't around."

"I won't keep you longer than needed. Should I let you know when it's, what, half-two?" It was one now. That would give her time to get back to wherever the house was.

"That would be very kind. Time is not particularly easy to wield right now." She settled on the bench, smoothing her skirts out. Vitus waited a moment, until she had stopped moving, then took the other end, leaving a reasonable amount of space between them. Before he did anything else, he tapped his pocket watch to set it to chime in due course.

When he looked back at her, she was watching him, steadily. Vitus had no idea what to do with that. He focused on unpacking his satchel, the lemonade, the box of baked goods, and then the small box with a few sample stones. She reached out a hand, frowning, then pulled it back. "You thought about bringing things."

"Yes." Vitus considered the question, as he took off his gloves, finger by finger. Or rather, not the question exactly, but what it implied. "You didn't expect that?"

"It's all been terribly awkward. Everything." Her fingers twitched, and she pulled them back into her lap, burying them in a fold of her skirt. "I want to go duel something, and I can't. It's not anything I can deal with that way."

Vitus didn't have a tremendous amount of experience here. The two grandparents he'd known who had died had been at the end of well-lived lives. They'd known it was coming. And in Grandmother's case, it had been as much a kindness. She'd been in a great deal of pain sometimes. "People expect you to feel and behave a certain way. And the customs help a bit, I suppose, but they're not enough by themselves."

Thessaly was nodding her head by the time he started the second sentence. "Just like that. Which is why I'm so glad you wrote, I just needed to be..." She glanced back toward where the house must be. "I needed to be somewhere else for a bit."

"I'm glad, then, that I could come out. It's a beautiful bit of countryside." He was not actually entirely sure where he was. He hadn't had a chance to look up the portal address anywhere.

She took pity on him, and added, "Northumberland.

Not terribly far from Hadrian's Wall, not that that's entirely identifying. There's a small magical village here. We're roughly between Hexham and Carlisle, not that we go to either very often."

"With a portal, you'd go to Trellech. Or London?" Vitus suggested.

"Both. But Trellech more. Magical families and all that. The house came down from Papa's side of the family." She shrugged slightly. "It will, well." There was a slow breath. "I suppose it's a good thing I like it. I shan't be able to go out for a bit, and then only to Mistress North's and back for a long while. Not that I want to go out and be social. Of course I don't, but this is rather remote."

Again, Vitus wasn't entirely sure what to say to that. Then he had an idea. "There's a theory - it comes up in some talisman work - about a space that's protective. Where you can signal what the rules are, what would be best for you. Mourning dress does that, but so can some kinds of jewellery or, I don't know. I gather from Niobe that there was a particular fashion for indicating things with hats a decade and a half ago."

Thessaly snorted softly. "Mama did that. We have the lists somewhere, I'm sure." She glanced at him, then she was frowning a little. "Why are you so easy to talk to?" Her tone was baffled, more than accusatory, but that didn't make it easier for him to answer. After a moment, she coughed. "I'm sorry, that's unfair."

"I'm glad you think so, though." Now Vitus had to go delicately. "It seems like perhaps you could use another friend or two. I don't know if that should be me, or if you'd —" He really did not know how to finish his sentence, and now he looked away.

"That's very kind of you." A moment later, he felt her

fingers brush the top of his hand, where it was resting on the bench. She had gloves on, of course, still, though then she looked down at their hands, and cleared her throat. "I'd love to try some of the lemonade, and perhaps a cake."

"Grief is horrible for the appetite. But it won't do you any good to be faint. That just makes matters worse." It was not the sort of conversation one was supposed to have with women, but it was also true.

"You're very pragmatic, aren't you? I like that." There was a dip in her voice, quieter and a little shy now. "Thinking about a stone you could offer. Bringing something to drink and eat and a blanket. I didn't give you much to plan with."

Vitus offered a half-smile. "The word orchard is actually surprisingly informative. It made me fairly certain we might want something to sit on. Apples do stain. I'm sure there are some around on the grass from last year still, or other things that would not be kind to clothing. And yet, we cannot turn to the apples for a little sustenance, unless you grow particularly early varieties."

"Not this far north, no," Thessaly said. "Or so I understand it. I am glad you thought through it. That is what I'm trying to say. I would very much like a stone. Sleep has been — well, mostly sleep hasn't, without a potion."

"Here, how about you take a look at the stones, feel them in your hands..." Her gloves were now off. This was a good time for that. "And then I can talk about what I might do."

"I'd be glad to, I mean. Your time is worth something, surely? And the stones?" When he glanced at her face, Thessaly was flushing.

"It is my pleasure. And Niobe said she'd be glad to cover the cost of the stone. None of these are expensive, we have plenty of all of them, it's...." Vitus turned his palm up. "It's the sort of thing we do for a friend. I suppose that's different from illusion work."

"A lot of what I do is delicate, you need to do it in the right moment," Thessaly said, a little distracted. "What are the stones?"

"That one is amethyst, that one is howlite. Both are good for sleep talismans, or ease. You could wear the amethyst with your mourning dresses, in a month or two, if you preferred. And I put in a piece of jasper, but that is more associated with guilt." As he said the last word, her eyes widened, and her hand twitched. He hadn't expected that at all. He took a breath, not wanting to rush her. "You might also just have a strong feeling about one stone over the other. Hold each one, take your time with it."

CHAPTER 31
JUNE 23RD IN AN ORCHARD

Thessaly hadn't wanted to let him see her reaction when he mentioned that word. Guilt. She was still coiled around it, snappish and unwilling to admit it, while also entirely unable to stop thinking about it. Thessaly was sure he'd noticed. She was doing horribly at hiding much right now. But he didn't say anything.

When he continued to be quiet, she glanced at him, then let out a breath and reached to take one stone. The amethyst, that was the right place to start. It was beautiful, shading from darker purple, more opaque, to something lighter, giving a sheen of purple to the light as she looked through it. It was a crystal, still, and she turned it around in her hand, feeling the edges of it, before setting it down gently.

Another glance at Vitus wasn't much help. He just sat there, waiting patiently. He wasn't quite smiling - that wasn't the proper emotion for the moment, anyway. But he wasn't frowning, either. There was something straightforward about him that she found refreshing. He didn't seem to hide anything from her, or want to. That was probably wrong. Most people she knew hid things, often quite a lot of things. Childeric was a visible example right now, or rather an exceedingly distant example, given that he was down at Arundel, presumably, and she was up here in Northumbria, almost on the border of Scotland.

Thessaly set that aside, deliberately, and picked up the stone that wasn't jasper. Howlite, he'd called it. "I don't know much about howlite?" Her voice cracked on the name.

"The lore about amethyst is better known, of course. All the stories about Dionysus, the uses against drunkenness or, in some tales, poison." Vitus's voice was clear and quiet. "Howlite forms in nodules. They were first named thirty years ago, in 1868, from a vein found in Canada. Magically, in terms of materia, it's good for focusing the mind. Meditation, turning inwards, if that's a tradition you favour, or calming and soothing, releasing tension. It looks a bit like turquoise in the veining and how it polishes, and it takes dyes well, for people who like that sort of thing. It's a good one to use as a worry stone."

Thessaly nodded, turning the piece over in her hand. It fit nicely in her palm, a cool curve that nestled in. But what she needed, perhaps, wasn't cooling, it was something else. Aunt Metaia would have advised something with a bit of spice, and that made her breath catch again.

Vitus did not comment on it, he just let the silence be, until Thessaly had to say something. "I was thinking cooling isn't what I need. And that Aunt Metaia would have recommended something with a bit of spice. She liked a curry or a bit of ginger cake for the purpose."

Now she was watching him, and he blinked once, then just nodded. "Those are the important things to remember, I think. The little moments, the good advice. It is good advice. I'm afraid the scones I brought along are berry, though."

Thessaly nodded once, then she considered him. "Have you lost someone you care about? You seem to have a much better idea of what not to say than many people. Given a somewhat small sample of examples right now."

"I'm glad I'm not saying the awful things," Vitus said. "Two of my grandparents." He hesitated, as if the next thing was more important. It was the sort of adjustment that in a duel would have told her a new approach was coming and possibly a new vulnerability to explore. "My mother's been quietly ill for a long time. I've thought, on and off, about what, what I'd need to be prepared for, if things got worse."

"Oh." That wasn't a thing she'd ever worried about, not with either of her parents. Or with Aunt Metaia, and well, that hadn't turned out that way. "Does it help?"

"If it means I'm not saying the foolish hurtful things to you now, then yes." Then he ducked his chin. "Would you hold the jasper, see what you think about it?"

Thessaly eyed it warily, but she'd tried the other two, and it wasn't as if Vitus didn't know she'd reacted. This one was a smooth, rounded piece. "A cabochon, yes? Is that also what you call it? I know the terms for jewellery." She didn't quite add 'of course' on there, but it was something women of her background and class learned in the nursery. How else could she evaluate what everyone was wearing, or an offered gift or token?

"Still a cabochon," Vitus agreed. "That's red jasper. Nothing terribly fancy, as stones go, but it is insistently itself."

She considered that, curling her fingers around it to enclose it fully, then opening her palm so she could cup both hands around it, the stone pressed between her palms. It felt good, deep down, in a way she hadn't at all expected. She felt it, for one thing, not that core of ice and guilt and solid misery. Not that everything was all better. No stone could do that. No talisman either, she knew that. But it was hopeful.

"This one, please." She didn't want to give it back, actually. She kept her fingers curled around it.

"Hold it for a little, if you like. Or..." He considered, doing some mental calculations. "You can keep that, and I'll make a talisman out of another piece. Would that help?"

Her fingers tightened around it, before she could even decide, her body acting for her like responding to an exchange in the duelling salle. That was a trained response, though, and this was something entirely instinctive. "Please. That's very kind." Thessaly swallowed, trying to figure out how to explain what she felt. She owed him that much, she felt, he was being so thoughtful and generous. "It makes me feel a bit hopeful. Like there's something on the other end of what I'm feeling now."

She couldn't look up at him, just down at her hands. There was a silence and a pause, then his fingers reached out to touch hers, lightly, just resting, as if he were ready to pull away at any moment. "I'm glad." She liked the sound of his voice, too. It was soothing, like the stone was. Warm like the stone was, too. "There's a bit of fire in that, red jasper has a lot of iron, and it's associated with Mars. Maybe that's the right amount of warmth for right now." There wasn't any pressure there, and that was something miraculous and wonderful.

Thessaly didn't want to move, and so she kept her hands right there, afraid any twitch would make him move as well. "How did you know it might help?"

"I wasn't sure? But when Niobe and I were talking about it, I wondered. And this morning, I trusted my instincts. Trained instinct, about what might suit." He shrugged. She felt the way his fingers moved. "Is this all right?"

"I like the way your hand feels." That suddenly seemed like the most intimate thing a person could say to someone else. She closed her eyes, concentrating on the sensations. "I do feel guilty. I've been wondering if something I said led to something Aunt Metaia did, and that meant..." She couldn't finish that sentence.

"That must be an immense challenge. Challenges, also for Mars. I'm sure you know that as well as I do." Still, his voice was gentle, just weaving along through the words he was choosing, nothing sharp even when he was saying difficult things. "Is it something you're going to solve right now?"

"Something I can't solve right now. Not for a while or ever, maybe." Putting words to that made her feel a bit better, even just naming that she might never know. "I suppose it depends on the investigation. And I heard they were busy with something else." His fingers shifted a little on her hand, and she looked up, frowning. He winced. She saw that. "Is something the matter?"

"The other case." Vitus considered, and now he turned his hand a little, enough she could slip her fingers into it. She shouldn't, but she did. There was no one here to see, for one thing, and it felt good, and she desperately wanted something that felt good right now. Not something that felt like an impossible chasm or even the ordinary itchiness and discomfort of mourning dress. Vitus let her. He didn't pull away. "Philip Landry was found dead in his flat. Two days ago, the evening of the twenty-first."

"Oh." Thessaly tried to figure that out. "We hadn't heard. How awful. And for his mother and his brother. His mother's, um..."

"Terrifyingly sharp?" Vitus said it with a little bit of humour. "Yes. I consulted with Philip a couple of weeks ago, and he was helpful. Kind, like you say I'm being kind. Not going terribly out of his way. It was easy for him, I think, but it made a difference to me. And now..." He cleared his throat. "Do you know the Landrys well?"

"Alexander and Philip, more than their mother. She is, as you say, terrifyingly sharp. And not very interested in things I'm interested in. Above all that? No, above is the wrong word. Beyond that. Not worth her time, which is entirely fair, honestly. But Philip is - was - an excellent duellist, and Alexander was coming along very well. Skilled by Schola standards, and improving every time."

"And you, then." Vitus hesitated. "You know, I don't know how to ask how good you are in the scheme of things. I've seen your illusion work, but not your duels."

It made her smile, or at least her lips gestured in that direction for what felt like the first time in months. Even if it had only been days, even countable hours. "Ranked in the first tier, the sort of thing where it depends who is at their best on a given day. Or location." She shrugged. "I've the advantage that we have no salle here. I'm used to duelling in a dozen different places. Other people have the advantage of their home salle. I've never been able to rely on that."

He tilted his head. "That's an interesting way to think about it. Adaptable to the situation, then. That seems useful. And with your illusion work, as well. Is that a linked skill?"

Thessaly considered that. It was, in a nutshell, the sort

of conversation she'd had a lot with Aunt Metaia and not very often with anyone else. Whatever this was, whoever Vitus was, she felt that way with him, comfortable with him, far beyond any sensible reason. And yet, the thing Aunt Metaia had urged her to do was trust that sort of feeling, whether it was in conversation, in magic, or in duelling. Not that they weren't the same thing sometimes.

"The adaptability to the moment, possibly." She gestured with her free hand, the stone held against her palm with her thumb. "Home is - it's a perfectly reasonable house, but it doesn't have deep roots. Mama and Papa were given it when they married. It hadn't been in the family that long. There are things I love about it, but..." Her fingers clenched a little against his. "Aunt Metaia's, that I'm going to miss a great deal. Besides missing her. Both. Separately and together."

CHAPTER 32

JUNE 23RD IN AN ORCHARD

Vitus kept finding himself not sure what to say, and having to trust that he wouldn't foul this up. He looked down at his hand, their hands, where his hand was resting on hers. "That must be terribly hard. My grandfather set up the house I live in, I'd have a terribly hard time leaving it. I will someday, probably, it's not big enough to marry and raise a family of my own. But not to go back, for a visit, Sunday dinner, whatever that looks like, that would hurt."

Thessaly looked up at him, and then just nodded once. "And that's different, for both of us, than somewhere like Arundel, where it's passed down generation to generation, in a specific way. Bryn Glas will go back to someone in the Powell line. I don't know who. But they probably will change the decoration, the garden, all of that. A lot of what I love about it."

"They have definitely not done much with the decoration at Arundel in a generation or two." Vitus said, offering it as a bit of amusement.

She smiled, so it had been a decent choice. "No.

Childeric says..." Then she swallowed. "Do you want me to continue that sentence?"

Vitus wasn't sure how to answer that again. He squeezed her fingers while he was thinking, hoping to reassure that he wasn't upset, while he worked through a little of it in his head. Then he gave up and cleared his throat. "I'd like to talk it out with you, if you don't mind. Now, sometime later, whatever you'd prefer."

Her other shoulder shrugged. "Now is as good a time as any, I suppose?"

Of course, that meant he had to figure out what to say. "I don't want to do something that would upset the Fortiers. I can't afford to, on any level. My father's the man of business of a number of their client families and associated families, for one thing, and I need to establish myself. They're not particularly interested in helping me - my style of work doesn't suit what they usually commission." That was a genteel circumlocution that did what was needed. He'd have to remember that. "But I can't afford to go against them. And I don't know what that means with you, or with Childeric, or what someone might be offended by." He didn't name the elder Fortiers. He didn't need to.

Thessaly considered that, chewing on her lip, though she also squeezed his hand back while she thought. He liked that. "Our agreement, the formal agreement, the one with oaths and signatures, is for marriage, for suitable public support, both ways around. Two children, preferably at least one boy, but I am not committed beyond the attempt. A standard sort of agreement there. Either of us might have other lovers, with discretion. And with suitable contraceptive charms, on both parts - the, what's the word? Not penalty?" She looked up at him.

"Consequences? Contractual obligations?" Vitus offered the two options cautiously.

"Contractual obligations will do." It wasn't what she had been thinking, but she went on. "Those. They're the same in both cases - the child adopted out or otherwise separate from the family concerns, whatever makes sense. Not in the line of succession for either family." She grimaced. "It doesn't seem kind, but I hope it won't be relevant, you know? The charms and potions are very effective these days. Beyond that, discretion. Nothing public, nothing that causes undue gossip. Again, also the usual sort of thing."

"So a dance in public is fine, a conversation. And that - meeting like this, that is also fine?" Vitus felt that was the place to begin.

"This is also fine. A conversation in a library, a bookstore, being seen at a duelling salle - not that you duel, that would actually be suggestive. A lecture or a concert, then, say. Or whatever in private, when no one can observe. I am..." She swallowed and looked away. "Constrained, at the moment. And also I don't want to do any of those things. They feel far too raw. I want to duel, but not be seen doing it."

"And the conversation here?" Vitus felt he needed to clarify this point. Or maybe he needed to hear her say what she wanted, there. "Or in the coming days? I would be glad to arrange to meet you, here or somewhere else, if you would like that. Only if you would. I don't want to be a bother."

"You are not a bother. You are very kind." She hesitated. She said nothing further.

After a long moment, a silence that went on, Vitus murmured, "At the least, it would be good to know how to get you the talisman when it is finished. A few days, maybe a week, depending on other work. It's not that it will take that long, it's that there are pauses between several steps."

"Sometime." She swallowed. "Sometime would you tell me about the process, about your work? How a piece goes together?" Thessaly looked up at him, and then she suddenly yawned. "I'm sorry, I'm so tired. But yes, come out and give it to me. Probably here, it's the safest place. Send a note when you're ready?"

"Your family won't worry?" That was the other thing. He didn't much want the Powells, or the Lyttons, or the Lytton-Powells for that matter, annoyed with him either.

"Oh, probably not. Mama's, I don't know. Distracted. If you'd rather, drop it at the Fox's Den and they'll forward it."

Vitus nodded. The clubs were useful that way. "I'll think about it." He considered. "And Childeric? Will he be bothered if he knows you're talking to someone else? Privately?"

"Oh, he might make a bit of a fuss if he notices. But that would involve him noticing. Besides, I'm fairly sure he's got his own pleasures on the side." Thessaly focused her attention on Vitus. "It feels horrible to say, but I'm sort of glad. I mean, I'm sure it will be fine, the necessary parts. He's good at picking up skills when he actually cares about them."

Vitus rather thought that Childeric was the sort who would pick up the skills about his pleasure, and not necessarily about his partner's. But that was certainly not something he was going to say at the moment. Then he nodded. "So. To sum up, you would like to continue to see me. Now is not the time for anything further, beyond this." He moved his fingers slightly. "But you would not object if, down the road, we both found that worth exploring more? Only if and when you're ready, of course."

She flushed. It was more visible with how pale she was.

"That. I'm glad you aren't pressing. I gather some people do."

Vitus snorted. He couldn't help himself. "It seems a poor way to begin what I hope will be a long friendship, perhaps more in time. And besides, we've already established you're the far better duellist, I wouldn't dare take liberties." Then he glanced at the bench behind her, considering. It wouldn't be terribly comfortable in that dress and that corset, but he could offer something now. "I do have that blanket, if you'd like to use it for a pillow. You could rest your eyes, at least."

Thessaly blinked at him. Then she did smile, like a rock cracking open and water pouring out, a myth of coming forth. "Oh. I would like that very much. If you're willing. Rather boring for you, though."

"I also brought a book. I packed exceedingly thoughtfully, as you have seen." That got him a squeeze of his hand, and then she moved to kiss him on the cheek, once, gently.

"You are kind, thoughtful." Her breath caught. "Please. A nap sounds like the best thing in the world, or whatever rest there might be." Vitus twisted to gather up the blanket and hand it over, as well as fishing out his book. Thessaly ended up tilted, using the arm of the bench as the framework for the pillow. She had folded the blanket to make it comfortable, and her hands curled up loosely against her chest. One of them still held the piece of jasper. She had refused to let it go or to put it away. It wasn't terribly comfortable, he suspected. Her spine was held straight by the corset and cut of the dress. But within a couple of minutes he could hear her breathing change, and he was sure she was sleeping.

He checked the time on his watch, and she had most of an hour left. Vitus opened his book, but he did not read much. He certainly didn't retain any of it. Instead, he alternated between watching her and thinking about what she'd said. He had in front of him direct evidence that she felt safe enough with him. Safe to fall asleep, safe to be honest, he thought, in several directions.

Vitus wanted more of that. For all she was a duellist, for all she was of Fox House, and the sort of sharply talented family that could take care of themselves, she trusted him to watch over her. Now, it wasn't likely there would be much risk in an apple orchard inside her family's warding. He still liked that trust, and he liked that she'd answered his questions.

And he also liked the answers. Of course, there were things he could not have with her. Not marriage, not children. He himself - as Mama kept reminding him - would need to marry sooner than later. It was a way to establish himself as fundamentally respectable and a reliable pillar of the community. But given that there was no one he was interested in, that could come in its own time.

It wasn't even that Thessaly had promised anything in specific - of course she hadn't, and of course he wouldn't press her. Or even ask about it. Not until she was out of mourning, until she smiled more freely again, until she wanted it. If she ever wanted it. In the meantime, he would bask in her friendship and in her inquisitive nature. And he'd look forward to the prospect of more conversations about magic and theory and what to do with it that made a difference in the world.

And perhaps he'd have a long conversation with Niobe about what sorts of things he might read up on that Thessaly would be interested in talking about in due course. More about stones, that was easy. She'd seemed rather interested in the variations, the way they worked in practice. He could certainly learn more about illusion work, and she might recommend some places to start in a few weeks. More about the materia that went into the salle protections, some of that was crushed stones, he knew that much.

His fingers came up to touch where she'd kissed. It had been fleeting, the kind of kiss he gave to his mother, or that he'd given to Grandmother. The kiss had been affectionate, fond. It didn't necessarily mean anything beyond that. But he'd be remembering it. He knew that. Vitus let out a little sigh. He had to keep a grip on himself. For his own sake, and for hers. He couldn't assume, even if at least he knew a bit more about the boundaries now.

In due course, the chime on his watch sounded a little imitation of a bird call. He cleared his throat. "Thessaly? Time to wake up." She stirred a little, but didn't wake, and he considered. Then he leaned over to touch her shoulder, her upper arm, just enough to move her. "Thessaly? It's half two. You needed to get back."

That got her blinking, rubbing her face, then pushing herself upright. She almost dropped the stone, then closed her fingers around it. "Did I sleep the entire time? I'm sorry, you must be so bored."

"It was a pleasure to keep an eye out. You obviously needed the rest. But you'd said you didn't want to be out here too long. Let me pack up. I assume you need to let me out of the warding, too." He then considered. "If I needed to leave something for you, would it be safe to leave it just outside the fence here? Tucked out of the way?"

"If I knew to come look for it." She was still a little muzzy from sleep, and she rubbed her face again. "A note to tell me to come look for it if we can't meet up." Then she reached for his hand, fingers curling under his palm. "I'd rather see you, though. If we can."

"If we can. I'd like that too, very much." There was nothing else he could say to that, so he didn't, just held her fingers for a long moment before he moved to pack up his things. "I should take the cakes?"

"I'm sorry I didn't try them. Or can I have one to eat on the way back?"

He handed it over and packed up the rest. She stood, brushing out her skirts, then went to the gate ahead of him, to let him out. When he was through the gate, she looked him over one last time. "Thank you." Just the two words. Then she closed the gate and turned and walked away.

CHAPTER 33

June 23rd

In the middle of the night

"Thess?" Thessaly had half-heard a noise, waking enough out of sleep to shove the jasper under the corner of her pillow. She did not know what time it was, besides still dark. She'd been asleep for a fair bit, more asleep than previous nights. There'd been some sound before her name, she was fairly sure of that.

"Mm, who?" Only as soon as she said it, she knew who it had to be. Who would call her that? "Hermia?"

The door cracked open - she could just see the edge of it crack open, a shadow against shadows in the waning moonlight. "Can I sleep with you? I woke up and..."

Thessaly hesitated. It wouldn't help her sleep, but she also would not leave her sister on her own, not like that. When she talked to Vitus next, she didn't want to admit she'd done that. She pushed herself upright, slipping the jasper into a small bowl on her bedside table. "Come, yes." That meant wiggling over to one side of the bed, making sure the sheet and light blanket weren't too tangled.

"I left a note." It wasn't like Hermia hadn't done this before, though not for a year or two. It had started when she'd read some of the historical stories about sisters sharing a bed, and wanting that closeness, instead of the way they were often so separate. Fitchley, her governess, tolerated it - she had a younger sister herself - and Thessaly was fairly sure that Mama and Father didn't actually know. They didn't care much about what went on in Thessaly's rooms or in the nursery, as long as they didn't cause trouble or disrupt anything.

There were quick steps across the floor, Hermia pausing to remove her slippers, her hair in a braid down her back and smoothed back by the nightcap. It was one of Thessaly's hand-me-downs, still good enough to be worn, but the lace had been mended twice. Then Hermia was in the bed, tucking her feet under the sheets and cuddling up close to Thessaly. Thessaly settled on her back, her sister's head on her shoulder.

"Sorry I woke you. Were you sleeping?" Hermia's breath tickled a little.

"I was. It's all right. I—" Thessaly's voice caught for a second. "I'm glad you came." She was, too. She was glad her sister trusted her to be there. Only, in a few months, next spring, she wouldn't be. She'd be in rooms in Arundel, away from her sister, away from her family, living by a different set of rules and assumptions. She might well have her own bedroom - she was fairly sure the Fortiers tended that way, though of course it wasn't a thing anyone could ask about. Mama and Father did, though their rooms adjoined, with a door between them. "Did you have a nightmare, or just couldn't sleep?"

Hermia was quiet for a long moment. "Both?" She

sounded uncertain at first. Then, with more confidence, she repeated it. “Both.”

“Do you want to talk about it?” Thessaly wasn’t entirely sure what to say, but saying something mattered. Vitus had done that for her today. It had left her with enough ability to cope to pass it on.

Hermia shrugged once, then she asked, “Are Mama and Father fighting with each other?” She’d had supper with them - it had just been the family.

“Neither of them has talked to me about it.” But Thessaly had eyes and all sorts of other modes of perception. “Yes. I don’t know what about, though.” Not that Thessaly didn’t have a few guesses.

“But you know more than I do.” Hermia shifted, and that was a little more comfortable. “What do you know?”

Thessaly considered where to start. Not that all of this was new to Hermia. But their parents had kept Hermia out of most of the more detailed discussions about the betrothal and everything that led up to it. Her situation would be different, in several ways. “Did Mama tell you much about how they went about planning for me?”

“No. And I was younger then.” Hermia sounded bemused. “She said time for that later. I’m not old enough to go to that sort of party yet. Tell me?”

No one had actually explained all of it to Thessaly, though Mama had outlined a fair bit. “You know that when Mama and Papa married, there were all sorts of negotiations for how that worked. The relevant inheritances, and so on.”

“Mmhmm. And that’s why we’re the Lytton-Powells, not the Lyttons, because Mama’s agreements were partly about the name.” Hermia’s voice got more uncertain. “And money?”

"And a bit about money. Grandfather Powell gave Mama a dowry, and when it was clear Aunt Metaia would not marry, he gave her the same. Toward materials, I think. And then when he died, things were split." Thessaly frowned. "Unevenly, I know that much, but I don't know the details. Because Mama had us."

"That's both fair and unfair, isn't it?" Hermia said. "And Father?"

"And Father's family had expectations. How things are done. What Father's expected to excel in and do. If either of us had been a boy, we'd have had different training. Illusion work, that's good for a woman marrying well. There are all sorts of social things where it comes in handy, especially when it's clothing and decorations, rather than lasting impressions, like Aunt Metaia."

Thessaly let her eyes close. It wasn't like she was seeing much in the dark. "But there's, I don't know how to put this. We have money, we're comfortable. A big house, with more than enough staff. Maybe not as many new dresses and gowns as we'd like, but quite a few. But we're not wealthy. Not all the jewels or magical treasures or whatever, like the Fortiers. Or the senior line of the Powells, or the Lyttons. And not..." This was the first time Thessaly had said this out loud. "Not a lot of stability, either, maybe. I'm not sure why."

"And no land magic, either. And being on the Council, like Aunt Metaia - and Cousin Owain - is power, but it's a particular kind, and it's not, um. What's the word?" Hermia did at least sound like she was following.

"Generational. Not really, no, though often families have people on the Council in succession. Quintessence Percival's grandmother, I think. Or maybe aunt, much older aunt?" Thessaly couldn't quite remember, and she certainly wasn't going to go look it up.

"So what does it mean for Mama and Father now?" Hermia was keeping up, that was the sensible next question.

"It means the balance of power between the families has changed. Um, think of it like a hand of cards. One card is out of play, so you have to look for other ways to make a hand that does better. Father's getting some pressure from his family, but I don't know about what. You know he won't tell us until he thinks it's time." If he ever did, not that Thessaly would say that right now.

Hermia nodded, her cheek rubbing against Thessaly's nightgown. "What was he like when he told you about the arrangements? When did he tell you, I mean, compared to when anyone knew?"

That was a good question, and one Thessaly had both been wanting to think about and avoiding, the more so since this afternoon. "On a practical level, it's a limited pool of people Mama and Father would consider as an ideal choice, in family terms. Of excellent family, ideally at step or more in power and influence up from where we are. And some of those people were already promised - Ignatius Knapton, say. Or people Father didn't want to align with, like Temenos Sibley or Gerold Teague, not that he's Heir. A couple no one was sure about - just not up to expectations."

"Mmm." Hermia wriggled a bit more into place. "And what sort of status mattered?"

"The peak of that is someone who's Heir now, or maybe a young and unmarried Lord. Or Lady, but it's not as if I could marry Genevieve Donovan and have children with her. Marrying a Council Member would be second best, but most of them are too much older and also too married.

Father put out some feelers about Romulus Heath, not long after he challenged, but I gather there were already arrangements in progress with Helica."

Romulus Heath was the youngest of the current Council, six years older than Thessaly, though Hestia Palgrave had been the most recent challenge, the year after Romulus. Romulus was a decent enough sort, if obsessed with alchemy and its implications for illusion work. With the benefit of hindsight and Childeric's recent behaviour, Thessaly was beginning to think that Helica had got by far the better partner out of it. They certainly seemed happy enough, with two young children at home, and Helica now free to focus on her own interests.

Hermia giggled a little. "Helica Heath is not the best name."

"That is the problem with marrying." Though Thessaly Fortier actually sounded well enough, even if it wasn't in keeping with the Fortier's preference for archaic, preferably Merovingian, French names. It sounded well enough in French, though, which was a start.

"Did Father ask you about that when he was considering it?" Hermia got back to the topic at hand.

"When he started, he asked if there was anyone I would prefer to avoid, knowing what I knew of them at Schola and otherwise. Romulus - we've chatted at some of the discussions for illusionists, but you know how we all hoard our secrets and particular practices." She shrugged, the shoulder Hermia wasn't using as a pillow. "There were a couple I asked him not to consider. People who have reputations as a rake, in the careless sort of way, or where I knew they'd refuse some of what I wanted."

"Like what?" Hermia's voice was softer now.

"At least a couple would want me to give up duelling.

Devote myself strictly to the interests of the family, even though duelling is - within sensible bounds - generally excellent for health and for magical capability." Thessaly hesitated. "It's not that Childeric and I are a grand love match. But I thought we could make a partnership of it, well enough."

The verb tense was telling, and for a second or two, she thought Hermia would miss the implications. Then, no, there was the voice by her ear. "Thought?"

The problem with her sister was that her sister was also very clever, in her own ways. Thessaly let out a breath. "I don't know what I think right now. He sent the oddest note, saying he was sorry about Aunt Metaia, but also very busy, he couldn't call. All the Fortiers are like that, I guess, but Mama does not know why, and it's not like we can ask." It occurred to her that maybe Vitus might hear more information than Thessaly had - if not immediately, in the coming days or even weeks. Though the Fortiers would be at the funeral. Childeric had said so. And if they weren't there, it would look awful in public.

"Mmph." Hermia sounded disgruntled. "That's not right. I mean, you and he get along, well enough?"

Thessaly nodded. "We have been. And back when we were making the arrangements, he was delightful. He took me out to supper quite a few times, we went to more parties. Childeric was charming. He paid attention to what I liked. Some of it was a lot of fun." She swallowed. "I liked people looking at us, wanting to be us, more than a little. And now, I don't know what changed. I mean, I don't know what I did wrong. If I did something wrong." That had been haunting her, more and more so.

Hermia moved, her breath now right on Thessaly's face. "You didn't. I know you didn't." It was said with all the absurd confidence of a sister who had trust in her, even if it was also one who couldn't possibly know the answer to that.

"Hermia, it's..." Thessaly let out a long breath. "It's complicated. All tangled up, like your embroidery floss was, last month after your teacher's cat got into it." It had taken three different sessions in strong light and four hands to untangle it all. "He's certainly acting like I did something wrong. Or something not right enough. And it's not the sort of thing I can ask Mama or Father about."

"No." Hermia settled down on her shoulder again. "They'd think you had done something. Only you don't. You're very precise about what you do. Out in public. It's why I watch what you do, and not Mama."

That was a fascinating image, because Thessaly looked to Mama, assumed Mama had it perfect. Aunt Metaia had always done what she thought best, which was decidedly not always the most proper choice by etiquette. "I don't have to solve it right now, probably. After all, if it got that far, Lord Fortier would talk to Father, and Father would talk to me, and I don't know. I wouldn't like it much, probably, but I'd know what I needed to do differently."

"Wouldn't enjoy being told, or wouldn't enjoy doing whatever it was?" Hermia asked. "And is Father going to arrange something like that for me?"

"Both. Probably both." Thessaly let out a breath. "The thing about me marrying well, sweet, is that it gives you more options. Less pressure to do it yourself. If you met someone you really liked, when you're properly out in society, you'd have more choices, so long as they were respectable." A talisman maker of good background, but not aristocratic, just for example, not that Thessaly would ever say that out loud.

"Oh." Hermia nestled in again, and there was a long silence. Just before Thessaly was certain her sister had fallen asleep, there was a whisper. "I don't want you to be miserable for that."

Thessaly had absolutely no answer to that, other than pretending she'd fallen asleep.

CHAPTER 34

JUNE 24TH

On Monday, Vitus spent the morning in Niobe's workshop before she shooed him out to do other useful things. He'd originally intended to go to the Faire, but he wasn't remotely in the mood. Instead, he went by the haberdasher his father swore by, to pick up a new tie and pocket square. He had a black suit, suitable for funerals, of course, but only one properly sombre tie. Two would be better, since there would be some people at both, almost certainly.

From there, he went off to the Four Metals house, arriving on the late side of the lunch hour. As he'd expected, there weren't many people there. Most would either be tending to whatever their business was, or out at the Faire. He settled down in the conversation room to read through the paper and a few other minor publications, and also to see who happened by.

He'd been there perhaps twenty minutes when someone went by him, past him, then stopped and backed up. "Just the man I remembered I wanted to talk to." It was

Merryn Penforth, looking particularly sharply dressed. "Do you have a minute, Vitus?"

Vitus had been to three evening gatherings, including that first one she'd invited him to. As she'd said, the topics weren't always to his particular interest, but the discussions around them were. He nodded, setting the paper aside. "Of course. Here or somewhere else?"

"One of the private rooms, if you don't mind. It won't be long, but there's a possible commission." And that, yes, he'd want to learn about without everyone listening over his shoulder, for all sorts of reasons. Vitus got up, slotting the paper back in place neatly, and followed Merryn down the hall. The layout was both like the Stream and not. There were no sleeping rooms upstairs, like the House clubs had for people who needed to spend a night in Trellech in a reliable spot.

Instead, this floor had a variety of meeting rooms, with the kitchen and staff rooms in the basement. The first and second floors held a variety of workshop spaces with smaller tools and materials. Four Metals as a society had a country estate, convenient to a portal, and that was where all the larger or more complex workshops were; the forge, the kiln, the carpentry shop, and several buildings Vitus had never ventured into.

The private room Merryn chose was small, but the decorative woodwork was pleasing. The walls were a shade of deep blue that Vitus found restful, and the two easy chairs were comfortable. She went in first, and Vitus flipped the sign by the door to show it was occupied, closing the door behind him. Merryn settled in the chair facing the door, and Vitus took the other. Then he waited. She had all the relevant information; he did not.

What Merryn did was look at him, her head cocked

slightly. "Two things, in fact. First, are you intending to be at Magistra Powell's funeral tomorrow?" She held up her fingers. "I gather you spoke with her briefly at the Council rites, and with her niece a little longer."

Vitus blinked. "You are well-informed." He nodded. "I was planning on it, yes." Someone from Fox House would dissemble here, and he couldn't bring himself to do it. Besides, it would be obvious tomorrow that he was there. Keeping it secret now didn't seem worthwhile. "May I ask why?"

"She was one of our own." Merryn's voice was a little clipped. It was the sort of tone that made Vitus sure this loss was personal to her, if not nearly as much as to Thessaly. "You know our customs?"

Vitus inclined his head. "I've not, in the past, but yes." It was the custom of the Four Metals to craft a chain, a link for each person mourning the death. They were made of hammered metal and left on the grave by someone with access, buried in the top layer of soil. "After the service?"

"At the country house, yes, in the metal shop. If you can bring your own gloves and such, that would be a help, but we'll have spares handy." Merryn considered him. "May I ask how well you knew her?"

"Not nearly as well as I suspect you did." Vitus inclined his head. "I'm sorry for your loss. I met her niece - Thessaly, the older of the Lytton-Powell daughters - at the St George's Day gala. And we've talked several times since. She was intrigued by the illusion challenges of lapis lazuli, and she had some questions for me about some of my work." There, that was neutral enough, though he suspected some of his emotion showed through somewhere. It certainly felt like it was all on display. And even more so once he remembered yesterday.

"Ah." Merryn's voice was suddenly very neutral. "I don't know Mistress Lytton-Powell well, but I know nothing against her. She's a braver woman than I am, making the marriage choices she has."

Vitus held still at that, and he was sure that showed as well. Then he took a breath, considered his options, and went for honesty, given he couldn't hide all his feelings. "We're on the way to being friends. I think she might rather need them."

Merryn gave him a sharp look. "I expect you're right." Her voice started neutral, but then she shook her head, as if shaking something off. "We would be glad to have you then, and you'd be welcome to tell her niece about our custom in due course, if you thought it the right thing."

"I appreciate that." Vitus hesitated. "May I ask whether you're the one arranging it, or just the one who spotted me?"

"I am the one who is helping arrange matters, but I also suggested you be invited. How's that?" She spread her hands, palms up. "We are still getting to know you again. Travel changes a man - and a woman - as I know myself." Her mouth quirked up. "I came back from a Grand Tour of my own. I promptly refused to marry the man my parents had in mind for me. Then I went sideways into an entirely different line of apprenticeship. I didn't know Metaia at school, but she was helpful in sorting out the apprenticeship, and by the time I finished, she was on the Council."

"Ah." Vitus considered that. "That would make a strong connection, that kind of help. And I gather she was generous with that, helping people find where they might do best."

Merryn's eyes gleamed for a moment. "A great loss, for many people. She kept the Four Metals part rather private.

She felt she could do more from the shadows. And she did like her illusions and tricking the eye. The sort who preferred to be underestimated." Merryn tapped her fingers on the arm of her chair. "She was supposed to be meeting Thirza. You've seen more of her, I think?"

"I have." Thirza Remmerton was an acclaimed crafter of pigments. There was some overlap between their arts, or at least the raw materia for them. And stones that weren't suited for talisman work could profitably go to pigment work. She wasn't a colourman - or colourwoman - making up inks, but instead crafted materials for artists and for magical use. "Ah." He now saw how the invitation must have gone, if Thirza had any idea of the connection. "That must have been terribly hard for her, as well."

"You're very thoughtful. We do like that, on the whole, you'll have a chance to say so tomorrow. She's taken it hard. They were close friends, comfortable friends, no masks, no illusions. Those are too rare a thing in the world." Then Merryn shifted, almost shaking out invisible feathers into something tidier. "The other question - or did you have anything else first?"

Vitus considered. "I also intend to attend Philip Landry's funeral." She'd been the one to suggest the introduction. He'd thanked her for it already. "I know the circumstances are mysterious - I was just reading the paper about that. But I know them, through the Fortier connections, and Philip was kind to me. And I feel for his brother."

"Ah." Now Merryn tapped her fingertips together, a little fidget, unlike her. "No one's seen any of the Fortiers outside their estates, I gather. Not since Solstice. And no one's sure why. I won't ask you to pass on information. I don't move in those circles, but I know enough of the risks. And no one's ever been sure what to make of the Landrys, though I agree Philip could be quite congenial in the right circumstance. Always that sense of distance, but congenial and willing to share in the ordinary line of things. If you notice anything unusual at the funeral you feel you can share, I'd like to know. There have been some odd orders for materia, as well, and we're not sure why."

Vitus considered this, the implications of the request. "You are one of the people keeping an eye on the Four Metals, then." It was a secret society at root, a collaboration of people bound by mutual interest and creativity as much as any oath. Leadership, such as it was, rotated, but the way it did was mysterious. There was a rota of people who made sure materials were reordered for the workshops, tended to any requests for the building, and resolved the rare interpersonal problem.

But mostly, events of the Four Metals were self-selecting. People went to the ones that interested them and ignored the ones that didn't. Vitus found it decidedly restful, more than the Stream, where everyone seemed to want to drag anyone nearby into their latest interest or idea. On the other hand, people had to keep things running, and that meant a few people coordinating.

Merryn snorted. "Guilty as charged. One of seven, as we usually do it, I have been this year. Keeping an eye on our more liminal members - people beginning or finishing apprenticeships - is one of my particular duties, though I'd have invited you along to supper, anyway. You're reasonable to talk to, you don't hoard your knowledge, and you're not afraid to explore new ideas." Then she considered. "I suppose that brings me to the second thing I wanted to talk to you about."

"Yes?" Vitus straightened a little. He wasn't entirely surprised by either Merryn or her actual role. He knew there were people doing those exact things. Knowing it was Merryn might lead him to ask her a few more questions in private at some point. She wasn't competition for him, as he wasn't for her, but she had an entirely different range of professional connections.

"There will be a new Council challenge, obviously. People are already considering it, as callous as that seems." She let out a huff of breath. "I know of someone who might be looking for talisman work. I can't say I entirely recommend him as a person. But as a client I think he'd be in a position to be of interest to you, and he's good for the fee. The sort who believes in paying well for skilled magical work, which is always a good quality in a client."

"Someone you know well?" Vitus asked, though that was a sort of sideways insult in there.

"Oh, someone you know. Same year at Schola as you, if I have the maths right. Theo Carrington."

Vitus blinked. "Fox House, my year, yes." He considered. "Rather skilled in Incantation, I think he finished his apprenticeship while I was away. Good family, not one that has reliably held a Council seat." Then he tilted his head. "Did he proposition you at some point, then?"

Merryn let out an exasperated breath. "Last summer. I was doing some work on the warding on the family estate. He took no for an answer, and he doesn't have wandering hands without asking, which is more than you can say for a number of men of that type. Not a problem you'd need to duck, and I don't think he'd dare try with Niobe if he called round."

"He already had a reputation for ardent pursuit of women at school. Though I will say, all the gossip I heard suggested that he takes a no in reasonably good grace. I didn't hear comment that he didn't. But I didn't hear whatever complaining he did in the dorms, of course. He wouldn't, to the likes of me." Vitus nodded. "I'd be glad to talk to him and see what he wants, a consultation. Not tomorrow or Wednesday, and I'd rather wait until the end of the Faire. Or I'll be at the Fortier booth Wednesday afternoon if that's convenient for arranging a good time." He'd be going from Philip Landry's morning funeral to the Faire, pausing at the Stream to change clothing and leave his case to be picked up later.

Merryn pulled a notebook out and made a few notes. "That's plenty to go on with. Correspondence to the Stream, or to your home? You don't have a workshop yet, do you?"

"To Niobe's, by preference, she'll forward on anything if I won't be in for a day or two." Vitus rummaged and pulled out a card which had the details, his name on one side, her workshop address on the other.

"Grand. I'll pass it along, give you my recommendation, and I hope he's the sort of client you're looking for. Do charge what you're worth, please, he'll expect it." Then she stood. "I must get along, people to see, orders to make. I'm glad I caught you, dinner next week, if things settle down?"

Vitus stood, getting the door for her, and agreeing that would be excellent if the world cooperated. Merryn took herself off promptly, and Vitus decided that burying himself in the library and drafting a few ideas for talismanic work for a Council challenge would be the best use of his time and mind for the moment.

CHAPTER 35

JUNE 25TH AT DINAS EMRYS

It felt strange and wrong to be here, and entirely different from just four days ago. Everything had changed, and nothing had changed. Oh, Dinas Emrys felt different. The solstice decorations had come down, all the flowers and charmlights and illusions. Thessaly and her family had been given time alone in the Great Hall, with Aunt Metaia's coffin. The hall had been hung with sombre black hangings, not even the usual heraldry.

Council Head Rowan had made sure they'd had time on their own, a full half hour. It wasn't useful to Thessaly. She'd stood in front of the coffin on her own, holding Hermia's hand, for a good five minutes, but nothing that mattered was in her head. That was not her aunt, that was not the living, breathing, laughing, teasing woman she'd loved. Who'd loved her, who'd cared about her, who had fiercely been determined that Thessaly should have the best life possible.

It wasn't the woman who'd loved colour and delighted in tricks and pranks, clever and elegant ones. It wasn't the woman who'd made her own way, despite what her family wanted, and chosen her own sort of power. And it wasn't the woman who'd wielded that power thoughtfully, not to make herself look good, but to accomplish what she thought mattered.

None of that was in the coffin. Just a shell, and the shell wasn't the same. So Thessaly had stood there silently, her arm through her sister's. She'd waited an appropriate amount of time, and then they'd moved off to one side, to let Mama have longer. Father had stood behind her, not interfering, but also not touching. Mama and Father had not quarrelled this morning, Thessaly thought, but yesterday had been full of undercurrents of tension and difficulty. Now, at least for the moment, they seemed to be a unified front.

Then they'd all been escorted off to a side room to wait while others arrived. The keep was quite large, and over the years it had been designed for a range of events, as well as whatever magics the Council tended to. One whole side of the downstairs was fitted out with parlours and waiting rooms with sofas and chairs. Mama had claimed the central chair, of course, with Father standing behind her. Thessaly and Hermia perched on the sofa. All of them were in deep black, even Hermia, who might have had an excuse given her age. Mama's veil entirely obscured her face, Thessaly's was more transparent, and Hermia was unveiled.

Thessaly had expected to see some of the Lyttons, her uncles and aunts and cousins, but they hadn't arrived yet, apparently. It might have to do with why Father was unhappy. This was a funeral, but along with everything else it was, it put the focus on the Powell family, not on Father's line.

There was a knock on the door, and cousin Owain appeared at Mama's quiet "Yes?"

He came all the way in. "The Fortiers wondered if they might speak privately, before the service. Everyone is arriving. We will begin on time, fifteen minutes."

Mama didn't glance at Thessaly, she just nodded. "Please. Thessaly, you might sit under the window, with space to talk to Childeric."

Thessaly obediently got up. She would not argue. Of course, she wasn't at all sure what Childeric might say, though it was something that he was here, and that his family wished to speak quietly. By the time she was settled on the seat under the high window, there was another knock, and the Fortiers were shown in. They were in proper black, of course, though Lady Maylis was not veiled, and Lady Chrodechildis wasn't either. They weren't family, of course, so it was black dresses but not the other trappings. Childeric and Sigbert were behind their parents, and Childeric immediately came toward Thessaly. She didn't see either Dagobert or Laudine Fortier, though.

She extended her hand, without rising, not entirely sure what else to do. He bent over it, taking her gloved fingers in his, kissing the air over the silk, then he met her eyes. "May I join you, Thessaly?"

Thessaly nodded once, before glancing over to see the Fortiers sitting near Mama and Papa. Sigbert joined Hermia on the sofa. The room was large enough she couldn't hear what they were saying, and she expected Mama couldn't hear whatever Childeric might share. Thessaly took a breath. She ought to say something, but she had no idea what words would make sense. She wanted to ask him why he hadn't even written again, why they hadn't called. Instead, he took her hand gently between his.

He was on good behaviour, then, doing everything as he ought. "I am so sorry we have not called, Thessaly. It is a significant loss, to you and your family, and to Albion. I know how much time you spent with your aunt." Those things were all accurate enough. Though he didn't actually have a good idea how much time she'd spent with Aunt Metaia, Thessaly realised. She'd never spelled it out for him, all the hours here and there when they'd had a chance. "I do hope you'll forgive my absence. There were matters on the estate that needed tending."

She inclined her head once. "I am glad you're here now. Are your mother and father explaining? I know they wrote."

Childeric glanced at them, turning his head slightly. "Making our apologies, yes. But we are here now. Your mother invited us to join the procession at the Powell cemetery." Mama had not mentioned it to Thessaly, never mind asked Thessaly's opinion. "I do hope I may offer you a proper escort there."

There wasn't anything to do but nod again. "I'm glad to know you'll be there. This is so awful, all of it, so overwhelming." It was expected for women to be emotional, and this gave Thessaly a reason - not at all feigned - to dab at her eyes with her handkerchief. Childeric squeezed her hand slightly, and it wasn't remotely soothing. Not like when Vitus had touched her two days ago.

"Have the Guard told you anything about what happened, or their investigation?" Childeric kept his voice quiet.

She shook her head. "Nothing. They asked a lot of questions, of course. I was the last visitor on the property. I'd got ready for the rites with her. Nothing beyond that."

"Ah." Childeric took her hands between hers. "You will let me know if anyone makes things difficult for you, I hope?"

It sounded like the sort of thing she wanted to hear, and

yet there was an odd note to his voice. He seemed almost to be repeating some speech from a dramatic moment in a play, or something learned out of an etiquette book. On the other hand, they were betrothed, and it would, in due course, be his duty to protect her in the ways protection might be needed. Or at least the ones he could offer, which was perhaps a more limited sample. She hesitated, and of course he caught the hesitation. "Is anything - erm, beyond the obvious - wrong, Thessaly? You aren't cross with me, I hope?"

Cross wasn't the word. She heard the echoes of what Aunt Metaia had said last Thursday. Thessaly heard the echoes of what Aunt Metaia hadn't said in words, but had been thinking. She heard all the silence of his absence, the days between them. She could play back that shambles of a note in her mind, word for word. Thessaly turned her head away, grateful her own veil would obscure things a bit, though it wasn't fully opaque. "It's all so upsetting. I don't know what I think right now, it's— I miss her so much."

"Ah." He did not have a pat answer for that, and she was grateful at least that he did not fumble toward one. Instead, he sat quietly, his hand still in hers. "I will call when I can, of course. When you wish to receive me. If your family is willing."

"Mama would approve. She did ask if you'd written, though not to see your note." There, she could give him that piece of information. He should know Thessaly had protected his choices in that small way. Before she had to think of anything else to say, there was another knock from the door, and it was time for them to be shown to their places.

Thessaly and her family were in the front row, on the right side, with the Council Members and their spouses arrayed on the left and in the rows behind them. She got only a glimpse of the hall, but the rows of seats were filled with people standing at the back. She glimpsed Aunt Metaia's staff, too, in black dresses or with black armbands, off in one corner at the back. They were all solemn but insistently there, with Mistress Collins maintaining proper etiquette for them all.

The form of the funeral was what Thessaly had expected from her grandparents on the Powell side. This bit of public formality was, well, public, a chance for comments, a eulogy of Aunt Metaia's virtues, a public ritual to chain together what needed doing. People remembered her, people kept her name alive. Whoever had made the final decisions had been sensible.

There were four speakers. Cousin Owain, for the family, because some people would have thought Mama speaking improper. And honestly, Mama was in no state to speak clearly. She kept dabbing at her face with her handkerchief under her veil. Council Head Rowan spoke next, about Aunt Metaia's time on the Council. She focused on the way Aunt Metaia had given unstintingly to their work and had lent her talents in expected and unexpected ways. Thirza Remmerton spoke about how good a friend she had been, how creative and how she'd always had a thought that improved a situation. Magistra Walder, Aunt Metaia's apprentice mistress, decades ago, spoke about the sorrow of outliving her, sharing a story or two from her apprenticeship.

Thessaly wished she could have spoken, but it would have been an incoherent mess, and she knew it. There was singing, because the Welsh sang, and the Powells sang, and enough people knew the tunes here to carry the harmony. Then Thessaly and her family were guided into a long line, to receive well wishes. That would last as long as it needed to. Then there would be the quieter family rites at the burial. And there would be more, at All Hallows, in October, remembering the dead of the year.

When it came to the receiving line, the Council Members had gone through first. Each of them had in fact taken a moment to share some brief memory with Thessaly, even those she knew Aunt Metaia had often argued with. Some of those memories sang more in her heart than others, but she appreciated the gesture, even the awkward ones.

Then had come those close to the family, the Fortiers and various others. They had other comments, how sad the loss, how unfortunate she was still so young. Then it was the rest of them. Before very long, Thessaly's feet ached, her back ached, and she no longer had any sense of time passing. There was always some new person to greet. One of the staff members from the Council stood behind Mama and Father, murmuring names, just loudly enough Thessaly could also hear them. She repeated enough of them to be proper.

She looked up, most of the way through, to find Mistress Collins. "Mistress. I am glad you and the staff could come. I hope you can come to the burial?"

Mistress Collins ducked her head. "Council Member Owain Powell made it clear we are welcome, Mistress, thank you."

"I hope that..." Now Thessaly didn't know how to ask. "There is no rush to change your circumstances?" It must be particularly hard for them to have their livelihood shaken, as well as their other losses.

"Council Head Rowan has made it clear we should remain until the new owner of the house can decide what to do. And she kindly made the necessary arrangements. Thank you for thinking of us, Mistress, few would."

Thessaly inclined her head. "You all took such good care of my aunt and of the house. I will miss visiting very much, not just for my aunt's sake."

"Very kind indeed, ma'am." Then the pressure of the people behind her meant she had to move along. Thessaly repeated the same comments to the other staff, more briefly, getting quiet responses back.

It wasn't until nearly the end of the line that she looked up again to see Vitus. He offered a quiet smile. "I am still so sorry for your loss, but I hope hearing others remember your aunt is at least some comfort." He'd already spoken to Mama and Father, of course.

"A little, thank you. And you saying so, also a comfort." She considered, then nodded at Hermia next to her. "My sister, Hermia. Hermia, this is Vitus Deschamps, who was kind enough to share a specific memory of meeting Aunt Metaia when he wrote."

Vitus moved along, but she was reassured, somehow, that he'd come. When everyone had filed out, they were escorted off to the portal. Once through and on the estate, they made a small procession with pallbearers and a formal carriage drawn by horses with deep, black ostrich plumes. It was all solemnity and a single repeated thump on a great bass drum.

There was little in the way of talking at the grave, which meant Thessaly didn't need to say anything. Each person there tossed in a handful of dirt, then poured a cup of water as a libation. There were other parts of the rites that would come later. There would be a distribution of hair for all those who wanted a lock for a memento, besides whatever other rituals Aunt Metaia had wanted.

When that was done, the brown earth heaped over the grave, there was a funeral luncheon just for the family at the estate. Thessaly perched on a chair beside Hermia, letting the adults talk quietly. Certainly, the older generation weren't much including either her or Hermia, so she might as well count as a child, never mind she was betrothed. She couldn't quite hear anything, or what she heard didn't seem to flow together. By the time they could leave, it was near enough four in the afternoon. She was glad to simply remove all her mourning clothing, unpin the veil and hat, and fall into bed.

CHAPTER 36

JUNE 26TH IN TRELLECH

Wednesday morning found Vitus - and a number of others - at another funeral. This one differed from the beginning, as it was being held in a small temple building near the Temple of Healing. It was one that could be set for a number of different practices, hallowed ground that was bound to no particular pantheon or faith or tradition. The Temple of Healing worked much the same way, but that was a much larger space. If Philip's funeral had been there, the mourners would have been lost in the vastness.

There was an entry hall, perhaps a third the visible length of the building, with double doors that opened into the main temple space. Candles had been lit, not just charm lights, and light shone in from skylights above as well. There were no seats, just a broad empty space with a coffin at one end, and simple illusion work of great statues and an Egyptian temple. Vitus wondered fleetingly who had done it, or if there were illusions in stock somewhere, brought out for all rituals of the appropriate type. There were a few benches along the walls, a gesture at seats for anyone truly in need.

Vitus had expected that Philip Landry's funeral would be small. Certainly vastly smaller than a sitting Council Member who died in the prime of her life, with an extensive family as well as numerous social connections. And that was before he counted up the lesser known connections, the others of the Four Metals he'd seen among the attendees. Yesterday, it had been hundreds, too many to count easily. Today it was dozens, maybe sixty at the most.

He was grateful that the quieter part of Metaia Powell's memorial had gone well, at least. He had met up with the others of the society who'd known her at the country estate. Each of them had beaten out a flat circle of copper, joining it by overlapping the ends and hammering it smooth, making a chain. His had a private word inscribed, the one he'd chosen at his initiation. It had been quiet but companionable in a way Vitus hadn't known he needed. A few people had told stories of Metaia Powell, but there had been a lot more of the wordless sounds of hammer on metal, or stamp and copper. No one had commented on how many of them cried as they worked silently.

From there, they'd gone out to the family estate in the twilight, to add the chain of links to the grave and cover it with dirt. The groundskeeper had been there, and as they walked back silently to the portal, he had filled in the last shovels of deep brown earth and was tamping it down. Vitus turned once, to hold the memory of it in case, at some future time, Thessaly might want to know.

Now, he stood in his best black suit, formal and uncertain. These weren't his customs, whatever the Landrys kept, he was sure of that. And it seemed that most of those there weren't sure what to expect either. The men stood still, the pose of people who knew uprightness was expected, literally as well as figuratively, while the women waited. Vitus found a spot about a quarter of the way back from the front, over to the left side. He took an occasional glance around, seeing a cluster of the Fortiers, and then - arriving just before the hour - Thessaly and her father. She was veiled again and entirely in black. He hadn't expected to see her here at all.

Outside, the bells chimed at the Temple, and then as the last of the strokes sounded, there was the sound of something else higher and sharper, claiming the space. Vitus couldn't see what it was or where it was coming from. A door from the back opened, admitting a man in long ritual robes. Then Henut Landry - it could only be her - and Alexander followed. Alexander was in black ritual robes, of a sort that anyone in Albion would recognise over a stark black suit. The white of his shirt collar was the only variation. Magistra Landry was in full mourning, with a dark veil that entirely hid her face and fell to her waist. She took up a place near the head of the coffin, with Alexander closer to the feet.

There was no announcement, certainly no explanation. Magistra Landry said one sentence, waited, as if the answer informed her of something. Then she began declaiming, pausing for an answer from Alexander. The two of them set into a dialogue of some kind, the sort that obviously formed some ritual purpose, but in a language Vitus couldn't even begin to parse. The respectful thing to do seemed to be to listen, but several people there shifted uneasily. Vitus could understand the desire there. He could feel the ritual energies building around him.

But he knew enough to know they weren't about him, they weren't touching him. He was standing on a steady rock in a stream, water rushing around him. The water would do as water did. He was above it all, untouched and unsplashed. Whatever they were saying went on, perhaps five minutes, enough for a few of the ladies to claim a seat on the benches and fan themselves. The air felt close, certainly, and there was incense in the air in a blend Vitus didn't know.

But then, the ritual magics, beyond what he'd learned at Schola and the few he used in his own work, weren't his specialty. He knew enough to know each part of this was doing something that mattered to the Landrys. Perhaps he would have a conversation with one of them - Alexander by preference - at some later date, and be able to ask. Perhaps he'd come across some reference that would explain it, in his reading about some other topic entirely. Most likely, he would live with the mystery of it. Not all magics were his to understand.

There were several sharp comments, the kind that if they'd been in English would have been scolding, even challenging. Alexander stepped backwards once, with the force of it, said something, then took another small step of retreat. Something in the language changed then, a different rhythm that shifted the energy one more time.

The ensuing silence lasted five beats of his heart. Then there was wailing and moaning, high and sharp and pitched, coming from every corner of the room. It was mostly women's voices, but a few men as well. They came forward, along the paths at the edges, weeping and crying out, until they formed little groups at the front of the room. It wasn't a Deschamps custom, but Vitus had heard of professional mourners, the role they played. The man who had opened the door at first then gestured. Magistra Landry and Alexander processed up toward the entry hall, and the other attendees were encouraged to move slowly past the coffin, for whatever final moment they wished.

The way the lines flowed, Vitus was toward the end, the people behind him coming around first. He saw Thessaly's father, her arm through his, then Thessaly glanced his way. He nodded once, minutely, but he didn't see if she made any gesture of reply before the angles changed again. One attendant gestured him into place, perhaps ten feet behind the Lytton-Powells, and he was focused for a bit on his own thoughts.

He was sorry for Philip's death. Confused by it, as well. There had been no information about what had happened, even in the announcement in the paper about the funeral. He had died suddenly, a brief biography, and of course no mention of Schola house or Trellech's clubs. He hadn't had those connections. The thing of it was, Vitus had hoped to know him better. The man had been clever, and even more than clever, thoughtful. That was rare, but the range of knowledge he'd applied in that one conversation had suggested he'd known a great many things Vitus didn't.

And all of that was lost now, all the chances they might have had. Besides the fact that no man of thirty-one ought to die suddenly, for no reason. All he could do was hold the memory and hope that mattered a little. He remembered that much of what he knew of Egyptian religion - assuming that carried over to the Landrys. That remembering the name mattered.

By the time he made it to the entry hall, he was in the tail of the gathering. Thessaly and her father had disappeared through the door to the outside just as he'd entered. There was no chance to greet her. The Fortiers, too, had entirely disappeared. Then he was up at the head of the line.

Vitus bowed to Magistra Landry, low and respectful. "I am sorry for your loss, Magistra, Alexander." He hesitated, but then trusted that instinct that had been lurking there. "I wish I could have known Philip better. Please, I am sure I cannot offer much in the way of help, but if I can, I hope you will call on my aid."

Some silent communication passed between the two of them. Then Alexander cleared his throat. "Would you wait a few minutes until we have greeted everyone?" It was an unexpected request, and puzzling, but an easy one to grant.

Vitus nodded. "Of course. I'll wait somewhere out of the way." He went and found a bench in the main temple room, sitting silently and reflecting. Not that he made any progress on any particular thought. They were chasing around inside his mind and refusing to settle in any kind of order.

When the room was empty except for the attendants and the wailing mourners had fallen quiet, he stood again, to save someone having to come find him. The entry hall was empty now, other than the man who had opened the ritual, speaking briefly to Magistra Landry. He waited until the man backed away, and Magistra Landry turned her body toward him.

It was eerie, knowing she could see his reactions - he was sure she was marking each move he made - and he could not judge hers a tenth as well. Alexander inclined his upper body, opening one hand in a gesture of invitation, and Vitus joined them.

"There is one thing you might help us with. Do you know a source for a piece of carnelian, of talisman quality, two to three inches long, an inch and a half wide?" It was an exceedingly specific sort of question. On the other hand, he had just done an inventory of all of Niobe's current stones.

Before he could figure out how to bring up the fact it was not his stock, Magistra Landry lifted a finger. "I will gladly pay, but my usual sources do not have such a piece on hand."

"I would be glad to inquire of Niobe. We have two pieces that might serve, if—" He cleared his throat. "Would you prefer to call by her workroom or for me to come by? I would want to double check the measurements and quality before presenting the piece."

"Alexander will call tomorrow morning. We have the other stones I wish." The 'morning' was a slight question, but Vitus nodded. "We thank you. For your care and your memory." That was a sharp nod of dismissal. Vitus bowed and withdrew. He set off for the Stream to change clothing into something suitable for his obligations at the Faire. And also to send a messenger to Niobe about the carnelian, with a promise to explain in the morning when he got to the workshop.

The whole thing had been unsettling, as if other people in the room had been weighed and found wanting. He half remembered the discussion in one of his Society and Culture classes. There'd been more detail in Ritual class a year or two later, about the weighing of the heart against a feather. What discomforted him most was that he wasn't the one being weighed. He'd have understood having that eerie feeling if it had been meant for him, but he was certain it wasn't.

Then he was at Portal Square, and he had to set the whole thing aside for the day. Perhaps tonight he'd be too tired to dwell on it. Or perhaps a night's sleep might shake something loose, he did not know.

CHAPTER 37

JUNE 27TH IN TRELLECH

Thessaly felt absolutely drained of anything good by the time she got to Thursday. Aunt Metaia's funeral had been exhausting and awful in so many ways, but it had at least been something she understood. Philip's funeral yesterday had been something entirely different, a duel she didn't know how to parse that used angles and attacks she'd never seen or felt.

Going had also caused an argument between Mama and Father. Thessaly had asked to go. She'd known Philip, not well, but more than the rest of her family, and she knew Alexander better than that. She'd duelled Philip, she'd talked to him, he'd been kind to her. One of the family ought to go, she'd argued. Mama had refused, and she'd even raised her voice about Thessaly going.

Father had argued back, out in the open, not in suppressed whispers and sharp tones. He'd said that whatever else they thought, having Henut Landry notice a slight wouldn't be a good idea. It was not the argument she'd expected at all. And it came after Father sharing the commentary circulating at Bourne's about how no one had trusted Philip Landry, not any of the right sorts.

But, illogically, he'd gone straight from that to insisting Thessaly make an appearance. He would escort her. It was not a social call; it was not forbidden by mourning custom. All of that was true, but it sat uncomfortably on Thessaly's shoulders.

Thessaly did not have the energy or the wits to figure out why her parents were being quite like this. Obviously, the Landrys were of the professional class, not the Great Families, and that mattered to both Mama and Father. She thought Father might have come up on the wrong end of Magistra Landry's sharpness at some point, the way he made a point of avoiding her when they were at the same event. But none of that ought to matter, when Philip was dead, and Alexander was mourning, and there were customs that indicated kindness and recognition of that grief.

She'd been glad to get Vitus's note, first thing this morning, that he'd come by the orchard gate at half-one, and if she could meet him, wonderful. If not, he'd leave the stone after a few minutes. She'd managed to get away - Mama was lying down in a dark room with a cool cloth on her forehead and Hermia reading to her quietly. Father was out, tending to some legal matter, something he and Mama had been talking about in private.

Thessaly was, therefore, down waiting at the orchard gate at quarter past, looking down the lane, hoping for a sign of Vitus. Then, right on time, there he was, waving one hand at her while he closed the distance. She opened the gate to him immediately, and he came through. "It's good to see you." Those were the first words out of his mouth, followed promptly by, "I hope you are all right, considering, and that yesterday was not too much of a strain? I have some Welsh cakes, if you care for them, and lemonade."

It was far more than Childeric had offered yesterday, or any of the Fortiers, during their brief afternoon call. They had been terse - polite, but terse - and they'd hurried out at the end. Thessaly ducked her chin. "I'm glad you came." It came out warmly, the way she felt that this was a momentary light in her life that mattered. "And please. I— food's still difficult, but the cakes sound worth trying."

"Should I set a chime for an hour? Do you need to be back at any point?" He knew the way to the bench now. He went a little ahead, kicking a fallen branch out of the way with one toe, sparing her the need to navigate it. She nodded, and he set the chime as soon as she sat down. A minute later, they were comfortably arranged on the bench, a small cardboard box of Welsh cakes open between them, and he had opened a bottle of lemonade for her.

It tasted like sunlight, the tartness the taste she hadn't known she'd be able to enjoy right now. Drinking it let her take a deeper breath for the first time in days. "Thank you." Thessaly tried to find words for something beyond that, and couldn't, settling back to "Thank you," again.

"I'm glad it's the right thing." Vitus crossed one of his legs over the other. "First, I have your talisman for you. It should ease things, but I wouldn't handle it much unless you're ready to sleep, especially right now, if that's been hard." He reached into the satchel he'd brought and took out a small jewellery box, opening to reveal a polished and inscribed stone, mounted to be worn as a pendant. "There's a soft ribbon in there, more comfortable for sleep, and—" He flushed, as if he were about to say something more indelicate than he actually did. "It might catch on your hair, a chain, I thought."

"Not many would think about that. May I touch it?" Thessaly waited for his nod and then reached out a finger to stroke the surface. It felt cool in the way a breeze felt in summer's heat. It was soothing, or it would be soothing, she was sure of that. She looked up to meet his eyes. "I can feel that it does what, I mean." She stammered over the end, and pulled her hand back into her lap, then had to reach out again when he closed the box and offered it to her. She let it settle in the fold of her skirts, where she could feel the weight of it.

"It can't take the grief away, but if there is some other way I could help, I hope you will tell me." He hesitated, then he reached out a hand toward hers, and she nodded. A moment later, his fingers were resting there. She turned her hand over, so their hands matched palm to palm. His fingertips brushed against the inside of her wrist, hers just fitting into the curve of the heel of his hand. It made her think, ridiculously - because the original was a dance, not a moment on a bench - of the line from Shakespeare.

"Palm to palm is holy palmer's kiss." It came out of her mouth before she could stop herself. It must sound silly.

Vitus said nothing for a moment, but he was looking at her, then he cleared his throat. "I treasure your touch. Whatever form pleases you." He inhaled. "Also, I have no desire to end like Romeo and Juliet. I am no Benedick, but that is a happier end to the tale by far."

It made her mouth turn up. She felt it. "I neither. And our families are not feuding, not like that. Dissimilar, that's a different problem. I don't think Shakespeare has an answer for it."

"We will make our own, then, whatever form it takes?" His voice angled up at the end, more uncertain, until she nodded. Then, more securely, he said, "Alexander came by this morning. His mother asked yesterday if I had a carnelian that would suit for something, and Niobe did. He seemed..." Then he stopped. "Were you as confused by the funeral as I was?"

"I don't know how confused you were, but I was very confused." Thessaly admitted it, relieved. "I am so sorry for them, for Alexander, perhaps most. He looked up to Philip no end. I'm not close to any of them, not friends, not even so much as you, now, but duelling and gatherings, the way you know people like that." She hesitated, then added, "Did you understand what they were doing? I know what it felt like, but I don't know what they were saying?"

Vitus blinked at her, his hand shifting a little under hers. "That's more than I got?"

"It was - the best way I can describe it was a duel, a ritualised duel. That they were both, um. Taking roles. Roles that were real, not, um, acted? To go back a few sentences. But that was also following a framework. I don't know what that was. I'm just sure that's what they were doing. And the Fortiers didn't like it. At least the ones who were there."

That made Vitus blink again. "I didn't get a good look at all of who was there. It would have been rude and obvious."

"And we can't ever be obvious, can we?" It came out of Thessaly's mouth like a quote from Mama, and she covered her mouth with her other hand. "Pardon. I sound like Mama. I really don't mean to. No, you were right. Everyone was on edge. Dagobert and Laudine weren't there, and I wouldn't have expected Garin, anyway. Lord Clovis, his mother, Lady Maylis, and both Childeric and Sigbert. Not Bradamante Nevill, Clovis and Dagobert's sister. But I saw her husband. He's had some business dealings with Henut Landry, I think, though not recently."

"This is why you being a scion of Fox House gives you some advantages. Besides the other." Vitus let out a breath. "What made you think they didn't like it?"

"I don't know exactly what caused it, but there was a point, part way through - I was maybe five or six feet away from Lord Clovis? - when all of them flinched. Like they'd all had a shock at the same time. Not Yves Nevill, though. He was right in front of me, and he didn't move at all."

Vitus was quiet for a long moment, long enough that Thessaly reached for another bit of the Welsh cake, breaking it off with her fingers awkwardly. She was ambidextrous enough for duelling and illusion work, and that did not actually transfer to cake. "I don't know what to make of it. Or if it's the sort of thing we really shouldn't pry about. Alexander said nothing about it today, just picked up the stone. He was polite, just—" Vitus swallowed. "He looked awful. More awful than you have."

Thessaly grimaced, but she understood what that meant. "Exhausted?"

"Exhausted. Like a tremendous duel or bohort match or something of the kind, something that had used all his vitality and then some, magically. And that had been emotionally challenging as well, not just hard work." Thessaly knew enough how that felt, though she was rarely allowed to exert herself that far. It was not considered ladylike. Vitus added, "Did you talk to any of the Fortiers after?"

"No." She considered that. "They wanted to leave immediately as soon as was minimally polite. I'd have said they'd seen a ghost or something of the kind, but I'm fairly sure they don't permit ghosts or such magical untidiness."

It made Vitus snort, briefly. Then he looked down at her hand, as if something had caught his attention for the first time. "Pardon."

"You were looking at something?" Thessaly was curious now, and this was a thing she could admit to being curious about. Also, she rather wanted a distraction from thinking about the funeral. And especially from how it had seemed like whatever magic was in the room was searching for something, illuminating something, like focusing sunlight through a lens.

"Pardon, I'm curious now. It's terribly forward of me, but might I have a look at your engagement ring? Properly, with my particular skills?" Vitus met her gaze evenly.

"You think there's something I should know about it?" She took a breath and then tugged the ring off her hand. He sucked in a breath, as if he hadn't expected that, then moved his hand, so she could drop the ring into his palm. He rummaged without looking in his satchel, pulling out a small leather kit and opening it one-handed, pulling out a jeweller's loupe. Of course he'd carry one, the same way Thessaly routinely carried a selection of vials of powdered materia with her.

Vitus took his time examining the ring, holding it delicately but securely between his fingers. "The usual sort of charms for a ring. Find it if it slips off, to keep it clean and such." The comment sounded like it was routine, that it was entirely what he expected. "A central - yes, that's a ruby, not a spinel. Doubly refractive, of course. But moonstone, among the diamonds surrounding it, that's interesting." His tone suggested a professional neutrality, or at least he was trying for one.

"Not what you expected?" Thessaly leaned forward for a second, then realised it would change the light he was using and made herself settle back. "It's a family piece, or the stones were. They had them reset for me."

"It's a ring about, well." Vitus looked up, flushing

slightly again. "The mix of male and female fertility, more or less. Though the ruby is dark enough and shading enough toward blue that it's a reasonable enough hue for someone of Fox House. Both ruby and moonstone have protective qualities, too. But, pardon. More protection of you as a thing to be kept safe for future intended use than, say, a ring chosen for happiness or joy or love."

Thessaly let out a puff of breath. "I suppose in the circumstances, I will take the protection I can get." She felt like the air had been knocked out of her. It wasn't a surprise. She hadn't expected romantic adoration in any part of this betrothal. But she had hoped for the space for it. Apparently, she was the only one who had, the only one foolish enough to think that was even a possibility.

"There's a little hope from the diamond. It's often used for clarity of thought, and for preventing misunderstandings." Vitus took one more look at it. "None of them are talismanic stones, that's what I was wondering. Or worrying about, I suppose." He admitted the last softly.

"I'm glad to know." She wasn't sure what she felt about the fact it wasn't a talisman. Was she not worth the bother there, or was it a nod to wanting her to agree to whatever she wore like that? There was no way to tell without asking. Thessaly held out her hand, and he slipped the ring back on after a moment's hesitation. She felt it settle again. "Both that it's not doing things I didn't know about, and what the inclinations are." Before she could say anything else, there was a voice coming up from over the hill.

"Mistress Thessaly? There's a caller. Your mother would like you to join her." That was Fitchley.

It wasn't remotely ladylike to swear, even the sort of language common at Schola. Thessaly stood, suddenly. "I have to go. Thank you so much for coming. And for telling me I'm not alone in thinking things strange. Wait until we've been gone a couple of minutes and then you can slip out. I left the warding so you could."

She bent, before she could think better of it, to kiss Vitus on the cheek. They were well back in the orchard. Fitchley wouldn't see Vitus. Then she was picking up her skirts a little and heading through the path, slipping the talisman in its box into the slit in her skirts and the pocket underneath. "Coming, Fitchley. Just a moment."

CHAPTER 38

JUNE 29TH AT THE DESCHAMPS FAMILY HOME

In some ways, it was good that Vitus was so incredibly busy. He'd made it out to the Faire each day for at least a few hours, and he had hopes that some of the conversations would bear fruit. He'd scheduled an initial discussion with Theo Carrington about work. And he'd spent his spare hours and minutes rummaging through notes about what kinds of things might be of interest and a sense of costs and time frame.

In all the interstitial spaces, he thought about that conversation with Thessaly and the two funerals. He'd also stewed on whether there was anything he could do that might help anyone that didn't involve inscriptions and rocks, which brought him back to Thessaly again. She'd sent him a note, yesterday, saying that the talisman was working very well. She'd had two decent nights of sleep. But it had been a short note, forwarded on from the Fox House club. Even he wasn't able to spend more than an hour staring at it to suck out every drop of possible obscured meaning, so he'd gone back to his professional needs.

The Council challenge itself had been set for the autumnal equinox, which gave everyone near three months to prepare, considered a generous term. It was Vitus's first time doing a piece for a challenger. But Niobe had done pieces for four challengers since Vitus had started his apprenticeship, and she'd explained the different potential approaches each time. Some people wanted something for protection from whatever happened in the challenge space, some wanted a way to bolster a particular magic or skill they had. Some wanted something more obscure, more about the mental aspect of the challenge than anything else.

Niobe's piece for Justus Livingstone in 1885 had been focused on having the knowledge he needed come to mind quickly and reliably, and he'd come out of the challenge successfully. And with a generous bonus to Niobe afterwards, too, actually, besides recommending her to others in need of talisman work. And her piece for the challenge in 1883 hadn't been successful. Hesperidon Warren had triumphed that day. But the challenger there had come out of it unharmed and able to try again another day. She'd been less generous, but it had still been a help to business. Vitus was suspecting Theo Carrington would want something more like protection. But part of what he was working through had to do with some newspaper references and general material about the family.

All of which meant that he was home on Saturday evening. His parents had received a last-minute invitation to join one of Father's clients for a supper at one of the restaurants that set up at the Faire. Vitus had laid out his papers in the library, half a dozen books spread out in front of him. He rubbed the bridge of his nose, because he'd read the same three pages five times and he wasn't getting any further.

"Anyone home? It's - oh, there you are!" Lucas swung the door to the library open before Vitus could do more than turn in his chair toward the sound. He stood, reflexively, and his brother came over, clapping him on the shoulder in a cheerful embrace. "I was wondering."

"We didn't expect you tonight. Didn't you say you had plans?" Vitus ran his hand through his hair, then tried again, because some of it, yes, was sticking up.

"My plans fell through." Lucas shrugged. "The girl I was going to take dancing has a more serious suitor. I wish her well." Vitus blinked at that, then pivoted and sat down on the end of the sofa with a soft thud.

"You were seeing someone?" Lucas hadn't mentioned. Though they didn't get a lot of chance to talk, Lucas had a limited amount of leave. That went triple for anything Lucas didn't want to discuss with their parents around. "Mama and Papa are at the Faire for a supper with the Bellrights. I don't expect them back until at least half nine."

"So we've got a bit. Half-seven now, if you didn't hear the chime. Look, how about I get a tray of cheese on toast, maybe an egg, and bring it back? You get yourself to a good pause with your papers." Lucas seemed in good humour, whatever the rest of his day had held, and Vitus certainly didn't have the wits to argue. "Ten minutes, maybe fifteen." He went off without waiting for more answer than a nod, and Vitus heard him heading for the back stairs and the staff's sitting room and the kitchen.

By the time Lucas came back with a tray, Vitus had cleared off the table. He'd stacked his books in a neat pile and had even fetched a bottle of wine and opened it. Nothing fancy, of course, but Papa prided himself on being a man who preferred wine and all its upper class connotations, over beer or ale or cider.

Lucas came in, beaming. "Here we are, then, that should hold us. Now, what has you here stewing over books?"

"Trust you to start in right away." The thing about Lucas is that he didn't dodge around delicate questions. From what Vitus had seen from his friends from Boar House, none of them were inclined to. It was just a question of how obvious the charge was. It suited Lucas well in the cavalry, where straight talking and common sense apparently went a long way.

"That's not an answer." Lucas leaned back, and Vitus focused on the plate in front of him, rather than look back at his brother. "Here, I'll start. I was walking out with a girl, but we both knew it wasn't serious. Magical, obviously, but she wants someone who'll settle down and marry sooner than later, and I'm not that. Eventually, I'm sure." He shrugged, then considered and undid his uniform jacket to end up in shirtsleeves, twisting to fold the jacket over the chair beside him. "You?"

It wasn't anything Vitus had said out loud, not to anyone yet. He'd barely said it inside his own head, because it was ridiculous and impossible and wouldn't do him any good. But here he was, and Lucas was asking, and Lucas was probably the only person he could say it to. "In confidence from everyone?"

"Everyone. I'll make oath on it, if you want." Then he held up his hand. "I swear on my tin soldiers."

That made Vitus laugh, meeting his brother's eyes. "A solemn oath, even more binding than one on the Silence. For you." Lucas grinned back at him and then just waited. He had grown both more patient and more determined since their nursery days. Vitus took a breath. "I've fallen in love with someone where it's impossible. And I'm worried about her."

He heard Lucas let out a huff of breath. "Oh." Then the tone of his voice changed. "Have a bite or two of food, some of that wine. And then tell me a little more, would you? Have you, anyone else?"

"Who would I tell? Not her, though she trusts me." Vitus took his brother's sensible advice, taking a few bites of his supper, drinking a swallow or two of wine, then setting the glass down carefully. "Thessaly Lytton-Powell. We'd talked about her before, but more now."

"Oh. Oh, Vitus." Those syllables were full of emotion, sympathy, and understanding. It was almost more than Vitus could bear. Except, like his conversation with Thessaly two days ago, it was far better to have company in the complexity. "Does she care for him? What does she think of you?"

"She's..." Vitus had to stop and figure out how to put that in words. "She's never said she loves him or talked about him like that. Thessaly's pragmatic? Of course she is. She's both a Lytton and a Powell." He turned his hand palm up. "Thessaly let me look at her engagement ring yesterday. No talisman work, which is curious, but of course it's harder to get that to take without her consent and understanding. But it was all coldly practical. Her role in having children, and protection of that goal, nothing about warmth or love or passion or whatever other emotion betrothal might suggest."

"There's a rumour - I can see if I can hear anything more about it - that Childeric Fortier has a mistress. If I have it right, a young widow. Her late husband was some sort of suitably skilled craftsman. I do not know what he's like with the maids. I wouldn't hear that sort of gossip."

"Nor I." Vitus said. It was the sort of thing someone might hear at a club, if they shared a club with whoever it was. It would come out either in their bragging openly about their prowess or in the whispers from people who didn't approve. But they didn't have an overlapping club or circle. "Why'd you remember it?"

"That's a long story, involving a prank, three barrels of beer, a log rolling contest, an elderly mule, and a three-cornered hat. Fortier got mentioned as a tangent, related to the hat. I think. I might have been more than drunk at the time." Lucas shrugged. "Every bit of information helps in a strategy."

Vitus snorted. "What you do when you're not here visiting?"

"Man's got to keep up with his schoolmates." Lucas shrugged, grinning amiably. "All right. So what have you done with this woman? Who you call by her first name?"

"She said I could!" It came out entirely defensive, and Vitus immediately blushed. "She's had a horrible time. I met her at the St. George's Gala, she did the illusion work for her own gown, her aunt's, and then we got to talking. She did an illusion on mine and asked if I'd come so she could work on a vein of lapis. Then we met in the library, and a couple of times since. Her aunt...." His voice trailed off.

"Metaia Powell." Lucas's voice was quiet. "I'm sorry for her loss. Haven't heard much about that, it's not the sort of thing for the loud gossip of Boar House, and I'm not around enough for the quiet to reach me fast."

"She was in Four Metals." Vitus offered it, knowing his brother would translate that. "And much liked, though she wasn't at most of our events. I'd never seen her. I suppose it would be tricky, as a Council member. I made Thessaly a talisman for better sleep. She said it helped." He couldn't help the way his voice softened at the end.

"You've seen her, then?" Lucas considered. "Without falling afoul of their mourning customs?" He was considering something. Vitus knew that tone.

"She asked me to meet her. A footpath along the back of their property, she lets me in the gate of the orchard. Well, she has twice. And she's sent notes, mostly via her club, for forwarding." Vitus considered. "She thinks in terms of strategy, she's a duellist. But she also - she let me keep an eye out over her, while she slept. And she kissed my cheek, two days ago."

Lucas was about to say something, then he let out his breath with an inaudible sigh. "I think that's a woman who could use a bit of your kindness, brother. Someone to lend a hand. But it's going to get your heart broken, and I don't like that."

"Don't think I have a lot of choice in that, really. I've been turning it over and over, like looking at a stone for where to carve, and I can't figure out anything that won't hurt me. I'd rather be her friend and ache than leave her alone." That was definitely the first time Vitus had put words to it, but he knew they were true.

"I'll keep my ears open, then, for anything that might be relevant. And I wish you well, even if I don't have a bloody idea what that looks like. Or could look like. You watch yourself, though. I don't need to tell you that."

"You don't." Vitus dropped his eyes to his plate again, remembering to take another bite or two before the toast was all sogginess. "I know it's dangerous. And not just to me, if they took the idea she was at fault. But it's not simple."

"You don't come in simple. Me, give me a cavalry charge. You can change the speed. You can change the angles, but fundamentally, it's you and the horse. And they only go at speed in one direction at a time. I don't know what to do with you and your inscribed stones and the nuance of this stroke or that line, never mind the people you're doing them for. But you let me know if you need a shoulder. Or, I don't know, someone with a shovel and a strong back."

Vitus shuddered at that last image. "Don't joke about that, please. It's been a week, and then some."

"Easy, there we go. Here, have a little more wine. And here, a strawberry or two. You've been working yourself into a fit, candle burning both ends, whatever else. Let me tell you a few stories, all nice and simple horses and foolish new recruits."

Vitus glanced up, then nodded once, before returning his attention to his food, letting Lucas's stories roll over him. By the time their parents came home, they'd settled into comfortable tipsiness, trading story for story. Some from school that hadn't come up, some from Vitus's travels, some from the Army. When Mama and Papa returned at ten, she immediately shooed Vitus up to bed, and he knew that was the sensible thing.

CHAPTER 39

JULY 5TH AT ARUNDEL

A bare ten days after Aunt Metaia's funeral, Thessaly found herself at Arundel. Childeric's family had insisted, via Mama, and Mama had made it clear Thessaly would go. It would apparently not ask of her anything outside the bounds of mourning, but simply going made a statement. Thessaly didn't think it would be a quiet gathering with Childeric and his parents and his brother.

Of course she went. She put on the black gown and the veil, because she didn't much want anyone to see her face or her expressions, and she went through the portal precisely on time, at noon. A footman met her at the other end. He escorted her silently down the long avenue lined with trees to the front of the house, then in and up the stairs, around a corner.

It took Thessaly a moment to figure out where they were, a gallery above the great hall, the original heart of the manor house. A great carved wooden screen let her see what was going on below, especially at the far end of the room, but she was sure no one could see her. There were two chairs set out, a table between them, but there was no one else there. Below, the only people she could see were servants, bustling around, finishing setting things up.

The footman bowed, and she blinked at him. "May I bring anything, Mistress? It will be a little while before things begin. The water closet is straight across the hallway from the door. You are asked not to go further than that. I will bring tea when the other guests arrive." That was even more baffling. It seemed she would be sitting here for some unspecified amount of time on her own. She hadn't brought a book, nor anything that might keep her hands busy, like embroidery. Not that the light was really good enough for that.

Thessaly would not be rude to one of the staff, though. "If there is a book you might bring - a classic story, perhaps? Or perhaps a regional history?" Either of those would be socially acceptable, and easy to find again if she wanted to continue reading whatever it was.

He bowed once and disappeared without a further comment. He returned in five minutes, handing over a copy of something bound in blue bookcloth that turned out to be a series of tales about Sussex folklore. It would do. From there, she was abandoned. She carefully folded the veil back from her face so that it lay over her shoulders, and began to read.

She was entirely on her own for over ninety minutes. She'd made a trip to the water closet, read most of the book. Then she'd gone back to read some of it again, and fretfully looked down below to figure out what might be happening. It was a particular sort of power to demand she show up that early, and then leave her to sit. Just after one-thirty, another woman entered the gallery.

Thessaly turned at the sound, then blinked. The light

was not bright up here, but there was more than enough to see that Laudine Fortier did not look well at all. "Mistress Fortier." She didn't rise. That wasn't proper. But figuring out what to say next was tricky. "I hope everything is all right. We've not seen you or your husband. Or Garin." Garin was honestly the easy one to talk about.

Laudine didn't speak until she'd settled into the other chair. "I'm afraid my husband has been unwell, but thank you for asking. Garin is well, however. He's enjoying himself at the Essex estate." She spoke precisely, her voice clipped. "I would have thought Childeric might have mentioned when he invited you."

That was a whole new knot. Childeric had said nothing to her since that brief word before Philip Landry's funeral began. Certainly nothing personal. And right now, she did not have the veil to hide behind. Before she could figure out what to say, before she had to figure out what to say, there were steps on the stone outside the gallery. There was an instant of an echo, and she heard Childeric's voice before she saw him. "Thess, can you come out into the hallway for a moment?"

His voice had a sharpness to it, the sort of tone that assumed he would be obeyed immediately, that she should already have been moving. Of course she stood, murmuring to Laudine something entirely unspecific, a muted "Pardon". Maybe she would be back, maybe she wouldn't be back. She had no idea.

She followed Childeric out into the hallway, between the stairs and the bathroom. Now she could see him clearly, but that didn't help. He was dressed for a formal afternoon, and not at all in mourning, not even a black armband. The cut was up to the mode, but the colours were far more common to Albion than to the non-magical. He wore a deep brown coat that brought out the highlights in his hair, trousers two precise shades lighter, and a waistcoat of golden brocade. All of it hinted at rich earth, and all complemented his hair, which fell loosely over the top of his shoulders.

"It's good to see you, Childeric." She swallowed. "I'm so confused, though, about—"

"Thessaly." He took her hand, pressing it to his lips and not letting her finish the sentence. "I'm so sorry I've not been in touch. It's simply been one thing after another. Don't ask Aunt Laudine about Uncle Dagobert, please. It's been such a trial, trying to find a Healer who understands discretion, and proper attendants str - up to the task." Thessaly was not sure in the moment if he'd meant to make that slip - strong, surely? - or whether he'd actually done so accidentally.

And she realised, in the moment, that there was no apology for the demand, none for making her show up early with no idea what to expect. There was nothing that was treating her as anything other than a playing piece on the board. Whatever the game he was playing was. Or whatever the game the Fortiers were playing was.

Her role in this was to duck her head and say something appropriate. "Oh no, I had no idea. How horrible! I do hope he recovers soon."

She barely got that out before Childeric was talking again over her last few words. "Now, Thess, I know you're going to be very pleased with what we're about to announce. That's why I wanted you to be here for it. Of course, in ordinary circumstances, you'd be down beside me. But I thought you'd at least want to hear it in the moment, so we can talk about it later."

Before she could ask what he meant - she felt very much

as if she'd missed at least six things she ought to know about - he tugged at her hand. He pulled her closer with a force that refused to let her resist and kissed her cheek. "Must go. I need to welcome our guests. We'll be starting at two." And then he had dropped her hand and disappeared back down the stairs, leaving her alone. At least that meant she could duck into the water closet again and tidy her hair and peer at her face in the mirror. She considered, then added an illusion to smooth out her features and mute any twitches of expression she might not actually want to show. Then she squared her shoulders and went back to the gallery.

"I beg pardon, Mistress Fortier." Thessaly sat again, automatically arranging her skirts. In the interim, more tea had arrived, and Laudine Fortier had poured for both of them, though she'd left the sugar and cream uncovered. Thessaly added sugar to hers, before looking up.

"You are marrying in. Please call me Laudine." It wasn't uncommon, in that kind of relationship, not that Thessaly would dare address Childeric's mother by her bare first name without an invitation given several times. But Laudine was wife to the younger son, and also younger than Dagobert, only about a decade older than Thessaly herself. The offer was very likely being made for several reasons. But if Laudine wished to make a bridge to the next generation that way, accepting it would at least provide some additional information. Probably.

"Laudine." Thessaly repeated it. "Thank you." She couldn't admit her utter ignorance of why she was here, could she? That would reflect badly on someone, and it was as likely to be Thessaly as Childeric. Such things flowed off him like water off a duck's back. "Childeric said he had to go greet the guests. We'd be starting at two?"

"Yes." The answer didn't help. There was no new information there. Then Laudine went on. "There is a charm near the far end. See that vase behind the chairs? It will project what's said near it up here, more clearly. We'll be able to hear quite well. No room for misunderstanding."

That hit home, and Thessaly considered the merits and flaws of throwing herself on Laudine's goodwill, and seeing if she could get an explanation of any kind. Doing so would be admitting to a number of things. It would mean showing weakness, and as a duellist she couldn't bring herself to do it. Certainly she couldn't risk it without being able to retreat to a stronger position immediately afterward. And she didn't have a stronger position to work with.

Instead, Laudine went on after a well-mannered and precisely measured pause. "I can't leave Dagobert for long right now. But I also thought you might like a little company, someone who understands the challenges of marrying into a family like the Fortiers. I remember how intimidated I was, and honestly, still am." As she finished speaking, the Dowager Lady Chrodechildis entered. She was wearing a stunning afternoon gown of deep gold and purple that echoed Childeric's waistcoat and hair. Laudine nodded down at her. "My mother-in-law, for example."

There was a note there, just for a second, the kind of thing that could be read half a dozen ways, that made Thessaly sure there was hatred there, or something close enough to it. And, she thought, recent, there had been nothing like that at the betrothal, or the other social events since. "I am fairly sure the entire family practices being intimidating. Like Childeric practices being charming." She kept her voice even, she thought, but Laudine raised an eyebrow.

"He has spent less time with you since the betrothal, I gather, and not much since - I am so sorry about your aunt, my dear. I gather the eulogies were lovely at the funeral. So many people recognised her as a sharp-eyed and intelligent woman. There was a great deal to aspire to, watching her." Laudine's voice had an odd note to it again, but this one was utterly baffling to Thessaly, so she only nodded, her attention focused on the guests she could see.

Like any well-trained woman of the Great Families, she could identify many of the relevant guests at an angle and a height. The Deschamps family was not there, nor anyone else of their tier - though she admitted she'd looked first for Vitus. But all of the direct client families were at least represented. There were dozens of people in attendance, standing in loose groups in the Great Hall. They could hear more conversation from near the opposite end of the room, as Lord Clovis and Lady Maylis joined his mother, and then Childeric made his way up.

Precisely at two, she was sure, a gong sounded, reverberating through the room. Then Lord Clovis spoke, everyone falling silent and his voice amplified until it was almost uncomfortable. "Family, friends, and allies, we welcome you here to Arundel on this glorious summer afternoon. The weather could not be better, the sun could not shine brighter. We gather today to announce that my eldest son, Childeric, has been accepted as a challenger for the open Council seat, upon the autumnal equinox."

Thessaly couldn't hear anything else for a moment, struggle though she might. There was a rushing in her ears. She felt faint. It was good she was already sitting down. Her fingers tightened on the arm of the chair, and if she'd been able to see her hands, they'd have been white to the knuckles. She forced herself to breathe with all the discipline of the physical she'd learned in the duelling salle. She counted it out relentlessly in her head until her body remembered how again.

"…. ask that you, who wish the family well, will lend your arts in preparing my son for this challenge. Of course he will triumph. He is the best and brightest of his generation, bred to the ancient magics. Now he is reaching for new forms of arcane understanding, like all the Fortiers before him, stretching back to the Conquest. And, we are sure, with his marriage to come, for countless generations to come."

There was a murmur from the crowd, and then Childeric stepped forward. "I am honoured at the opportunity, especially while I am yet so young. Naturally, I wish to lend the strength of my magic to the lands beyond our own estates. I am sure magic herself will grant me every success."

Thankfully, the speeches - brief as they were - were over, and it appeared to be time for Childeric and his parents to circulate. Laudine opened her mouth once, then settled back with a quiet. "Perhaps, in due course, when it is appropriate for you and my husband is more recovered, you might call for some further conversation, if you wish?"

Thessaly nodded, grateful not to have to navigate the conversation. She could hear snatches of comment now, only when people approached to speak with Lady Chrodechildis. One bit stuck with her, though. Two.

"What have you heard about the other challenges, then? I suppose there's no actual competition." That was Jacquetta Montague, a cousin twice over to the Fortiers, once by marriage.

Pascal, her husband, scoffed. "No one of note, I'm sure you'd agree, Lady Chrodechildis." He was showing off, flattering beyond reason. "I've heard Cyrus Smythe-Clive means to make a go of it, but honestly, he's lost all sense since the death of his wife. Perhaps he finds that an easier way to end himself than anything else. Not a man made of bravery. And I heard something about Theo Carrington. There was a bit of gossip about him asking around about talisman makers, but surely someone who has skills, like Childeric, won't need that sort of thing."

Thessaly had already had a proper respect for a well-made talisman, but the last week of sleep had made her sure of it. She bit her lip, turning her head so Laudine couldn't see. She thought a talisman from a competent maker could do quite a bit of good, even if no one was sure what happened in the challenge itself. Perhaps she'd ask Vitus about it at some point. She'd not seen him since he'd given it to her, just exchanged a note each. She'd had a terrible time getting a note out without being obvious about it.

Eventually, the conversation faded down, and the guests dispersed to refreshments and more conversation in the garden. Laudine slipped out when that happened, murmuring that someone would come escort Thessaly out in due course. And adding, just before she left, "I do hope we'll have time to talk further. When you're ready."

That escort turned out to be ages later, near half-four, when one of the footmen came and walked her out. There was no one visible at all as she made her way to the portal. None of the family, none of the staff, as if everyone had disappeared. The entire afternoon left Thessaly feeling like she was missing several key pieces of information, while having others shouted in her face. She certainly didn't like how she felt about Childeric at the moment, or how his entire family had managed this announcement.

CHAPTER 40
JULY 8TH IN TRELLECH

Monday after lunch, Vitus was working on some simple talismanic cufflinks, the kind meant to help someone present themselves to their best advantage. They were popular as an item. On the owner's side, they were an affordable touch of magic, or a considerate gift for a man the purchaser was fond of. On the maker's side, unlike some pieces, people often wanted a range of colours. Make one set that someone liked, and they'd come back for pairs to match whatever they wore. Or, depending on the design, a range of needs - a set for eloquence, a set for clear thought, and so on.

Other talisman makers found them a challenge because of the small size and the need for precision. Even Niobe preferred other forms, given the choice. But Vitus rather liked the complexity of it. First, in finding two stones that matched or in some cases cutting and shaping two appropriate pieces from a single stone. Then it was a matter of arranging the talismanic inscription where it would be hidden, doing the enchantments to bring it to life, and setting the stones. Fiddly, detailed, even finicky, but rewarding to do right.

He heard the bell from the front door ring, and Niobe went to see who it was. She came back looking bemused a minute later. "Magistra Landry to see you, Vitus. She asked for a few minutes' conversation. I showed her to the office."

They rarely used Niobe's office, only for the sort of formal consultation and negotiation that needed privacy or a lack of interruptions. Otherwise, they conducted business in the front room at the counter. Niobe picked up her tea and nodded. "I'll be out front. Let me know if you need me to step in."

Vitus coughed. "Erm. Yes." He paused in the small water closet under the stairs to wash and dry his hands and check that he looked presentable. Then Vitus went off to the office, inclining his head as he closed the door behind him. "Magistra Landry."

Magistra Landry was in full and imposing mourning dress. Of course she was. She had left the veil down over her face, and she had a walking stick with her of ebony wood with a pattern traced or embellished in copper around the handle. Vitus sidled around to sit in the chair behind the desk without stumbling or turning his back on her. Once he sat, he cleared his throat. "I hope the carnelian piece suited your needs? Alexander knew what was wanted. I was impressed by his knowledge for someone not in our field or a related one."

He thought something in that might have amused her, just slightly, though it had the quality of a cat amused by a mouse it was about to pounce on. Even if he couldn't see her face, the intent came through clear as day. "It did suit, and you were accurate about its quality." She considered for a moment. "Alexander has departed on his Grand

Tour, and I am tending to various necessary pieces of business."

Vitus assumed, quite reasonably, that she had some reason for turning up here, and without an appointment. It was a bad idea to turn away a potential customer, and a worse one to anger someone whose scope for magic was powerful but not well known. He had a well-developed sense of self-preservation, as Niobe put it, as well as a growing sense of proper development of his professional reputation. "A talisman, magistra?" He wasn't sure if that was what she meant, but it was a neutral enough inquiry given where they were.

"Tell me, when we spoke some weeks ago, you were looking for your own quarters. May I ask if you have found a flat that meets your needs?"

It was an odd question in several dimensions. If it were a stone, it would be an irregular mass, a bit of copper or some other metal rather than an orderly crystal. Her memory must be phenomenal. It had been an ordinary conversation, small talk, and she had had a great many other conversations and more important things since. He took a breath. That was always a good idea when meeting an unexpected question or statement. "I am still looking, magistra."

"Ah." She did not expand on the question or the reason for the question. Of course she didn't.

Vitus struggled to figure out what else to ask about. She had already mentioned Alexander, but in a manner that did not encourage further conversation along that line. He was curious about their funeral customs, but it didn't seem the sort of thing one could ask about politely, certainly not without an opening. And the part he'd kept thinking about - Thessaly feeling it was a ritualised duel - certainly wasn't the sort of thing he could come out with on his own. Instead, he folded his hands in his lap and waited.

He thought she might well wait him out, but after he'd counted to forty-three, she inclined her head. "You might do me a favour, then." He thought she would not expand on that cryptic statement, but then she went on just before he could bring himself to ask. "And you have a question. Ask me that first."

Vitus swallowed hard. He was not deft enough to dance around who he'd been talking to, and revealing that he'd been talking to Thessaly would indicate all sorts of things. On the other hand, lying to Magistra Landry seemed an entirely disastrous idea. He cleared his throat. "Mistress Lytton-Powell is by way of becoming a friend. After the funeral," no need to specify which one, "she mentioned it seemed to her much like a ritualised duel. I am curious about your customs. They are not familiar to me, but I hope they brought you - and Alexander - some comfort."

Before she answered, she lifted the corners of the veil, folding back the near-opaque fabric to show her face. "Not comfort alone, but yes. I am glad we could give Philip the proper rites, can continue to do so. We could not do the same for my husband years ago." Then she placed her hands back in her lap. "When you speak to Thessaly again, please convey my appreciation of her insight. She is correct on that point."

Magistra Landry spoke politely and precisely, but Vitus was clear it was an order and that she would somehow know if he failed to do so. He nodded. "Of course, Magistra. When I have the opportunity again."

Her nod this time was rather like patting a dog on the head in praise, but it was a fraction less terrifying to contemplate. "The customs we use go back millennia, and we are a people who value the power and weight of our rituals and obligations. And, how shall we say," For the first time, he remembered that English surely was not her first language. There was that slight hint of feeling for words and her accent and rhythm shifting. "A ritual drama enacted. Yes, that is the word I want. The library here in Trellech might have something about it."

Vitus nodded. "I appreciate that, Magistra." Then he sucked in his breath, working his way to bravery. "You said I might do you a favour?" He didn't offer to do it, he wasn't foolish like that. He'd been trained out of it, but especially with anyone who wielded word and magic this competently.

"Philip's flat." Now the words came out sharp and edged. "His landlord refuses to break the lease. I have matters to attend to. I do not wish to be bothered with remembering to deal with it, month in and month out. If you would take over the lease, it would allow me to turn my full attention to other concerns."

Vitus felt himself go pale, just for a moment. "I had not expected, I— pardon. May I ask the particulars?"

"Oh, I do not expect you to take it unseen. And if it eases you, I can assure you my son did not die there." Vitus had read the newspaper coverage. His body had certainly been found there. She named the monthly price and noted that the lease would renew the following March. Next, she listed off what was included and what was not, in clearly enunciated words. He scribbled down the numbers and notes as she went. It was on the higher end of what he thought he could afford. But if the groundwork had already been done for the kind of warding he'd need, that would be a savings.

Then she paused before continuing, her voice deepening a hair. It wasn't softer. Soft was not a word that would apply to her, but more familiar. "I will remove his personal items, and whatever of the furniture you do not want to keep. You are welcome to whatever books on his shelves are duplicates of the family library. You have seen the sitting room. There is a workroom and a small bedroom, along with a bathing room and kitchen. Meals can be had from a woman in the flats next door, or there are various eating establishments nearby. And it is the proper sort of place for your stage of business."

Vitus sucked in a breath. "Philip told you I asked him a little how he had chosen it then." She inclined her head, but said nothing. "If I may look at it, especially with an eye to the protective enchantments for our work. If it is agreeable, I would ask Niobe to join us."

"Magistra Hall? Certainly. Would tomorrow afternoon suit? Or I suppose you will need to ask her. Tomorrow or Wednesday. I would like until the fifteenth to move what is coming to my home, but I would pay August's rent for you, in turn."

It was an especially generous offer, and that made Vitus suspicious. Or certainly wary. He wasn't entirely sure if suspicious were the proper term. Finally, he had to say something. "I am certainly interested in looking, Magistra."

"Good." She waved a hand. "And if you take it on, if you find some small thing that the movers missed, I can trust you will return it to me. That would not be true of many."

That put a somewhat different picture on it, and Vitus relaxed. It showed, because she snorted, almost amused, though there was nothing like a smile on her face. "You worry there is some unspoken cost, like one of your fairy tales. Grimm, Perrault, something of the kind."

"I try to be a sensible man, literate in the tales we tell about what is dangerous and what is safe— safer." He changed the last word at the last moment, and it got him an approving nod. "Something magical, Magistra, or some other item?"

"Paper slips behind furniture or into odd places so easily. Or small things. There is a ring Philip often wore I have not found. A copper band with a central turquoise, and lapis lazuli inlaid on either side. It had no particular meaning, except of course that all things such as we wear have meaning." That, on the other hand, was a deft nod to Vitus's own work and profession. Then she tilted her head. "You find it easier to know I have some particular wish, there? That you know I seek something in making this offer to you?"

"Oh, yes, magistra." Vitus didn't hide his more active relief. He tried to figure out a way to put this, the way a Fox would put it, rather than his own straightforward Salmon. Then he gave up and said what was in his mind and his heart. "It is much less confusing, magistra, to know you have ulterior motives. Or rather, I assumed you did, but to have an idea of them."

She was silent for a good thirty seconds before she nodded once. "Philip enjoyed his conversations with you. You treated him with due respect for his skill. I would rather you benefit than some other." Then she rose and lowered the veil over her face again, hanging in perfect flowing folds, not that any piece of her clothing would dare disobey. "You may escort me out and confirm when you will see the flat with Magistra Hall."

"Of course." He stood as she did, a bit hurriedly, then moved around the desk and her chair to get the door. Niobe was willing enough - even without explanation - to agree to see the flat the next day, and they made the arrangements. Vitus waited at the door, watching Magistra Landry until she reached the end of the courtyard alley, then turned into the main street.

When he came back inside, Niobe had gone back to the workshop, and Vitus set the warding on the door. He automatically made more tea, bringing it back with him, his head spinning. Niobe looked up at him, then silently went to go pour a glass of the medicinal brandy from the decanter in her office, putting it in front of him. "Will you take it?"

"Probably." He knew he would, unless it had some irredeemable defect. "The light is excellent, the space agreeable. The rent is in the range I was hoping for, if at the high end. And - I do not think she is someone I wish to anger."

Niobe shook her head. "No. She is the sort whose attention cuts. Better to have her think well of you." She considered. "No more work for you this afternoon. You can focus on looking at the warding specifications and what we need to know about the walls and foundation and all. I think you should be fine, given that neighbourhood, but we'll want the details handy."

"Yes'm." Vitus let out a breath, and set the larger and more complex problems aside for the moment as best he could.

CHAPTER 41

JULY 12TH AT THESSALY'S HOME

"What did you tell Aunt Laudine?" Childeric's comment came out as an accusation as soon as they were alone in the garden. They hadn't even sat down yet. Actually, they hadn't even made it to the bench on the far side of the garden, where Thessaly was aiming. It had a reasonable amount of shade.

He had come to call that afternoon. Mama had apparently expected him. She had told the two of them to go out to the garden; the weather was pleasant. Mama herself had barely left the front parlour other than to sleep since the funeral. She kept the lace curtains closed, letting in only filtered light. Thessaly was worried about her, but every time she'd tried to encourage Mama in something else, she'd been sent away.

Now she felt even more isolated. Not that she wanted to have this conversation with either of her parents nearby, or Hermia. It was complicated enough as it was. She was coming to this duel on the wrong foot. Certainly, she had no advance preparation other than what she had available to her at all times.

Thessaly squared her shoulders and took a breath. She was not prepared for this, but there was no need to make foolish missteps by rushing. "She assumed you had told me more than you did. That wasn't hard, Childeric, given that you told me basically nothing other than when to come through the portal." His expression hardened, and Thessaly added, "I can't support you in what you're doing if I don't know what it is. Or avoid putting my foot in my mouth. I'd asked after her well-being and your uncle's, and she was surprised you hadn't mentioned that."

Childeric stood abruptly, going to stare pointedly at a rosebush, his back to her. He folded his hands behind his back, everything rigid and unyielding. She didn't beg him to turn around; she didn't try to soothe him. Instead, she sat there, fingers running over the ridge of her betrothal ring under her glove, thinking about what Vitus had said about it. Protection of what she was contracted to do, not anything about warmth.

He stood there for a long time, but she was more patient than Childeric was. She'd trained patience just as much as she'd trained in casting illusions or in duelling. She'd had the discipline and care for the art form that meant endless rounds of practice. Childeric wanted to rush in and do something visibly heroic, then depart stage left, pursued by an admiring crowd. No, stage right. He thought the left side of his face was handsomer.

Finally he turned around, and he was all smiles. Thessaly thought suddenly of what Aunt Metaia had said, the afternoon before she died, about when Childeric turned the charm on, when he thought he needed to. He took several steps back over to her, perching on the bench again and reaching for her hand. "Do forgive me, Thess. I wanted to spare you the strain, considering, well, everything." The last word sounded a little hollow, but Thessaly wasn't sure if she entirely trusted her own judgement on that point, not right now.

"I'd rather know. Especially when it comes to inviting me to anything with your family. I feel so awful when I've not met their expectations. Or yours." She threw that last phrase in on a hunch, and she saw the way his expression changed into something uncomfortably approving. "It's so hard, with Aunt Metaia gone, and Mama - well, Mama's taking it very hard. They were close. But I'm marrying you, and I need to know the things that matter there."

He patted her hand, the way you patted a horse on the withers to settle it. "There, there, oh, I suppose when you put it like that, it makes sense." As if her feelings had to do with her being a weak and emotional female who needed special attention. She might well be emotional at the moment, but she felt she had good cause. "There, there, Thess. No, you're right. I am sorry I didn't give you more warning about the announcement."

Thessaly considered her options, all of them, even the distasteful ones. She could concede the field, forgive him, and go on to talk about something else. That would set a horrid pattern for the rest of their lives together. Also, she was fairly sure Aunt Metaia's ghost would come and haunt her every night, or something of the kind. That wouldn't do at all.

The second option was probing a little, with a decided leavening of praise, about why he'd chosen to do the announcement then and that way. What he hoped for with the Council, too, because she was fairly sure he wasn't actually prepared for the work involved. Not that Thessaly knew all the details. But she knew there was a fair bit of work.

Meetings, for one, and Childeric did not have much patience for meetings.

Third, she could confront him, and that would end messily, and Mama would be upset about it besides. Possibly also Father. She was entirely unsure how to weight things with her parents right now. They weren't behaving like they had. Not with each other and not with Thessaly either. Possibly with Hermia, but Hermia was doing her utter best not to be a trouble to anyone and mostly in her room or the nursery.

Put that way, her choice was clear. She couldn't dither about other variations, she had to stay nimble and keep moving forward. Whichever direction forward actually was, which was definitely part of her problem here. Thessaly took a breath and let it out. "Can you explain more of it now to me, please, so I understand better? I'm sure I'm missing something. Why you did the announcement that way, why you couldn't tell me in advance, so I knew what to expect. You've been very distant, and I know you're worried about your uncle, but is there something else?"

That last part hit a sore spot for just a second. She saw him react the way he had at the funeral, a sudden jolt, and she still didn't know what it meant. Then Childeric shook his head, his smile false for a moment, then warming. "That's a lot of questions. Let's see. Well, first, Maman and Father wanted to make a fuss over it. It's not every day anyone gets a shot at a Council seat."

No, since generally it meant that one of the Council had died. Retiring was a possibility, but the sort of people who made it onto the Council were the sort of people who didn't understand the concept of retirement. Aunt Metaia had been teasing Hereswith Rowan about it for years. Council Head Rowan was in her early seventies. And she'd had a whole separate career in the Ministry, doing diplomatic work, before challenging for the Council. Thessaly did her best to sound cautiously full of questions. "And why now? I mean, of course you want the chance, that much is obvious, but you're very young for it. I mean, I know enough about all of them, and how long they've been on the Council."

"Of course you do, dearest." He patted her hand again. "Who knows when the next chance will be? It could be years, a decade. Now, right now, I'm in the prime of my youth. I can devote myself entirely to preparations - Father and Maman have worked up a whole schedule for - with - me." That, now, was a telling admission. "They've even got Andreas Fulton to come in starting next week."

Andreas Fulton was an excellent duellist, but not necessarily an excellent trainer. Thessaly had done three master classes with him and then decided that her time was better spent in most other pursuits. Even, say, flower arranging, which was almost never her choice if other options were available. Given the fee he'd likely asked for, he'd flatter Childeric, give him a few tips that might be some use, and not do any harm. She nodded. "I hope that goes well. He does know quite a lot."

"And, of course, it would be a feather in the hat for the family. You understand that one, of course. The connections, the influence, everything that we want." Now instead of patting her hand, he curled his fingers around it, the angle not quite comfortable for her, but she didn't try to rearrange.

"Oh, I can understand that, yes." Thessaly cleared her throat. "And the announcement? That's what really hurts, Childeric, that I had no idea. And it was Aunt Metaia's seat. I know it isn't personal, but it feels personal."

His face froze for just a moment, then he squeezed her

hand. "I am sorry, dearest. I handled that badly. And Maman has scolded me. You needn't do the same." As if his mother and Thessaly were interchangeable. Or rather, as if Thessaly's feelings about this didn't matter at all. "We really have been terribly worried about Uncle Dagobert. Aunt Laudine's done all she can for him, but he's in a bad way. An orderly with him all the time, someone who knows all the right charms in case, well, he gets it in his head to do something dangerous."

None of that prevented Childeric from sending a note, even if making a call was not feasible. Thessaly nodded. "I'm sorry it's been so awful. Your aunt and uncle intimidate me a bit - like your parents, I mean, I am sensible about their skills and magic, and properly respectful. But I've enjoyed talking with both your aunt and uncle when we've had the chance. And it must be awful for Garin."

"There you go, being soft-hearted. Now, I've answered your questions. And it's not as if this particular problem will come up again, will it? You're not likely to be in mourning again - that's what made it so tricky to navigate. And of course, I'll not be challenging twice for the Council." He sounded so confident and self-assured, and Thessaly couldn't bear the sound of it.

"Just, please, keep me informed? A note, if you can't get away. I really do want to back you up. That's my role now we're betrothed, and certainly once we're married. And I can't do that if I don't know anything about what's going on. Please? Can you promise me that?" She did her best to look endearing and gesture at the fact he held all the cards here.

Childeric leaned forward and kissed her cheek, a proper, gentle sort of kiss, but impersonal for all that. "I'll see what I can do. Sigbert's not holding up his end, he keeps disappearing while we've business to tend to." It wasn't any sort of promise at all, and she knew it. He must know it. "Now, Maman and Father would like to invite you to supper at some point, when you feel it's appropriate. When are you starting up with your apprenticeship again?"

"Just the family, not a larger party?" Thessaly felt she needed to check. It had only been three weeks, not yet a month. "I'm resuming the apprenticeship on Monday, but just going straight there and back." She glanced up toward the windows. "Mama's taking Aunt Metaia's death very badly. I do feel I need to be here to support her."

"I suppose that's reasonable enough. Maman thought you might like a little time at Arundel, on your own. Perhaps the Friday and Saturday? You can choose whatever quiet amusements you prefer, have luncheon and supper with us. Father reminded me it'd be best for you to become familiar with the land and the land magic sooner than later, of course. A few walks, a look at the less public parts of the manor?"

The problem, Thessaly realised, was that she could scarcely ask for more information and then turn down the first offer of it. She inclined her head. "I'm - well, I'm not sleeping as well as I'd like, or any of that. But if you'd like me to visit you and your family, I'm sure we can arrange something for a night or two. And Arundel is lovely in the summer."

"There, see how easy that is? It will give us more time to talk." He patted her hand again, looking triumphant. "Perhaps we might walk, and I could tell you more about what plans we have for my preparation."

Thessaly didn't argue. That took far more energy than she had, and besides it seemed a poor strategy. Instead, she nodded, let him stand, and then accepted his arm as they progressed moderately around the circuit of the garden. There were robe fittings for protective clothing, discussions about which of the family talisman pieces might suit rather than a commission. Childeric had his duelling training, and then a number of other skills. Someone with a bit of planning sense had clearly had a hand in the arrangements. But the events that excited Childeric were mostly not the more sensible end of the scale.

It all seemed decidedly rigid, as if there was a path with no space for her, crowding her off onto the verge. And while it was pleasant to be outside, she found the whole conversation oddly draining. It was as if she'd turned into a shadow of who she preferred to be in the course of the hour they spent together.

CHAPTER 42
JULY 16TH IN TRELLECH

On Tuesday morning, a messenger brought a note around mid-morning. Niobe was sorting the mail, tried to open it, and failed. "This one's for you. And charmed, as well. Do you need the office?"

Vitus blinked at it and then recognised the handwriting. "I don't think so? I don't know?" He pressed his thumb against the wax seal and felt it give way when the magic identified him properly. Of course, she had a note or two from him to use as the anchor for that, enough.

The note from Thessaly was the sort of thing anyone could read without a hint of the overly personal. She was letting him know she'd resumed her apprenticeship. Of course, she still wasn't making social calls. It also made it clear she'd be available to discuss the question of lapis lazuli illusions at some agreeable time. More to the point gave the hours she'd be at her apprentice mistress's. It was not quite a formal engraved invitation, but it was the same sort of thing.

"Mind if I finish promptly at half-four today? I can do

some more research tonight." Vitus peered over the letter at Niobe.

"You were going to do more research tonight, whether or not you finished here early. Go on with you when it's time. You'll be in tomorrow?" Niobe leaned her elbows on the wood of the counter nearest the hall.

"In a little late - I'm meeting the landlord first thing to walk through and get the keys and get set on the warding. Magister Gordon says he'll be able to do the workroom next week, he thought Wednesday." He couldn't move materials in there until then, but he could figure out the rest of the space. For the moment, he planned to continue living at home. But he'd arranged with the woman in the flats next door for lunches, and for a weekly cleaning.

He had been able to figure out, as soon as he'd talked to her, that she relied on the money, and every bit helped. He'd have a bed in the bedroom, in case he had a late night in Trellech for some reason, a meeting or lecture, but he liked seeing Mama and Papa regularly. And Lucas, when Lucas could get away for the evening.

At half-four, he was packed up and ready to go, and by quarter to five, he was outside Thessaly's apprentice mistress, waiting on a bench nearby. Vitus didn't actually have much of a plan from this point, though they could perhaps go find a bench somewhere out of the way. Or Thessaly could tell him when to come back, when her apprentice mistress was around to chaperone.

Five on the dot - as the Temple bells were chiming - Thessaly opened the door and came out. She was wearing mourning, of course, the sombre black, though her veil was pulled back over the back of her head. She glanced around, then before he could approach, caught sight of him and came in his direction. "Vitus. Have you been waiting long?"

"Just a few minutes. I thought catching you might be easier than passing a note back and forth. I would, of course, love your advice on the lapis lazuli question. Would you like to suggest a time, perhaps?"

She hesitated. He felt her fingers shift on her arm. "Perhaps a walk. We're not far from the parkland." Then she considered again. "Or if you don't mind a bit more of a walk, the cemetery?"

The cemetery was a bit more out of the way, and her dress would also not attract any attention there. He suddenly realised that he knew where her aunt was buried, and she might not know he knew. "I know your aunt's buried at your family estates. Are there others you visit here?"

Thessaly raised an eyebrow, then nodded once. "Shall we?" They set off walking south, curving through the Ministry quarter, to the southeast gate. There were benches just outside the cemetery. Thessaly kept going through, then following one of the twisting paths between tombstones and monuments until they were in one section not yet in use as a burial ground. There, she found a bench, settling onto it with grace. "We should be private enough here, don't you think?"

Vitus was very curious how she knew to come just here, but he couldn't figure out how to ask. Instead, he cleared his throat, nervous. "I hope you are doing all right? Is it difficult to be back at the apprenticeship?"

"Yes, and no? Though two days is not a lot of information to go on. Yesterday was exhausting. Today I was glad I was out of the house. Mama won't notice when I come back, as long as it's before supper, and Father's out until at least then." She added it as if it was information he had any right to, but he supposed she might not want him worrying about that.

"And a bit of fresh air is probably also good for you." That was a truism, but it made her smile a little and incline her head.

"I do come here sometimes - my nanny is buried here. And I sometimes leave flowers for Magistra Ventry. Gods know not many other people will."

Vitus blinked. "The Council Member, I assume?" She'd died a few years ago, what, 1883, and she had been widely regarded as a complete terror.

"Mmmhmm. Aunt Metaia didn't exactly like her, but she respected her. Magistra Ventry didn't have much family, and she lurked in corners like something out of a Gothic novel, but—" Thessaly's shoulder twitched. "That doesn't mean she should be forgotten."

Vitus hesitated, then reached to rest his fingers on her wrist for a moment. She immediately turned her hand so he could hold it, making her own willingness obvious. "No." He considered. "You know them in a different way than most people. The Council." Then he coughed. "I'm sorry. If you'd rather not talk about it, just say so."

There was a silence, Thessaly looking out across the grass. "Most people don't ask. Don't think to ask. I think most people forget the Council are people, before anything else. Whatever dances of power and magic and illumination and the land there are, we start as people. Aunt Metaia didn't tell tales out of school, as the saying goes, but she talked about the other things that came up. Books, or a particular anniversary, or a meal together. She didn't like all of them. I'm sure not all of them liked her, not as friends or even as allies. That's different." Thessaly added to him. "I mean, the number of the Council who are Fox House."

“I do know the difference.” Vitus said, earnestly. “Some of the time, anyway.” He added a moment later. “We are friends, and I hope also allies. Both.”

Thessaly tilted her head. “Both.” she agreed. “And that’s more than I have with Childeric. On both counts, I rather think. He and I had an odd conversation on Friday. I’m still thinking about it.” Then, before Vitus could change the subject or even say anything at all, she went on. “I was thinking back to the challenges I know about. I remember Aunt Metaia’s, though I wasn’t there, but everyone talking about it. But I was only nine. The more recent ones...”

Vitus cleared his throat. “Pardon, you should probably know sooner than later, even though it’s not directly relevant. I’ve been commissioned to make a talisman for Theo Carrington for it. We’re still working through the parameters, but he’s agreed to my fee in principle.”

Her eyes flashed. He couldn’t tell if that was tears welling up or some other emotion. She looked away from him, out across the clipped grass again, and he couldn’t read her expression at all. Her hand stayed in his, though. Without turning back, she said, “Childeric announced that he is challenging without talking to me about it privately at all. Without thinking about the fact it might be a tender thing, that it’s Aunt Metaia’s seat. Was her seat.”

“Oh.” There wasn’t a great deal Vitus could say, except that he rather wanted to go punch Childeric. Only Vitus’s hands were part of the core of his profession. He wasn’t actually good at punching anyone. And while Childeric might not be the duellist Thessaly was, he’d had more training at it than Vitus had. Wrestling with Lucas in childhood only went so far toward an understanding of the martial arts. “Do, please, stop and tell me if I’m that dense, please? I work with rocks. I try to be more observant than they are."

Something in that made her turn her head back, and then she was smiling, honestly smiling. "I don't expect you'll have that problem, no. For several reasons." Thessaly shook her shoulders out. "Can I tell you anything that might help?"

"I wouldn't ask you to, um. Divide your loyalties?" Vitus wasn't entirely sure how to put this.

"The way I see it - this is more the Lytton side of the family than the Powell side, though honestly, it's a tad hard to tell - it's not a division. Childeric hasn't asked me anything of the kind, and he's had the opportunity. There are notes we were talking on Friday - he did actually come and call. He has all the available information that I might be a resource. I won't tell you anything I wouldn't tell him." Then she wrinkled her nose. "Well. Probably. I'll have to think about that more. But we're not likely to get to any of that right now, in an overview."

"As you think suitable and fair, then." Vitus said, promptly. "Honestly, I'm interested in your analysis, seeing as you are a Powell and your aunt's niece. You know things I don't. Third, you're of Fox House and trained in that sort of analysis several times over."

That made her snort and almost smile again. Then she lifted her other hand, ticking off the people. "The ones I know about going back to 1880. Romulus Heath, Hestia Palgrave, Justus Livingstone, Quintessence Percival, Hesperidon Warren - he has Blanch Ventry's seat - and then Eustace FitzAlan and Esme Garrison."

"I've always heard FitzAlan with just his last name. Or the title. I suppose 'Eustace' explains it." Vitus offered. "And they have a range of specialties. And does that make a difference in the challenge?"

"Oh, yes. Aunt Metaia wouldn't talk about hers, of course, but what she did say is that she thinks it's a puzzle that has a number of possible solutions. And part of the question you're answering is how you go about that kind of puzzle, and part is what you're willing to risk solving it. But it's not an obvious, easy proportion, you understand? Sometimes people risk things they can't afford. Sometimes they try to bluster through a solution instead of picking a route they could do more with."

Vitus nodded slowly. "So while protective magics might be worthwhile, ones that granted clear sightedness or the ability to see the path forward might be even more valuable?"

"How not to waste your energy charging at stone walls, is what both Aunt Metaia and Magistra Hereswith said. The people who are actually clever don't keep doing the same things over and over again when they don't work." Thessaly shrugged. "What do you know about those seven, then, and I can fill in the gaps?"

That made Vitus consider what he knew that might matter. Like anyone who'd put the time in, he could reel off their names and families and their Schola house and their known specialties. But that wasn't enough, clearly. And yet, those were things someone like Vitus might know. He'd seen all of them, at the rites at various times, he'd spoken briefly and formally to a few. But he was having trouble making the patterns connect into anything useful. It all came out as opal or amber, amorphous rather than the precise crystal structures of something like diamond or corundum.

CHAPTER 43
JULY 16TH IN TRELLECH'S CEMETERY

While Vitus took a moment to think, Thessaly had to do the same. Not about the recent Council challenges. She was fairly sure what she'd say, and most of it was at least nominally accessible from public sources. Instead, she was thinking about how different this conversation felt with Vitus, compared to Childeric a few days ago.

For one thing, it was an actual conversation, as opposed to a duel with a badly matched opponent. And the more she thought about it, the more frustrated she was by Childeric. Not just not telling her, not thinking to tell her, in advance. That was a whole other wound she'd come back to. But even when he'd shown up to call, he hadn't thought to ask if she could be any help. He kept walling her out of anything that might let her take steps toward him.

She'd agreed to the marriage for all sorts of reasons, practical ones and being fairly sure she could build a life she liked with him, whatever he decided to do with himself. Now, she was questioning many parts of that. He'd sat through the negotiations, the same as she had. He'd signed the agreements three times over, ink and magic and oath. She'd thought that was about her becoming a Fortier, and instead she was finding herself stuck in some impossible in-between space that left her unsure where to find solid ground. In the middle of the river, balancing precariously on an unsteady rock, that was the metaphor she wanted.

Vitus cleared his throat. "I appreciate this. Being able to talk through it with someone other than Niobe. Are you comfortable before I start? I'm sorry I didn't think to bring anything."

"It is a cemetery," Thessaly pointed out. "They discourage that sort of thing." Then she glanced down at their hands. "I like this. How we're sitting, how we're talking. The spaces of it." She couldn't bring herself to come out and say it was the connection of it, the simple, decent humanity, but that, too. She hoped he understood.

"I do too." He hesitated, as if he might have said something more. "Romulus Heath three years ago, Fox House and Alchemy, but also Illusion, yes?"

Thessaly nodded. "There has been a lot more fuss about keeping people out of magical spaces, the last decade or so. That's part of what Aunt Metaia did, and Romulus Heath does it too. Good to not just have one person to rely on." She shivered. She could feel it being obvious, because no one had talked about death as a particular problem, but of course it was. "Not likely in the current batch of candidates, though."

"Wait, you know who else?" Vitus blinked at her, his fingers tightening on her hand. "Childeric. Theo Carrington, as I said."

"Cyrus Smythe-Clive has put in his name. And Heliotrope Masterson." When he blinked at her, uncertain, Thessaly said, "Incantation, and I gather she wasn't a bad bohort player. Not a duellist, older than you, I don't know that you overlapped. Fox, of course. I don't know what her plans are, though. Maybe one or two more, but there's still time." She nudged his thumb with hers. "Go on."

"Hestia Palgrave, Owl, to mix things up a little. She's a warding specialist, and I suppose that goes with the illusion needs, doesn't it? I gather her challenge was unusually short, actually. Quiet, I guess that's how people describe it in some of the write ups later."

"She's quiet, so that doesn't surprise me. Not unfriendly. Actually, if you get her talking about one of her interests, she can go on. But more the sort who needs to be drawn out than someone who wants to be the centre of anything." Thessaly nodded. "Justus Livingstone?"

Vitus snorted. "Also an Owl, the sort who lives and breathes a library. He's a researcher, first and foremost, I can see how that might be handy. Though I'm fairly clear he didn't have to fight for his challenge, did he?" Vitus tilted his head. "I'm thinking about what you said about puzzles that can be solved in multiple ways. What your aunt said, I mean."

"Like that. Because even just the three we've named have different skills. And the challengers. Cyrus isn't a horrid duellist, but it's not his best skill, he's a ritualist. Or was. I'm not sure he knows who he is, though I think he's close to finishing his apprenticeship." Now that she thought about it, that implied that he was both more clever than was immediately obvious. And also that he could be extremely dedicated, given the death of his wife and the devastation he still clearly felt. "And Childeric's not a very good duellist, so if he's relying on that, he's going to have problems."

"Also Incantation, isn't he? Like Theo." Vitus turned his

free hand palm up. "Quintessence Percival, which is a name that always makes me stop and wonder about nominal determination as a theory. Also a ritualist, and I know for a fact he's in Animus Mundi."

Thessaly nodded. "He's written a few papers for their journal. Later to challenge, but that meant he came in with more experience. If Cyrus is getting assistance or advice, I bet it's from him. Cyrus's apprentice mistress is close to the Percivals."

"Fox House analysis," Vitus said, very gently. "It is fascinating to see it at work." Then he stopped, another of those hesitations, before he went on, determined. "Hesperidon Warren."

"Also Incantation, though he makes something of a show of his duelling skill. I've seen him a few times. He's not bad, though not quite as good as he'd like everyone to think. But he doesn't like duelling women at all." Thessaly considered that indicative of the man, how he won most of his bouts, but through a certain do-or-die determination rather than having the best skills.

Vitus contemplated that for a moment. "Also a bit later to challenge, yes? Do you think it makes a difference if someone's younger or older?"

"Hereswith Rowan had a career in the diplomatic service, before." Thessaly said. "I've heard her talk about it - the Crimean War. She saw the decisions being made, and she decided there had to be a better way. Which meant the Council, to do what she thought needed doing. As she said, the trouble with that sort of motivation is that it also meant she was determined to challenge to become head." She had to look away at that. Her eyes were tearing up. She remembered, she loved, those more informal conversations on the comfortable benches out in the garden or the comfy chairs in the library, with Aunt Metaia and Magistra Hereswith. Or sometimes there would be one or two other people, just talking away and letting her hear.

Vitus nodded, slowly, then he reached out his hand to touch her cheek. "I'm sorry. That's a memory, a good one, but it hurts right now."

"Good and hurts." Thessaly agreed, taking a breath before she looked back at him. "I'd rather, I mean. Not duck around talking about it? FitzAlan is also a duellist, also the warding and protective magics. He coordinates a lot with the Guard and Courts, when someone has to do that, but I've heard he had quite a, um. The sort of youth where he had to leave the country a couple of times because of duels of questionable illegality."

"Wait, what?" Vitus blinked, and his hand dropped down to cover hers, so now both of his hands were curled around her gloved one. "There must be all sorts of stories there. Not just about him."

Thessaly nodded. "Oh, there are lots. Books of them. Sometime when we run out of other topics, I could tell you about them. If you like." Then she tried to make sense of his expression, which had gone odd again, like a horse straining against some command, or a hound. All the training going one way, and all the instinct wanting to run in another direction entirely. "Are you all right?"

"Yes? No? I mean, I'm fine." Vitus swallowed. She could see him do it. "There's something I keep thinking, and I can't."

Thessaly wasn't sure what to do with that at all. "Thinking is usually not the problem. Doing might be, but thinking is different."

"Oh, this is a problem, too. Even with what you've told

me already." Vitus looked down at their hands, then back up at her.

"Is it something you can tell me?" Thessaly wasn't sure what to do with this. She could feel emotion in the space between them. She could tell there was something there that had weight and took up space.

"I would like very much to kiss you. And I am not, because—" His voice stalled.

Oh. That put a particular light on things. Thessaly glanced around, wanting to make sure no one had come up behind them. Then, spacing out the words carefully, like the jet beads she was wearing hung on silk thread, she said, "I would like very much to be kissed. By you."

Before either of them could think better of it, he leaned in, kissing her lightly on the lips. He didn't press at the kiss, though when her mouth opened to him, he explored that, just a little. One of his hands shifted to her upper arm for balance, and he took his time. It was nothing like the kisses she'd had with boys at school, and especially not like Childeric, who had always had his own ideas about how things should go. This wasn't a duel. This was setting up magic together, reading the other person to make something together, something only they could do.

She wanted more of it, but then she remembered where she was. Where they were, and she pulled back reluctantly. Vitus let her, though he left his hand on her arm, turned more intimately toward her. When she could speak, she asked what she most wanted to know. "What does that mean to you?"

"Before I say more, nothing I say obligates you to anything. And you've been clear about your agreements, and." Then, before he could go on and blather, he swallowed and managed something simpler and tangled, all at once. "I'm quite sure I've fallen in love with you. And I want the best for you, as lovers ought. Tell me what you need from me, it doesn't matter if you requite me or not, and I will do my best to make that happen."

He was putting all the power in her hands. All his skills, all his thoughtfulness, all his kindness. Thessaly took a deep breath and then met his eyes. "I don't want to hurt you. For you to be hurt. And I..."

Before she could say anything else, there was a call from over behind Vitus's shoulder. "Thessaly? Thessaly Lytton-Powell, is that you? Goodness, girl, what are you doing all the way out here?"

She pulled back with a jerk, and Vitus dropped her hands and rearranged himself. It was someone who knew Mama; she was sure of it. Possibly others. Before she turned to face that new challenge, she got out the words she needed him to hear. "I want more time with you." She couldn't say what she felt for him yet, beyond that, beyond yearning for that, but she wanted so desperately to find out.

Then she was standing, brushing her skirts out, and figuring out who was approaching. "Oh, Mistress Pembroke." She gestured at Vitus. "Master Deschamps was kind enough to escort me. I was making a few visits. You're here to tend your sister's flowers, aren't you? Might I lend a hand?" She wasn't at all sure how much Mistress Pembroke had seen. But perhaps the conversation over the grave would let Thessaly do enough illusion work with word and implication that the older woman wouldn't spread gossip near and far. It was a narrow hope. The Pembroke sisters, all five of them still living, loved to pass along their little tidbits.

Vitus stood beside her, and he bowed. "My pleasure, Mistress Lytton-Powell, as always. Mistress Pembroke." He touched his hat and then he was making his way back to the path and up and around, without looking back. Thessaly realised he was like Orpheus determined to do the thing that was needed now, an Orpheus who had learned from earlier mistakes and would not look back for anything, an Orpheus whose love rang deeper than all the doubts and uncertainties of their world.

If you enjoyed *Enchanted Net* and would like to read more of this series, please sign up for my mailing list to get all the latest news and fun extras.

Enchanted Net is the first book of a trilogy. *Silent Circuit* will be out on November 15th, 2024 and *Elemental Truth* (the last book, with the happily-ever-after) will be out on December 13th, 2024. Get the rest of Thessaly and Vitus's story!

Your reviews (on whatever review site you use) are much appreciated, too!

Read on for more historical details about this book and how it fits into other tales of Albion.

AUTHOR'S NOTE

Thank you so much for joining me for the first book of the Mysterious Fields trilogy. I promise Thessaly and Vitus will have their happily ever after by the end of Book 3, *Elemental Truth*. It's just going to take them a minute to get there.

My thanks as always to Kiya Nicoll, my editor, who has done everything from editing to consulting on Egyptian funeral rites as done by the Landry family, to helping me make sure the through lines on the plot did what we wanted. My other early readers all made excellent comments to help tie the trilogy together. Particular thanks to Elise Matthesen, as well, for not only a great deal of plot discussion but for making certain my mentions of gemstones and other mineralogical delights were accurate.

~

This trilogy is the earliest point at which we've seen the Fortier and Landry families, but it's certainly not my first set of books dealing with them. You can find a complete list on my website (at https://www.celialake.com/book/enchanted-net/) at the bottom of the page.

Eclipse is set in 1924-1925, and includes Isembard (Laudine and Dagobert's younger son) along with Alexander (in his 50s). Alexander is the focus of *Best Foot Forward* in 1935, as well as Nocturnal Quarry in 1938. *The Magic of Four* includes Isembard's son Leo as one of the main characters. And then, as I noted, *Grown Wise* is focusing on events in 1947, and features rather a lot of Ursula (Isembard and Thesan's daughter) and her Uncle Garin.

The attentive reader who is familiar with some of my other books will also notice some familiar faces and names. Niobe Hall, Vitus's apprentice mistress, appears in *Facets of the Bench* in 1927, much later in her life. Those who read about Margot Williams from *Bound for Perdition* (1917) and *Three Graces* (1945) might remember her maiden name was Lytton. She's mentioned as still being in the nursery during the discussion with Thessaly's uncles here.

~

GEMS, TALISMANS, AND STONES

Obviously, there are quite a few references to gemstones and talismanic magic in this book (and that's going to continue through the trilogy, given Vitus's profession). There is a tremendously long history of using stones (of various kinds) for magical purposes. For a starting place, I drew heavily *A Lapidary of Sacred Stones: Their Magical and Medicinal Powers Based on the Earliest Sources, Includes More than 800 Gems and Stones* by Claude Leconteux as well as *Stars and Stones: An Astro-Magical Lapidary* by Peter Stockinger. The former - as you might guess by the title - is extensive. The latter is more focused, but goes into more detail in some places.

The way that stones are used varies across time, but talismanic stones in Albion in this period draw from different approaches. Part of it is the innate tendency of the stone (as determined over centuries and via experimentation). Each stone usually has a handful of related attributes, many of which overlap with other stones (such as the selection that Vitus considers for better sleep).

Lore also associates specific kinds of inscriptions for particular purposes. For example, to pick something not at all relevant to the trilogy, there's this description (taken from the Laconteaux book): "etched with the moon and sun and hung about the neck with hairs from a synocephalus and feathers from a swallow, it protects one from evil spells. Magical properties are increased if set in gold or silver and if a man on horseback holding a sceptre is carved on it." If that seems like a lot to put on a gemstone, yes, I thought that too. (A synocephalus has the head of a canid.)

Vitus and Niobe are mostly using something between those two extremes: designs that align the specific focus of the stone to a particular purpose, which are then enchanted with appropriate ritual. There's a reason talisman making is a long apprenticeship - people not only have to master gem cutting, but also the ritual and incantation magics relevant to the work.

On to the chapter notes - quite brief for this book!

~

CHAPTER NOTES

Chapter 1 : Many of the **Fortier** customs draw - as Thessaly notes - from their Merovingian and Norman ancestors. The Merovingians were an early Frankish dynasty, before the Carolingians. One line of lore has them descended from a sea monster (Merovech, where the name comes from), and they were known as the "long-haired kings", for not cutting their hair. Very in keeping with Albion's general preference for long hair as holding magic. Many of the social customs of the Fortiers are drawn as much from French as from British sources.

The **mazurka** is a common dance of the period - not quite as energetic as seen in the Addams Family movie, but more energetic than the waltz, and full of the little hops and kicks Thessaly describes.

Chapter 2 : A word about the **clothing** might as well go here. Victorian clothing can sometimes be extremely specific as to silhouette (especially of the sleeves and bustle), changing year to year in this period. I now have a fairly vast collection of images stored for 1889 and 1890 so I could stare at them and figure out a description. If you'd like to learn more, Mimi Matthews (also a romance author) has a fantastic series of blog posts talking about details on her website, and also has a non-fiction book discussing the period, especially clothing and customs.

Chapter 16 : The **Weald** is a geological and geographic feature that runs a little bit north of the magical Arundel. It was heavily used for sheep grazing and farming into the 20th century. It now has a number of vineyards. Arundel as a magical estate is a little north of Arundel Castle. The manor is about a mile directly north from Amberly. The estate is in the chalky downhill of the Weald.

Chapter 18 : When I was trying to figure out the state of **electrical transmission** in 1889 (for a passing reference in one of the lectures here), I got extremely confused by two references to the Willamette Falls transmitting electricity, one in 1889 and one in 1890. It turns out that the first one was direct current transmission and the second was alternating current.

Thank you so much for starting this journey with me! The second book of Thessaly and Vitus's story (*Silent Circuit)* will be out on November 15th, 2024. *Elemental Truth* (the last book, with the happily-ever-after) will be out on December 13th, 2024.

There are some elements of the plot that Vitus and Thessaly never fully see: some of those will be explored more in *Grown Wise,* Ursula Fortier's romance in 1947 (nearly 60 years later). That will be out in May of 2025.

My newsletter has all my updates and news, as well as additional information about where I am and what I'm doing online. Until next book, happy reading!

Also by Celia Lake

The Mysterious Fields Series - Victorian

Enchanted Net

Silent Circuit

Elemental Truth

The Mysterious Charm Series - 1920s

Outcrossing

Goblin Fruit

Magician's Hoard

Wards of the Roses

In The Cards

On The Bias

Seven Sisters

The Mysterious Powers Series - 1920s

Carry On

The Fossil Door

Eclipse

Fool's Gold

The Hare and the Oak

Point By Point

Mistress of Birds

The Mysterious Arts Series - 1920s

Bound for Perdition

Shoemaker's Wife

Perfect Accord

Facets of the Bench

Charms of Albion - Victorian standalone

Pastiche

Sailor's Jewel

Four Walls and a Heart

Land Mysteries - 1930s and 40s

Best Foot Forward

Nocturnal Quarry

Old As The Hills

Upon A Summer's Day

Illusion of a Boar

Three Graces

The Magic of Four

Other stories

Complementary

Winter's Charms

Forged in Combat

Learn more about the world of Albion and future books at my website, celialake.com. Additional information linking characters, places, and timelines is available at my authorial wiki at bit.ly/

celia-lake-wiki (or get there from my website under the menu that says "more information").

Sign up for my newsletter to be the first to hear about future books and learn about fascinating bits of research. Happy reading!

www.ingramcontent.com/pod-product-compliance
Lightning Source LLC
LaVergne TN
LVHW050923080826
845145LV00001B/187

* 9 7 8 1 9 5 7 1 4 3 2 5 5 *